COMPULSION

ALSO BY MICHAEL STEWART

Belladonna

Grace

Far Cry

Monkey Shines

Prodigy

Birthright

COMPULSION

MICHAEL STEWART

HarperCollins*Publishers*

HarperCollins books may be purchased for educational, business, or sales promotional use. For information, please write: Special Markets Department, HarperCollins Publishers, Inc., 10 East 53rd Street, New York, NY 10022.

FIRST EDITION

Designed by George McKeon

Library of Congress Cataloging-in-Publication Data
Compulsion / Michael Stewart.—1st ed.
  p. cm.
ISBN 0-06-017767-5
1. Man-woman relationships—New York (N.Y.)—Fiction. 2. Married women —New York (N.Y.)—Fiction. 3. Marriage—New York (N.Y.)—Fiction. 4. Children—Death—Fiction. I. Title.
PR6069.T464C66 1994
823'.914—dc20   93-30908

---

94 95 96 97 98 ❖/RRD 10 9 8 7 6 5 4 3 2 1

For Martine

COMPULSION

1

THE GIRL RAN HEADLONG down the center of the street, dodging the oncoming cars. She ran like a wounded deer, in a staggering, pain-crazed jink. Awkwardly, too, with her right hand pressed tight to her left breast. Her blonde hair, wild and damp, half smothered her face. The red silk night robe she wore gaped open as she ran. A large wet patch, too dark to be perspiration, circled the breast she clutched. Beneath the robe she was naked. Her feet on the melting asphalt were bare.

At the intersection she flashed a glance over her shoulder and, veering onto the sidewalk, redoubled her pace. Her steps were leading her toward the seething traffic of the FDR Drive, toward the headlong hurtling millrace of cars and trucks.

No one was around to notice her. All eyes in the neighborhood were trained upon the broad, brown East River beyond where, once every minute, a dazzling speedboat ripped through the water, glinted briefly in the heat haze, then roared away in a cloud of fumes and angry turbulence.

Today a powerboat race was taking place around the island of Manhattan.

People watched from high-rise apartments, from yachts and tugs, from cars in wasteland parking lots bordering the river, but scarcely from the footbridges or the sidewalks or the pedestrian overlooks. For days now the temperature and the humidity in the city had been locked at the hundred mark, and no one willingly ventured more than a few steps out of the air-conditioned cool.

Except this demented, half-naked girl with unshod feet and sweat-clotted blonde hair.

And, some way behind, a man following her. A man in a black shirt buttoned to the top.

The girl was limping now, clutching her breast and trying to hold the robe closed about her, but now and then it fell open, revealing the lean naked belly and soft inner thighs smeared a glistening red. The sidewalk was searingly hot, yet she didn't appear to feel anything. She blundered into a lamppost but careened on without halting. She seemed pursued by a demon in a world of torment all her own.

She reached the end of the street. Ahead, a chain-link fence barred her way. Beyond, across a stretch of wasteland, the traffic poured in an unending stream along the riverside expressway.

She glanced behind her again. The man was closing on her. With a small cry she began frantically to scale the fence. She caught her hair, she tore her robe, but finally she managed to tumble over the top and drop to the ground on the other side. Scrambling to her feet, she zigzagged away across the wasteland, through the grimy cans, hubcaps, and other roadside jetsam.

The traffic flowed four lanes broad in each direction. A low parapet wall separated the girl from the stream coming in on her left. She climbed onto the wall and stood teetering for a moment. Then abruptly she jumped down into the traffic and, mindless of the danger, fled out across the lanes. Cars swerved, horns blared, tires screeched. A white limousine clipped her glancingly with its fender. The force spun her round. She stumbled, but picked herself up again.

Reaching the central reservation, she clambered over the crash barrier and set off through the opposite flow of traffic. One car swerved in mid-lane, sending the truck behind skating fifty yards along the curb.

Somehow she made it to the other side. A few steps took her across a narrow pavement to a low concrete wall. Below flowed the brown East River. Way out in the middle of the river, another powerboat, its prow high as if straining for liftoff, speared through the water and disappeared with a growl into the shimmering heat.

The man following her had found a pedestrian bridge. He ran up the iron steps, but at the top he halted. Dull sunlight sheened the perspiration on his face and balding head. He seemed unable, or maybe unwilling, to help.

Then the girl jumped. One moment she'd been standing on the concrete wall, her arms waving to steady herself. The next she was gone from sight.

The man on the bridge leaned forward. He screwed up his eyes and scanned the water. For a while he could see nothing. Mid-river, unaware and unconcerned, a silver-blue powerboat sliced through the water like a spearhead. The wake fanned out behind it, but then, just as the first wave lapped the embankment, there she was, the dot of a blonde head looking suddenly so tiny and diminished, raised briefly by the swell, and then lost from view, leaving only an arm visible, a pale fragile arm with its fingers outstretched, reaching upward, clawing the air.

Above the growl of the receding powerboat there now came another sound: the mechanical threshing beat of a helicopter. It was the airport shuttle, appeared from nowhere. It hovered briefly above the drowning girl, its wings beating a circle as smooth as a millpond around her. The man scarcely breathed. But no: abruptly, it tilted up its tail and, indifferent to the drama unfolding below, nosed away toward the terminus landing pad.

The girl reappeared far into the middle of the river. Her arms were flailing the water feebly. She was now just a pinprick bobbing in the wash.

Again came the low, throaty roar from the left, and the razor prow of another powerboat surged out of the heat haze. The speck of human life lay directly in its path. Behind the spray-lashed windshield, the crew stood at the controls, leaning forward in their safety harnesses, but the nose of their craft rose proud of the water and they could not see what lay immediately in front. Their eyes were set anyway on a point far beyond, on the smudge of black fumes that was the rival boat ahead and, way further still, on the final finish line.

The boat was closing inexorably fast. The girl's arm flashed briefly, pale against the brown water . . . and an instant later it was gone, ridden down beneath the hull of the boat and lost among the rush and turmoil of its wake.

The man's gaze lingered on the stretch of water. He watched as the frothy bubbling gradually subsided. He looked for some sign of the body, but he saw nothing. He stood there for a long while as one boat after another passed over the spot. Finally, rubbing his eyes against the glare from the water, he turned away and slowly headed back the way he had come.

The body of the girl was never recovered. River police conducted a routine search of the embankments and the regular notification was sent to the Port Authority, but the current in the river that day was unusually strong, being aided by a forceful easterly wind, and it was concluded that the body, or what remained of it, had been swept out to the ocean.

One local paper carried a short report deep on an inner page. The incident was given a brief mention in a radio station news round-up. In their log the race organizers made note of some minor damage incurred by a craft encountering a "hazardous floating object of human identity." But otherwise the incident went unremarked.

Witnesses testified to the crazed, demented look on the girl's face as she leaped to her death. No one else appeared to be involved, and on the police file a verdict of suicide was recorded. It was one of a spate of suicides that week, all readily ascribed to the overpowering heat.

No one came forward to identify the unknown jumper. No missing person matched her description. Six days later, however, a maintenance crew inspecting an effluent discharge point in the river recovered a torn red silk night robe snagged in a water-level grille. The garment bore the label, *Designing Woman*. A small, high-class fashion salon on Madison Avenue at 70th Street.

Once the girl was identified, her next of kin would be noti-fied and the case satisfactorily closed. But had the body been found, the file would have remained open. Not because there was any doubt about the verdict of suicide. But because of one unusually macabre piece of evidence suggesting that she might have been driven to it.

For even the most cursory examination would have revealed

that the body had been mutilated in a very curious manner. The entire left breast was missing, and though the exposed area of glandular tissue would by then be quite white and bloodless, it would be clear that the breast had not been sliced off in the collision with the powerboat but removed deliberately in a fashion indicating careful and expert surgery and, moreover, from the condition of the flesh left raw and bare, that the ablation had been carried out *in vivo*.

2

"I HAVE A LIEUTENANT PORTILLO here to see you."

The voice of her assistant came strangled and tinny over the desk intercom. Joanna gave an involuntary start.

"A police lieutenant?"

"A cop, Joanna. Are you in?"

Joanna waited for the eddies of alarm to subside.

"Show the gentleman up, Cheryl."

Her hand was unsteady as she reached for her compact and checked her appearance. She closed her eyes for a moment and drew a deep breath. For God's *sake,* she muttered. This isn't anything. A routine tax check on one of the girls. Maybe Stephen hasn't paid a parking violation. Maybe the cop is selling tickets to a police charity dinner.

It was just that, coming today of all days . . .

The door opened, and Cheryl, a freckled redhead with moon-size glasses, pregnant, and breathing heavily from the climb, ushered in a lean, olive-skinned lieutenant. She rested her weight on a filing cabinet as he came forward, a black zipper bag in his hand. Flashing his identification, he laid the bag on the desk between them and pulled out a tattered red garment.

"Recognize this?"

Joanna gave a muffled gasp. Of course she recognized it. She had selected that exquisite fabric herself at a silk factory in Canton. And Designing Woman was the couture house which she'd set up five years ago in that painful no-man's-land after losing her first husband.

"Yes, it's ours," she said. "But I don't understand."

"You have a record of who bought it?"

"It's a sample. We're launching our own design collection. This is the night robe in the range." She bit her lip as the practical implications began to sink in. This year, the New York Fashion Week was madly early. "We only have one garment in each design made up. It's fitted for the girl who's going to model it. This was sized for Cristina."

She cast a hard glance at Cheryl, who was shifting uncomfortably on her feet.

"Cristina asked to borrow it," replied her assistant meekly. "For a special event. A private event," she added.

Joanna turned to the lieutenant.

"We let the girls borrow from stock once in a while. But never, of course, lines we haven't shown." She held up the flimsy garment. It was ruined. "Cheryl, call her up right away."

The lieutenant intervened by taking out a notepad.

"Okay, let's have her full name."

"We'll sort it out between ourselves, Lieutenant," said Joanna.

"Would you describe her as tall, blonde, with bluish eyes, in her early twenties?"

"Really, Lieutenant, I'm not going to make an issue."

Cheryl obliged with an answer.

"That's Cristina," she said.

He nodded his acknowledgment, then he cleared his throat.

"Mrs. Lefever, this garment was recovered from the East River. The description fits with a young lady seen in the FDR Drive area, around two in the afternoon, the Saturday before last . . ."

"Wearing a night robe in the afternoon?" queried Joanna.

"Before she climbed over the embankment and threw herself into the river and got chewed up by a powerboat."

"Oh my God."

"A straight suicide. The body's not been recovered. We just want to know who she was. For the record."

Just then the phone rang. Joanna watched it but did not move to pick it up. Echoes from the past were stirring in her mind, terrible and unforgettable echoes that she never seemed able to silence.

Eventually Cheryl stepped forward and answered the phone. She cupped her hand over the mouthpiece.

"Milan," she said. "You want to take it?"

Joanna seized the excuse. An order for cloth had been mislaid in customs and Milan was sending a replacement quantity, but there was a variation in the batch color. . . . She struggled to focus on the issue, but all the time she was watching the lieutenant as he cast his eye around the small office, scanning the filing cabinet cards and the memos clipped to the pinboard, the photographs of models posing on sets and parading down catwalks, and everywhere, in piles on the desk and taped to the walls, sketches for the new collection to launch herself as a design house of which the red silk robe, now lying in shreds on the desk between them, was the centerpiece. He leaned forward to examine a photo showing Bella, then aged seven, with her father, then fit and well, horsing about together in the pool at the beach house in East Hampton. And beside it, a snap of Stephen with his arm around a silver gorilla, taken on the field expedition to the Ruwenzori mountains in Africa on which she'd accompanied him, two years ago, in an attempt to put the trauma of their child's death behind them. She could see the lieutenant trying to work it all out. She could read the conditioned suspicion of the policeman in the way his eyes narrowed as he glanced from one photo to the other, deducing what it meant, how it all fitted.

Unnerved, she abruptly excused herself and hung up. She turned back to the lieutenant.

"I'm sorry, what were you asking?"

"The name of this girl, ma'am."

"Ah, right." She rose to her feet and walked stiffly over to a filing cabinet. "Her name is Cristina Parigi."

She took out a file card and scanned it quickly.

PARIGI, Cristina. 101 W. 89th St. Apt #7, NYC 10024. Age: 22. Height: 5'10". Bust: 38". Waist: 25". Hips: 36". Shoes: 6. Hair: blonde, shoulder-length, wavy. Eyes: Gray-blue. Experience: photographic assignments in "Vanity Fair," "Tatler," "Dallas Society"; fashion modeling for Ralph Lauren, Ungaro . . . References: none.

She handed the card to the lieutenant with a frown.

"She was young, attractive, healthy. She had everything in the world to live for. It's terrible."

He turned the card over and back again.

"Parigi. That's kind of unusual."

"A working name, I guess," she suggested.

"And when she wasn't working?"

"Girls come into this business for many reasons, Lieutenant. We don't ask."

Cheryl chipped in. "She once mentioned she had folk in Paris, Texas."

The lieutenant looked up uncomprehendingly. "Excuse me?"

"Paris. You know: Parigi." The assistant chided him with a teasing smile. "You don't speak *any* Italian, Lieutenant Portillo?"

"Call it a working name." A brief smile passed across his face, then vanished. "She gave no address for her folks?"

"None at all."

"Anything untoward happen to her recently? Money a problem? She used drugs?"

Joanna conjured up an image of the tall, blonde girl with the gray-blue eyes, high cheekbones, and broad sensuous mouth. There had always been something enigmatic in her manner, a strange aloofness and self-containment. But she'd hardly known her. She'd used her on and off to model for private clients, but she was bred for the catwalk and was to have been the star turn of the show.

"She first came to work for us six months ago," she offered. "She'd just arrived in New York and I think she found it tough making a living in this town. But I'm sure she wasn't into drugs."

Her assistant agreed. "She kept herself to herself," she added. "Her parents died in a car accident just before she came up here. I don't think she had many friends. I got the feeling she was lonesome. You can look like a goddess but deep down you're always alone."

A brief silence fell. This had been spoken from the heart. Cheryl was set for the loneliness of a single parent: the father of the child was a married man who'd refused to have anything more to do with her on hearing she was pregnant.

The lieutenant gave her a brief, appraising glance. He scribbled for a moment in his notepad, then folded it away.

"Did she work for any other fashion houses?" he asked.

"They all do," replied Joanna. "You could check with the agencies."

"Yeah, I guess we could."

"I can give you a list."

"Thank you. I'll remember that."

Wait a minute, thought Joanna. The lieutenant is closing the file. That isn't good enough. He should be finding out why this wicked tragedy happened at all. But then, from his viewpoint, the girl might have been young and healthy and full of promise, and no doubt someone somewhere would mourn her death, but she was, after all, just another suicide case, one jumper out of the columns of all ages and types throwing themselves like lemmings off buildings and bridges throughout the nation every day of the year.

The lieutenant rose to his feet and held up the file card.

"May I take a copy?" he asked. "And you have a photo?"

"Take the officer downstairs, Cheryl, and give him all he needs." She rose and reached out her hand. "Let me know if I can help any more."

He thanked her and moved to the door. There he turned back and held her eye. His tone was pensive but his gaze was penetrating.

"They all have mothers, all those crazies who blow themselves away. How do *they* feel? I always think of that." His gaze seemed to grow still sharper. "You're a mother, Mrs. Lefever, aren't you?"

"Well, yes."

"Say your own kid dies bad. Would you ever get over it?" He wiped a cuff over his perspiring forehead and replaced his cap. "We'll be in touch, Mrs. Lefever."

Joanna checked her watch. Past ten o'clock already. She was going to be hard pressed to get out to East Hampton and back in time for the reception at the Frick in the evening. And make the detour to pick up Stephen from the Department on the way, too.

She pushed aside the fifth cup of coffee Cheryl had brought her and scanned her list of the day's calls. She'd made an early start that day and, despite the interruption from the police, she'd covered the most urgent tasks. She'd checked with the printers that the invitations for the show had all been mailed, she'd called the caterers and discussed the canapés and cocktails, she'd phoned Milan and told them to stuff the replacement consignment, then called an old friend of her father's who promised to turn the entire New York Customs warehouse system upside down and find the missing package, and she'd faxed her agent in Hong Kong to contact the silk farm urgently for another roll of the red silk fabric. It was all problems and crises. At times she wished she'd kept the business a small, high-class retail salon and not entertained the grand illusions of a full design house. But it was too late to have such thoughts now.

Finally, she checked through the small thicket of yellow notelets stuck to shelves and magazine covers—*Manhattan Gown Hemline, Serena @ Harper's & Queen, Hair Appointment Paolo, Press Seats*—and, satisfied she had covered everything urgent, reached forward to the intercom.

"Cheryl, would you ask Galton to bring the car round? I'll be down in five minutes."

She stepped into the small dressing room that led off her office and began to undress. The room was hot and airless, for the air-conditioning couldn't penetrate the closely packed racks of clothes stored there to make way for the collection. Standing in front of an oval cheval glass, she kicked off her shoes, took off her pale cotton suit, and slipped out of the beige camisole top. Then she reached for a black linen day dress and black shoes. As she bent to step into the dress, she caught sight of her reflection in the glass, her dark coppery hair falling free, her mouth a slash of carmine against the black silk slip, and the slip itself stretched at the seams in front where her breasts hung full. An image passed through her mind of a painting at a recent exhibition, a rich, sensuous Bonnard entitled something like *Jeune Fille Nue à sa Toilette*, a painting full of maidenly innocence on the surface and yet seething with suppressed sexuality beneath, and she felt a powerful kinship with that pubescent girl whose outward chasteness masked her inward sensuality. No one reached the soul of her flesh. When Stephen touched her now, he touched only her skin. The inner ferment remained out of his reach.

It hadn't always been that way. Her first summer with Stephen had been an idyll of days of laughter and nights of love. But that was the past Stephen, the foreigner in the other country, beyond the frontier that had drawn itself across the map of her life in the small hours of one morning two years ago. Two years to the very day.

The terrain of their life together, once so lush and rich, had grown rough and sparse. After all the rage and recriminations and the attempts to pass the parcel of guilt, a great freeze had fallen between them like the descent of an Ice Age, locking them in a dance of opposition from which they were unable to break apart. Eventually, mutual need and a profound weariness of spirit had brought about a conditional truce. In the process, their love had changed. It had become a bond between two conspirators, each a constant reminder to the other of what had passed. Sex between them had dwindled to an occasional encounter conducted in the dark and the silence. This didn't seem to worry Stephen. He rode above it all, unmoved. He reasoned it away. Feelings such as guilt and regret, he'd say, were unknown in the animal kingdom. A bereaved swan might die of a broken heart, but never of remorse. That was a human construct and counter to nature. But what about *human* nature, Stephen? she wanted to scream. For her, a day never passed without her feeling the sharp pang of loss and the sickening stab of guilt.

And yet her body raised its own cry. In the heat of the city in August, already suffocating by mid-morning, with the air swollen with unslaked lusts, how could anyone be deaf to the clamor of the flesh or deny the raw tug of desire? Her hand slipped down to her inner thigh, to the naked skin above the rim of her stockings. She drew in her breath sharply at the touch, and a convulsive shiver ran through her belly as slowly, gradually, her fingers began to ascend.

Then, abruptly, she straightened. This wasn't the time; this wasn't the *way*.

Breathing heavily, she hastily zipped up her black dress and stepped shakily into her shoes. From her jewel case she selected a black pearl necklace and spent a while clumsily fumbling with the clasp. She touched up the edges of her lipstick with a liner pencil and ran a comb quickly through her hair. Then, glancing in the mirror, she reached for her black clutch bag and made for the door. Within a moment she was downstairs, across the deep-

carpeted salon and battling her way through the solid wall of
heat outside to the cool, leather-scented interior of the waiting
limousine.

Madison Avenue was gridlocked. Angry motorists with fraying
tempers leaned on their horns. A burly traffic cop, the spine of
his blue shirt darkened with sweat, looked on with lassitude and
indifference. Cocooned in the cool, Joanna settled deeper into
the comfortable seat. The exhaust fumes sucked in from the cars
in front, mingled with the steamy smell of hot wet asphalt, sent
her head lightly spinning. She looked forward with yearning to
the tranquillity and peace of the Garden of Remembrance.

At last they broke free of the traffic and cut across to Park
Avenue. Behind, the majestic white Pan Am building seemed to
float suspended on the shimmering heat haze like a celestial
citadel; ahead stretched the broad avenue in a succession of
rises and dips, its perspective strangely condensed by a trick of
the light.

She reached for the car phone and dialed Stephen's number
at the Department. A hundred to one he'd forgotten to bring
with him the black tie she'd put out earlier that morning. He
could at least make some effort. You couldn't just turn your back
on these things. Damn what they did in the animal kingdom.

The phone rang and rang. Where was he? Where was his secretary? He hadn't even switched on his answering service. He's
in the "zoo," she thought, that vile labyrinth of cages and pens
hidden out of sight on the roof of the Department building. He'll
be with Orson, or Charlie, or Marlene, or Lana. Talking to his
chimps in sign language. *How do you do? One banana or two?
Get your finger out of Lana's whatsit, Charlie, or are you trying to
say something?* God knew why the world thought *that* was so
brilliant.

Eventually, a girl answered. The voice was unfamiliar.

"Dr. Lefever's phone," announced the girl.

"Is he there, please?" asked Joanna.

"Oh, hi, Roxanne. No, I thought he was with you."

"It's his wife."

"Oh, excuse me, I thought . . . " The girl broke off, flustered.
"Shall I say you called, Mrs. Lefever?"

"No message, thank you."

Joanna replaced the phone in its cradle. She looked out of the window, but now she seemed to see nothing. They swept past the canopy of their own apartment block and distantly she noted the new Irish doorman was on duty, but otherwise her thoughts were turned in on themselves, and even when the car braked violently to avoid a truck that had jumped the lights, she hardly broke her self-absorption.

Oh, hi, Roxanne . . . excuse me, I thought . . .

Dear God, not now. Not on this of all days. Not on the day our child returned to earth and dust.

Abruptly, she leaned forward.

"Make a turn here," she said in a firm voice. "We'll go straight to the crematorium."

She returned late and hurriedly took the private elevator to the apartment. A heady fragrance of lilies and potpourri met her when the doors opened, and she paused for a moment in the cool of the hallway to make the mental transition. Still lingering in her mind's eye, like the afterimage of a bright sun, was the small marble memorial tablet. What had possessed her to agree to consigning her little treasure to the flames, with nothing returned but an urn of ashes to be immured behind a pitiful plaque in a row of other plaques in a common Garden of Remembrance? Why hadn't she insisted on a burial, so that she could at least stand in front of a grave, albeit a cot-size grave, and think of her tiny infant lying there and pretend to herself that it was simply and painlessly asleep? In that, too, she'd let Stephen have his way. She'd been too demented at the time to resist. God, how bitterly she regretted it.

She glanced around her to regain her bearings. Far down the corridor she could see the diminutive figure of Maria, the Puerto Rican maid, polishing the ornate glass double doors that led into the drawing room. From a further room came the sound of Bella's voice, on the telephone.

The apartment itself still bore the stamp of her grandfather, the founder of the family fortune, although she had got rid of much of the furniture which she'd inherited with it and now the place represented a fairer balance between her own possessions and Stephen's. His was the collection of nineteenth-century watercolors and the Georgian mahogany furniture, sent over from England the week before their marriage, just as his were all those dreadful masks—voodoo masks, African tribal masks, theatrical masks, death masks, and God knew what besides—which she'd finally banished to his study walls. Hers was all the silver and china, the Bruges tapestries and the Oriental rugs, the antique damask drapes and other heirlooms she'd insisted on keeping. Most of the rest—certainly all that was modern, such as the Morris Louis canvas and the Henry Moore bronze—they had bought together, albeit with her money, with the result that each room was in an individual style of its own and the whole presented an amalgam of periods and tastes. Stephen said it represented the perfect expression of two diametrically contrary personalities. He should know: his field was all about the covert content of behavior, the message behind the mask.

She looked at the gilt mantel clock. Fifteen minutes, at most, to shower and change. She'd leave without Stephen if he didn't show up in time, damn him. Abruptly she headed down the corridor. The apartment internally more resembled a house, with a broad staircase rising from the hall to the upper floor. The living room gave onto a large roof terrace, and leading off it, and reached also from the hall corridor, was the kitchen, a large high-tech room in chrome and white granite which served as the focus of family life.

There she found Bella, sitting on a bar stool, with her long fair hair hanging loose and dressed in nothing but a T-shirt and panties. She was painting her toenails as she spoke on the phone. She looked up momentarily and pulled a face. Not at Joanna, whom she hadn't noticed come in, but at Stephen, who was standing on the other side of the central island filming her with a video camera. He hadn't seen her either. Bella began pouting and wiggling her shoulders at the camera. She wasn't just teasing, she was flirting.

Joanna stepped forward. Bella saw her first and quickly wound up her phone conversation.

"Mom," she began as she hung up, "can't we go to the beach house tomorrow? Lorri's dying to come."

"We're going Friday, darling. I can't make it before."

"But it's so boring here. Everyone's away."

"Lorri isn't."

"Everyone with any sense in this heat," grumbled the girl.

Joanna turned to Stephen.

"Put that thing away, Stephen. I want to speak to you."

"I'm working," he replied smoothly, continuing to film.

"Stephen," she warned.

"Videophones are coming, and we're looking at how telephone habits will have to change. Nose picking's out, Bella."

"I wasn't," objected Bella.

He trained the camera on Joanna.

"And they'll have to learn to smile sweetly."

"Bella, darling," said Joanna, "isn't your wildlife program on now?"

"All right," sighed the girl and headed obediently for the door. "Why don't you just say you want a fight with Stephen, and I'll go?"

Stephen continued filming Bella until the door closed, then he put the camera down and went to the fridge.

"Vodka?" he asked, taking a bottle from the freezer. "You look as if you need one."

"Where were you? We had an appointment."

"Long or short?"

"Where were you, Stephen?" she repeated.

He handed her a vodka tonic. She refused it. He set it down on the island between them and raised his own glass.

"Down the hatch," he said in his infuriatingly bland English manner. "You know," he mused, staring into the fizzing tonic, "I think Bella would do brilliantly at drama college. She's a natural."

Joanna felt her temper rising.

"Don't try me, Stephen. You know why I'm mad. It was the least you could do."

He lowered his glass and fixed her with a slow, steady gaze. Beneath his thick dark brows his eyes hardened and his jaw clenched, but his smile never faltered.

"This need you feel to relive it all, Joanna," he said, "it truly worries me. You really should consider therapy."

"You just could have had the balls to face up to it this once, Stephen. Today of all days."

"It takes balls to face up to realities, Joanna," he sighed sadly. "All this maudlin dwelling in the past is, frankly, a cheap, cowardly way out."

She stepped forward and, before she realized what she was doing, slapped him hard across the cheek.

"How dare you say that!"

He gave no reaction to the blow, only inclined his head slightly and studied her with a look of professional concern.

"Joanna, the baby's dead," he said in a quiet, reasonable voice. "It's dead and buried. You have to come to terms with that."

"Luke is *not* buried," she retorted, her voice trembling. "And for me at least, his memory is not dead."

"Joanna, life must go on."

"What kind of a life?" She checked herself. "Any father with an iota of feeling would want to pay his respects."

"And that means an annual pilgrimage to the shrine?" he queried, reverting to a tone of pleasant detachment. "That's an interesting measure of parental feeling. Please go on."

"I can't take you in this mood, Stephen," she snapped, turning on her heel. "If you're going to be like this all evening, don't come. I'd rather go without you."

She left the room and went off down the corridor to the stairs. She was conscious of Stephen following behind, waiting for the next turn in the argument. He could be so maddeningly unengageable when he chose. He provoked quarrels just so as to observe the dynamics at play. He did it in company the whole time, and he left people in awe of his brilliant intellect, when all he'd really done was drop a piranha into the goldfish bowl and sit back and watch what happened. You never knew what he was really thinking; he rarely declared himself openly. He presented a permanently moving target. A psychological *agent provocateur.*

"Anyway, you'll find the party boring," she said as she turned up the stairs. "You know how you hate money talk."

"Money *is* boring. It's all about how to get it, and when you've got it, how to keep it. Never how to *use* it."

"And you, of course, know all about using money. Other people's money."

She checked herself again. This time the argument would only lead down the inevitable track about her family and their very mixed feelings about him, how they'd fallen for his charm but remained suspicious of his motives. The fact was, he didn't speak their language, the language of money. His wealth was his brains. It would raise the issue of the moment, too: the Foundation. Just that morning she'd had a call from one of the venerable old trustees querying whether endowing a chair in Behavioral Crypto-psychology at Columbia University was absolutely and entirely in keeping with the spirit of her grandfather's legacy.

She swept into their large, cool bedroom and kicked off her shoes. Stephen followed, declaiming.

"Any moron can make money," he was saying. "That's merely a craft. Spending it properly is an art."

She cast him a sweet smile.

"That's more like the English snob I know and loathe. On the other hand," she offered casually, "you could always call up Roxanne. Take your video camera and have yourself a party there."

He shot her a quick, uncertain glance.

"If I didn't know you better, my sweet, I'd say you were just a mite jealous."

"Should I care? What you do with your time is your business. Except when you have a commitment to me."

She turned and faced him, one hand on her hip. She noticed he adopted the same stance. She changed position, and consciously or unconsciously he changed his own, too. You couldn't live with Stephen without learning about the giveaway clues of body language. Posture echo, he called this. A subliminal message signaling appeasement. Ah, she thought, I've touched a nerve here. His visit to this girl may have been wholly innocent, but he's as guilty as hell by intent.

"Who is she, anyway?" she went on. "Roxanne: sounds like a bar of cheap soap."

"She's a graduate in the Department. She's the one working on nonobserved telephone behavior."

"Ah, telephone sex. Something else for your Behavioral Crypto-whatsit?"

She had undressed to her slip. She turned her back to him, conscious of his eyes fixed upon her. The only thing to which Stephen was vulnerable was irony. That was his Achilles' heel. She, too, had made her own study.

She went to the bathroom and stepped into the shower.

"Funny you should say that," she heard him begin, but the sound of the water drowned out the rest of his words.

She yielded herself to the sensation of the water beating down upon her skin. She felt strangely light and elated. She was even looking forward to the evening ahead. She had ruffled Stephen's careful mask of composure, and without broaching the danger zone. By an unspoken accord, they kept out of the truly forbidden area. But that, at root, was the bond that kept them together. The thing they had done, the thing they'd had to do, and which haunted her, waking and sleeping, every moment of her life.

She didn't hear him come into the shower. She was barely conscious of the moment the pounding of water on her flesh became the touch of hands. She felt the hands begin slowly soaping her body from behind, molding her breasts and rounding the contours of her stomach and thighs, then gradually, inexorably, working between her buttocks until, abruptly, with a smothered gasp she felt herself lifted off her feet with the force of the thrust and all sensation blotted out in the downrush of the cascade.

Before they'd even reached the party, however, the harmony of the aftermath of lust had dissolved to pain and disappointment.

They had taken the car, although the Frick Museum, where the reception was being held, was only a short distance away. Galton would drop them there and they'd take a cab home, or maybe even walk. Despite the evening hour, the heat was still fierce, and Stephen, who had been brought up in a drafty rectory on the Norfolk coast of England and profoundly disbelieved in air-conditioning, had the window of the limousine wide open. She was telling him the tragic news of the day, Cristina's suicide, but she couldn't tell if he was listening. He sat with his tie loosened, his collar slack, and his head craned out of the open window to catch a cooling breeze.

Something caught her attention and she found her voice trailing off. She leaned a little closer.

At first glance, the reddish marks on his neck looked as though the collar had been chafing the skin. Then abruptly she realized. There was no mistaking the particular pattern of fingernails.

She recoiled and, turning away, stared out of her own window. She said nothing. She'd often suspected he was seeing other women: she'd had hints now and then, as she'd had today. In practical, realistic moments, she'd even accepted that, sooner or later, he'd start looking elsewhere for the kind of sex he couldn't get within the framework of their marriage—simple, easy, uncomplicated sex, without the burden of unspoken issues and a subtext of awkward complicities. Even sex such as they'd just had in the shower carried its own context, born as it was from frustration and dissonance. She'd always told herself she would understand when it happened, and in her mind, in advance, she had forgiven him. Until it happened and the proof was in black and white, she would give him the benefit of the doubt.

But now the evidence stared her in the face. She could not pretend it away.

I was right, she thought with a distance that surprised her. He *did* have it off with that girl, the two-faced cheating hound.

Somewhere within her stirred a swell of pain and rage, but she wouldn't let it surface. She wouldn't scream or scratch his eyes out or throw him out of the car into the moving traffic. She just wanted to look at him, to study objectively this man who had spent the afternoon with a girl and come home and possessed her not twenty minutes before. Every line of his body reeked of arrogance, every movement filled her with disgust. She felt almost physically sick. He went off screwing girls, leaving her to shoulder the guilt, to carry the cross. That was his way out, and it was far the worse infidelity.

Sitting stonily still, she slowly began to do the trick she used to calm herself. Gradually she withdrew from her own body, like a camera pulling slowly back, until she saw herself from a distance, a figure with shortish dark copper hair, dressed in a Karl Lagerfeldt dogtooth suit, sitting in a limousine, legs crossed and hands folded, looking out of the window as the car pulled up outside the ornate wrought-iron railings of an imposing gray stone city mansion.

And when the man beside her sprang out to open the door

himself and ushered her out with a show of old-world chivalry, she saw this figure that was herself climb out and walk up the steps slowly, like a disembodied soul, her expression blank and her feelings buried deep within, and with nothing in her manner or her gait suggesting in any way that she was about to embark upon a portentous experience that would turn her whole life inside out.

3

Joanna stood beneath a large Rembrandt self-portrait, a glass of Roederer Crystal in her hand, listening distantly to the familiar cadence of cocktail party chatter. From the cool, cloistered hall behind floated the gentle strains of a Haydn quartet. All about her in the large, ornate salon, groups of besuited men and bejeweled ladies formed and re-formed in an ever-changing flux. Some lone individuals roamed free, heedless of the dangers of leaving the pack, and quickly fell prey to the suave young executives circulating with morocco-bound portfolios and soft talk of bond yields and stock ratios. The party was being hosted by a leading Wall Street investment bank to announce the donation of a multimillion-dollar Van Gogh to the museum, and the opportunity was being milked for all it was worth.

Joanna had gone along at her father's request. He was away on high government business in Tokyo, and she was there to represent the family trust, itself largely invested in works of art.

Stephen was there ostensibly to lend his support. But he was also ambitious—he'd turned down the offer of a chair in England to take up a visiting professorship at Columbia University—and he appreciated better than his colleagues back home the omnipotence of money in academic life. He was at that moment talking up his work to the president of a multinational software corporation. Later, she would ask him how the conversation had gone, and he would play diffident and pretend they'd only talked on an elevated plane about theory. She looked around the room at the others present, at the art collectors and gallery owners, at the ubiquitous faces of the New York social set, and at the occasional movie star and titled foreigner invited to lend the party a touch of class, and she smiled to herself. One of Stephen's fondest traits was his uneasy, English love-hate relationship with money. Money corrupted the academic's pursuit of knowledge, and yet it was the stuff that enabled it. Such a dilemma, both moral and philosophical, and seen *as* a dilemma, was inconceivable to anyone else in that room.

Her eye fell on a Corot on the far wall. They had a Corot in their bedroom. Just as fine, too. Well, frankly, they were all much of a muchness. Correction: *she* had the Corot. She frowned. The thing cut both ways. Sometimes she felt as if her money was like a third person in their lives: there was her, there was him, and there was *it*, her money . . .

A man was watching her.

. . . like the Other Woman . . .

A man standing by the painting, staring at her. Devouring her with his eyes.

She lost her train of thought. An involuntary shiver rippled through her. She hadn't noticed the man all the time she'd been looking at the picture. He seemed to have materialized out of nowhere. He didn't move a muscle, he just stood studying her greedily, voraciously.

Flustered, she looked away quickly, not wanting him to think she'd actually been staring at him. She kept her gaze averted, but all the time she could feel his eyes burning into her across the space between them. And, though she could hardly place it at once, she could sense his *smell*, a faint, musky odor dimly redolent of hot desert nights or the fur of a wild animal.

A waiter came round with champagne and as she held out her glass she cast the stranger a quick glance.

He was still there, consuming her with the full intensity of his gaze.

She was slowly catching fire. Invisible flames jetted out from his eyes, spreading around and through her, igniting her. She raised the glass to her lips but held it there without drinking, then slowly, like an automaton, lowered it again. She could not break the stare. She barely registered how he looked or dressed, for her whole focus was caught in the mesmeric grip of those penetrating, smoldering eyes.

When finally she tore her gaze away, she felt dazed and flushed. Her pulse drumming in her temples, she made an effort to reenter the talk around her, but she kept mishearing remarks addressed to her and dropping threads of the conversation. She was conscious of Stephen subjecting her to a puzzled scrutiny. Conscious, too, at some subliminal level, that the man in black had moved away but not left the room, rather that he had just moved round so as to observe her from a different angle, that he was, in effect, circling her, like a predator round its prey.

An image suddenly came to her, an image of herself observed from the outside. She was naked. All around her the men and women were fully dressed, and she alone had nothing on, not a slip nor stockings nor shoes, nothing except her pearl choker. Her naked skin, soft and pale, contrasted strikingly with the crisp dark suits of the men. Yet no one seemed to find it odd. They talked among each other, and indeed to her, as though a naked woman wearing nothing but a pearl collar were a perfectly normal feature of any gathering of the kind. All the while the stranger continued slowly circling, picking his steps, biding his distance, biding his time, too, while she suffocated with terror and anticipation, until the moment of his choosing when he would step forward and with one swift movement take hold of the choker and, tightening his grip around her neck, draw her forward and downward so that she was bent with her buttocks raised and her sex agape, and thus, beneath the incurious gaze of all those onlookers, with one long and savage thrust this perfect stranger would take possession of her.

"Joanna?"

Distantly she heard herself addressed.

"Don't you agree, Joanna?"

Giddy, she struggled to return to her senses. She composed a bland, all-purpose reply. It clearly made no sense in the context, for a brief silence fell, then someone else intervened smoothly and the awkward moment passed. For a while she made an effort to participate, focusing her attention on the group about her. Finally, she edged herself out of the conversation and summoned the nerve to cast a glance around.

He wasn't there.

Under the pretense of scanning the pictures, she slowly turned full circle.

The stranger was nowhere to be seen. Not by the Corot. Nowhere near the Rembrandt. Not among the group where a long-legged waitress stood serving canapés.

Above the rising hubbub came the sudden, sharp hammering of a gavel. She looked up. The liveried master of ceremonies who had announced them one by one on arrival had now taken up position on the dais at the far end of the room. On his left stood the benefactor, on his right the beneficiary, and behind, veiled by a velvet curtain, the work of art itself.

"Ladies and gentlemen, your attention please," began the sonorous voice.

Joanna felt a stab of panic. She was trapped. There would be speeches, presentations, the unveiling, more speeches and toasts. Once the ceremonies had started, there was no escape.

Avoiding Stephen's eye, she turned to the couple closest to her and murmured an excuse. She slipped away through the crush of guests and made her way to the mahogany and gilt double doors that led to the central hall. There she paused briefly and scanned the sea of faces, all now turned toward the dais. Would she even recognize him? He was tall, she seemed to think. And quite slim. Dark hair, sleeked back and receding, balding even, dark suit, black shirt buttoned to the neck.

She turned away, afraid of being caught. Caught doing what? By whom? This was absurd!

Her heart was pounding. What was she doing? Yes, of course: she was going to the restrooms.

The museum had formerly been a private city mansion, and the rooms led from one into another in a circuit around the cloistered central hall. All were empty but for the custodians at their posts. The music had stopped for the presentation, and in the silence she felt conscious of the clack of her heels on the marble and oak floors. She turned left into a smaller gallery.

He wasn't there, either.

Quickening her step, she headed for the next room. Suppose she did come upon him, what then? She couldn't appear to be looking for him. And the restrooms were in quite the opposite direction. Perhaps she had lost something on her way round earlier. An earring? Quickly she unclasped an earring and slipped it into her clutch bag. She entered the room, but the stranger was not there either. She moved to the next gallery and, caught under the eye of an attendant, reached a hand to her ear and feigned to scan the floor. The attendant came up and asked solicitously if he could help. Blushing with embarrassment, she mumbled something and backed away out of the room into the central hall, where she hid in the shadow of a large stone column. She was shaking all over. What in God's name was she doing?

From the main salon came a ripple of laughter, followed by polite applause. She sank against the column. She couldn't go back in there. She couldn't face those people, the superficial chatter, the forced conviviality. She'd find Stephen at his little party game, dropping ironic poisoned bomblets into the conversation to liven it up, observing the reaction, and she'd watch the others trying to work out where he was coming from, whether to laugh or take offense or just attribute it to some inscrutable English sense of humor. She'd have to ease him away before he got out of hand, and then he'd insist they went out to a restaurant for dinner, where he'd drink rather too much and put on a brilliant show of talk and wit and she'd remember once again why she'd fallen for him in the first place, then they'd go home to bed, avoiding *that* issue, and up in the morning to an early start, digging Bella reluctantly out of bed, then off to the salon or to the midtown design studio. . . . She knew it all so well. The content of any day might change, but the form remained the same. She couldn't go back to that suffocating routine. Not now. Not just yet.

She had to get out into the open. She'd walk home. The air would be cooler by now. She'd stroll the streets quietly. Just until she'd recovered her composure. Resolved this madness. Put herself back together.

On the broad steps outside, with the city lights brightening against the falling dusk, she paused. Turning left would take her in a direct route back to the apartment.

She turned right.

She sauntered to the end of the block. The final fiery rays from the dying sun were filtering through the trees of Central Park, etching the towering skyline beyond in violet. The heat of the day still shimmered off the buildings and lingered in the sidewalk paving, and in the silky air she sensed the throb of imminent excitement. She walked slowly, pausing from time to time to look about her. She felt strange and distanced, at one remove from the world about her.

As she turned the corner away from the park, she was dimly aware of a limousine with darkened windows parked across the road. Perhaps some acuity of hearing picked up the soft electric whir, or maybe the glass caught a glint of sunlight as it was low-ered, but she looked across and saw the back window slowly descending. It wound down to its fullest extent. Nothing hap-pened for a moment. The interior was a pool of darkness. But even at that distance she could sense the dark flames of eyes boring out at her.

A hand emerged. It reached out from a black sleeve that seemed all of a substance with the darkness within. Slowly a fin-ger beckoned.

She froze in her tracks. Her head was spinning. She felt giddy, disorientated. Her grip on the world was crumbling. A veil of blindness was falling over her, paralyzing her senses, robbing her of her will.

She took a step forward.

It was not Joanna Lefever who crossed that road with the trance-like gait of a sleepwalker. It was not Joanna who watched as the car door opened of its own accord, slowly, so slowly, and who hesitated on the very brink of the act she was about to com-mit. Voices belonging to a different person and speaking of another life echoed distantly in her mind. *You can't do this! You're a respectable woman of thirty-six with a family and a busi-ness and responsibilities on all sides, you don't know who this man is, he could be anyone, it could be a setup, he could have a knife or a gun or a lethal disease, this is crazy, dangerous, insane.* But louder than any voice was the throb of her pulse, the surge of her blood, and the uncontrollable, visceral urge drawing her with absolute inevitability into the dark unknown.

She entered the car. There was that musky aroma again, the warm, alluring smell of an animal's lair. She heard the click of the door closing behind her and the soft *phthut* of the electric locking device. The darkness within was alive and moving, like the inside of a living body. A hand guided her to her knees. The carpet was thick and soft. She swayed back against the leather upholstery. Her body was in a fever. It would explode in flames at a touch. She felt turned inside out, from her sex to her scalp, inverted like a ripe fig with its skin folded in and the raw engorged flesh exposed.

The hand had found her breast, naked beneath her slip. Fingers evaluated its weight and substance, lingered for a moment cupping its round solidity, then traced a path up to the nipple. Fingernails dug gently into the hard, swollen tip. The sensation was excruciating. She felt as though a net of hot wires was tautening the sinews of her inside thighs and drawing together up through the pit of her belly, through her chest and lungs, to this single focal budding point.

His voice seemed to come from inside her head. It was soft, modulated, caressing.

"Exquisite," the voice said slowly. "Does this beauty have a name?"

Her mind was whirling, her senses were spinning. Who *was* she, what was she doing there? She didn't know. She was lost.

From some unfathomable depths of her being, far from the reach of reason and sense, she heard herself answer. Her teeth were clamped on the flesh of her hand, and the name came out muffled.

"Cristina. Cristina Parigi."

He might have heard her, he might not, it made no difference, nothing mattered, she could do nothing, think of nothing. She waited in agony during the long, laden silence that followed. Then gradually the grip on her nipple winched tighter, prizing a gasp of pain from her lips, and she found herself slowly being drawn forward by the very apex of her breast, forward and down, until she was kneeling over the seat, with the leather pressing cool against her naked front and her buttocks forced up and apart and a hand slowly working its passage toward the aching inferno between.

4

IN THE SHAVING MIRROR, her figure framed by the open door of the bathroom, Stephen watched Joanna dressing. She moved briskly, with determination. Today it was a sleeveless, body-hugging dress in a hot mix of pink and orange, a far cry from yesterday's somber blacks and grays. She stretched a long leg onto the end of the bed and bent forward to roll on a stocking. A sprawl of sheets on the bed bore testimony to the morning's brief and unexpected moment of passion.

He looked back at his face in the mirror. Today he could be mistaken for fifty, not forty. True, he'd drunk too much at dinner the previous night. But the fact was, too much sex knocked the stuffing out of a man. It was downright unfair. Sex regenerated a woman: she could arise from her bed of lust, shower and dress, and go out into the world, refreshed and reconstituted and ready to do it all over again. Or not even rise from her bed and yet still do it all over again, he thought with an inward groan as he recalled Joanna's insatiability, her *greediness*, that morning. By its very nature, the act subtracted from a man but added to a woman. Thinking of it like that, a man might well end up resentful of womankind.

He glanced back at Joanna in the mirror. She looked so damned *fresh*. She was even humming to herself.

"You sound chirpy today," he said. "I wonder why."

"Maybe not why you think," she responded archly.

"I haven't seen that dress before. I like it."

She looked up.

"You have, Stephen, and you don't."

He went through into the bedroom, toweling his face hard, punitively.

"How can you possibly say I don't like it? Since when has one person been privy to another's consciousness?"

She turned aside to hitch her stocking top to the garter belt. A cream cutaway belt, he noted.

"Last time you said it reminded you of a baboon's behind."

"Exactly. A sexual invitation."

"To another baboon." She appraised his state of undress. "You'd better get moving or you'll miss your ride."

"Miss a ride with you?"

"Don't be cheap. And don't look at me like that. Come on, shift your ass."

He couldn't move. Something about her filled him with both wonder and outrage. She seemed so complete in herself. The same as when they'd made love earlier. She hadn't wanted *him*, she hadn't needed *him*. He'd been just a vehicle for her own gratification. He could have been a total stranger. Here again, sex was different for men. Physiologically, they were designed to be promiscuous, to spore indiscriminately, indifferent to the identity of their mate. But by nature a woman should cleave to one man for her sexual fulfillment. It wasn't right if she went off into her own private world where anyone would do.

The sight of Joanna's naked upper leg filled him with the urge to despoil her, to ruffle the crisp neatness of her appearance, to send her out into the world filled with his seed, bearing his mark. He reached out and, grabbing hold of her, hauled her down onto the bed. Though she'd never admit it, sometimes she liked it rough. The sheets still gave back faintly the warm scented odor of their earlier coupling. Pinning her down with one hand, he ran the other coarsely between her legs.

But she slipped from his grasp and stood up, flushed and irritated.

"For God's sake, Stephen," she muttered, smoothing down her dress.

"Come back," he growled. "I want you."

She glanced down to where his towel had come adrift.

"You don't. You just want the idea of it." She softened and rubbed a hand through his curly dark hair. "So very you."

He pulled away and lay back, affecting a sudden, amused indifference in an attempt to regain some dignity.

"Did you know, the female orgasm is unknown among animals? It only exists among humans. Doesn't serve any reproductive purpose. Not a survival mechanism. It's purely for pleasure. What's the evolutionary value in a woman coming?"

"You lie there and work it out," she said, pouting into her dressing-table mirror as she put on her lipstick. "Maybe you should do some research on it. You're well qualified, Stephen."

He chose to ignore the barb.

"I suppose it started with Eve and the deal with the serpent," he mused. "The apple as the forbidden pleasures of sex."

"Another one for the proposal?"

"Joanna, there's a whole field of crypto-sexology no one's explored yet."

"Well, I'd give that one a miss."

"Sweetheart, your trustees aren't the only font of dough."

"Then look elsewhere," she responded crisply. "That might be easier all round."

He climbed off the bed and casually reached for a shirt, letting the conversation drop. He wouldn't pursue that line.

Out of the corner of his eye he watched her carefully. Something about her was different. He could read it in the way she stood, in the tilt of her head, in tiny details of her posture and unconscious hints in her mannerisms. She seemed less vulnerable, less dependent.

"You pay your beloved a compliment," he began again, feigning hurt, "and look what you get. I only said I liked your dress."

"Stephen, do get a move on."

"I mean it's a pleasant change from yesterday. Not so funereal."

"Today's a new day." She glanced at her watch and headed for the door. "I'm going to be late. The car leaves in five minutes. With or without you."

With that, she left the room.

For a moment he stared at the doorway after her. Ever since the tragedy she had depended on him for reassurance, for comfort, for absolution. He couldn't number the hours he'd spent telling her in a thousand different ways that they had no reason, no *right*, to blame themselves. Had she finally come through?

He hurriedly pulled on his trousers. He'd better indeed shift his ass. He had a hell of a day at the Department ahead of him, and it'd be a miracle if he came through *that*.

"Praise the Lord I say, praise Him in your hearts and souls, ye children who dwell in uptown Manhattan. Verily it is a blessing to share the word of the Lord with you fellow sinners on this Friday morning. Hallelujah, praise the Lord, I'm a believer . . . "

Over the soundtrack came a sudden howl of laughter.

Stephen pressed a button, and the video monitor froze frame. The screen was split into two images. The left half showed a television evangelist, garbed in a designer surplice, his eyes uplifted to the studio ceiling in an attitude of fervent supplication. The right half showed a young man with an elongated, lopsided face and a shock of raven hair, filmed with a concealed camera as he watched the evangelist perform. The young man was an aphasiac: he was incapable of understanding words as such, but he had developed, by compensation, an incredible ability to read people's meaning through their expression, their gestures and posture, through the hidden tone and inflection of their voices. He could grasp the expressive content of utterances, something that could never be faked in the way that words themselves so easily could.

And here he was, laughing at the evangelist. For the evangelist was lying.

Stephen rewound the tape a few inches.

". . . praise the Lord, I'm a believer . . . "

Again he froze the frame, then keyed in an instruction that magnified the evangelist's face until it filled the screen. A glance showed him he had here what he was looking for: distinct micro-momentary bilateral asymmetry. The musculature on the left side of the man's face was tight and knotted, the eye screwed almost closed beneath a hooded upper lid and the lips folded in on themselves so as to render that side of the mouth almost lipless, while by contrast the right side of his face was slack, almost gross, with the eye wide and staring, the pupil enlarged and the whole lip formation peeled back to the gums.

Everybody's face, divided down the middle, presented two different halves, of course: that was hardly surprising since each was controlled by a different hemisphere of the brain. But such an extreme dissonance as this revealed a profound incongruity between the man's words and his thoughts. He was uttering one thing and signifying another. The grimace would last no more than a fleeting fraction of a second, but that was long enough to reveal the true state of his mind. His face was giving the lie to his speech.

Stephen sat forward, focusing his concentration. Another keystroke superimposed a grid matrix on the screen, and with a cursor he began to take measurements. Then, calling up a computer graphics package, he divided the face vertically down the middle and replicated each half upon the other so as to create two separate and different faces, one composed of two left sides, the other of two right sides.

He was so absorbed that he did not hear the door open behind him. A hand on his shoulder made him start violently.

"Don't let me disturb you."

He looked up to find Don Weitzman, his dean and departmental professor, stooping over him. Weitzman leaned forward and peered at the screen through his thin rimless glasses.

"Nice pair of composites you got there, Steve," he said sweetly. "Libelous, of course."

"I don't intend publishing," replied Stephen.

"I didn't hear that." The dean pulled up a chair. He addressed the screen, casually, after a pause. "You heard they're not reappointing the Psychophysiology chair?"

"Hang on while I kill this." Stephen hit a series of keys and the original face returned to the screen. Then, discreetly, he touched a switch. He coughed to conceal the quiet whir of a motor starting up. "Yes, I heard rumors," he acknowledged.

Weitzman pinched the bridge of his nose. His long, angular face twisted with discomfort.

"We all know what that means," he frowned.

"Change is opportunity. Isn't that what you always say, Don?"

"Sure, opportunity to get one's ass kicked if one is not very careful." He continued at the screen, "I believe in your work, Steve. It has truly great potential. I wouldn't want to see your ass with the boot up it."

Stephen felt his pulse quicken.

"Are you trying to tell me something I should know, Don?"

"No, no." The dean waved his long, bony hands. "I just came by to see how you're getting on. We haven't had a chat for so long."

Stephen raised an eyebrow. They'd met virtually every day for the past months. In the corridor, in meetings, in the elevator, at parties, and entertaining visiting academics.

He gestured around the large, cluttered room. The shelves were stacked with film and videotapes, the desks groaned under books and journals, the walls were papered with printouts and computerized visuals and memo slips with ideas to follow up and references to check. Beside the window, which gave a view over the treetops of Central Park, hung a WANTED poster he'd once made as a private joke, showing two left and right facial composites of a female chimpanzee taken during the act of coitus.

"Well, you can see."

"That's what worries me, Steve. It's all so dissipated. You're scattering your fire. Academic success is all about *focus*."

"Focus pocus! Where's your lateral thinking?"

Weitzman finally turned and met his eye.

"I'm thinking about your visiting professorship coming up for review. I remember all the pizzazz when you joined the Department, how we all said getting you was such a coup."

"And what do you all say now?" Stephen was smiling, but inside his stomach was knotting.

"The stuff you did on chimps, decoding the body linguistics of primates—that's decent, solid, *focused* research. It's why we bought you. But all this 'Somatype' business . . . "

Somatext," corrected Stephen.

"It's shooting at the moon."

"Listen, Don," said Stephen, leaning forward. "Forget chimps. What can you do with a vocabulary of three hundred words? Plus, you know very well, chimps can't *lie*. We can, though. We do all the time. We're masters of deception. The hidden message behind the spoken words. The tongue says one thing the face another." He felt his enthusiasm running away with him as usual. "Decoding the human crypto-language, Don, and harnessing it into a scientific diagnostic tool, that's the project of the century. It's to behavioral psychology what the Human Genome Project is to genetics."

"And look how many guys are working on *that*. Worldwide. Round the clock. With billions of dollars behind them."

"This could be that big."

"If your name was James Watson. Sure, you don't have to have a Nobel to get to first base, but you've got to get known. That means, *published*." The dean shook his head. "Remember all that stuff you did on lie detecting with criminals? Comparing the statements under sodium amytal with what you got from your spy-in-the-room gizmo here? Brilliant, but what did you do with it? God, man, you never even wrote it up."

"Publishing papers is intellectual wanking."

"Publishing papers is publicity. It is also a measure of performance, Steve," the dean added in a warning tone. "Your trouble is, you flit from one project to another without putting down your marker."

"I'm after the big one, Don."

"Then you'd better be after the big bucks." Weitzman looked back at the screen and spoke casually after a pause. "All okay on the family front?"

Stephen swallowed. He understood. He didn't want to talk about the Foundation project. He wasn't quite sure where he stood with Joanna's trust.

"Fine," he responded crisply.

"That's not what I came to talk about. I just want to see results. Results in print. Right?" He rose and went to the door. There he turned and added, as if by afterthought, "I have a faculty heads meeting on Thursday on next year's resources budget. Would you write me a note on your own project load, Steve? With practical suggestions," he added sweetly, "on how you plan to fund it?"

Stephen listened until the footsteps had disappeared down the corridor. He got up and paced the room. He felt angry, cornered. Academic inquiry should proceed on many levels and in many directions. In a field such as his, you couldn't afford to specialize too early: you had no way of telling which avenues would turn out to be fruitful and which would be culs-de-sac. Damn the man, he muttered to himself. What had he *really* come to say? What had he really been signaling?

He returned to the video monitor and rewound the tape he had been secretly recording from the camera concealed in the monitor itself.

"I believe in your work, Steve. It has truly great potential." True or false? The tone of voice gave that one away. But he wasn't really interested in Weitzman's personal feelings. He scrolled forward again until he located the passage near the end where the dean had remarked, *"That's not what I came to talk about."* He froze the frame, then amplified the image until the dean's lean, angular face filled the screen.

Instantly it hit him. The bilateral asymmetry. The transparent dissonance between the spoken words and the unspoken message. He bit his lip. Weitzman had come to talk about one thing only: how he was going to screw a major endowment out of Joanna's Trust to set up a new department, in a new building of its own, with a dozen research fellowships and a team of assistants to support them. He'd really only just floated the idea as a possibility, but it had been interpreted as an offer, and somehow the offer had become a pledge. . . . Winding back again to the earlier part of the conversation, he realized that the message had been patently clear all along, the threat barely veiled. The university considered his work academically and financially unproductive, and this endowment was the quid pro quo for renewing his post. No Foundation, no full professorship.

He slammed his fist on the table in despair. What kind of a fool had he been to give such a hostage to fortune?

Joanna spent the morning in the midtown area, at the former textile showroom where her designers and cutters were working flat out on the show, and it was approaching noon before she reached the salon. She asked Galton to drop her on the corner of 68th and Madison, and she walked the two blocks to the burgundy and gold awning.

She stopped to buy a bagel from a street vendor, something she rarely did. She slipped a ten-dollar bill to a vagrant begging on the sidewalk, something no one with anything of value on their person was advised to do. The heat shimmered off the streets, sickly with car fumes and steamy with the air-conditioning exhaust blowing from every shop front, yet she inhaled it all with a deep, secret, inner joy she hadn't sensed for years. All around reverberated the babble of city life, the cacophony of car horns, the shouts of insult and greeting, the ceaseless maniacal roar and grind of heavy machinery, but it sounded to her like music, a triumphant symphony celebrating vitality and life. She was conscious the people she passed were casting her uncertain glances, and for a moment this disconcerted her, until she realized it was because she was smiling. She could feel it in the muscles of her face. A small, private, internal smile that kept bubbling to the surface and betraying hints of the secret she harbored.

Fifteen minutes in a dark car with a perfect stranger.

The very phrase excited her. The words carried a thrilling, hypnotic power. *Stranger*. She whispered the word in her mind. A *strange* stranger. Silent. Unspeaking. Almost invisible in the dark. An unknown presence. And unknowable: that seemed to be part of the unspoken pact between them. She didn't even know his name.

And he didn't know hers.

She slowed in her tracks. No, that wasn't exactly right. He didn't know the name of the person walking down Madison Avenue at this very moment, the person with a husband and a daughter and a couture salon on the next block. The person he knew, whether by name or not, was entirely different. The one she had assumed. The one who had existed only then, in that darkened car, for fifteen short minutes of eternity.

Joanna arrived in the shop braced for the usual battery of messages and crises. The showroom was filled with middle-aged Japanese ladies, hunting in vain for the smallest sizes, and she slipped discreetly up the stairs to her office at the rear. She paused on the way through Cheryl's office to pick up her messages.

Cheryl was on the phone. She put a hand over the mouthpiece.

"I'm holding for that lieutenant," she explained.

"What's happened?" Joanna asked quickly.

"I thought we should get the other two back."

"I'm sorry?"

"Cristina signed out two dresses as well. If we don't register our claim, they'll get cleared out with the rest of her stuff."

Joanna picked up her messages and headed toward her own office.

"Put it through to me, Cheryl," she said. "I'll handle it."

Her assistant transferred the call. On came a recorded voice asking her in tones of plastic politeness to continue to hold. For a while Joanna waited, but with increasing disquiet. She wasn't ready. She hadn't thought it out. She didn't want to speak to the lieutenant. She didn't want to speak to anyone about Cristina. Even when Cheryl mentioned her name, she'd felt almost resentful that anyone else should have a claim on her. Cristina Parigi was, somehow, *hers*.

Abruptly she hung up.

They'll get cleared out with the rest of her stuff. Cheryl was right. Someone was bound to go in and sort out the girl's possessions. A sudden, unaccountable wave of alarm swept over Joanna. She went to the filing cabinet and took out the card she'd shown the lieutenant the previous day. There it was: *PARIGI, Cristina, 101 W. 89th St. Apt #7 . . .*

She held it carefully, almost reverently. It was more than just a ticket to redeem two summer dresses borrowed from the salon stockroom by a freelance model on the house's books. It was a form of entitlement to Cristina herself.

5

OF COURSE, she was merely going to reclaim her property. Stock that belonged to her shop. Just so there would be no misunderstanding or confusion when the relatives or friends of the unfortunate girl came to sort out her belongings.

So Joanna reminded herself as her limousine swept across Central Park. Yet why was she being so secretive? She had told Cheryl she was meeting Bella for lunch downtown at the Union Square restaurant. And, earlier that morning, she'd sent Galton off on a lengthy round of deliveries that wasn't strictly necessary, though she'd also had a twinge of fear—fear of what?—and she'd waited for him to come back and drive her over himself. Galton was her "ex," as she liked to call him; an ex-black belt, ex-club bouncer, ex-bodyguard, ex-villain. In his past, he had cracked safes and skulls, picked locks and pockets, and generally busted ass the length and breadth of the state. And yet he had a soft, even sentimental heart: he was devoted to his family and fiercely loyal to her. With him, she felt safe wherever she went.

Yet though she wanted him at hand, she also wanted to do this thing alone, unseen. She deliberately gave him the wrong street number, and as the car reached West 89th Street, she asked him to set her down at the far corner of the block and wait for her. She walked the rest, trying as far as possible to keep out of his line of sight. And when she found the house, she stood for a long while in the shade of a tree on the other side of the street, studying it as she weighed up what to do.

Number 101 was a large brownstone, one of a row of similar houses originally built as family homes but long since converted into apartments. Little distinguished it from its neighbors. The front steps were painted red rather than left the natural stone, and at the top stood a pair of concrete ornamental tubs chained to the wall and filled with wilting geraniums, but the facade with its grimy, muscular elegance matched those on either side and even the gate piers bore identical scrawls of graffiti which, similarly too, no one had troubled to clean off. Whereas with the other houses a low parapet wall enclosed a paved strip to form the front yard, here a self-conscious attempt at landscaping had been made using raised flowerbeds in sinuous brick shapes, planted with heat-stricken shrubs woven in with discarded drink cans and cigarette packs and other flotsam off the streets.

As she watched from opposite the front door opened, and a young man carrying a suitcase in each hand and a pile of mail between his teeth hurried down the steps and headed toward the main avenue. A while later, a woman with the olive coloring and squat build of an immigrant maid arrived and let herself in, and a minute later appeared briefly at the first floor window.

At last, Joanna broke cover and slowly crossed the street.

By a quirk of numbering, apartment #7 was the basement. As the first floor of the house was entered up steep front steps, the basement floor was virtually on a level with the street. It was reached by a narrow brick path that led between the shrub beds and down two steps to a separate and heavily fortified front door.

Joanna rang the bell. There was no reply. She rang it again, to make quite sure. Quite possibly Cristina shared the apartment with another girl, or perhaps a boyfriend. She turned to the window and, cupping her hand against the glass, peered in through the security gate.

The room, an open-plan living room, stretched the full depth of the house, for a glow of daylight came in through another, smaller, window at the far end. As her eyes gradually adjusted, she began to make out more of the details. In the center stood a large, deep sofa, with a phone resting on the arm, its cable at full stretch, and an open diary beside it. On the floor lay a discarded bath towel. To one side stood a desk with an answering machine, its message light flashing intermittently. On a table scattered with fashion magazines, Joanna could pick out various other items: a bottle of nail polish, a hair dryer, a bunch of letters, a half-drunk glass of orange juice. A spiral staircase led downstairs from the center of the room, presumably to the bedroom. Beyond, in the far corner, stood an exercise bicycle. And forming an alcove along the left wall was a built-in kitchen and, in front, a breakfast bar on which stood a coffeepot, a mug, a plate, and a cereal bowl.

This was a single household. A bachelor girl's pad.

She tried the door. Stupid, but she tried it. She stared dumbly at the double Union lock. What was she expecting? A note saying the key was under the doormat? What was she there *for*?

Conscious her behavior might be causing notice, Joanna retraced her path. Instead of turning away, however, she found herself climbing the front steps. Through the barred window of the front door she could see a row of metal mailboxes in the hallway. Maybe she could get at the girl's mail, she told herself, and that might give a clue to the reason for her suicide. But then, was *that* the reason she was there?

On the wall beside her was an intercom with names and apartments listed on the panel. Some force impelled her to reach forward and press the buzzer marked #1.

A woman's voice in a broken accent came over the system. It was the maid.

"Hello?" she demanded.

"Delivery for Parigi," called Joanna.

"Miss Cristina live downstairs," came the reply.

So the maid, for one, hadn't heard about the tragedy. Maybe they weren't particularly neighborly here.

"No reply downstairs. I need to leave it in the hall."

"I ask Madam, but Madam is out. She comes back maybe in one hour."

"Look, just press the button."

"Who is this, please?"

"Open the door!"

There was a muffled tutting, then a *click*, and abruptly the receiver went dead.

Joanna turned away irritably. This was crazy. She only had

to give Lieutenant Portillo a call, mention her father's name, or not even that, and the dresses would be quietly and discreetly returned.

But the dresses were not the point: they were just the pretext. They had nothing to do with why she was really there. Or why she had to get into that apartment.

She headed through the ferocious, unabating heat of the city streets back to the waiting car. As she approached, Galton climbed out and held the door open for her, but she didn't get in.

"Galton," she began. "A double Union lock. Would that be something you're familiar with?"

A grin slowly spread over the chauffeur's face.

"With my eyes shut, miss," he replied.

She gave him the correct address and watched him disappear, pantherlike, down the street and out of sight. She waited for what seemed an inordinately long time. She could have sat in the air-conditioned cool of the car, but she was too restless. Instead, she paced up and down beside the car, yearning for a cigarette and wishing she hadn't given it up. She looked at her watch for the tenth time. Where was the man? Maybe that conscientious maid had seen him breaking in and called the police. Maybe he hadn't got the plastic card or the keys or whatever gear he needed . . .

Finally, quite suddenly, he reappeared out of nowhere. His grin was broader than ever.

"Open Sesame," he said.

She smiled.

"See you shortly," she replied.

Nothing had been touched, it seemed, since the twenty-two-year-old model had left the apartment ten days before, made her way across town to some intimate assignation and tragically ended her life by throwing herself into the East River. If the police had been to the apartment, they had left no traces of their visit. Certainly, no friend or relative appeared to have been in for anything.

The place smelled airless and stale. A skin of mold had dried in the base of the coffee mug and the half-eaten cereal in the bowl was furry with mildew. Half the glass of juice had evaporated away, leaving a pattern of hard orange rings on the inside. Instinctively, Joanna opened the far window to let in the slight breath of wind that was stirring. She shoveled the cereal into the wastebasket and was washing out the glass when she checked herself. What was she doing? She was acting as if this were her own home.

She picked up the mail lying on the occasional table and glanced through it. A subscription circular from *Time* magazine. An American Express statement with the warning in heavy print, visible through the envelope, *Overdue: Remit at Once.* A card from Kwik-Kut on Columbus, *Your #1 Choice, 24-hr. See-U-Safe Service, Agent for Fort Knox Alarms.* All unopened. And, lying beneath a postcard from Hawaii signed "Dizzy," a front-door key. A Union key. She picked it up quickly. Less quickly, she put it down.

She looked about the room, stirred with a confusion of feelings. She was an interloper, stealing her way into a stranger's domain. Even the dead were entitled to their privacy. Any minute she might be discovered. There'd be steps on the path, then a key in the lock . . .

Suddenly the phone rang.

She started violently. It rang three, four, five times, then the answering machine cut in.

"This is Cristina," the voice played. "I am not available to take your call right now, but leave your name and number and any message and I'll call you back as soon as I can."

Cristina was there in the room. Disembodied. Speaking from the grave.

The machine gave a beep, and a mature woman's voice came on, sweetened with a seductive purr.

"Hi, honey. Listen, have I got one for yoo-hoo! His name is Robert Holtzheim. He's from D.C., he's hunky and he's loaded. And I mean *loaded.* I've told him, it's strictly no touchee. Suits him just fine. You'll see, honey." A trickle of a laugh. "Just take plenty of lipstick. You're to be at the Ambassador, suite two oh five, tonight, ten o'clock." The voice dropped a tone. "Play it right, and you can retire on this one."

Joanna stared stupidly at the machine as it whirred and clicked and finally went silent. It was eerie: Cristina was gone, but her life was carrying on as though she were still alive and well. The maid upstairs, the credit-card companies, and the friends sending her mail, this man on the phone: they acted as if nothing had happened to interrupt the continuity of her existence. A person's life should end definitively with their death. But Cristina's seemed to keep on growing, like the hair and nails on a corpse.

Joanna turned abruptly and headed toward the spiral staircase. She'd get the dresses quickly, and go.

Below ground, a mysterious, fantastical world existed. Here the light of day was not seen. The stairs ended in a small passage painted a shiny black and lit by a hidden constellation of tiny lights. Behind a closed door lay a small storeroom piled with old fashion magazines, packing cartons, suitcases, and a jumble of discarded clothes and shoes. Opposite was the bathroom. There, the walls, the ceiling, and even the floor were made of mirrored glass and lit, it seemed, entirely by small bulbs like a Broadway dressing room.

Ahead, through a tassel curtain lay the bedroom. Joanna fumbled for a switch. The low reddish glow seemed at first to materialize out of nowhere, but as her eyes grew accustomed, she saw it came from within a kind of tent of translucent fabric like mosquito netting which overhung the bed and was gathered in swathes at the corners to form a canopy. The bed itself, which was unmade, had deep red satin sheets beneath a pale embroidered coverlet, so that at first glance she fancied the sheets were steeped in blood. At the foot stood an oval cheval glass, tilted to reflect onto the bed itself. Beyond lay chairs strewn with clothes and underwear and, lost in the deeper shadows, were panels of dark mirror glass that formed the doors to hanging cupboards and reflected the canopied bed in a dozen different facets. Joanna suppressed a shiver. It felt like walking into a subterranean womb.

Her fingers touched another switch, and suddenly thin pencil beams pierced the shadows. On the bedside table stood a bottle of tablets: sleeping pills, in a mild form. Nearby lay Linda Goodman's *Star Signs*, facedown and open at Gemini. Her own sign. A small silver photograph frame stood propped against the bedside light. It showed a smiling girl with a couple: no doubt, the parents. The girl closely resembled Cristina but she had dark hair. So, there really was a sister.

The phone lay on the bed and, beside it, several letters. Demands for payment. One was from the telephone company, giving her fourteen days. Another was from a real estate firm, threatening eviction if the outstanding rent was not paid. Cristina was clearly in debt all around. And yet it was hard to believe. The wardrobes were bursting with expensive clothes, the furniture and furnishings were all of costly imported quality, and the whole style and decor of the place betrayed high living tastes. Perhaps her income didn't live up to her tastes. Had debt driven the poor girl to take her own life?

Joanna caught sight of the time on the bedside alarm clock and stepped briskly over to the wall of mirrored wardrobes. There were cocktail dresses, leather miniskirts, smart party frocks, long evening dresses, ball gowns, a tight wet-look catsuit, a pinstripe business suit, casual daytime dresses, silk jacket and pants suits and, in one wardrobe by themselves, an entire collection of glitzy sleaze: backless cocktail dresses, others whose neckline plunged to the navel, vampish dresses with skirts split up the thigh and black lacy teddies designed to be worn alone beneath a jacket.

Joanna recognized all the labels, but the sheer quantity was astonishing. Had Cristina really bought all these garments? Had she worked for these other salons and borrowed the clothes? Or deliberately purloined them? Did she have a rich lover, or several rich lovers, who kept her in the style of apparel to which she was evidently well accustomed?

Within a couple of minutes Joanna had located one dress bearing her own label, *Designing Woman*, itself representing a few thousand dollars at retail price. She hadn't yet found the other.

As she opened the final pair of mirrored doors, she stepped back with a stifled cry.

A dozen faceless white heads stared out at her from the middle shelf of the closet. For a moment she thought she had stumbled upon a gruesome cache of severed heads, until she realized they were merely polystyrene dummies acting as wig stands. All but one supported a wig. The wigs were of different lengths and styles. And all were blonde.

Joanna understood. The girl in the photo with dark hair had been Cristina herself. She was a blonde under false pretenses.

A sudden surge of panic gripped her. She was going beyond the bounds. She shouldn't be there, discovering these things.

Something terrible was going to happen, she'd be trapped down there in that bizarre, sensual dungeon. . . . Grabbing her dress, she headed for the door. There she paused to cast a final glance over the room. On impulse, she stepped quickly over to the bed and snatched up the rent demand letter. Then she turned out the lights and hurriedly retraced her steps through the black tunnel, up the spiral stairs and into the daylight.

As if some beast from the netherworld were at her heels, she hastened through the living room. As she passed, she grabbed the front-door key and, without a further backward glance, let herself out of the door. She slammed the door shut, double-locking it behind her. Then, slipping the key into her purse alongside the letter from the realtors, she hurried up the path into the open, where she broke into a fast walk, crossing and recrossing the street until she had reached the waiting car and distanced herself from the apartment and its strange, disturbing allure.

But later that afternoon, she wrote out a check for the unpaid rent. She put it in an unmarked envelope, without a covering note, and on her way home that evening she slipped it by hand into a mailbox on the street.

6

"CLAMS WITH WILD RICE and salad. How does that sound?" As she began unpacking the groceries, Joanna caught Bella's expression. "We're having supper together for a change."

"I told Lorri I'd go to a movie with her," said Bella.

"Invite her over. Stephen will be back soon, too. I left him a message." She pushed aside a pile of mail and newspapers to clear the work-top. "You can go to your movie tomorrow."

"About tomorrow, Mom," began Bella more tentatively. "Lorri and I were thinking . . . "

"Darling, don't start again. You know I can't leave till Friday. I've got too much to do."

"We'll take the Jitney."

Joanna poured half a glass of wine from the fridge and topped it up with soda.

"You're both just sixteen. I'm not having you staying there on your own. That's final."

"Stephen can take us, then. He thinks we're crazy sticking around in the city. What's the point of having the house if we don't use it?"

"Stephen's got a lot on. Don't pressure him."

"He can bring his work."

"Here, angel, you can start rinsing the lettuce."

Bella toyed thoughtfully with a tail of her blonde hair.

"You're not comfortable when it's just Stephen and me, are you?"

"Don't be absurd! I love to see you together. You don't need me around the whole time."

"Well, then."

"Just go and call Lorri. And okay, I guess we could go on Thursday, at a pinch."

While Bella was out of the room, Joanna began preparing the clams and rice. Eating together was an important and neglected ritual: it brought a family together and sustained the elemental relationships. Life was always so hectic and fragmented: it was too easy to browse separately from the fridge, snatching a bite here and there, without settling down for any serious time to share their day's experiences and restore their bonds.

Bella returned, biting her lip.

"The movie ends today," she said. "Lorri doesn't want to miss it."

Joanna went to the fridge.

"You'd better have something before you go."

"Actually, Mom, I had a gyro on the way home."

She closed the fridge. "When does it start?"

"I said I'd meet her in ten minutes."

"You'd better get going, then. Do you have money?"

"Sure." She kissed her mother. "Sorry, Mom. We'll have feasts together every day next week. Midnight barbecues on the beach. Right?"

"Of course," she smiled. "Take care, angel. Don't be back late. Look in when you come home if I'm in bed."

"Bye, Mom. Love you."

In a moment, she was gone. Joanna listened as the elevator doors closed and the soft whirring of the motor finally stopped. She looked back at the food she was preparing, her appetite gone. She'd wait until Stephen came home and they'd finish making it together. They had their own bonds to restore.

She topped up her glass of wine and took the pile of papers and mail into the living room, where she put on a compact disc of Pavarotti arias and sank into the sofa. The phone kept ringing, and every few minutes Maria, the Puerto Rican maid, came in to deliver a message or ask some question about the arrangements for the coming week, and in between all of this momentary images of Cristina and her curious, seductive apartment kept flashing across her mind, so that it took her a good half hour to cover the correspondence.

Finally, she came to the last of the mail. It was a postcard of Niagara Falls. She turned it over and glanced at the signature.

Oh my God, she muttered aloud.

Quickly she skimmed the message.

Dear Mr. and Mrs. Lefever,

Remember me? It only seems like yesterday, amazing isn't it.

Canada didn't work out. Got into a bit of trouble, had to move on. I'm coming back to New York. We need a talk. I'll call when I hit town. See you.

Karen.

P.S. The Falls are something else!

For what seemed like minutes, Joanna sat absolutely still. She read and re-read the postcard, her stomach knotting with dread. The phone went again, but she did not pick it up. Distantly, she heard Maria answer it and, a moment later, her footsteps coming down the corridor, and from somewhere far outside herself she called out to say she wasn't in. Her thoughts were locked in their own closed circuit, oscillating between the specters dredged up from the past and anxieties about the implications for the future. In God's name, wasn't all that over and done with? Karen had no right to turn up again in their lives like this. They had an *understanding*. Stephen had seen to that.

We need a talk. What was the young nurse after?

She glanced at the clock on the mantelpiece. Stephen should have been home by now. She badly needed to speak to him. Maybe he hadn't left work yet.

Just as she was reaching out to pick up the phone, it rang. She started violently. She snatched it up.

"Hello? Who's that?"

"Hi, sweetheart. Everything okay?"

His voice was silky, smooth, almost jocular. In the background, indistinctly, Joanna could hear sounds of someone else. He had company in the lab.

"I was just about to call you," she said.

He must have sensed the tension in her voice, for his own tone grew serious. He spoke closer into the phone, and she imagined him signaling to the other person for silence.

"What's up?"

"I . . . " she broke off. This wasn't the moment. "Are you going to be long?"

"Be long?"

"For supper. I bought some clams." She paused. "Didn't you get my message?"

"Ah. Yes. That's why I called." He adjusted quickly. She could almost hear the machinery of his mind working. "I'm a bit tied up here. Don wants a report for the faculty board on Thursday. I'm sorry."

"It'll have to keep, then," she said quietly, looking at the post-card in her hand.

"No, you go ahead and eat," he replied quickly, misunderstanding her. "I don't know when I'll be through."

"Stephen . . . " she began again, then checked herself. "Forget it."

A brief silence fell.

"Well, see you later, then," he said.

"Whenever."

"Hey, come on! This is work."

"I'm going now, Stephen. I've got work to do, too."

She put the phone down and went to the kitchen to refill her glass. His tone of voice, so patronizing, so self-righteous, filled her with rage. She'd just received this disturbing, *sinister* card from a figure from their past and now, the very time she needed him, where the heck was he? Writing one of his eternal reports for the faculty board.

Like hell he was. With someone else in the room?

Then she realized. He wasn't even at the Department. He hadn't picked up the message at all.

With a sense of detached curiosity, she called his number at the Department. As before, she got his answering machine. She'd been right. It all figured. He'd only called just now to fore-stall *her* calling *him*. To establish his alibi.

Abruptly, she tore up the postcard and dropped the pieces

into the wastebasket. She didn't need his help and support. She didn't need *him*.

She went out onto the roof terrace and stood for a while staring out over the panorama stretching far into the distance. All over the city the night was coming alive, its pulse quickening. The smell of excitement, a humming, violet smell, wafted up out of the deepening dusk. It rose from the dark blot of the park and from the swirling ferment of headlights coursing the streets. High above the horizon, tiny specks of planes flashed briefly in the fast-fading afterlight, while higher in the heavens the first stars sparkled bright against the infinite indigo night.

As she stood against the railings, scouring the city night-scape, she had the powerful sensation that this was not a random mass of a myriad fragmented entities but a vast single living organ, pulsating with a single, hypnotic rhythm, drawing her toward itself with a magnetic pull. It was a lover calling her, wooing her, a siren seducing her with its song. *Come to me*, it seemed to be saying, *merge with me, lose yourself in me*.

A light breeze brushed her bare arms, its touch like a whisper of chiffon. She shivered and drew a step sharply back from the rail.

From deep inside the house a clock chimed. She counted nine strokes. One hour to ten o'clock. One hour in which to heed, or to ignore, the call to madness.

The Ambassador was the kind of hotel frequented by Europeans in search of the old, aristocratic America. Formerly the town mansion of a rail baron turned philanthropist, it conveyed the atmosphere of a discreet private club for the very wealthy. Its presence was announced not by sidewalk canopies and grand spot-lit foyers but by a single brass wall-plaque. Nor was it entered by automatic plate-glass doors that whisked invitingly open at the approach of a passerby, but by a single, solid oak door whose function was precisely the opposite, to ward off prying eyes and keep out the gross uninitiated public.

The door opened at Joanna's approach by an invisible doorman, robbing her of the final second of choice.

Shaking with fear and anticipation, she stepped into the cool inside. At a glance she took in the paneled walls, the soft leather armchairs, the fine wall-hangings and drapes and the lavish floral displays. About a dozen people, mostly men in groups of two or three, sat in the front lounge, talking quietly. She scanned their faces quickly, in case there was anyone she knew. Beyond, in a room more resembling a gaming den, she could make out several figures sitting at a bar. Would she recognize anyone? She swallowed. Dressed as she was, in dark glasses and with her hair restyled with gel, the real question was, would anyone recognize *her*?

A man wearing a pinstripe suit and tortoise-shell spectacles, evidently the floor manager, glided toward her out of nowhere. A practiced glance clearly told him she was not a guest newly arriving.

"Good evening, madam," he purred politely.

She returned his greeting with assumed indifference. Inside, she was in turmoil. Maybe he would stop her, question her. The practiced glance flicked over her once again, appraising her in a different way. A knowing eye lingered briefly over the low-cut, lace-trimmed bodice she wore beneath the pink silk jacket, then descended to her hand.

Oh my God, she thought: my wedding band!

She slid the hand behind her back and, summoning all her nerve, stepped boldly across the deep-carpeted foyer toward the elevator. The man seemed to dissolve into the background from which he has appeared. She felt a shiver of power and possibility. Maybe she was going to bring it off! Maybe she could do anything, be anyone, and no one would ever know!

The doors whispered closed and quickly she began wrestling with her wedding band. The floor level indicator had already reached ten before she managed to free it and slip it into her pocket. Calming herself, she began to focus on the danger, and the excitement, that lay ahead. The room, a large, low-lit sitting room, was empty. On an escritoire stood two bottles of champagne chilling in a bucket. The curtains were closed. Hunting prints covered the fabric-lined walls, a large mahogany cabinet concealed the television and a pair of deep sofas faced one another across a coffee-table on which stood another effusive display of flowers. A typical five-star hotel suite. Joanna had stayed in dozens like it.

"The champagne is open. Help yourself."

The voice came through an open door, from which filtered a dimmer, reddish glow. Evidently this was the bedroom. She glanced behind her at the door, measuring the distance. Yet the madness that had lured her here now drove her onward. She was possessed, beyond recall. Gripped beneath this compulsive spell, she found herself slowly crossing to the escritoire and pouring herself a glass of champagne. Her hand was shaking. She swallowed back the wine, refilled the glass and stepped cautiously toward the bedroom.

In the overmantel mirror as she passed she paused to check her appearance. She spiked up her hair in front a bit more, checked her strident lipstick, adjusted her dark glasses. The bracelet she wore, a paste copy of the gold diamond original in the safe at the East Hampton home, looked suitably gaudy in the context. And the jacket, the bodice, the tailored pants, and black ankle boots, these were the best approximation her wardrobe could offer of how a high-class hooker might dress.

A faint, complicit half-smile eddied round the corners of her mouth. The face of Cristina returned the smile.

The voice from the bedroom cut in again. Polite, modulated. "Come in here, would you?"

In the doorway, she stopped. The room was in darkness but for a lamp on the dressing table with a red shade. Reluctantly she removed her dark glasses, but even so it took her eyes a moment to adjust. A tall, handsome, fairhaired young man was standing in the shadows by the bed. He was fully dressed. The bed, large and sumptuous and also made up, lay between them. The words on the answering machine flashed through her mind: *strictly no touchee.* Her mouth was dry, her hand trembling, as she frantically tried to imagine what he would require of her and whether, indeed, she would bring herself to perform it. In that room with its ambiguous light and its atmosphere suffused with erotic tension, she felt her own boundaries diffusing until she didn't know for certain how far she would go and where she would draw the line.

He made his requirements very explicit. She was to undress to her slip, sit at the dressing table and make herself up in the mirror. She had to sit exactly as he specified, leaning forward so that her mouth alone was in the light and so that he could also see it reflected in the mirror, and until he gave her the word to stop she was to apply lipstick to her lips, pursing and stretching them as she did so, then touching up the edges with lip-liner and finally dabbing off the surplus on a Kleenex, then carefully clean it all off with lotion and cotton-wool and repeat the process again. That was all. What he did for himself in the shadows went unseen and, but for muffled grunts of pleasure, largely unheard.

When finally she made her escape, after the shockwaves had subsided, she felt curiously, and dangerously, elated.

7

JOANNA LAY IN THE SHADE of a broad acacia tree, her eyes closed, listening to the soft *plash* of the ocean lapping against the shore. A light breeze stirred the leaves above her, dappling the shadows with chinks of sunlight and flickering a dull, hypnotic red through her eyelids. From the boathouse she could hear distant cries and laughter from Bella and her friend as they worked at baling out the old sailing dinghy, while from afar off in the house, through an open window where Stephen was working, filtered occasional snatches of Italian opera. From time to time a boat would drone past in the distance, and once in a while a plane whispered high across the sky, but otherwise nothing disturbed the drowsy torpor of the afternoon.

Random images came floating into her mind, images of the night at the Ambassador hotel. Four days had passed since, days in which her memory had worked and reworked the experience.

As she lay reclined on the sun lounger, she pictured the scene as she'd hastened to go, how the young man had wanted her to stay and talk—only talk, goddammit—and made a grab at her wrist and her diamond paste bracelet had snapped. She recalled how she'd been seized with a sudden panic to get out of that room, afraid maybe of being unmasked, and how she'd snatched up the white envelope placed prominently on the mantelpiece—what had possessed her to do that? She hadn't gone there for the money—and fled from the suite, along the deep-carpeted corridor, down the elevator, and finally out of the hotel and into the heat of the night. She thought back, too, to how she'd been so filled with a confusion of feelings, so torn between relief and shock and pity, that she hadn't been able to face returning home at once but had gone on to a club instead, where she'd spent an hour, maybe two, drinking daiquiris, a drink she normally detested, until slowly, moment by moment, she'd come back down to earth. And how, in a dark corner of the club, she'd opened the envelope to find it contained five crisp one-hundred-dollar bills which, the following day, she'd paid into American Express to the account of Cristina Parigi against the balance of her debt.

Now she was here, at the beach house in East Hampton, a hundred miles away in body and a million miles in spirit, surrounded by her family and friends and neighbors, swimming in the cool ocean and cooking barbecues and sleeping long and late, and somehow, against every proper expectation, all was well, everything was all right. She had come through intact, unscathed, even enhanced. At first, she had felt profoundly disturbed. Disturbed, partly, at having uncovered a dark and dangerous side to herself, a repressed, unnatural thirst to escape into fantasy, to have sexual adventures with strangers, adventures involving no contact and no names and conducted in virtual silence, and, to remove it yet further from reality, to do it apparently for money. Or was it deeper still, a sublimation of guilt through the submergence of her self in another persona? Endless convoluted psychological theories suggested themselves until her head seemed ready to burst, but none seemed to fit. The undeniable fact was, she felt *good*. In putting on Cristina she had taken off Joanna and shed Joanna's emotional, guilt-ridden baggage. She felt exonerated, liberated. How could that possibly be bad? The small secret smile began once again to unfurl within her, and a warm glow of triumph spread through her body. She was glad of what had happened that night. Bizarre, shocking, wonderful, it had its place in the scheme of her life.

She opened her eyes.

Ahead in the ocean, the two girls, now joined by the boy from the neighbor's house, were wading waist-high in the waves, struggling to launch the boat. Bella looked up, laughing, caught her eye and waved. From the house behind, snatches of music still floated across the lawn and sands, while on the shoreline some way away she could see Stephen, in a florid pair of Bermuda shorts, standing idly skimming pebbles across the water. He turned, as if sensing her gaze upon him, and smiled. She returned the smile. He beckoned her over. Slowly she rose to her feet and stepped out into the hot sun. She made her way across the burning sand to the edge of the ocean where he stood and, slipping her arm around his waist, laid her head gently against his chest and sank contentedly into his familiar embrace.

She had been wanting to do it for two years, but until now she hadn't had the strength.

The morning was already hot, giving promise of a day hotter still than those before. Stephen was out in the dinghy with Bella and Lorri; they'd gone with rods and lines and tins of bait and a mission to catch the lunch. Joanna had driven down to the nearby mall to buy a stock of basic provisions, and specifically several large packs of garbage bags. She hurried back: she wanted time alone to do this.

The house, a two-story clapboard construction, had been altered and added to throughout its life so that now it sprawled in all directions from its original core. A former owner, an admiral of the fleet, had built an octagonal observatory tower on the ocean face, to which Stephen was fond of retreating to observe the stars or the shipping through a telescope. More recently, a large conservatory had been erected on the opposite flank, in which orchids and other plants more common to an Everglades climate flourished. The only building work they themselves had undertaken was on the upper floor, where they'd reshaped the rooms at the south end so as to create a specialized hospital facility, complete with a small clinical diagnostic lab and an adjoining suite for the live-in nurse. The door still bore the painted wooden sign Bella had bought back from a summer camp in the Adirondacks. It read, *Luke's Room.* For two years that door had been kept locked.

Joanna now took the garbage bags and went upstairs. Fetching the key from her jewelry case, she made her way along the corridor to the baby's room, just as she had done every hour of the night for all those terrible, heartbreaking months. Quickly, before the memories could swamp her, she unlocked the door and stepped inside.

The suffocating, airless smell of a hospital hit her, a smell that always evoked desperation and panic in her. Hurriedly she threw open the window. The incoming breeze scattered the crop of dead flies lying among the film of dust on the sill.

She looked around the bare room, deciding where to begin. Contractors had stripped out the medical equipment in the days that followed the tragedy, and now only indentations in the carpet and trailing wires and tubes showed where the cardiovascular monitors and the fluid filtering systems had been positioned. Close to the window and giving a view over the ocean—although the poor infant could never see it—stood the specially modified cot, now just a frame and mattress, and a small cutout mobile which swung gently on the breeze from the open window. The walls near the cot still bore brightly colored posters with pictures of rabbits and apples and clowns and toys and other objects that featured in a normal child's world but were never to feature in his. Further away from the cot, the walls were covered in a different way. Here, instead of nursery posters there were graphs recording body temperature and blood pressure, charts noting dosages and frequency of medication, and printouts giving the activity and state of each one of his tiny vital organs, all showing a gradual, irreversible downturn and all terminating in a sudden, abrupt ending.

She moved fast.

Down came the posters and the charts, the pictures and the printouts. Into the bin liners went the mobile he'd probably never been able to focus on and the soft furry toys his hands could never manage to grasp. Next, she attacked the chest of drawers. Flannel cot-sheets, cellular blankets, pajamas still in their wrappings, little white vests, tiny pairs of woolen socks and mittens, all these she hauled out and thrust into garbage bags. She upended a drawer full of presents into yet another bag, the tribute brought by well-meaning but unknowing friends to honor the birth: a small pillowcase embroidered with the initial L, a silver teething ring in a pale blue Tiffany's box, a book of Psalms from some devout neighbors inscribed:

To Luke Carrington Lefever,
born August 19th, 1990.
May this bring you a Life of Joy in the Love of God.

She rammed the Psalm book down hard in among the rest of the trash. A life of joy? The love of God? Bitter, empty words.

Finally, she stood up and cast a final glance about the room. It looked desolated but cleansed. In the morning, she'd get decorators in. She'd have it painted pale yellow, a bright, optimistic color. And turn it back into a guest bedroom. Give it life again.

She turned to the door. Her hand on the doorknob was trembling. Inside, she was weeping. Weeping with sorrow and yet also with relief.

Downstairs, she could hear doors slamming. The sound of girls' laughter filtered up the stairs.

"Mom, where are you?" came Bella's voice. "See what we caught!"

"Coming, darling," Joanna called back.

She closed the door behind her and was about to lock it by habit when she realized. She flung it wide open and, propping it open with one of the garbage bags, she headed away with a quick, light step toward the stairs.

By Sunday the first hint of a crack in the grip of the heat wave seemed to open up, but it was to prove a false promise. The sky abruptly darkened around mid-afternoon and dry thunder rolled around the low-lying hills, but the wind barely quickened and not a drop of rain fell to quench the parched land.

The two girls had gone off to a soda bar with the neighbor's boy, whose name was Eddie, and Joanna was in the conservatory, picking flowers. Stephen had drifted in to join her. He was standing inspecting a tall, broad-leaved plant.

"Interesting how many structures in nature are helical," he mused. "See the way these leaves grow on the stem. Exactly how genetic building blocks are organized." A silence fell, punctuated by the distant growl of thunder. Getting no response, he switched his attention to what she was doing. "Those are pretty. For the people tonight?"

"I don't feel like going," she replied. "I can't face a crowd. You go, though."

"But you're for throwing a party ourselves next weekend."

"That's repaying hospitality. Today I just feel like being quiet."

"You're crazy going back to town tomorrow. Stay the week here. Cheryl can run the show without you."

"I need to be on the spot."

He came closer and put his nose to the lilies she'd cut.

"Who's the lucky fellow, then?" he smiled.

She elbowed her way past him. She was taking the flowers to the Garden of Remembrance later.

"Ah, I see," he corrected himself. His change of tone showed he'd understood. Then he frowned. "Actually, I *don't* see."

"Stephen, would you pass those pruning shears?"

"I mean, one moment you're clearing out the shrine, and the next you're paying homage at the grave. Not that I disapprove. It's just that I feel—"

"I'm not sure I care how you feel, Stephen. How I deal with these things is my own business."

"Aren't you being a bit inconsistent?" he persisted. "When people behave in two contradictory ways at the same time, it generally means there's some internal conflict that's not properly resolved."

She turned to him and held his eye. She felt she understood something about him for the first time. It came as a flash of insight, lucid and compelling. Stephen had presented himself as a tutor figure to her, as a professor, adviser, therapist, guru, mediator, priest. His motive was to control her thoughts and feelings, and he achieved this by making himself the filter through which she interpreted herself, the mirror in which she understood herself. He relished that role, and he played up to it perfectly. She'd fallen for him at first precisely because of it. She'd admired his mind and been flattered by his attention, she'd envied his intellectual power and been shamed by the comparative inadequacy of her own. Just when she might have begun to see through his academic brilliance as superficial sophistry, the tragedy had occurred. In fact, though she hardly dared admit what it implied, the tragedy had occurred largely *because of* his brilliant mind and persuasive argument. After it, she'd been so destroyed within herself that she had needed all the support and help he could provide. She had looked to him as adviser and therapist, she had depended on him as guru and priest.

Maybe now at last she had grown beyond the need.

Why now? What had happened to create the change? The question sent a shiver through her, for even as she formulated it, she knew the answer. She knew very well what had recently changed in her life.

"I feel perfectly resolved," she replied quietly.

He handed her the shears with an easy shrug. She knew that mode of assumed nonchalance. It meant he was deeply affected.

"Well, I think you deserve all the credit. You've broken free from all that mawkish living in the past. That takes guts. You've seen the light, and you've gone for it. Good for you."

She selected a flower and cut the stem with sudden, vicious asperity. I don't need you to endorse it, Stephen, she thought to herself. I don't want you to congratulate me for having the guts, for seeing the light, for doing what you've been pestering me to do all along. Whatever I've done, I've done by myself, on my own, in my own way. Don't try and claim credit for my triumph.

She looked up again. She gave him the faintest of smiles. It was a mask, and behind it she was safe, untouchable.

"Thank you, Stephen," she said. "You're very kind."

A lengthy silence fell. From time to time he made as if to speak, then seemed to think better of it. She was conscious that he was studying her carefully. Perhaps he was wondering if her last remark was ironic, or perhaps he was puzzling over the apparent new and sudden shift in the balance between them. She hardly cared. She wouldn't *let* herself care. She had cared too much, for too long. Now she was out of his reach, out of the reach of her own blame and guilt. She had a secret, and she harbored it closely in her heart. And in this secret inner world she now lived and had her being.

Returning to the city was like coming down with a tropical fever. Hotter and more humid than ever, the city seemed on the verge of suffocation. Crime soared with the temperature, and nerves were at breaking point. Even the very streets were cracking up, causing water mains to burst, adding to the fears of a water shortage. Yet Joanna was glad to be back. She felt closer to herself and the danger.

Business at the salon was seasonally slack: regular customers were away on vacation and trade was mostly from passing tourists, and even they were fewer on account of the insufferable heat. Most of the preparatory work for the show had now been done and Cheryl was coping competently with the outstanding details, so Joanna decided she would return to the beach house mid-week. Meantime, there was the Sunday party there to organize and a host of minor domestic tasks to attend to.

She spent the first morning at the apartment on the telephone. She invited neighbors and friends from nearby and others vacationing within reach, including a leavening of clients and business contacts. One of their neighbors had a house party that weekend and asked to bring a guest. She left a message with her father's secretary on the off chance that he could move up his flight home and come along, too. When she came to counting the acceptances, she was astonished to find the total approaching a hundred. Then she applied herself to organizing caterers, a marquee and band, flowers and garden flares, and all the other paraphernalia of a summer evening party.

Running through her address book a final time, she found she had overlooked the Friedmans. Warner Friedman was chairman of the board of trustees, and Stephen might find it useful to meet him in a relaxed social setting. She called the law firm he ran, and in a moment she was put through to his office.

"Ah, Joanna, I'm glad you called," opened the venerable attorney. "I wanted to speak to you about your proposal to set up a foundation in," he groped for the phrase, "whatever the hell it is."

"Stephen's proposal," she corrected, meaning to stress its credibility.

"But it has your support, I take it?"

"Of course. It's just the kind of thing Grandpa meant his money to be used for."

"The kind of thing," he agreed. "But is this the *actual* thing?"

"What are you saying?"

"Joanna, I've discussed this at length with the other trustees and I have to tell you I'm not getting a lot of support for the idea."

"You've got to swing it, Warner. Stephen's stuck his neck out."

"We're talking ten million dollars! I'm thinking of Bella. And other future children you may have. It's a hell of a slice of the trust to give away."

"It leaves enough. And there's a tax break."

There was a pause.

"Joanna, I don't quite know how to say this to you . . . "

"You're *turning it down?*"

"I'm afraid so. I tried everything I could, believe me. But the consensus was negative. Your vote would make no difference."

She gave a deeply troubled sigh.

"God knows how I'll break it to Stephen."

"Just tell him we're a load of old-fashioned fuddy-duddies whose science education stopped at second grade."

"Then how can you possibly judge?" she snapped. She checked herself, realizing the issue was political, not academic. "Listen. You've got my vote. Suppose I get Harvey on our side. One more and we'd have stalemate. Then you'd have the casting vote, Warner." There was another pause. She waited with a sinking feeling as he did nothing to fill the silence. "I see. Well, then, I suggest *you* break it to Stephen. You explain it, and let him hear your reasons. And try and find something more convincing than saying you had an arrested education. I'm very disappointed in you, Warner."

"I'm sorry, Joanna. But as trustees we have to act in the best interest of the Trust as we see it. That's what we're paid for."

"I'm very disappointed in your decision, then." She brought the conversation to a close. "See you on Sunday."

"I look forward to it. Good-bye, Joanna."

She poured herself a long, cool drink and went out onto the roof terrace. Stephen would be mortified. It had only been a passing idea of hers at the start, and then only a couple of million dollars to endow a chair, but Stephen had typically latched onto it and built it up into the inflated, grandiose scheme it had become. Worse, he had built it up in his mind into a reality. He despised the trustees as backward, retrogressive bigots and, again typically, he had no time to listen to their opinions, ignoring the fact that, backward and bigoted though they might be, they controlled the strings of the purse. She'd warned him, but he'd made commitments to the faculty before he'd properly secured the other end. In so many ways he was a child. He believed that justice and enlightenment always prevailed in the end. He ought to know better. In this world, most of the time, the moronic inherited the earth and the meritorious didn't get a look-in.

In the background she heard the phone ringing. She didn't move, knowing she couldn't catch it. In this city, no caller let a phone ring more than five or six times. Time was too precious.

But it rang on and on. For a while she assumed Maria would pick it up, but then guessed she was out shopping. Finally, fearing it might be Bella and something was wrong, she went back inside to the living room and picked up the receiver.

There was a silence from the other end. For a moment she thought the caller had hung up just as she'd reached it.

"Hello?" she said into the void.

Then came a voice she knew, the voice she had been dreading. A flush of perspiration prickled her skin.

"Mrs. Lefever? It's me."

"Who's that?" she demanded, knowing full well.

"Karen."

"What do you want?" she croaked.

"Did you get my card? I bet you were surprised. It's been so long. Well, two years isn't so long, really. I've thought about you every day. How is the family? Mr. Lefever? And Bella? She must be sixteen by now. Doesn't time fly?"

Joanna was gripping the phone so hard her fingers ached.

"I have nothing to say to you, Karen. I don't want to speak to you, and I don't want to hear from you again."

"Hey, this is just a friendly hello. I just got back to New York and I thought, I must see how Joanna and Stephen are getting on. Maybe they have another baby by now. Or one on the way."

"I'm hanging up."

"You wouldn't, Mrs. Lefever. Not after all we've been through together. And seeing as I need help."

"Listen, Karen. I don't know what you want, I don't *care* what you want, but I've got nothing for you." She fought down the hysteria rising in her voice. "Leave us alone! As far as I'm concerned, it's all in the past. Finished. I don't want any more to do with it. I don't want to hear from you again. Ever. Do you understand? Good-bye."

She slammed down the receiver. The world about her seemed to lurch and sway. She felt physically sick.

Images began crowding her mind like a flock of birds flapping around the inside of her head, pecking at her brain. She was back in the delivery room at the clinic, and the baby was coming, and in the middle of the daze of pain and the pandemonium of her senses she caught the look in the obstetrician's eyes above his green mask and saw his brow tighten in a frown of concern, she saw him exchange a quick glance with the nurse and her eyes reflect alarm, and then suddenly everybody about her crashed into emergency gear, equipment was wheeled up, instruments clattered on metal dishes, nurses prepared syringes, then she felt the sudden sting of a needle and a wave of oblivion blurred out the scene, while all the time inside her she was screaming, aloud but unheard, *What's happening? What's the matter? What's wrong with my baby?*

And she thought of the room at the beach house she had just cleared, of the clothes and toys and nursery pictures stuffed in black garbage bags and awaiting collection, of the painters, too, who had gone in that very day to wipe out the last memories and breathe new life into the house.

She sank onto the sofa and beat her temples with her knuckles. Was she ever going to be free?

She'd received a call from Lieutenant Portillo, just to update her. They'd drawn a blank on the Cristina Parigi case. The body had still not been recovered, no missing persons reports had shown any correlation and no one had come forward as next of kin. They'd visited the apartment, he said—some fancy goddamn bordello it was, too—but they hadn't turned up anything useful. As the case stood, he could not warrant expending further police time.

She ran the conversation back in her mind as the cab rattled across the park to West 89th Street. On a detached, uninvolved level, she was genuinely sorry. Everyone had someone who loved them and cared about them. Cristina must surely have had a person like that in her life, someone who had a right to know. She ought to do her best to find this person and make contact. Maybe a message on the answering machine might provide a lead. Or she'd find something among the papers the police had missed.

On another level, she couldn't help feeling secretly pleased that the girl seemed untraceable. For, in truth, she was neither detached nor uninvolved.

She asked the cab driver to drop her further up the street and, again, she walked the remaining block. As she reached the house, however, she gave an abrupt start. In the street outside stood a moving truck. Men were loading it up with furniture. She rushed forward, but when she saw the men carrying a large sofa down the front steps from an upper apartment, and not the basement, a flood of relief overwhelmed her. In that instant, through her own instinctive reaction, Joanna realized how deep her involvement went.

She waited until the men were back inside and slipped unseen down the path to the door of the basement apartment. With a precautionary glance through the living room window, she let herself quickly in.

Twilight was falling, but she didn't turn on the lights. As her eyes grew accustomed to the penumbra, she saw with shock the results of the police "visit." Magazines and mail were scattered over the floor, drawers were turned out and their contents ransacked, the sofa was upended and several of the cushions were ripped and slashed apart. It was only when she saw the fridge door open and, looking closer, found the ice compartment had been plundered that she realized that this had been a drug raid. They'd presumed a drug connection in Cristina's suicide. They'd turned the place over and, finding nothing, walked out and left it.

Left it to *whom?* No one seemed to hold any claim over Cristina or her possessions.

The way lay open and clear.

First, she needed a drink. With a lingering twinge of guilt, she poured herself a large, neat vodka. Stolichnaya, she noted—her own favorite brand—but of course there was no ice. She took a gulp of the tepid spirit and sank back into the sofa. She drew a deep breath and let it out slowly. Every second longer she spent there, the place seemed to belong to her more. In the low, undefined light, she had the feeling that the edges of her own body had somehow grown diffused and begun to merge with the space about her, so that she was part of the objects around her and they, in turn, part of her.

After a while, she rose and began to tidy up the grosser signs of chaos, shoveling the contents back into the drawers and righting the fallen furniture. She wandered around the room, familiarizing herself with the silent voice of the place. She examined objects one by one. She traced a finger in the dust on the surfaces as she passed and felt the fabric of the curtains and upholstery. There was a coherence in it all, a pattern that seemed, strangely, fitting. It was like putting on a favorite coat long forgotten in the closet.

The message light was flashing on the answering machine. She hesitated, torn between her earlier pledge and an inexcusable feeling of resentment at being intruded upon.

She pressed the button. "You have two messages," announced the synthesized voice.

The first was from Dizzy, the writer of the postcard from Hawaii. Dizzy was drunk. She was back in town and they were having a party at Sam's place—whoops of laughter in the background—and Cristina just had to drop everything and come on over, or did she mean come on over and drop everything? The message ended in a garbled slur. The time-and-date indicator showed it was three days old. Dizzy had not left a number.

The second voice was also a woman's. She recognized at once the sweet, seductive purr.

"Hi, honey, so what in the name of Saint Priapus did you *do* to young Robert? He's calling me every hour, on the hour. You blew his socks off—and not just his socks, either. He's an open pocketbook, honey, and he's crazy to see you again. So do us all a favor and *call me*, huh?"

She stood for a while without moving as the secret feeling of elation once again spread through her.

She was Cristina. The mask fitted.

It was almost too dark to see now. She felt her way to the stairs and slowly descended into the black womb of the house. In the bedroom she turned on the low, seductive lighting and stood by the bed for a moment, looking at her reflection faceted in the mirrors all around. She tossed her head, ran a hand through her hair, did a little pirouette. She was a perfect Cristina.

The bedside table had been searched and the sleeping pills were gone, but the bed, with its disheveled crimson sheets, remained untouched. She stroked a hand over the cool satin. Feeling a wave of weariness coming over her, she gently laid herself down on the edge of the coverlet. The faintest perfume arose from the pillows: a floral fragrance, still fresh, the scent of a young woman. She lay back. Above her, from an indefinable source, shone the low red glow, diffused through the muslin drapes. She kicked off her shoes and stretched out further onto the bed.

She closed her eyes. A feeling of great calm came over her. She was a boat detaching from the land and drifting away into a vast, limitless ocean. All the guilt and the grief, the shame and the sorrow, lay left behind on the shore in the husk of her discarded body, while her own true essence, pure and light and unfettered, floated free and formless upon the gentle waves.

She awoke from a light, dreamless sleep and sat up with a start. Then she remembered where she was, and she sank back into the warmth and security. She was safe in her hideaway, beyond the reach of the world, beyond the reach of Joanna.

She gave a yawn and stretched. As her hand reached out between the pillows, her fingers touched a small, flat object. She took it out to see. It was a lizard-skin credit-card holder. Unclasped, it opened to reveal transparent pouches packed with credit cards. All held cards except the last. She leaned up on her elbow and angled it to the light.

It was an identity card.

Apprehensively she slid the card out of its pouch and switched on the bedside light. She drew in her breath.

The photo on the card was Cristina all right. But the name was entirely different. *Courtenay Ann Chambers*, she read. *Place of birth: Paris, Tx.*

8

THE INVITATION WAS FOR SIX O'CLOCK and, at three minutes past, the first guests arrived. Stephen was still upstairs, in shirt and underpants, struggling with his bow tie. He was always late: to an English gentleman, he said, punctuality smacked of unseemly eagerness. "If you were less of a chauvinist snob and settled for a clip-on bow tie," Joanna retorted, "you'd be like any well-bred American gentleman. On time."

She stood on the broad lawn at the back of the house, welcoming the guests as they were ushered through the house and emerged through the open double doors. She wore a long dress made of crimson silk crepe and a short white sequined jacket, with a string of diamonds and the gold diamond bracelet out of the wall safe. Bella stood beside her, in a classically simple pale blue evening dress. It was one of Joanna's own and, as she noted with that confusion of alarm, delight and envy of a mother watching her daughter growing up, it fitted fully and perfectly around the bust.

At her side hovered a waiter with a tray of cocktails. Behind, from the marquee by the pool, filtered the sounds of a small band tuning up, punctuated by the chink of cutlery and the soft pop of corks. All around the gardens, tracing the walkways that wove through the shrubbery and lining the broad stretch of open grass that led down to the shoreline, stood the stakes of garden flares as yet unlit. The evening was close and humid, and all about her seemed cloaked in a thin mauve heat-haze stolen in from the ocean.

She shook hands, she exchanged kisses, she embraced old friends and greeted new ones, she was on cocktail-party automatic pilot.

"So glad you could come, Merrily, you're looking wonderful, it must be love, hi, Gabriel, good to see you, how's the shark fishing this year?, I loved that piece in *Forbes,* hello, Tony, Denise, that's a wonderful frock, Merrily, Gabriel, do you know Tony and Denise Burton?, Tony's heir apparent at Burton and Frankel . . . "

An arm grasped her round the waist from behind and a hand spread against the flat of her stomach. It was Stephen in a black tuxedo, oozing smiles and bonhomie.

"Good evening, Merrily, Gabriel, Tony, Denise. That's a truly fascinating dress, Denise,"—its neckline plunged to the navel, revealing two perfectly hemispherical silicone orbs—"could it be one of Joanna's new secret weapons?, first things first, what can I offer you? Here we have the house cocktail, champagne and a mystery ingredient, tis just this side of legal, but if you don't fancy living dangerously, Manuel can fix you something more tame . . . "

More guests kept arriving. Stephen, she noticed, was sinking the cocktails with ominous rapidity. He drank when he was frustrated and depressed, and he drank when he was elated and optimistic. She bit her lip, remembering that the family lawyer would be appearing through that door at any moment.

During a short lull, she slipped her hand in Stephen's and drew him to one side. Together they surveyed the party scene. The first mix of introductions, lubricated by the cocktails, seemed to be going well, and bursts of laughter exploded on all sides like firecrackers. From time to time the caterers or musicians would come up to her to check details of the arrangements, but all was going without a hitch. Bella had slipped away and was standing by the pool, talking to Eddie with great intensity. The rich smoky aroma of the barbecue arose in the air, mingling with the rising volume of jocularity.

A waiter passed, and Stephen swapped his empty glass for a

full one. Joanna wasn't drinking. He raised his glass in a solo toast.

"Looks like we've got ignition," he said. "You certainly throw a good bash, sweetheart."

She laid a restraining hand on his arm.

"Go easy. You're among friends."

"Friends?" he snorted.

"Come on, relax." She squeezed his hand.

"You know," he said with a fragile chuckle, "the thing about you lot is you're all so damned *sure* of yourselves. Such certitude. I don't know whether I feel pity or envy."

"It's all faked. Underneath, we're all a mess of anxieties and neuroses. You of all people can surely decode that, Stephen." She cast him a careful glance. He was in a worse state than she'd imagined. He knew Friedman was coming, of course; maybe he had guessed the trustees' decision. "Listen to me, Stephen," she continued urgently, meaning to prepare him for the news. "You could quit your job tomorrow if you wanted. Screw Don Weitzman and the rest. We don't need the money."

From the quiet despair in his reply, she knew she'd touched the right nerve.

"I need the work, Joanna. I need the *challenge*."

"Columbia is convenient, sure, but there are a hundred other universities. And the whole wide world outside the ivory tower." Beyond him, she could see a new group of guests emerging through the double doors. She tightened her grip on his arm. "Just remember who you are. You're brilliant, and if they don't appreciate that, then stuff them. You don't need the hassle. Remember all the shit you used to give me? Take a dose of your own medicine."

She turned and steered him back to welcome the new arrivals. *Remember all the shit you used to give me?* She could hardly believe these words came from her own lips. For as long as she could remember, she'd looked to him for strength and reassurance. Now the balance was tipping the other way. They could talk it through properly later, but right now he was clearly in no state to hear he had been turned down. She'd intercept Warner Friedman as he arrived and tell him to hold back. Tonight was not the time to break the news.

Several more people arrived in quick succession, and once again she went through the welcoming ritual, shaking hands, embracing, exchanging compliments, offering drinks, effecting introductions, before returning to repeat the same with the next guests.

Last came a handsome young couple from West Hampton. Randi was a professional tennis player and Greg a Wall Street investment broker, and they had brought their house guest along with them, an athletic young man with close-cropped fair hair and classic chiseled features.

The house guest stepped forward in his turn to be introduced.

"Joanna, Stephen," said Greg, "I'd like you to meet a good friend of ours . . . "

Joanna stifled a gasp. She took an involuntary step back.

". . . Robert Holtzheim. Robert's weekending with us. Robert, may I introduce Joanna and Stephen Lefever . . . "

With her senses blurring and her head spinning, she found herself stretching out her hand and looking into those boyish blue eyes.

The blue eyes sharpened, the pale brows furrowed. Across his face, in quick succession, flitted expressions of shock, disbelief, recognition, embarrassment. A violent blush reddened the lean, fresh cheeks.

"Hi," he stammered. He reached out his hand clumsily and shook her by the fingers. His hand was moist. "Thanks for having me along, Mrs., uh, Lefever. Looks like a great party."

He lingered over the handshake, searching her face for a prompt. Stephen, typically, sensed an atmosphere. His face was smiling, but his eyes were reading.

"You've met before?" he inquired.

"I've never had the pleasure," replied Joanna firmly. She gestured quickly toward the waiter and his tray of cocktails. Keep talking, she thought, and get rid of him. "Would you care for a champagne cocktail, Stephen calls it Chinese Whispers, after the nightwear range in our new collection, it has a mystery ingredient, God knows what, ginseng or pickled snake or something, what is it, Stephen?"

"Three penis brandy," said Stephen.

"Whose were the other two?" chuckled Greg.

"Actually, it's sake, I saw the bottles," she continued hurriedly. "And of course we have scotch, wine, anything else you'd like, Manuel will fix it, and then come and meet some people, I think there are a few you won't know." She caught sight of the catering manager heading toward her through the throng. "Would you excuse me a moment? Stephen, you see to our friends."

She slipped away and intercepted the manager. She drew him back to the marquee and stayed there inspecting the layout of the buffet at unnecessary length until she'd recovered her composure. What a stupid, impetuous idiot she'd been! New York was a *small town*, for God's sake. She could at least have disguised herself better. She reached for a glass from a passing waiter and drained it at a gulp. Fortified, she felt more resolute. All she could do now was see it through. After all, at one level of truth, Joanna Lefever had *not* met this boy.

From that moment, the evening turned into a nightmare.

Down by the pool she came upon Bella, sitting at a candle-lit table sipping orange juice and still locked in close conversation with Eddie. They were planning to take a year off between high school and college and travel around the world together. She sat down at the table and joined in. She heard herself offering encouragement and precaution by turns until she realized that each piece of advice she gave contradicted the last. Travel broadened the mind, but the world was a dangerous place. They were far too young, but then hadn't she herself been all over Europe in her teens, spending a semester at a finishing school in Switzerland, and even once got to China and Japan? Then again, she'd been in the company of her father on one of his business trips, whereas Bella was proposing to go just with Becky and Eddie. What if they fell ill? Or just fell out?

"Mom," sighed Bella patiently, "there are such things as airplanes and credit cards. Even if there weren't in your day."

"Oh, I'm before the steam age," she managed to smile.

All the while she was concentrating on not looking around. When finally she glanced up, she immediately spotted the figure of Robert at the far end of the pool. He was standing alone, glass in hand, fixing her with an intent stare. As she caught his eye, he began to move forward. Abruptly she stood up and, with a promise to talk more about it later, headed back toward the thick of the gathering.

To avoid being intercepted, she took a circuitous route along a path through the shrubbery. The flares were now lit and, with the twilight falling fast, they cast pools of yellow and red light that lent the gardens an atmosphere of dangerous enchantment. She walked quickly, fearing the footfall behind her or the face springing out from the shadows. As she emerged into the open again, she stopped dead in her tracks.

Not ten yards ahead, in opposing positions on either side of the old stone sundial and clearly locked in an acrimonious dispute, stood the two figures of Stephen and Warner Friedman. Stephen was leaning forward, his shoulders braced like a boxer's, and his hands hanging menacingly at his side. The chairman of the Trust faced him, his gray-bearded chin thrust forward and his tall, thin body, as rigid as a board, inclined slightly backward as if instinctively keeping out of reach.

And, moving into her view from the side and cutting off her access to the main group, prowled the solitary, searching figure of Robert Holtzheim.

The band had begun to play, and people were gathering in the marquee for the buffet. Joanna was inside, gliding to and fro, exchanging a word here and issuing an instruction there. She paused briefly to talk about drama schools with Merrily and the art investment market with Tony. She called Bella over and asked to turn on the pool lights. Spotting Warner Friedman entering the marquee, alone and flushed, she cast anxiously around for Stephen, but he was nowhere to be seen. She had to find him. On the way she got caught by Greg, who said with an untrustworthy smile that his house guest had been asking all about her, what she did, where she lived, how long she'd been married and, gee, anyone would have thought she was an old heartthrob from school days, which maybe she was, was she?

With a dismissive laugh, she finally slipped out into the flare-lit night. She searched first the area by the sundial, but there was only a couple embracing in the moonlight. She headed down to the pool and glanced in at the changing rooms, but finding no one she hurried on, aware that her absence from the party would soon be noticed. She was growing worried. She hadn't realized until seeing Stephen's state tonight just how far he had actually committed himself. The idiot had put his ass on the line. With all the drink he'd taken on board, Christ knew what crazy thing he might think of doing.

She quickened her step. The shadows loomed out at her. Ahead, the waves crumpled softly onto the shore, paused at the turn, then ebbed with a hiss. A brief sheet of lightning flickered in the sky, followed an interval later by the distant dry rumble of thunder. She reached the low headland from which she could see the frothing rim of the shore and, beyond, the oily black sea. To her right lay the low clapboard boathouse. She screwed her eyes to scan the shadows.

Yes, maybe . . .

She hurried closer. She was right. He was there. She could see him in outline. He moved, and his figure was lost against the darkness of the building. The poor fool. God knew, he'd probably got a bottle of scotch and was drowning his sorrows. He'd end up drowning himself if he wasn't careful.

"Stephen?" she called. "Are you okay?"

She had reached the boathouse and skipped up the five steps onto the boardwalk that ran around it, when suddenly, out of the shadows and directly into her path, stepped a different figure.

Robert Holtzheim.

She recoiled with a choked cry. He moved closer. The moonlight silhouetted him from behind, so that she could not see his face.

"At last," he said slowly, his eyes boring through the dark. "The *madame* of the house."

She fought to recover her composure. This was an impertinent, uninvited guest who was overstepping the mark.

"I'm not sure I like that remark," she said tightly, backing away.

"Relax. I'm not about to cause a scene. I'd just like a talk. The talk we never had."

"You're mistaking me for someone else."

"Oh no. It's you all right."

"I've never met you in my life. Now, if you don't mind . . . "

"Your voice. Your face. Your mouth. Why, even that bracelet."

She contrived a short, mocking laugh.

"Tiffany's sells bracelets like these by the dozen."

"Look, don't feel embarrassed. What's wrong with a little moonlighting on the side? Many ladies in your position do it. Maybe they're bored with their husbands, or their husbands play around. Stephen looks like he's got a roving eye . . . "

"Get out!" she hissed.

"Easy, easy. Don't worry, I'm not going to blow the whistle. I want to see you again. Listen, I'm in town next week. How about Tuesday, same time, same place?"

"Did you hear me?"

"Now, hold it. I *could* make this very uncomfortable for you. Believe me I could, Cristina," he added nastily.

"Out!" she cried hoarsely. "Out of here at once. If you're not off my property in three minutes, I'll call security."

Before he could respond, she spun round and walked away with all the dignity she could muster. A few yards into the darkness, she broke into a run. Briefly she turned to catch a glimpse of the young man staring after her, mortified and angry, but already she was scrambling up the low headland, along the path between the tussocks of wiry sea grass, and finally up the broad stretch of lawn that led toward the salvation of the house.

Outside the marquee, she paused. Trembling and sick, she steadied herself against one of the ropes. Someone came up and asked if she was feeling all right. An arm steered her toward a chair. But she couldn't sit down. She had to find Stephen. She asked this person and that, but no one had seen him. She felt out of control, caught in a spiral of noise and light and surrounded by mad, meaningless voices and crazy laughter.

There was a roll on the drums and a clash on the cymbals, and the band struck up a different tune. Distantly she recognized the introductory bars of *Stormy Weather*. Someone blew into a microphone, and a cheer rippled through the gathering as a soft, velvety voice took up the melody. The sound of that extraordinary, magical voice penetrated her senses. She was aware of a hush of awe falling gradually over the audience.

She looked across the throng to the platform. It was Bella singing. She stood very upright, very still, with her long blonde hair curtaining her face and the microphone held close to her lips. Such poise, thought Joanna fleetingly, and such composure. What had happened to the child she'd known? Grown up without her realizing it, when she was looking the other way. As she had been for the past two years.

She scanned the sea of admiring faces. No sign of Stephen. She glanced back across the gardens. None there, either. With a flush of anxiety she thought of Robert. She must never again risk her two lives crossing like this. But what if he refused to leave? Suppose he came up to her in front of her guests and caused a scene? Or spread some scandal through Randi and Greg? She'd get the security staff to check him physically off the premises, and meantime she'd make herself scarce.

She headed toward the house. Behind her, the song had come to an end, the final bars drowned in a burst of applause. People began dispersing, some to the barbecue, others to the lawns and pool. She wished she could stay and congratulate Bella, but she couldn't chance it.

Indoors, she spoke to the security supervisor and sent him off to deal with the unwanted guest. In the marquee, the band had now kicked into a furious hillbilly romp, and through the open doors and windows rose a wild frenzy of whoops and cries. Somewhere on the patio a glass smashed. From the pool came a thunderous splash, accompanied by peals of laughter. The party had reached criticality. From here on it would run under its own momentum.

She went deeper into the house. She had to hide until she knew the coast was clear. But there were people everywhere: in the conservatory a couple was locked in intense and intimate conversation, in the library a group of men lounged smoking and talking business, while throughout the halls and corridors, in the kitchen and scullery, staff and helpers scurried back and forth. Finally she was driven to seek refuge and solitude up the narrow, winding stairs that led to the small octagonal observatory in the tower.

She closed the door of the observatory behind her with a sigh of relief. She did not turn on the light: with windows on all sides, there was enough light from the moon and from the flares and party lights below. This was the perfect retreat. Here she could see and not be seen.

Built higher than the adjacent roof, this room commanded a watchtower's view of the front and back of the house. She now focused her attention on the front yard for signs of the unwelcome visitor departing. For a while she watched the pool of light on the gravel driveway in front of the porch, but saw neither comings nor goings. She scanned the rows of cars parked haphazardly along the drive and under the pine trees. Suddenly her gaze froze.

Deep in the shadows she glimpsed movement. She peered closer. A figure was standing close into the trunk of a tree, watching the house. It was a woman, she felt sure. A snooper, a prowler, a gate-crasher? She screwed up her eyes but she couldn't make out any more.

Then she had an idea. The telescope!

She swiveled the instrument round on its pedestal and, directing it toward the tree, peered into the eyepiece. All she could get at first was a dim blur, but as she managed to adjust the lens, leaves and branches sprang suddenly into focus, magnified a hundredfold. She combed the grass and the under-trees, sweeping the telescope back and forth, but whoever it was had vanished. Then, by the stone pillars at the entrance to the drive, the telescope picked up a group of three men. Two were burly security guards and the third was the angry, truculent figure of Robert Holtzheim being escorted into a car. A moment later, the car turned full about in a shower of gravel and sped off out through the entrance, and the two security men returned alone.

She heaved a sigh of relief and turned to the door. She could return to the party now.

As she was about to leave, she glanced down at the throng in the gardens at the rear of the house. She paused. Somewhere among that whole tapestry of light and movement was Stephen.

She turned back to the telescope.

Images sprang to her eye in intimate close-up. She followed the passage of a vial and spoon being handed around a group in the shadows of the marquee. She watched Gabriel and Tony shaking hands on a deal. She penetrated the further darkness to find a figure bent double, vomiting into the shrubbery. She homed in on the pool, where she discovered Bella and Lorri swimming in the nude, their two pale, lissome bodies underlit by the pool lights, and Eddie standing on the side, his clothes dripping wet. She focused further away, on the ripple of froth at the shore's edge, as bright as a string of pearls in the moonlight, on the dark outline of the boathouse, on the dwarfed and wind-scoured bushes that lay along the headland path and on the hidden pockets of soft, grassy sand in between . . .

She whipped the telescope back.

Two figures were lying among the grass in a shallow sandy dip, entwined in the act of coitus. The man lay atop the woman, his dark hair disheveled, his jacket thrown aside and his white shirttails heaving up and down with each thrust. Beneath writhed the woman, her blonde hair thrashing to and fro, her long naked legs, pale in the moonlight, raised above his shoulders, her mouth agape in an inaudible moan and her dress torn off her shoulders to reveal her breasts, perfect hemispherical orbs standing perfectly upright in defiance of natural gravity . . .

It's Denise, she thought, the cheating little harlot, being fucked into next week while Tony is up at the party, talking business with Gabriel.

The man turned his head. His face was in shadow, but just visible. Teeth clenched, mouth screwed in a wince of pain, or ecstasy, it wasn't possible to tell. Rupture, or rapture: was it *ever* possible to tell?

He raised his head, like a wolf baying to the moon.

It was Stephen.

Stephen is fucking Denise, she heard herself think. And I am standing here, watching him.

She let out a small involuntary cry. It came out strangely like a laugh. In a way, it *was* funny.

She kept her eye pressed to the eyepiece. Stephen was flagging now, but Denise wanted more, she was doing the thrusting now, heaving him up and down on her like a sack of potatoes. He was having to clutch onto the grass to stay on the ride; his face was contorted, his neck sinews strained like whipcord, the veins on his temples stood out like knots. Why was he putting himself through this? Was it really a measure of virility, riding this bucking, fucking bronco? Suddenly and very obviously he came. But she was insatiable. She wanted on and on. She must have been screaming out loud, for he clamped his hand over her mouth. She grabbed the other hand and forced it to work between her legs. A long series of convulsive spasms racked her body and slowly she grew still. He climbed off her and fumbled with his pants. She stretched out, luxuriating in the aftermath. He looked around nervously, checked his watch, rearranged his clothes hurriedly, and rose to his feet. As he fiddled with his bow tie, he signaled to her to hurry up, too. Eventually she rose. She was naked to the waist. But instead of pulling up her dress, she wriggled it over her hips and let it drop to the ground so that she stood before him completely naked. She pressed her body against his in a brief, clinging embrace, then she turned and walked away, slowly and with a high step, her breasts bobbing and her ass undulating and her blonde hair flowing like a golden mane, down the path and along the headland and across the sandy beach and finally into the water, where she waded in up to her waist and then slowly, exquisitely gave herself to the ocean.

The party was drawing to a close. From the back came the sound of equipment being dismantled and folding chairs stacked; from the front, raucous farewells and car doors slamming. Joanna stood in the hallway, bidding good-bye to the departing guests. Stephen was lurching around outside, seeing people to their cars. He hadn't addressed a word to her in the two hours since he'd returned, flushed and unsteady, from his escapade on the beach. While the party had been in full swing, they'd managed to steer clear of one another, but now that everyone was leaving they were being forced together like fish in a dwindling pond. Yet still he contrived to avoid her, and she was glad that he did. She saw an almighty storm ahead, and she wasn't going to have it break in public.

Finally she waved off the last of the guests from the porch and turned back indoors with a weary sigh. How had it gone? She couldn't tell. One never could with one's own parties. It was well past one o'clock and enough had been drunk to float a fleet, and on that measure it had been a success. For her, however, it had been a nightmare. And the nightmare wasn't over yet.

The catering manager came up to her with an unctuous smile.

"I hope everything was to your satisfaction," he began.

"Everything was just fine, thank you."

"Is Mr. Lefever available?"

She could tell he was after payment. He wasn't to know that in this household she wrote the checks.

"Come with me and I'll see to you."

She led the way down the corridor and into the small, comfortable study which she used as an office when away from town. The lights were dimmed, bathing the book-lined walls and the velvet upholstered wingback chairs in a rich red glow. She stepped over to the leather-top desk and switched on the glass-shaded table lamp. The manager hung back deferentially in the doorway. She reached into the top drawer and took out a checkbook. Then she looked up.

It was the holdall she saw first. A black Adidas holdall lying on the Turkish rug. Then she saw the feet, in worn white trainers and bobby socks. Then the legs, slim legs, folded casually, in tight scuffed jeans. And as she gradually raised her gaze, she saw to her alarm, comfortably established within the arms and wings of the chair, with a drink in one hand and a look of cool defiance in her eye . . .

She felt the blood drain out of her.

"Karen!" she breathed. "What the hell are you doing here?"

"Hi, Mrs. Lefever." The girl's voice was quiet, polite. "I guess you weren't expecting me."

"How did you get in?"

"Through the front door."

"I'll deal with this gentleman and see you out again."

"Do carry on, please." The girl stood up and gestured around the room with her glass. "Nothing's changed. Same smell, too." She sniffed the air. "New banknotes."

"Be quiet."

Joanna scribbled a check and handed it to the caterer. She hustled him out of the room, then turned to face the girl. A giddy sense of déjà vu overwhelmed her, catapulting her back two years, back to the same room. The same girl, auburn-haired and freckle-faced, standing in the same position, then in the crisp uniform of a nurse, not a travel-worn sweatshirt and jeans. The same conversation, too, she suspected, and to the same purpose. And rising like a tide in her own heart the same horror and guilt, still as fresh as ever.

She held the door open. She was shaking with shock and outrage.

"I must ask you to leave," she croaked hoarsely. "Go now. Don't make me have you thrown out."

Karen smiled, ignoring the threat.

"Tell me, has my room still got that weird old bed with the inlay stuff?"

Joanna brushed past her and went to the desk. She'd ring through to the kitchen and call in the security guard. Or better, get someone to fetch Stephen. Drunk or sober, he'd sort out the little bitch. He was in this up to his eyebrows, too.

The checkbook lay still open on the desktop, and she swept it quickly into the drawer. Karen noticed.

"I wouldn't," she said sweetly. "You'll need that."

Joanna snatched up the phone, but then she hesitated. She cast the girl a long, calculating look. So, this was the figure she'd glimpsed in the trees, watching the house. She'd had her pickings before, and she'd come back for more. She would always be back. She'd always be there. The voice at the end of the phone. The card in the mail. The figure in the dark, watching. The pitiless reminder, the living reproach.

She replaced the receiver and sank back into the chair. She had to be rid of this girl. She'd do anything, pay anything, to buy silence of mind and peace of heart.

Gradually she recovered her composure. She reached for the checkbook. This was a business arrangement. Everything had its price. Five, ten, twenty thousand: what did it matter?

She spoke quietly, without looking up.

"Close the door," she said.

Joanna stood in the dark beside the bed, deciding whether to undress there or go to another room. A shaft of moonlight through the curtains fell across the sleeping form of Stephen. He lay facedown in the pillows where he had collapsed, fully clothed. She watched his body rise and fall in rhythm to his snoring. The nasal rattle at the inhale, the agonizing suspense at the cusp, then the long descending whistle of the exhale. Such a hateful sound, so egotistical, so disgustingly *male*.

The storm had only half broken. Perhaps the rest would break tomorrow. She no longer cared. Stephen could do what he liked. He had his own problems and his own way of dealing with them. She had hers. Everything with him came down to expediency. For him, the issue of Karen was not one of con-science but of strategy. Not of guilt but of guile.

"*Ten thousand dollars?*" he'd expostulated. "You're out of your brain!"

"I made a decision," she'd retorted, though she knew it was fatal to engage in direct argument with Stephen. "I wanted rid of her."

"I warned you, Joanna. I said she'd come back for more. And here she is, and you give her another hunk of dough. Why should *this* ten grand shut her up? Wait till twenty becomes fifty, then a hundred."

"It buys you off the hook, too, Stephen."

"I'm not *on* the hook, for Christ's sake!"

"Oh yes you are. Don't try to wash your hands now. What would *you* do? Call her bluff? Buy her off with a research grant?"

"I'd get on top of it."

"On top of *her*, you mean!" she'd laughed hoarsely.

"Don't be crude."

"No, no, let me guess how you'd do it. You'd take her down to the beach. At night, in the moonlight, with a few drinks inside her. Pump away on the sand and grass, then she'd go off skinny-dipping in the ocean, where hopefully she'll drown, and you pull on your pants and fix your tie and saunter back whistling. Sounds familiar, you cheating pig?"

"Don't talk to me about cheating! You're the cheat, you and your fucking Trust! You and Friedman are hand in glove. You knew their decision all along. You pulled the plug on me. My sweet and loyal wife."

"That's a lie, Stephen. I did everything I could to swing it for you. They're just a bunch of reactionary deadheads. I can't help that."

"Lucky you don't have to go to Friedman for ten grand. Or is blackmail easier to sanction?" He had taken her by the shoul-ders and was shaking her violently. "Joanna, Joanna, why did you give in to her? It's not the money, it's the thinking behind it. Bribing her off is accepting she's got something on us. It's an admission of guilt, Joanna, and we've got nothing to feel guilty about."

She'd begun to weep. Silent tears were pouring down her

face. She sank onto the bed, her head in her hands.

"I just can't live with this thing hanging over me all the time. I simply can't handle it."

"Sweetheart, you need help."

She'd shaken her head in sorrow and defeat.

"We both need help, Stephen. You think you've got over it, but you haven't. You're running away just like I am."

A long exhausted pause had followed, and then, quite suddenly she'd flung her arms around him and drawn him down onto the bed beside her, with the tears streaming down her face, and sat hugging him as though her very life depended on it. They were lost in a fearsome and terrible wood. They worked all their grief and fury out upon one another, but in reality they were fellow sufferers in a common tragedy.

And then, abruptly, he'd fallen asleep. Just like a candle snuffed out or a light switched off. His body went limp and he crumpled onto the bed, and within a few seconds he was snoring loudly and deeply in this interminable, mind-numbing rhythm, in-pause-out, in-pause-out.

She tugged off his shoes and pants, loosened his shirt and pulled the coverlet over him, then she went slowly over to her dressing table to take off her makeup. As she sat down in front of the mirror, a sense of ultimate hopelessness swamped her. She was trapped. Trapped in the past that kept returning. In the person she was and, for all her efforts, couldn't escape. In the world she inhabited, in the husband she saw drifting away, in the daughter she felt slipping from her. She felt the hysteria rising within her like a vast bubble, threatening to burst her apart like a puffball. She was going mad. Slowly, surely, and inescapably mad.

She sat, shaking with impotent despair, helpless to control herself. As she looked up in the mirror, through a blur of tears and running mascara, she saw her own face dissolve and its features, the eyes and nose and mouth and cheekbones and hair and all that gave it its identity, somehow lose their distinctness and take on a kind of general plasticity. She could be somebody else, she could be nobody. She could be anybody except the person she was.

An idea struck her. It seemed the necessary thing to do.

She reached for her purse and took out the identity card

she'd found in Cristina Parigi's apartment. She tilted it to the moonlight. *Courtenay Ann Chambers. Place of birth: Paris, Tx.*

She reached for a pair of nail scissors and with a quick, deft movement she cut the card up, first in half, then in quarters, then she cut the quarters in half again, and finally she took the small handful of shreds across to the bathroom and, wrapping them in a bundle of tissue, flushed them down the toilet.

9

CRISTINA STROLLED GENTLY through the labyrinthine paths that crisscrossed Central Park. She was in no particular hurry. The sky was leaden and heavy, portending the long-awaited break in the heat wave, but her steps were light and her heart swelled with delight. Weeks of dry weather had parched the grass and turned the foliage a premature autumn hue, yet for her it seemed as if spring had freshly broken.

She skirted the reservoir and crossed the inner-ring road, dodging joggers and cyclists, then headed toward the majestic skyline that flanked the park in the south. She paused by the baseball field, now reduced to a dust bowl, and watched a game in progress. A kid with quick Moroccan looks sidled up to her and offered her a Rolex. A burly spectator with lecherous eyes engaged her in over-friendly conversation. A couple of players practicing ball whistled at her as she moved off. She walked on, her feet dancing over the baked earth. The dry electric air seemed to crackle with excitement. God, she loved this city.

Walking down Fifth Avenue, she glanced at her reflection in the shop windows. She tossed her head, swinging long blonde hair like a mane. Her white summer dress, tight around the bust and belted at the waist, flared wide at the skirt and flowed loosely with each stride. The light of a secret joy flickered at her brightly painted lips, and behind her dark glasses her eyes were smiling.

At Sixtieth and Fifth she stepped through a set of revolving doors into the air-conditioned cool of the Midtown Manhattan Bank. She waited her turn in line, then deposited a large check into her account. From a service desk she requested a set of personalized checks and signed the requisition form with a rapid, practiced hand, *Cristina Parigi*. Finally she filled out a standing order to the credit of Roxby Realty Management Inc. for the rent on Apartment #7, 101 West 89th Street, handed the form in at the service desk. Her business done, she left the building.

A short cab ride took her back to the Upper West Side. She chatted with the driver the whole way there, and even continued for a while outside the apartment. She paid him, giving him an oversized tip, and climbed out. She gave the maid at the first floor window a friendly wave and slipped up the front steps and into the hall to collect her mail. More bills. A circular from Time-Life. An invitation to an opening at the David Blum Gallery on East 57th Street that coming Friday—posted four weeks ago, according to the date stamp, and evidently gone astray. A reminder card for a dental appointment. A winter holiday brochure. The usual stuff. Taking the mail, she went back out and down the path that led to her own apartment.

Once inside, she poured a glass of orange juice and Perrier and checked the answering machine. Then she went down the spiral staircase, along the starry corridor, and into the bedroom. She kicked off her shoes and wriggled out of the white dress. Naked but for a thin slip, she went to the end closet and opened the door. Very carefully she took off the blonde wig, unhooking the small hidden combs that held it in place, and laid it on the polystyrene dummy. She sat down at the dressing table and took off the hair net and shook her copper dark hair free, then wiped off the bright lipstick, the mascara and eyeliner and put on a lighter shade. She changed her earrings, swapped her rings and watch back, put on her pearl necklace, and brushed out her hair. Then she reached for the crisp gray Chanel suit on the bed. Finally, with a quick glance in the mirror, she retraced her steps up the spiral stairs and into the living room. Pausing only to finish her drink and reset the answering machine, she picked up her purse and headed out through the door.

Joanna hurried up the path and out into the street. With never a glance behind her, she walked briskly to the corner of the avenue, where she hailed a cab and gave the driver the address of a high-class couture salon over on Madison Avenue.

The next few days flew past in a frenzy of activity. The show was barely a week off, and there was a mountain of last-minute details to attend to. More invitations had been sent out than seating was available, in the expectation of refusals and no-shows, but they had been inundated with acceptances and Joanna had exercised all her charm and persuasion on the manager of the Essex Hotel, not without a certain eloquence from her checkbook either, to switch from a conference room to the ballroom. It meant revising the catering arrangements, replanning the sound and lighting, redesigning the dressing area layouts, and even rechoreographing the show itself to allow for a larger parade and a longer catwalk. Fashion was theater, after all, and garments were judged as much by their staging as their style.

On the Friday, toward the end of the day, Bella came by. She arrived in the middle of another crisis. Cheryl had been on the phone all afternoon, Joanna had exhausted her own contacts, and a mood of despair and exhaustion hung over the cramped office.

Joanna looked up over the top of her reading glasses as her daughter came in.

"Hi, Bella. This is a nice surprise. Grab a drink." She gestured toward the office mini-bar. "God, will I be glad when it's over and nothing else can go wrong!" she sighed fervently.

Bella sat down on the typist's chair opposite. She swung her legs onto the desktop and snapped open a can of 7-Up.

"What's up this time, Mom? You look like it's terminal."

Cheryl, at the desk in her own office, cupped her hand over the phone and called through the open door.

"Morris says he can offer Belinda, only she's taken up weights and put on muscle."

"No, no, she's got to be slim. Lissome. And blonde." She cast Bella a weary smile. "Louella—that's the replacement for Cristina—just snapped a tendon playing tennis," she explained. "We've called every agency in town. The girls are all too tall, or too short, or too busty, or too skinny."

"Alter the clothes," Bella suggested.

"At this stage, darling, you fit the girls to the garments, not the other way round."

"Slim, lissome, and blonde, you said? How about five-seven and a hundred and twelve pounds, blonde, pretty cute figure, reasonable looks, long legs?"

Joanna understood, and smiled.

"No way, angel. But thanks for the thought."

Bella called through to the adjoining office.

"Cheryl, what do you pay the girls?"

"You're too young," protested her mother. "Besides, it takes training."

"Come on, Mom, it's a cinch. You just prance up and down the catwalk showing off and giving the audience the eye."

"Showing off the *clothes*," she corrected. "Anyway, the audience is mostly women. Raddled, middle-aged fashion hacks."

"Sure. Come to ogle the young bodies."

"That's the other thing. Louella was modeling nightwear."

"I don't care. Anyway, Stephen says if you've got a good body, be proud of it."

"Is that what Stephen says?" she queried pointedly. "Well, it doesn't mean you should parade it around. People can get all kinds of wrong ideas." She glanced at her watch. An old client just around the corner had ordered a dress, and she'd promised to take it round by the end of the afternoon, herself. She rose to her feet. "I have to go out for ten minutes or so. Stay, and we'll go home together."

"I'm meeting Eddie in an hour."

"Ah, Eddie."

"For heaven's sake, Mom."

"I didn't say anything." She kissed her daughter on the forehead and went through to her assistant's office. "Cheryl, is Mrs. Danzberg's dress ready?"

She hurried out through the shop and into the street. The sky was blackening from the east, and the buildings stood out in bright, false sunlight like a photo in negative. She crossed the street and made her way to an apartment building just a block away.

Stephen says if you've got a good body. . . . She frowned. She'd always encouraged Bella to have her own relationship

with Stephen, and it had warmed her heart to see their friend-
ship blossom. Bella had been ten when Tony, her father, crash-
landed his Cessna in fog one November night, coming in to a
private landing strip at the Hamptons. It was a terrible age to
lose a father, yet she'd come out of it with a strength and maturity well in advance of her years. She'd taken to Stephen the
moment he'd been introduced. Stephen had become the father
she had lost, just as after the second tragedy two years ago, she
herself became the child that he had lost.

But recently she'd had her anxieties as she watched Bella
emerge from the chrysalis of adolescence into really a remark-
ably beautiful young woman and Stephen at the same time
degenerate into a faithless womanizer. Especially now, having
witnessed that scene of blatant infidelity on the beach the other
night, could she really *trust* him? He was so clever, so sophisti-
cal, he could twist the very thoughts in a person's mind inside
out. And for all her emotional strength and maturity, Bella was
so innocent in worldly affairs. When a man like Stephen told a
sixteen-year-old girl she should be proud of her body, wasn't he
really saying, "Come on, don't be shy, don't be ashamed of showing yourself in front of me"?

She shuddered. The idea was too vile to contemplate.

She checked herself. This was pure paranoia. There was no
objective evidence. To judge by that silicone slag the other night,
Stephen's extramarital tastes would be satisfied by a blow-up
rubber doll. His birthday was coming up shortly: maybe she had
just the present for him.

The memory of that terrible night quickened her step. She'd
said nothing further about it to Stephen since. The truth was,
she felt strangely untouched by it. She had her own refuge, and
nothing need reach her now. If she felt anything, it was sorrow
for him. Could he really find consolation in a quick drunken
fuck on the beach in the dark? If that was his refuge, how empty
it must be.

She was a few minutes late back to the salon. She handed
the check she'd collected to her manageress and was calling
upstairs to Bella to tell her she was back when the soft background music in the salon abruptly changed to a loud, vampish
beat. The mirrored door to the changing rooms opened and out
stepped a girl holding a carnival mask in front of her face, her

blonde hair piled high, and wearing the red silk night robe that was the centerpiece of the show. The girl swept past her and walked down the plush carpet, swinging her hips and shoulders, and pirouetting to display the garment this way and that with all the style and grace of a professional mannequin. She was perfect. And the robe fitted like a glove.

Joanna caught her breath. The hair, the figure, the way she walked . . . It was Cristina, returned to the flesh. She felt dazed, disorientated.

Cheryl was at her elbow, smiling.

"What do you think? Will she do?"

"Who sent her?" asked Joanna, recovering.

The girl waltzed up and slowly lowered her mask.

It was Bella.

"Do I pass, Mom?" she asked.

"You're . . . breathtaking," replied Joanna, swallowing hard. "Whose idea was the mask?"

"If they can't see your face, they can't see *you*," replied Bella in a matter-of-fact voice. "You could be anyone. Or no one."

Joanna nodded. She understood that very well.

"Cheryl," she began, feeling a shiver of excitement of a new idea unfolding, "how quickly could we get a bunch of masks like this? We could give the show a carnival theme. Rio style. No, Venice. Grander, older, more decadent, more *anonymous*. Say, we start on the street with the evening wear and end in the bedroom with the nightwear. The message is, "You can be any woman you want." We'd need to change some of the music. Rework the choreography a bit. And find some suitable props."

With growing enthusiasm, she began detailing all that would have to be done to bring it off, and it was only when she finally paused for breath that she caught the patient, wry look in Bella's eye.

"So do I get the job, Mom?" asked the girl.

"Darling . . . ," she began. "Let me think about it."

"The idea is copyright. No me, no masks."

"I've thought about it," smiled Joanna. "You'll need to take some lessons. Cheryl will set that up. Dress rehearsal Monday." She paused. "Don't get hooked, angel. It's no career for you."

"It'll go toward my trip. Two grand is half the ticket."

"Two thousand dollars? Who said anything about that kind of money?"

The girl smiled sweetly.

"Top model rates, Mom. You always say you've got to pay for the best."

"I don't know where do you get the chutzpah from," groaned Joanna.

Bella leaned forward and kissed her mother on the cheek, then spun round and waltzed off back through the mirrored door, leaving Joanna shaking her head in amused incredulity. Yet the image was disturbing, too: Bella's resemblance to Cristina was extraordinary, chilling. Maybe she was just projecting her own obsession. Or worse: this was paranoia emerging again. Earlier she'd felt threatened by her daughter's relationship with her husband, now it was her daughter usurping her secret self.

After Bella had gone, she turned to Cheryl. What had *she* seen?

"You know," she confided, "Bella gave me quite a turn. For a moment I thought she was someone else."

"So did I," agreed Cheryl. "She looked a dead ringer for Louella."

Joanna stayed behind after the staff had left. She poured a glass of Schweppes from the mini-bar in her office and glanced at her engagements for the evening. Outside, a pneumatic drill that had been pounding all day had at last fallen silent, and above the purr of the air-conditioning only the cleaning woman vacuuming downstairs could be heard.

She felt strangely restless. Perhaps it was the image of Cristina suddenly resurfacing. She'd been too busy all week to allow herself more than a passing thought to those dangerous, forbidden excitements. That evening at six, she was due at a commercial reception at the Italian embassy and, at eight, a supper party hosted by the editor of *Vanity Fair*. She didn't feel like doing either. She'd have liked to go to a movie with Bella and take in a pizza afterward. Stephen had a late meeting with Don Weitzman. This was the crunch meeting, he said: the showdown on the Foundation issue. Poor Stephen: he was such a brilliant academic but such a lousy politician. How could he have painted himself into a corner like that?

She reached for the phone. She'd interrupt his meeting and suggest they meet for dinner. It was time they talked, alone and properly. Away from home and the phone and the other distractions that always got in the way. And, for once, over the first drink of the evening, not the last.

She just caught the Department switchboard as it was closing for the night. There was no reply from either Stephen's or Don Weitzman's extensions. She was transferred to the front reception desk, to be told Stephen had left two hours before. Weitzman was on the Coast, at a conference at Berkeley.

She replaced the receiver slowly. She understood. Would she never learn?

She reached into the mini-bar and topped up her glass with vodka. She sat down at her desk and picked up the carnival mask. For a while she toyed with it, considering it from this angle and that, holding it to her face and looking out through the eye slits at her reflection in the mirror. She thought of the apartment on the other side of the park, of the heady sense of liberation she'd felt going around town as Cristina, and she began to feel the familiar thick, swollen sensation like the tug of erotic desire uncoiling inside her.

Her pulse drummed a louder beat. The pull was becoming irresistible.

Abruptly she swallowed back her drink and went through into the stockroom. There she searched the rails until she found the dress Cristina had borrowed, still in its protective polyethylene wrap. Folding it carefully over her arm, she returned to her office for her purse, then headed downstairs. With a parting word to the cleaning woman, she let herself out into the oppressive, thunderous evening and hailed a passing cab.

From the living room upstairs came the twangy refrain of a country and western folksong. In the gaps between the tracks, faint echoes of the thunder brewing up outside filtered down to the red-lit subterranean bedroom where Cristina stood, inspecting her appearance in the mirror.

The result pleased her. The blue silk chiffon cocktail dress set off her wavy blonde hair perfectly, and the matching blue

stilettos lent her legs an extra slenderness. She checked her
complexion, feathering in the edges of her eye makeup and dabbing her lips on a tissue to tone down the gloss. Then she stood
back and began to work on her posture. She practiced holding
her body in a more angular stance, her head high and one
shoulder projected forward. Out of the expression in her eyes
she coaxed a blend of desire and disdain, and she experimented
with various ways of shaping her lips until she hit upon the
right mixture of aloofness and allure. She took another sip of
iced vodka and sang along with the music for a while, whooping
and lamenting in exaggerated fashion until she cracked up with
laughter.

She went up the spiral staircase, taking the stairs awkwardly
in the high heels, and idled about the room for a while. She settled on the sofa and leafed through a magazine until the disc
came to an end, then she flicked through the channels on television without finding anything she wanted to watch. She glanced
through the red leather personal organizer lying by the phone.
In an inner pouch she found several engraved ivory visiting
cards bearing just her name in palace script, *Cristina Parigi*,
together with the phone number. Business cards for a girl in her
business. She laid them on one side. She might be needing
them.

What did a single girl do on a Friday night, all dressed up
and nowhere to go? She would call someone up. She began
through the address-book section, then abruptly tossed the personal organizer aside. She was unconsciously looking for names
Joanna knew.

Her eye lit upon the mail lying on the coffee table. The bills,
the dentist's reminder, the circular from Time Life and, with its
beveled edge protruding from beneath the pile and revealing her
name in looped handwriting, *Cristina P . . .* , the invitation to
the opening of a show at the David Blum Gallery. Cocktails and
canapés, six to eight. Friday.

Tonight.

Joanna knew the gallery. Warner Friedman bought works of
art as investments for the Trust there. Perhaps the fact he and
David Blum went to the same synagogue had something to do
with that. The gallery specialized in early religious art—icons
from the Byzantine period and medieval works of the crucifix-

ion of Christ and the torments of the saints and suchlike. They
traveled on loan to museums or stayed locked in the vaults. She
would never have them hanging in her own house.

And the gallery, of course, knew Joanna. David Blum was an
occasional visitor to the Park Avenue apartment. Curiously
enough, he seemed to get on well with Stephen. He'd befriended
Stephen during his first months in New York and offered him
an open door when everyone else connected with her family
were offering him a cold shoulder. They always seemed to have
a lot to say to one another, though what on earth a behavioral
psychologist and a dealer in macabre medieval art had in common was beyond her.

But the gallery clearly knew Cristina, too. How well?

And come to think of it, how did Cristina, being in the pro-
fession she was, know them?

She stood up and caught a glimpse of herself in the overmantel mirror. The blonde hair, the look in the eye, the angle of
the head. . . . As she held the eye that met hers in the mirror, she
felt the small, wild inner smile rising within her.

Abruptly she turned back to the coffee table and slipped the
invitation and the visiting cards into a small evening clutch bag.
As she headed for the door, a sudden flash of lightning sheeted
the windows and, a long count later, a slow barrel of thunder
rolled across the sky. Grabbing an umbrella, she let herself out
and, with the first fleshy drops of rain smacking down around
her, hastened down the sidewalk toward the avenue.

The gallery was packed. Half the New York art society seemed to
be there. Most stood with their backs to the walls, come for the
party and not for the pictures. The gallery had been designed to
exhibit contemporary art, and although subtly spotlit in a way
that brought out their full richness, the early medieval works on
display, painted as they were mostly on wooden board with
sable-hair brushes and using gold leaf and rare earth pigments
rather than on massive canvases using airbrushes and industrial
acrylics, seemed diminished to the scale of small jewels on the
broad expanse of white wall.

She hovered at the entrance, her nerve faltering. Here and
there in the crowd she picked out a familiar face. She fingered
her blonde hair uncertainly. The escapade was fast losing its

wild allure. She might be dressed for the part, she might have concealed much of her face behind dark glasses and some of her age beneath layers of foundation, she might tell herself to walk young, stand young, think young, but could a woman of thirty-six ever convincingly pass herself off as one of twenty-two? Bella was closer in age than she was . . .

But it was too late. A hat girl had taken her umbrella and collected the invitation. A waiter was offering her a tray of drinks. More guests were pressing in behind her.

Then through the crowd, his hand outstretched in greeting, stepped David Blum, the gallery owner. He was a short, balding figure with thick frameless glasses, moist lips, and a complexion like a polished stone stretching from jowels to pate.

"Hello, how are you? Glad you could come. You have a drink? That's fine. Now, remind me, you must be . . . "

She took a breath. *Be the mask,* she told herself.

She extended her hand and replied with a trace of a soft Southern drawl.

"Hi, I'm Cristina Parigi."

"Ah, Miss Parigi. It's a pleasure to meet you at last." A light frown wrinkled the polished brow. "I heard you weren't too well and couldn't make it along tonight." He withdrew his hand. "Nothing contagious, uh?"

He managed a chuckle, but his eyes were sizing her up and down, hard and critical.

She returned the smile steadily.

"Nothing you won't have already had, Mr. Blum," she said.

"Yes, ahem, that doesn't preclude much." He chuckled again. "Well, who would you like to meet? You know who's here, of course."

"I'd most like to look at the works. I'm fascinated by late Byzantine icons. I heard the Hermitage is quietly offloading onto the market." Hold on, she told herself. Don't push your luck.

"The stuff's shot. Been festering away in damp warehouses since the Bolsheviks looted it." He considered her more carefully. "You're very well informed, young lady."

"One picks things up."

"Ah, of course, I see." He nodded, evidently satisfied. "Well, do excuse me. I'll catch up with you later."

He moved to greet fresh arrivals and she headed off toward the paintings. She turned to find him glancing back at her, puzzled and curious. He looked quickly away.

She sauntered along the walls, stopping before each painting in turn. But her thoughts were elsewhere. Her pulse was racing and her hands were damp with perspiration, yet inside her head reverberated a tiny voice of triumph, *I did it! I pulled it off!* A surge of confidence swept through her. You only had to make anodyne remarks and people built their own rationalizations around them. "One picks things up." "Ah, of course, I see." What did he see? He'd filled in the gap for himself.

She was so absorbed in her thoughts that she scarcely noticed the man standing beside her, studying her. Somewhere deep in her consciousness a faint smell of musk stirred an echo, but it was his voice that struck her first. Slow, soft, hypnotic.

"Really quite fine, don't you think? As an example of its type."

My God, she knew that voice!

"This little painting inspired one of Piero's great frescoes at Arezzo. Do you know those frescoes?"

She turned.

She saw who it was.

The dark hair, sleeked back and receding, the dark suit, the black shirt buttoned to the neck. And those deep, dark eyes burning like acetylene flames.

She opened her mouth to speak, but no words came out.

"Piero della Francesca," he continued easily, covering over her silence. "Maybe you know that he was named after his mother Francesca, who trained him. In the early Renaissance, pupils often took their master's name. Ruskin called this the 'prettiest instance of all.'"

"I . . . I didn't know that," she stumbled.

She looked back at the painting to hide her face in case it should betray the turmoil of feelings within her. She had to play for time while she worked out how to be, *who* to be. Talk about the painting, she thought.

She looked closer, trying to make sense of the narrative depicted in the work. It portrayed a plain earth grave surmounted by a wooden cross and beside it the figure of a man kneeling, with the same figure again in the distance carrying a large branch. The scene was set in a stylized rocky landscape, with praying angels depicted in profile hovering in a circle all around.

"I can't place the story," she said finally, her throat dry.

"It's the death of Adam," he replied. "Adam is dying, and Seth goes to the Paradise Terrestrial to ask for oil of mercy. The archangel Michael gives him instead a branch from the apple tree out of Eden. Seth comes back and finds his father dead, and plants the branch on the grave."

"But that's a cross," she objected, latching onto a sudden idea. "How could Adam's grave have a cross on it? That's surely anachronistic."

"Ah!" He smiled. "Time condenses in primitive art. Just as you have Seth in two places at once—here, carrying in the branch, and also there, kneeling at the graveside. The branch later *becomes* the cross. It's the legend of the True Cross. You know of Jacopo Voragine? The *Golden Legend*? No? Well, the branch from Eden grows into a great tree, but the Queen of Sheba has a prophetic vision of the crucifixion and tells Solomon, and Solomon has the tree chopped down and buried deep in the earth. Centuries later it is rediscovered and, of course, the wood is used to make the cross of Christ."

She was hardly listening throughout this recital. All those feelings that had consumed her at the reception at the Frick museum came flooding back. And with them the memory of what had happened afterward. The perfect encounter with the perfect stranger.

"Although," he was saying in his soft, silken voice, "you can't really appreciate the true intensity of the color through dark glasses."

She gave a start. She couldn't remove her glasses. They were the mask. The moment lengthened. She knew there was no alternative. Slowly, abandoning herself to the inevitable, she took off the glasses and met his gaze.

His eyes narrowed and his expression grew keener. But he said nothing. Not by the slightest hint or flicker did he betray whether he recognized her. He merely stood there, just as before, consuming her with his gaze, devouring her with his being. Once again she felt as though she were slowly catching fire. Invisible flames jetted out from his eyes, spreading around and through her, igniting her. She raised the glass to her lips but held it there without drinking, then slowly, like an automaton, she lowered it again. But still she could not break the stare, and when finally she tore her gaze away, she felt dazed and flushed, betrayed by her naked desire.

She handed her glass to a passing waiter and refused another. There was nothing more she wanted from this party.

She took his hand as though to shake it. Holding his eye as she did so, she lifted the hand up and pressed it briefly to her breast, the breast by whose nipple he had drawn her toward him in the darkened limousine that hot and steamy night, then released it, and with the barest shadow of a smile she turned and left him.

And within a minute she was out of the building.

The storm that had been impending for so long was breaking across the city. Lightning shimmered off the glass facades of the high-rises, and the thunder reverberated down the avenues like the splintering of a great forest. The rain was now falling in heavy, sheer curtains, and in the streets a ruthless warfare for cabs was being waged.

Directly outside the gallery building, however, stood a stationary cab. Its engine was running and its roof light indicated it was unavailable for hire. Inside in the semi-dark sat a passenger, and though constantly importuned by other pedestrians in need of transport, the driver made no attempt to move off.

The cab stayed waiting for five minutes. Five minutes became ten. Traffic was congesting, and buses and limousines honked angrily as they swung out to avoid the obstruction. Any moment the police would arrive and move the cab on.

Finally a figure in a dark suit and black shirt came out of the building through the swing doors. He stood hesitating beneath the canopy as he cast about the street. Perhaps he was assessing the rain and the crowd, or perhaps looking for someone.

The window of the cab lowered. It lowered slowly down to its fullest extent. A hand emerged, a slender woman's hand. The hand reached out from the darkness within. And slowly a finger beckoned.

The man saw. He moved forward, slowly, without hurry, as if he had been expecting this. The crowd on the sidewalk seemed to part to let him through. As he reached the cab, the door opened. He climbed inside. The door closed firmly, the window rose and the cab pulled out into the sluggish stream of traffic.

The darkness within was alive and moving, like the inside of a living body. The woman drew him backward and down onto the torn plastic seat. She pressed her lips greedily against his, devouring his mouth and cheek and neck. Her urgent fingers were already reaching for his belt and loosening it. The man reclined, abandoning himself to pleasure. She slipped to her knees and took him in her mouth. The cab lurched violently to the side, throwing her aside, but strong arms reached for her and drew her bodily back. Hands pulled up her dress and tore down her panties. Her buttocks were being lifted up, her legs parted, and with a sudden sharp stab she felt herself impaled upon him.

The rain drummed on the steel roof, the wipers kept up a rhythmic swishing sweep, the tires of cars outside threw up hissing sheets of spray, concealing the man and the woman from prying outside gazes and all but the widening eyes of the driver framed in the rearview mirror. The cab rocked and bucked, rocking and bucking them with it. Faster and faster he drove her, until she felt herself lifting off like a balloon from its tether, rising up and up, above the jostling and the jolting, above the noise and the crush and the rain and the thunder, up above the sheer-rising blocks and up still further into the very eye of the storm where all was suddenly quiet and silent and still and all she could hear was the distant, drawn-out cry from her soul.

She came back to earth like a feather falling in the void. She became aware that the cab was pulling up. Through the rain-blurred window she could make out the large brownstone with the familiar graffiti on the gate piers and the pair of concrete ornamental tubs on the porch step. Dazed, she hastily re-arranged her clothing and reached for the door handle.

He was sitting back in the corner, his face lost in shadow. He made no move to stop her, he made no attempt to ask her name or suggest they met again. He said nothing. Not a word had passed between them during the entire journey. Nothing needed to be said. What had happened was complete within itself.

And yet such a miracle was too good to leave to the chance

of another random encounter. From her clutch bag the woman quickly took out one of the visiting cards and handed it to him. Then she opened the door and stepped out. As she turned, she saw him glance at the card. He looked up sharply, visibly startled. His eyes narrowed as if he were striving to read her thoughts, but still he said nothing, merely held her in the grip of a tight, penetrating gaze while she leaned forward and slowly closed the door.

She stood on the sidewalk in the pouring rain, watching the cab taillights disappear. She had left her umbrella inside, but the thought hardly registered. Within moments she was drenched to the skin, but still she stood there, her face upturned to the pounding rain and her whole being alight with joy.

10

STEPHEN SLAMMED THE DOOR so hard the office partitioning shook. A videotape perched precariously on the edge of a shelf toppled down. He stepped forward and kicked it across the room. He kicked the swivel chair, sending it crashing into the monitors on the far side. He picked up a pile of fan-folded print-out and slewed it out across the floor and punched a hole clean through a box file with his fist.

"The stupid fucking miserable bastards," he cursed aloud. "The petty politicking moronic assholes!"

That toad Weitzman was behind it all. He'd railroaded the faculty heads. He'd nobbled the chairman of the Appointments Board. A pained frown to this one, a sorry shake of the head to that one, and in went the knife, right in between the shoulder blades.

Seething with rage, he thought back to the meeting he'd just left. He'd stood in the dean's office, with the knife sticking right out of his back and the dean himself facing him across his billiards-size desk, his face wreathed in false regret and his clammy hands flapping in a gesture of helplessness.

"You have my deepest sympathy, Steve," he was saying.

Deepest sympathy, *bullshit!*

"As I've said before, I truly believe in your work, Steve. It has genuinely profound implications for behavioral psychology and, indeed, for humanity at large. . . "

Anyone who said "truly" and "genuinely" with every breath was neither true nor genuine.

"I did all I could for you, Steve. Trust me."

Trust you, you two-faced creep?

"But the Board was minded to take the view that it would not be consonant with the Department's strategic objectives—"

What kind of crap was this?

"—to sanction a renewal of your post."

Stephen gave a filing cabinet a savage kick. It left a dent.

Why couldn't Weitzman just have said, "Listen, pal, sorry but you're fired"?

More to the point, why did he hide behind all this camouflage and not tell the real truth? That Stephen Lefever hadn't delivered the dough he'd promised and so he was getting the ax. That the Department had budgeted for this vast benefaction and the vultures had already begun carving it among themselves, and now the Board had to retract in embarrassment with egg all over their faces? Why couldn't Weitzman be honest enough to admit, even off the record, as one colleague to another, that the real reason had nothing to do with how much or how little Stephen had published, nor with the quality of his work or considerations of "strategic objectives," but with how many fucking dollars and cents he could pull in? Why? Because Don Weitzman was like the rest. A stupid, miserable, petty politicking moronic asshole of a bastard.

The difference was, Don Weitzman had his ass on a chair. And Stephen now did not.

He cleared his desk. He'd been fired, and he was leaving. He wasn't going to wait out a period of notice while the rumors flew around and colleagues started cutting him dead in the corridor. He commandeered a load of chests and packing cases from the janitor and into them he threw all his books, journals, papers, videotapes, notes, and records. He worked fast, fueled by rage. By shortcircuiting the internal wiring he blew up his specially designed spy-in-the-box camera. Five minutes at the computer terminal erased all trace of his files from the mainframe data base, and those papers that would not fit into boxes went into the trash bin or through the shredder.

By mid-afternoon, his office was cleared, the packing cases were down in the basement storeroom and all that remained to show that he had ever inhabited the place were the tape marks and dabs of blue tack on the walls where posters and charts had been fixed up and a small army of white plastic coffee cups, arranged in increasing order of moldiness, lined up along the window sill.

He glanced for the last time at the laboratory wall clock. It was coming up to four o'clock. He'd say his good-byes to the innocents and go out and get drunk.

Not wanting to meet anyone in the elevator, he took the stairs up to the zoo, as the penthouse was known internally, and let himself in with his electronic pass card. Inside, the odor of fur and urine, intensified by the heat beneath the roof, evoked in him the familiar blend of excitement and repulsion.

Cages lined the walls on one side. Large and airy, they were fitted with perches and swinging grips and treadmills and divided into separate areas for feeding, sleeping, and defecating. The chimps were housed one to a cage, with a screen between each to prevent social contact and so upset the delicate control of the experiments. They flew crazily around at his approach, chattering and squealing in excitement. However much their environment was enriched, life in captivity was never like life in the wild, and boredom was a real problem with such intelligent creatures. In fact, most laboratory animals could be persuaded to do almost anything for the promised reward of a simple glimpse out of the window.

He went slowly along the row, speaking to each in turn in the sign language he had developed with them, an idiosyncratic version of Ameslan, the language of the deaf and dumb. Hand up, palm outward: *Hi, Orson*. Finger wiped across the smile: *you okay, Lana?* Clenched fists to heart: *love you, Marlene*. Marlene was his favorite. She had such bright, quick eyes and— goddamnit, he of all people shouldn't be anthropomorphizing— the closest thing to human expressions he'd ever seen. In fact, in comparison with that toad-featured Weitzman she was *super*human.

He reached toward the cage. The chimp's long, slender arm extended toward him. She stretched forward her small hand, so delicate and nimble. It was covered in fine honey-color hair, its palm and pads a soft leathery black. Human and chimp touched fingertips.

Bye, Marlene, he signed. *Take care. Be happy.*

A look of puzzlement, then profound sadness, filled her large hazel eyes. She cocked her head on one side and waved her small paw in the return sign, *Bye.*

He slowly retraced his steps. He felt he was saying good-bye to innocence. The world had started going wrong when the brain of australopithecine man stepped over the critical threshold and endowed him with the talent that, above all else, characterized modern man: the ability for deception. Guileful though these high primates were, they were incapable of actively lying. Yet a human child of two was already exercising his inborn gift for duplicity. And by adulthood, by the time he was a Don Weitzman or a member of an Admissions Board, the gift for counterfeit and falsehood was practice perfect.

He closed the door quietly and retrieved the pass card from the lock. This time he took the elevator to the ground. At the lobby, he signed himself out for the last time and handed the receptionist his staff parking pass, the keys to his office, and his night-security ID card, with instructions to have them sent up to the dean's office. But somehow the pass card to the chimps' house stayed in his pocket, unsurrendered.

He took a cab to midtown, to an Irish bar between Radio City and Eighth Avenue which he frequented. Roxanne's apartment was just a block away, and by habit this had become a watering hole where he regrouped his forces after her passionate onslaught in preparation for the return to normal life. He was greeted by the barman with his usual drink, a large, straight Jamieson's without ice. He hoisted himself onto a bar stool and, swallowing the drink in one, passed it back for another.

He looked around the dim-lit dive. High in one corner of the bar hung the inevitable television with the inevitable ball game loudly in progress. No one was watching. In the deeper recesses, two men wearing heavy construction boots were playing pool. A group of truckers lounged on stools further down the bar, conversing in grunts. Stephen downed his second drink and called for a third. There was one trucker bigger than the other two combined. His belly hung over his belt like the dewlap of a turkey and the low growl he emitted reminded Stephen curiously of the mating grunt of an adult gorilla. He listened closer. Yes, the same inflection, the same timbre, even the same interrupted rhythm. There was evidence that relics of Neanderthal man lived among us, but a throwback to the primates . . . ?

He was sinking his fourth glass and pursuing some fanciful theory of evolution that would blow the world of science apart when he realized the beefy trucker had climbed off his stool and was sidling along the bar toward him. His expression was distinctly ugly. It only filtered through Stephen's dulled wits that he had been staring at the man in a way that might well be construed as provocative when a vast sweaty pancake of jowels thrust itself right up against his face and the grunts transformed miraculously into human language.

"Take a good look, pal, 'cos then I'm gonna bust your ass."

He drew back, instinctively apologetic.

"I'm sorry. I was, uh, daydreaming."

Daydreamin'! Don't you get fancy with me."

"Look, I said I'm sorry, it's a misunderstanding . . . "

The blow knocked him off the stool. He didn't know where it came from or even where it hit him. One moment he could smell the man's breath, the next he was on his back on the floor and struggling to his feet. A hand the size of a baseball mitt grabbed him by the shirtfront and hauled him to his feet, then propelled him backward through the bar, knocking over stools as he went, up the steps and out of the door, and flung him like a bag of garbage onto the sidewalk.

He sat on the pavement in the broad daylight, with pedestrians hurrying indifferently past him on either side, his head throbbing violently and his body aching in every muscle, and all he wanted to do was to laugh. A man gets fired from his job. He clears his desk and bids farewell to his true friends. He closes the door on the ivory tower and goes out into the real world, seeking normal consolation like any normal guy, and what happens? He gets kicked out of a bar and ends up sitting on his ass on the sidewalk, rocking back and forth, chuckling and shaking and heaving by turns like a crazy escaped from a sanatorium.

It would be really funny if it weren't so damn unjust, he

thought, sobering a little. He'd been betrayed. Joanna pulled the rug. Of course she could have fixed it. It was *her* money. The Trust was just a tax dodge. Did she have any idea her refusal might cost him his job? It was all very well for her, her job was a dilettante hobby, a rich woman's diversion, a handy form of practical psychotherapy. No one could fire *her*. She had no boss, no board, no shareholders to answer to. The show could flop and no one would say anything . . .

My God, Joanna's show! It was today. He'd forgotten all about it.

He glanced at his watch. In a few minutes it would be starting.

In the cool marble temple of the hotel restroom he did what he could to repair the damage, but there was no concealing the livid swelling over his right eye and the dirty scuff marks all over his pale linen jacket. He sleeked back his hair with pomade and sprinkled eau de toilette liberally round his neck and under his arms, but the cold water he splashed on his face began to sober him up dangerously and he made a detour to the ball-room by way of the bar, where he re-primed the pump.

The show was well under way. At the door he was stopped by a security guard who eyed him suspiciously and moved to block his path.

"Your invitation, sir?"

"Would you mind?"

Beyond the guard's burly frame, he could see the rows of people seated on either side of the raised catwalk. Some were men, Lagerfeld clones with polo necks and pigtails, but most were women, a bitchy, over-tailored sisterhood frowning over their designer spectacles and jotting notes with their Cartier poison pens. And down the center of the catwalk, the floor itself lit like an aircraft landing strip, sauntered a tall, leggy blonde wearing a diaphanous chiffon evening dress and holding before her face a Pierrot carnival mask.

"Your invitation, sir?" repeated the guard.

"I'm Stephen Lefever."

"Is that with an *L* or an *F*, sir?"

He looked at the man for the first time. Close-set eyes, ears like cabbage leaves, mouth like a sphincter. A Neanderthal relict.

"Am I to take that as a serious question?"

"I have to check the list."

"Does the name Joanna Lefever ring any faint bells?"

"Excuse me?"

"Mrs. Lefever just happens to be giving this goddamn show, and by extension that means paying you, and she just also happens to be my wife." He spotted Cheryl circulating in the background and beckoned to her. "Cheryl, explain to this zealous goon."

Cheryl gave the nod and at once the caveman lumbered aside. She took in Stephen's appearance at a glance.

"What the heck happened to you, Stephen?" she asked. "Got mugged on the way?"

"Something like that," he muttered wryly. "How's it going? Where's Joanna?"

"Backstage." She waved a notebook. "It's going great. The fashion editors are clucking and the buyers are buying. What more could you ask?"

"Nothing, Cheryl, nothing at all," he said, then he remembered irony was dead before Cheryl was born.

He followed her into the ballroom and took up position in the twilight behind the seated rows. He hailed a waiter for a large scotch and no ice, and when it came with the inevitable ice he fished the cubes out and dropped them into the waiter's jacket pocket. Cheryl tossed her head of red hair and laughed. The light danced over her freckled face and softened the long line of her neck, and Stephen wondered why he had never looked at her in *that* way before. His eyes descended routinely to her breasts, now fuller than ever. She'd always been a big girl, upholstered on a scale surprisingly generous and ample for so slender a frame. With her bionic breasts and boyish ass, she'd always struck him as the perfect hermaphroditic construct. Now, as his gaze descended to her belly, revealing her transformation into ripe earth mother, she appeared to him more desirable than ever. What was it that men fancied about pregnant women? Not just that well-woman glow, but something deeper, something sunk deep in the archetypes of the human psyche.

He was getting drunk again. He could tell when he heard himself thinking garbage.

A tall, feline black model was stalking the catwalk now, holding a black mask to her face. He knew all about masks. He'd made a lifetime's hobby of collecting them, and one day he would write the definitive deconstruction, entitled something like *The Semiotics of the Persona*, with a footnote in the mass-market editions explaining that the very word *persona* was the Latin for a "mask." It was all to do with the negation of individuality and the sublimation of ego to image. Or some such crap. The girl was undoubtedly more exciting *with* the mask. With it, she could be anybody, or just nobody. Without it, she was simply the particular person she was, no more and no less. Maybe that was why people mostly made love with the lights out.

"Cheryl, tell me something. Do you fuck in the dark or with the lights on?"

The question went unasked. Cheryl was craning forward as far as her bulk would allow her. A hush had fallen over the chattering crowd. A tall young girl, barefooted, with her blonde hair brushed out as if for bed was strolling demurely down the catwalk. She wore a red silk chiffon night robe and nothing underneath, for the shadowy hint of her pubic triangle could be seen through the material, as could the palest pink suggestion of her areolas. She, too, carried a mask, but hers was all white, a facade of chastity contradicted by the provocative scarlet robe.

Stephen was stunned.

"Jesus," he breathed. "Who's that?"

"Magic, isn't she?"

He watched, mesmerized by the sinuous movements of her hips, the arch fluidity of shoulders, the whole composite of waif and whore she projected. The hush from the crowd broke only when she finally disappeared back into the Venetian *palazzo* that formed the backdrop to the show.

Stephen swallowed back his drink and, excusing himself, made his way to the far end of the room. There he slipped behind the curtains and along a corridor at the back to a door on which was pinned a handwritten card, *Dressing Room*.

He let himself in.

It was like walking into a *hammam* at the fall of Babylon. The atmosphere was clamorous and frenetic. On all sides, half-naked girls were scrambling in and out of clothes, battling with buttons and fluffing up flounces, while around them fussed a whole hive of dressers and makeup artistes and hair stylists. Everywhere, all the time, appeared the figure of Joanna, directing, approving, straightening a hem here, giving a cue there. And over by the curtained tunnel that led up onto the stage, with her back to him and her arms raised in the act of pinning up her hair, stood the girl in the red night robe.

Stephen stepped forward and blundered into a tailor's dummy. A nearby girl tittered. Others looked up. The girl in the red night robe turned. Stephen froze in his tracks.

It was Bella.

"Stephen!" she exclaimed in delight.

At that moment Joanna loomed into his field of vision. She scanned him up and down, her face black with fury. Her mouth was full of pins and it made her words come out distorted.

"What the hell's happened to you?" she demanded.

"Spitting tacks, dear heart?' He raised his hands in mock self-defense. "Just a joke."

"Look at the state of you! I hope no one's seen you."

"I've had a tough day."

"And you're drunk! For God's sake, Stephen." A rising crescendo on violins heralded a change in music. The grand finale was about to begin, and the girls were getting into line for the final parade. Joanna turned back to the melee. "Do me just one favor, just keep out of sight."

"Afraid I'll get up on stage and moon?"

"Don't push it, Stephen."

"Where's your sense of humor? It's carnival time!"

He grabbed the tailor's dummy by the waist and began to tango with it around the crowded room, weaving in and out of the dressers and artistes and up to the line of girls. Bella was laughing, holding her hand to her mouth in the alluring childish way she had. The others had begun to giggle, too. He held the dummy tighter, its pole pressed between his legs. The girls' laughter rose higher and higher to his ears, and with it arose a wild, crazed hilarity within him. *Don't push it, Stephen.* Why not push it? Why not push the whole crazy madness over the edge?

Some demon was possessing him, driving him onward. He didn't recognize this clowning lunatic as himself. From outside he watched himself as he snatched a mask and, holding it up as the dummy's face, swept away, spinning and turning, down the curtained tunnel and out into the sudden dazzling explosion of light and the full public gaze of the catwalk.

A gasp shivered through the gathering, followed by buzz of chatter. Was this part of the show? Comic relief? Or just a drunken interloper creating a hideous embarrassment? No one knew, and no one dared yet give a verdict. Then someone recognized him, and the whisper went around. This was Joanna's husband. Was it intentional, then?

But Stephen was past caring. He danced with abandonment. He was clown and comedian. One moment he was mimicking the girls doing their catwalk parade, the next flirting with the dummy as though it were a living woman. He caressed her, kissed her painted face, swept her nimbly off her feet, sank her onto her back, then whisked her off again in a crazy whirlwind of steps. A nervous titter rippled over the audience. It rose to a chuckle, and here and there broke sporadic peals of unashamed laughter. The laughter spread and swelled, and with it came the applause that rose to a peak as finally, with an extravagant flourish, he stripped the dummy of its mask and tossed it into the audience, then swept off the stage and down the curtain tunnel and straight into the thunderous face and implacable fury of Joanna.

Mature modern couples separating did not scream and shout. Mature modern couples talked it through in careful, controlled voices. The mature modern man left his home not to the sound of ranting and raving, the smashing of crockery, and the slamming of doors. He left to the soft buzz of the house phone and the polite voice of the doorman informing him that the cab, which his mature wife had called, had arrived for him.

Nor did the mature modern woman eject her husband and his clothes separately. There was no undignified flinging of shirts and pants out onto the landing or the emptying of drawers into the street below. Instead, she packed a suitcase for him with the clothes and shoes and shaving gear he would need to get him started in his new life, the meager but sufficient suitcase of an immigrant arriving at Ellis Island, and she set the suitcase up beside the front door—this side of the door, what was more, so that he would have to take it over the threshold himself and thereby perform the act of leaving home voluntarily.

And the mature modern husband took the meager but sufficient suitcase in one hand and in the other a briefcase concealing a bottle of whiskey, and made as dignified an exit as was possible for one who felt he was really sleepwalking and that none of this was happening in the real world but rather in a realm of virtual reality in which he had only to flip a switch or pull some plug and he would find himself back on the rails of his known and normal life.

Such a man now found himself alone in the hallway. The suitcase, an old and battered crocodile-skin object of which he was curiously fond, perhaps by reason of feeling old and battered and crocodile-skinned himself, stood waiting by the door. Through his mind went the things he felt he should be feeling, the words he should be saying. Not that any words from him would be heard, let alone heeded, for the mature woman had retired upstairs to her boudoir, her business done, the drone shown the door. As his hand reached to pick up the case, he had the sense that a moment of personal history was in the making and that, by all rights, he should be surrounded by cameras and reporters eager to record his parting statement.

But all he did was eructate. Loud and long, he belched.

The sound echoed like a gunshot around the hall, amplified by the mirrors and polished furniture. It was probably heard in the kitchen, where the daughter of the house was watching television with the volume turned up, perched on a bar stool and picking at a bag of potato chips, misreading the relative silence as the calm of a truce rather than the stillness of a battlefield after a massacre. Very possibly the belch was audible in the boudoir upstairs, too, where the mature woman was at that very moment wiping off her makeup with a cleansing pad and dabbing the trail of mascara off her cheek where it had run a little in a moment of tearfulness as she'd closed the door on this chapter of her life, before applying the night face pack, the thick cosmetic lard that sensitive wives used only in secret when their menfolk were away on business trips or expelled from the marital bed.

This mature modern man closed the door of the apartment softly and stepped into the private elevator. He took the elevator down to the ground, just as he had countless times before, crossed the large vestibule, his metal heels snicking on the marble floor as they always did, exchanged a courteous "good night" with the doorman and climbed into the waiting cab.

There the driver asked where he wanted to go. He hadn't thought that far ahead. Where did such a husband, thrown out onto the street at one o'clock in the morning, actually *go?* A hotel? A club?

On the spur of the moment he gave the address of a small condominium just round the corner from the midtown bar where, earlier that afternoon and a lifetime ago, the terminal phase of the day's downward spiral had begun.

The building, a tall redbrick apartment block, had a double door entry system designed to filter out the less intelligent, or perhaps merely less persistent, muggers and rapists. The first door led to a large hallway, manned during daytime by a receptionist, beyond which stood a further door with a separate intercom board. It meant callers had to identify themselves a second time, giving the person being called a chance to change their mind.

Stephen paid off the cab and, holding his suitcase under his arm so that it wouldn't look so completely the thing it was, pressed the button marked 77-A. An age passed before the girl's voice crackled over the intercom, sleepy and irritable.

"Whoozat? Whaddya want?"

"Hi, Roxanne, it's Stephen."

Silence from upstairs. For God's sake, he'd only been in her bed yesterday afternoon. How many Stephens did she know with English accents? Did he have to spell it out?

"Stephen Lefever," he amplified.

"Hi, Stephen. This is a lousy time to call. Have you any idea what time it is?"

"Look, could we talk inside? It's Gotham City out here."

"Stephen, I've gone to bed."

"Alone?"

"Just me and a couple of U.S. Marines. What do you want?"

"I want to see you. To be with you. To spend a whole night with you."

"You should have called. I'm not presentable."

"I should hope not. Kick the Marines out and let me in. This is a dawn raid."

"Oh, for God's *sake*."

The door opened at the buzz, and Stephen crossed the hall to the second door. He pressed the button again.

"Give me two minutes," she said, and hung up.

He paced the hall. What the hell was he doing there? He took a long slug of the whiskey. That wasn't a question to be asked. He gave her five minutes, not wanting to appear over-keen. Another minute, and he'd have been asleep on his feet. Or worse, sober.

She appeared at the apartment door in a long, flowery wrap-around robe, her raven hair let down to her shoulders and her ice-blue eyes steady and watchful. He drew her toward him to kiss her, and felt the familiar stirring of arousal as the prow of her breasts flattened softly against his chest. She had put fresh makeup on, and she averted her lips to avoid a direct kiss, sending it wide of the mark. He sank his face into her warm neck, where the sharp scent of musky perfume, its alcohol as yet unevaporated, overlaid the sensual smell of slumber.

"Where's Joanna?" she asked.

"Joanna?" he echoed, burying his face deeper into the warm flesh. "Who's Joanna?"

She must have registered the significance of the suitcase, for she pulled away and fixed him hard with the iceberg eyes. Perhaps, too, for the first time she took in his general drunken and disheveled condition.

"Stephen," she began, "whatever's going on between you and her—"

"Nothing's 'going on' between me and her."

"Just leave me out of it. Don't bring your marital problems here. The way we work suits me fine. If you want to change the rules, count me out. I'm not into heavy involvements."

"Roxanne, sweetheart, relax," he murmured, drawing her to him again. He ran his hand between the folds of her robe and cupped her rubbery naked breast. "Do you think I don't know all that?"

"So long as it's understood, okay?"

"Suits me. Now, can we go somewhere more comfortable?"

The demon that inspired him to extravagant feats of performance earlier that evening now turned against him. For all the licentious mumblings in her ear, for all the little depravities he promised and the exquisite obscenities he threatened, alas, the passion obstinately refused to make the small but critical leap from word to deed. Everything was wrong. He was drunk and exhausted, he'd been kicked out of a job, a bar, and his own home all in one day, and he was with a girl who wanted sex, whom he himself had aroused to want sex, when all he really yearned for was just sympathy and comfort, to lie alongside a naked girl, to feel the warmth and reassurance of a lithe young body, to fall asleep with a soft kiss on his lips and a child, all trusting innocence, in his arms. He wanted anything in the world but this, lying there with all his bodily forces in mutiny, ransacking his brain for fantasies that might work to stir his reluctant flesh, crying out in rage at his own body for forsaking him at this of all times.

It was to no avail. Neither his own strenuous effort of mind nor her own vigorous efforts upon his body did more than raise a momentary response that refused to be sustained. Finally, she gave him a resigned kiss and, saying she had to be up early, turned her back and went to sleep. Within a moment her breathing was rising and falling in the slow rhythm of gentle slumber, leaving him lying awake beside her but hardly daring to touch her, sweltering with anxieties he hadn't known since adolescence, wondering if the day's crises had triggered a sudden onset of the male menopause. He ransacked the library of his brain once again for fantasy images potent enough to work sooner or later or at least sometime during the night and enable him to take the girl in her sleep and so salvage something of his pride and honor.

But sleep itself was to rob him of that last hope. The next thing he knew, it was morning. Roxanne was standing over him, a glass of orange juice in her hand, all dressed, repaired, her hair up, and ready to face a fresh day. He shielded his eyes from the glare of the daylight. The movement sent stabs of pain through his skull.

"Here, drink this," she said. She regarded him with a nurse's detached eye. "You look like shit."

"I feel like shit." He drank the juice. "Sorry for crashing in on you like that. For crashing out on you, too."

"Forget it. What are friends for?"

Oh-ho, he thought, here we go. It's "friends" now.

"Yes, well, it was either you or a park bench in Union Square." He saw she was taking him literally. "Just kidding. You know how it is when a guy leaves home."

"I don't. I don't want to know, either."

A brief moment of awkwardness followed.

So," he said, mustering a cheerful tone, "you're off to the Department."

"If you shift your ass we could share a cab."

"I'm not going in. Not today." He squinted out beyond the window at the morning breaking bright and fine and full of fresh hope. He felt dull and flat and full of despair. "As a matter of fact, I've resigned."

"You quit?" She looked aghast.

"It was me or Weitzman. The Department isn't big enough for the both of us."

"Are you crazy, or what?"

"Don't look at me like that. I can get a dozen permanent professorships. I've only got to pick up the phone. Right now, I'm a free man. Let's have dinner tonight and do something wild."

She took him by the hand. He knew what was coming.

"Stephen," she began almost tenderly, "don't let's spoil things. Remember what I said last night about not being into heavy involvements?"

"Heavy? I feel light as air. You know what they say, 'Today is the first day of the rest of your life.' That's me, sweetheart."

"Who are you kidding? You're in deep shit." Her eyes hardened. The concern they expressed was partly for him but mostly for herself. "Where do you plan on staying?"

"Well, I thought maybe, just for a day or two, you know, till I get things sorted out . . . "

"Stephen, you can't stay here. I've got a friend coming in from the coast tonight."

"Ah. I see."

"No, you don't. She's a girlfriend. From high school days."

"And you don't want her to meet me. I understand. She

might write home and tell Mom her little girl's having an affair with the prof."

"We're not having an affair, Stephen. And you're no longer a prof."

"What *are* we having? An uninvolved, uncommitted professional acquaintanceship with occasional sexual asides?"

"Occasional," she muttered pointedly. "You can say that again."

"Okay," he challenged, knowing that persistence was fatal and yet unable to stop himself, "we'll stick to the old routine. Let's meet back here this afternoon. Three o'clock?"

"Sorry, Stephen. I've got a seminar." She packed a pile of books into a holdall and collected her purse and keys. Then she leaned forward and kissed him lightly on the forehead. "You're a really sweet guy," she said. "I'll always remember our afternoons."

He pulled away urgently.

"Come on, Roxanne. What's the matter? Nothing's changed."

"Everything's changed, can't you see?" She went to the door and turned. "There's bagels and stuff in the fridge. You know how to let yourself out. And turn off the air-conditioning when you go."

With a smile and a wave, she was gone. And a moment later the front door closed with a firm and final clang.

He lay back on the pillows and pressed the empty glass of ice to his aching temples. *Everything's changed, can't you see?* Typical of bloody women. A man and his function were inseparable in their minds. Roxanne wanted him *qua* afternoon lover and *qua* academic hero. Should the lover falter in his lover's duties or the hero professor forfeit his laurel crown, he no longer fulfilled his role and down came the guillotine.

He looked about the room, trying to focus on anything that would keep his thoughts away from Joanna and what had been said and done. He let his eye roam over the paper globe lampshade in the center, the busy-lizzie on the windowsill, the graduation day photo and the Chomsky textbook lying on the dressing table among the lipsticks and perfume bottles, the holiday postcards tucked into the mirror above, and on the bedside table the threadbare teddy bear, a relic of childhood, propped up alongside the framed photo of Mom and Dad . . . He groaned. He'd been here before a hundred times. Was he condemned to spend the rest of his life in and out of bedrooms like this, the uniformly predictable bedrooms of girls half his age?

The glare of the morning light sent arrows shooting through his head. He closed his eyes, but the pain remained. For the real torment lay inside him: the torment of remorse, of loss, and of loneliness.

11

HARD WORK WAS EVER the best therapy, and Joanna threw herself into her commitments at the salon with every ounce of her energy, hoping thereby to leave no chink of time or strength for reflection.

The show had been a triumph.

From the closing moment, they faced a deluge of inquiries and orders. Agents and distributors from the east coast to the west, buyers for boutiques and chains from the north border to the south, even representatives from across the world, inundated the small offices in Madison Avenue. And if there were ever moments when she would reach instinctively for the phone to touch base with Stephen or unthinkingly accept an invitation for a dinner party or a theater engagement for them both, any deeper reflection was quickly drowned in the urgent flood of phone calls and faxes, of orders and invoices and delivery notes. Then there were those that had been canceled or gone astray, or unwittingly offended delicate vanities in a trade noted for sensitive personalities, not to count the hundred and one other pressing claims of a business that had, quite simply and literally, taken off overnight.

And yet, in the moments snatched in between the meetings and the phone calls and the crises, she recognized the irony of her situation. Her work, the thing that Stephen dismissed as her "rich bitch hobby," and something at a deep level she cared nothing at all about, was an extraordinary triumph. Her personal life, which *did* matter deeply, was a complete disaster. How could it all be so upside down?

For a whole week she managed not to think beyond this. Hard work did prove good therapy, and she retired each evening so exhausted that she was asleep as her head hit the pillow. In the morning she woke to find the circus had already begun. She'd go downstairs to find the floor of her study awash in faxes from Tokyo and Sydney and other markets of the opposite time zone. She'd curse the machine and swear she'd disconnect it, but she never got round to doing even this small thing before the first calls came in from the office, where Cheryl was already at work, having come in from Brooklyn at dawn, or Bella was stirring and wanting to talk about the strange dreams she'd been having or, harder still, face her endless questions about Stephen, what she'd said to upset him, where he'd gone, when he was coming back, whether he *was* coming back and, frankly, how stupid and childish they both were.

One day she woke to a silent phone and fax machine and a sleeping daughter, and she realized that it was Sunday. In the strange, unnatural truce that settled momentarily even over such a godless city as this on the Lord's day of rest, she allowed herself, for the first time, to think and reflect. She made herself a glass of herbal tea and took it back to bed. Piling the pillows against the bedhead—not on her side, for there were no his and her sides anymore, but in the center where she now slept the night—she lay back and closed her eyes and gradually let her mind wrap itself around the reality of what she had done to him, of what he had done to her, and what they had done to themselves.

Her natural response as a mother was to draw together with her daughter, and in the days since they had become a household of two, for all the claims of her work, for Bella's sake she strove to fill in the gaps which Stephen had left in their family life. She evolved a new breakfast routine, typically, in which instead of independently grabbing what they wanted from the fridge they sat down together over the cornflakes and toast and talked.

"So, what shall we do today?" she asked that Sunday morning, refilling Bella's glass of juice. "We could go to the beach house. Or do you want to go to basketball?"

"It's okay, Mom," replied Bella. "I know you're busy."

"I'd love to take you. You'll have to show me where, though." Stephen normally took her for Sunday morning basketball practice. "We could meet up with Lorri for brunch."

"I'm seeing her tonight."

"Again? There can't be a movie left you haven't seen. Hey, there's a new exhibit at the Museum of Natural History. Something on the origins of man. Wouldn't that be useful for your vacation project?"

"There's no point."

"We can buy a guide book," urged Joanna. Anything scientific, again, was implicitly Stephen's province. "There's got to be plenty of stuff you can read up for yourself."

A moment's silence fell. Joanna stared into her coffee, Bella stared into her juice.

"Mom," began the girl without looking up, "how long is all this going to go on for? I mean, what's the big deal? He was only having a laugh. Everyone else thought it was really funny. No one got upset except you."

"Darling, one thing you've always got to have in a marriage, and that's respect."

"What about give and take?"

"It can't be all give and no take."

"That's not fair! Stephen does his bit. He doesn't have as much money as us, but he shares what he gets. Do we honestly share ours?"

"Of course I do! This whole apartment was bought with money from the Trust, but half belongs to Stephen. You know that."

"Then how come he was the one who had to quit? I'll tell you. Because it's really your place, not his."

Joanna reached for her daughter's hand, but thought better of it.

"Angel, marriage isn't easy. But it helps if you start with someone who is, well, *like* you. Take your friend Eddie. Just as an example, I mean. Eddie comes from the same background. You look at things the same way. You've got similar interests."

"You mean, we're both rich little WASP brats."

"If you must. But a man like Stephen is, well, more chancy. He and I come from different cultures. Different backgrounds with different value systems. We're different *people*."

It was Bella who reached out her hand and took her mother's.

"Mom, you don't need to say all that. You know it's not true. And even if it was, it wouldn't matter. You love him."

"I did love him, I admit."

"You still do. You know you do. Otherwise you wouldn't get so steamed up."

"I have a right to be steamed up. His behavior was utterly reprehensible."

"He got drunk. People do."

"That's not all."

"I suppose you mean his little flings?"

"Bella! What do you know about that?"

"I'm not blind, Mom." She paused. "I think men have affairs because things aren't right at home. Cheating doesn't make things break down. It's because they already have."

Joanna flinched. This was getting too close to home.

"What can I do?" she snapped.

"Call him up, Mom. Meet him for dinner at Mortimer's or one of your other old haunts. Say you're sorry."

"Why should I? I'm not sorry. He's the one who should grovel."

She caught the petulant tone in her own voice and felt momentarily ashamed. She knew it was because actually she felt on weak ground. She steeled herself with the memory of catching him *in flagrante* that night on the beach. Her blood boiled. She wasn't going to go all soft and forgiving now.

"Anyway," she said flatly, "I don't know where he is."

It wasn't true. She'd had a hunch and called the Athletic Club earlier in the week. And she'd been right: he'd checked into a room there. She'd just wanted to make sure he was somewhere reasonably okay. And perhaps to know where that somewhere was.

"Leave a message at the Department," said Bella. "He'll pick it up."

She looked out of the window at the city skyline beyond. It seemed suddenly so close, crowding in on her.

"Times like this, I really feel like getting out of town," she said.

"Nobody's stopping you. You're a free agent now."

"Shall we, then?"

"Sure." Bella munched thoughtfully on a muffin. She didn't seem inclined to move. "You've made it through far worse times," she went on. "When Luke died, Stephen was wonderful."

"That was a long time ago."

"Anyone would think it just happened yesterday."

"What do you mean?"

"That's when it all started going wrong, isn't it?"

"How can you say? You were only fourteen at the time."

"I live in this place, too, Mom. I hear everything that goes on. I think Stephen's right. You've never really got over Luke's death. But what about Stephen? I don't think you ever thought how tough it must have been for him. Luke was his child, too. His only child. You at least had me."

Joanna stood up and began clearing away the plates. This was an area she distinctly wanted to avoid. Bella had instinctively put her finger on the root of it all. But there was no way Joanna was going to go into that, even if it made the expulsion of Stephen seem unreasonable and abrupt in the girl's eyes—*stupid and childish,* as she'd said. Whether this was a breakup in their marriage or just a temporary separation, she knew there was nothing she could do to mend it. Everything that ever could be said between her and Stephen already had been said. They had fought and cried and made up time and time again, and now she was just too tired, too weary, too despairing of hope, to reengage the issue. She had given up. They simply shared too much of a past, and nothing would ever erase that. Bella could never know about it and, short of telling her, there was no explanation of the breakdown that would ever satisfy her. For her, Stephen's sudden departure and the silence between them would remain forever inexplicable and absurd.

She sought a way to turn the conversation.

"You're sure smart," she said. "You need to understand human psychology to make it as an actress."

Bella rose, too, and cleared away her plate and glass.

"That's another thing, Mom," she said casually. "I'm not sure about drama college any more."

"There's no hurry to decide."

"I've been reading some of Stephen's books. This whole behavioral psychology kick is really interesting."

"If that's what you really want to do," conceded Joanna. "Now, why don't we get ready to hit the road?"

She finished clearing away the breakfast, then went into her study to collect a few things for the trip. An urgent fax had arrived, and she was about to deal with it when she checked herself. Dammit, couldn't she give Bella just one day of her full concentration? This recent upset in the girl's life had cut deeper than was apparent on the surface. Maybe she understood something she herself didn't. Something about compassion. Maybe her advice wasn't so bad after all.

Leave a message at the Department. He'll pick it up. No, but she could make contact in another way. She scooped up the pile of mail addressed to Professor Lefever and put it into a large envelope, then went upstairs and packed a selection of shirts and socks and underpants into a sports bag. She'd deliver them to the Department, rather than let him know she'd run him to earth at the Athletic Club. From the bathroom she threw his special Trumper's eau-de-cologne and, returning to the kitchen downstairs, added the box of Turkish Delight she'd bought him the other day. A food parcel wasn't to be construed as a suit for peace.

Finally, calling to Bella that she was ready, she picked up her car keys and headed for the door.

She decided to drop the things off at the Department later, on their way back in the evening, when there was less likelihood of running into Stephen by accident. However, they met heavy traffic and, because Bella was already late for her date, they couldn't make the detour, so the bag and the envelope stayed in the car awaiting another opportunity.

The day they spent at the beach house was just like the old times. They swam in the pool, had lunch by the ocean, and spent most of the afternoon pottering around the coastline in the small sailing dinghy. She herself was a poor sailor, nowhere near as competent as Stephen, but she was determined not to be shown up. She fell into the water and got half concussed by the sail beam, but she gritted her teeth and kept on laughing, and when finally they maneuvered the small craft into the rickety boathouse and climbed out gingerly onto the rotten boards and the earth beneath her feet had stopped rocking, she felt a genuine glow of achievement. No one, not even the fond unworldly philandering fool she'd married, was indispensable.

As the afternoon wore on, Bella grew impatient to get back to the city. Joanna found herself strangely anxious to return, too. She couldn't at first think why: she had no reason to look forward to the strain and confusion of life there. They packed up, locked the house, and climbed into the car. It was only as they pulled onto the freeway and Bella asked what she planned to do that evening herself that she realized.

"I think I'll have an early night," she lied.

"Come with us, Mom. You love Jack Nicholson."

"I'll probably call up Warner and see if he can make it for a late drink," she said, laying the ground for an alibi. "I've got things to discuss."

"See a lawyer on a Sunday night? You'll pay triple rates."

"His Sabbath was yesterday."

"But his partner's a goy."

"And his wife's a client, darling. You've no idea how much she spends in the shop each month. *He*'d certainly be interested to know."

"Mom, surely you wouldn't!"

They exchanged glances and laughed. For a while they were united in a mood of girls' camaraderie, joking and kidding and reminiscing about the days before Stephen had arrived on the scene, talking for all the world like two sisters rather than a mother and her daughter. It reached the point that the mood of fellow feeling could only be sustained by an exchange of confessions, and Joanna was on the point of finding some elliptical way of sharing her most precious and personal secret when Bella abruptly broke the spell.

"You aren't thinking of divorcing Stephen?" she demanded bluntly. "Is that what you're seeing Warner about?"

"Well, it has to be considered," replied Joanna, coming sharply down to earth. "When things break down irretrievably . . . "

"Who says it's irretrievable? Don't be so *stiff*, Mom. Cool off for a bit, okay, but don't pull the plug."

Joanna glanced across at her daughter's strong, defiant

expression. It was so easy for the young. Everything came fresh to them, unburdened with the echoes of the past and its heartaches. Then she looked away. She couldn't answer her. The girl had a fair point. Was it right to rob her of the man who stood as the father in her world? If Stephen made another life, would Bella be part of it, and would that be the same?

Abruptly she reached forward and turned on the radio. She didn't want to pursue this line of thought. She didn't *want* Bella to be right. She didn't want to have to treat with Stephen, to reopen the case, to exercise the fairness and forgiveness of a reasonable adult. She knew it was hopeless. The seams of hope had been mined bare. But also, though she scarcely dared admit it, part of her *wanted* to be intransigent and unreasonable. Part of her wanted to see Stephen as a bastard and as the guilty party and to consign the marriage to irretrievable breakdown, so as to justify what she now wanted for herself. To justify what she was going to do that very evening.

"Find a tape," she said, switching the radio off. "Something horribly deafening."

She should have heeded the warning signs.

She should have recognized the hidden voice in that urge to return to the city as evening approached, when that very morning she'd been equally desperate to flee it. She should have observed herself with an objective eye as she lingered in the shower longer than she was wont, as she powdered and perfumed her body with unusual care and, even though she would be changing it all within the same hour, took particular pains selecting her underwear and dress and shoes. She should have read the significance of how finally she slipped out of the apartment without leaving Maria a word or Bella a note, how she blushed like an adolescent when the doorman downstairs complimented her on looking so good and how she gave him an address downtown to pass on to the driver in the waiting cab which, around the next block, she amended to a street on the Upper West Side. Certainly, when she reached the apartment and found the plain handwritten note on the doormat and felt her legs suddenly go weak and a flush of ache and panic swirl through her so forcefully that she couldn't stay sitting down for more than a moment before rising to her feet again to wander about the room, pausing every few steps to regain her breath, just as though the note had brought her confirmation of some incurable illness, which indeed in one sense it had, then, if ever she knew anything about herself, she should have recognized the symptoms, and understood.

She was in love.

Hopelessly, helplessly, in love.

In love with the danger of the unknown. In love with the freedom of being unknown. And simply, unashamedly, in love with lust.

The note gave an address on the far East Side. It was written on a plain sheet of paper, folded in half. It bore no name, either of the sender or the addressee, and was signed simply with the single letter, *L*.

The handwriting was extraordinary. It was calligraphed in a Gothic italic hand, with the capital letters elaborately flourished with serifs and scrollwork in the manner of a medieval illuminated manuscript. It read simply:

I hold your hostage.
Ransom it in person.
Tonight, at dusk.

And, as a clue, at the foot of the page was drawn a small and mysterious symbol, like the seal of a ring or the archive stamp on a precious book, which revealed itself under scrutiny to be a tiny drawing of an umbrella.

She smiled to herself as she reread the note in the cab that took her back across the park the very way she had come less than half an hour before. This time, however, the cab went past the Park Avenue apartment and headed east over to First Avenue, where it doubled back half a block and set her down outside a gaunt and grimy stone building, one of a row of similar town houses that for the past six decades had somehow evaded the bulldozer.

She paid off the cab and found herself suddenly alone on the sidewalk. The house stood before her, dark and forbidding in the fast-falling twilight. The upper two floors had evidently been converted to form a single living space, perhaps a studio, and here the windows ran from floor to ceiling and angled back along the line of the roof. Black blinds screened the front elevation, and the only light coming from the building at all was a yellowish glow that filtered through the panes in the roof.

She hesitated. She looked about her uneasily. Two young blacks were eying her from the stoop of the house opposite. A prowling car drew up alongside her, and in the streetlight she glimpsed a telltale gleam of greed in the driver's eye. Instinctively she clutched her purse more tightly. This wasn't a neighborhood in which to be hanging around as night fell. Down the road, beyond a tattoo parlor and a shop advertising "Marital Aids," she could see First Avenue, a bustling river of lights and traffic. Fifty paces would take her to a cab and to safety.

Ransom it in person. Tonight, at dusk.

She could hear his voice, that soft, seductive, lethal voice. She could see his eyes, those black, piercing, hypnotic eyes that ate into her soul. She felt sick and breathless. Her limbs were trembling. She was melting inside, the very substance of her body turning to liquid.

The door lay ahead, black and unmarked. Ten short paces, across the sidewalk and up the steps, would bring her there. She found herself staring at the door with the fixity of a trance. Her vision seemed to be tunneling, blanking out the street and all else around. Gradually, as though driven by an outside power, she found herself moving forward, across the sidewalk, up the steps, and onto the threshold of the black door.

The intercom beside the door had just one button. It was likewise unmarked. With trembling hand, she pressed it.

The soft, seductive voice came over tinny and cracked.

"Who is it?"

She drew a breath. A mist seemed to be closing in around her. Her own voice came out in a hoarse whisper.

"Cristina."

A brief pause followed. Then abruptly, and so loudly it startled her, the door buzzed open.

She let herself into a narrow hallway lit only by a dim, tasseled lamp set upon a sideboard. In the air hung the odor of linseed oil and turpentine and faintly, beneath it, she detected the cool, churchlike smell of gutted candles. Ahead lay a staircase, lacquered a deep gloss black, its shape almost lost against the deep maroon and dull gold damask wall coverings.

She waited. No one came.

Strains of early music, perhaps a Monteverdi lament, filtered down to her from an upper floor. The sound seemed to cast a spell of enchantment around her, luring her up from the dark underworld in which she found herself. Gradually, like a sleepwalker, she began to ascend the staircase. Step by step she went, drawn toward the reedy, plaintive music and the glow of light far ahead that gently intensified as she approached.

In the doorway she stopped, stupefied.

The room, a single vast space formed of the entire top half of the building, was partitioned not by walls but by curtains, thickly flowing drapes of rich dark hues of magenta and ultramarine and black and vermilion, that hung from poles and beams like the backdrops on a theater stage. The only lighting came from a scattering of low table lamps set around the room, creating small pools of warm colored light.

In the center stood a low platform on which was set a couch draped and cushioned in a pale embroidered Oriental fabric, and beside it lay a bronze urn filled with fruit. A few feet away stood an easel bearing a canvas marked out with faint grid lines. And beyond, almost lost in the shadows but not concealed, stood a large finely wrought brass bedstead with coverlet, sheets, and pillows all in black.

All this she took in at a single sweep. But he was nowhere to be seen.

Then she sensed a slight movement in the shadows to her side and, turning with a start, she saw he was standing there, watching her, fixing her with his deep, magnetic eyes. Once again the faint notes of musk rose to stir her senses. She waited for him to speak, but he said nothing. Without releasing her from his gaze, he reached forward and held out a glass to her. It was frosted with cold and contained a clear yellowish liquid. She took it. She didn't ask what it was. She didn't want to know. Aphrodisiac or poison, she would have taken it.

He raised his own glass and swallowed it back in one. Holding his eye, she did the same. A fiery spirit burned through her throat and exploded in her stomach, leaving behind an aftertaste redolent of broad grassy plains. As he refilled her glass, she caught a glimpse of the label: Zubrovka, bison grass vodka.

He refilled his own. But instead of drinking it, he held the glass forward, slowly, inch by inch, across the space between them, until the frosty surface was touching the tip of her breast. She could feel the nipple surging erect, stretching against the thin silk of her shirt, and she felt a flush of shame at such an involuntary response, such a blatant betrayal of her body's desire. He pressed the glass harder against her breast, flattening the flesh. She knew it was wetting the silk, rendering the material transparent. She caught her breath as a sheet of pain streaked through her. The icy cold burned like flame. Yet she stood there, unable to move, scarcely even able to breathe.

Finally, an eternity later, he took a step back. For the first time he spoke.

"Take that off, if you please," he said quietly.

Slowly, button by button, she began to undo the blouse.

He stood back in the shadows, watching her. His eyes glinted hard, but his stance bespoke indifference. This was a familiar, even a routine, occurrence to him, his body language seemed to be saying. For her, however, it was terrifyingly new, unknown territory. She had never undressed in front of a man in this way before, at his word and under his gaze and while he himself remained fully clothed. And yet it struck a chord within her deepest desire, so that when finally she let the flimsy silk garment drop to the floor and, after another interminable torturing silence he spoke again, she was powerless to protest.

"And now the rest," he said.

Reaching round to the side of her short, tight skirt, she began undoing the zipper. The skirt joined the blouse on the floor. Next followed her shoes. And then her stockings, garters, panties, until she stood before him, entirely naked. Involuntarily, she placed a hand to cover her sex, but he reached out from the shadows and gently removed it. Her mind flashed back to the very first moment she'd seen him, at the Frick museum reception, and she'd imagined herself standing in the company of all those people, quite naked, her soft pale skin striking such a contrast to the crisp dark suits of the men. In the same unreal way now, she was conscious of her nudity standing out pale and vulnerable against the heavy dark fabrics all around her, here in the house of her stranger lover.

He led her to the low platform. There, focusing a light upon her, he began subjecting her naked body to a meticulous examination. He moved around her slowly like an expert appraising a marble statue, touching her gently here and there, testing her skin, feeling her flesh, evaluating its texture, exploring its contours. She shivered at his touch, yet far from flinching she proffered herself to his scrutiny, reveling in the inexpressible thrill of being relieved, however briefly, of the burden of her self and the interminable voices in her mind and, instead, of being reduced to a simple unknown, a creature with no identity and no function beyond the giving and gratifying of pleasure.

His hand lingered on her naked inner thigh, then gradually by infinitesimal degrees it rose toward the crux of her body. Higher and higher traced the fingertips. She caught her breath as though she were stepping inch by inch into a freezing ocean, only here the ocean was boiling. Abruptly she felt the hand enter her sex, sliding in with shocking ease and drawing a gasp from her throat as the fingers drove home, and the next thing she knew she was cupped by this hand and being half lifted upward and gently propelled backward and down onto the couch, onto her back, with the man's weight bearing down upon her and the hand no longer a hand but thrusting flesh alive within her.

12

STEPHEN AWOKE FROM THE NIGHTMARE in a swelter of terror. Through bleary, aching eyes he struggled to make sense of his bearings and to convince himself that this unfamiliar room with its dull, anodyne furnishings was indeed the real world, not the starkly vivid realm of the dream.

He had dreamed about Luke again. This time had been one of the worst. The setting was a sculptor's workshop. His infant son was lying on the bench before him, encased from head to foot in a plaster cast, all except for two holes for its eyes. It was alive inside the cast and struggling as much as the rigid body-cage would allow, and in its eyes—this was most terrible—there was an expression not so much of terror as of sorrowful puzzlement that those who loved it so much could be doing such a thing to it. Joanna was there, comforting it. She was weeping, but she was powerless to stop him. For he knew what he had to do. Beside him lay a bowl of fresh plaster, already beginning to set. Sick with horror and yet driven by a compulsion beyond him, he scooped a handful of the plaster and pasted it over the eyeholes, first one and then the other, covering the tiny bright-flashing eyes, smothering their little lights, then scooped out more and pasted it on top of the last, and on and on by degrees until the whole was like a smooth, unbroken pod. Then suddenly it all changed, and *he* was inside the plaster cast, immured in that dark and rigid encasement, unable to turn or twist or stretch a muscle, unable even to draw breath to scream. . . .

He lay back on the small, hard bed and waited for the ceiling to come into focus. The bright morning light seared his eyes. He closed them again, but that only intensified the painful drumming inside his skull and sucked him back into the world of the nightmare.

He raised himself on one elbow and squinted at his travel alarm clock. It read ten-twenty. Beyond, on the floor, he could make out the pile of clothes where he'd dropped them, returning soused and spent in the early hours. He realized he was still wearing his socks.

He struggled to remember what had happened the previous night. If he could reconnect the continuity of himself, it would finally give the lie to the dream.

It all seemed so distant. Vague images as from a half-forgotten film drifted to the surface of his mind. A party. A casual pick-up, more exactly, this Barbie Doll clone had picked *him* up. She'd taken him back to her apartment. She'd had a friend. When they'd drunk the champagne he'd brought, they'd gone on to piña coladas—God, he was going to retch—then all fallen into bed together. He'd excelled himself, doing a stallion's duty at serving each in turn. He groaned aloud. Men had got it all wrong. For them, ithyphallic prowess was the measure of a good fuck. But what had it done for him, running that sexual marathon? Women had the right idea, they rated a screw not by what they gave but by what they got. And those two girls, having got what they wanted, turned their backs on him and got on with enjoying each other. Spent and superfluous, he'd finally crawled out of the apartment, hailed a taxi, and headed for home. He'd arrived outside the Park Avenue apartment base, before he realized he'd unconsciously given the wrong address.

He stretched luxuriously, his toes reaching the two corners of the bed. There were compensations. He'd forgotten how good it was to wake up in one's own bed, alone. The warm emptiness in his loins and the dull soreness in his groin testified to his newfound state of life. He was a bachelor again, footloose and fancy-free. He felt rejuvenated, revitalized.

No, he didn't. He felt older than ever. He felt a dry husk, drained of its juice. To hell with being footloose and fancy-free.

He'd done all that. It was one thing to have affairs when you were married, to dip in and out of illicit beds and return home to a warm core of stability, but quite another when the core was cut away and bed-hopping became a function of sexual vagrancy. Right now he wanted to be at home, in the bed where he belonged, in the sheets, goddammit, that he'd bought from Pratesi with his first paycheck, lying alongside the warm and softly scented body of the woman he loved . . .

Correction, *a* woman he loved.

He didn't love *her*. He couldn't love her. She'd screwed up his life, she'd fouled up his career. She was a *witch*-bitch. She was a neurotic hysteric with a pathological guilt complex. He was well rid of her. He'd already sacrificed too many years of his life trying to build a marriage on those insecure and shifting sands.

He hadn't seen it at first, of course. No one ever saw the truth in that heady springtime of new love when hours spent together flew like minutes and hours spent apart crawled by like weeks.

But the death of their baby had brought out the truth. Or rather, the death of *her* baby. She never spoke of *his* baby, or even *our* baby. Just as it was never *his* pain and grief and sorrow and heartache, but always *hers*. He was a man, and men weren't allowed to have feelings, other perhaps than of the heroic kind. Men had to be strong and supportive and immovable as rocks. But just when they were strong and immovable they were then accused of being unfeeling. *Any father with an iota of feeling would want to pay his respects*—in his ears still echoed her words that day, the second anniversary of Luke's death, when she'd gone alone to the crematorium. True, he'd forgotten. True, too, he'd been enjoying carnal company while she'd been in prayerful solitude. But that wasn't the point. She never knew how he had wept for the infant. She'd never seen his tears, for he'd never allowed her to see them. He'd grieved alone and in private. To expect him to provide the strong shoulder to lean on and the next minute to accuse him of not having any feelings at all, just because for her sake he'd kept them hidden from her. . . . The thought filled him with indignation. The selfishness of the woman! The self-centered egotism! Yes indeed, he was well rid of her.

As he lay with his eyes half-open, listening to sounds of the plumbing in the next-door suite and, beyond the uncurtained windows, the rumble of traffic flowing along Central Park South, listening, too, to the petty and petulant tone of his own self-justification, he was filled with a sense of the vastness of the world and the limitlessness of its explicability and, measured against that, the paltriness of this one miserable hung over human being lying in bed with his socks on in an anonymous hotel room in the middle of the morning, raising his puny voice in futile rage against life and love and humankind and struggling to throw up specious rationalizations to excuse himself and shift the blame to anyone around him. There *was* a truth and a true explanation for everything. Mental mudslinging and outpourings of chauvinistic bravado were no solution, just as the companionable bottle and the casual bed were no escape. The subconscious was not to be cheated, its truth would always out. There was no hiding place from the nightmares.

If ever he were to rise beyond the state into which he was fast degenerating, he must apply his mind, with objective honesty and fair reasoning, to the deeper questions of his life. How did he really feel about Joanna? Was there truly no point in trying to get back together while the mess remained unresolved, after he'd broken his spirit over the past two years trying to resolve it? Was this, then, a stalemate he'd have to sit out until something or someone else entered the equation and helped Joanna to see the truth? And, finally, had he himself really come to terms with Luke's death and his own part in it, or was he, as she'd accused him, just running away?

He put on a robe, swallowed a handful of Tylenol tablets and took the elevator to the swimming-pool floor. There he sweated for thirty minutes in the Turkish bath, punished his flesh under the high-pressure water jet for a further five, then swam ten lengths of the Olympic-size pool. Sick and giddy, he staggered back to his room, dressed, then went out to a café round the corner where three fried eggs and mountains of hash browns, washed down by gallons of weak coffee, provided the ballast his stomach needed.

For the first time he looked at the day and saw it was fine and fair, with just the first hint of the changing season in the air. Taking a few deep breaths, he set off toward the open greenery of the park with a lighter step. He felt just as he had the very first occasion he'd set foot in that city, in the summer vacation before going up to university some eighteen years before. He'd arrived overnight on a student charter flight, and he recalled standing at exactly the same spot at the foot of the park, looking around him with the surreal, glazed eye of the unslept and thrilled with excitement at the majestic beauty of the city and, above all, at the fearless expression all around of raw human strength and energy. It was a spiritual experience, and it confirmed his belief in the unshakable omnipotence of man. Nothing was beyond his reach. Nothing stood outside his understanding and, ultimately, his control.

Returning to England to take up an arts place at Cambridge, he switched to the sciences and ended up obtaining a first-class degree in psychology and zoology. His doctoral thesis on gestural communication between capuchin monkeys took him to Latin America, where he could observe the creatures in the wild, and then on to a research fellowship in the States, where primate studies were the most advanced in the world.

It also led him to break up with the girl to whom he was engaged, a girl clever enough to understand him and sweet enough to love what she saw. Only years later, here in New York, did he realize she was the only person he'd never *pretended* with. At the time, all that seemed taken for granted. She was doing her doctorate in history, and her research was rooted in England. His future lay in America. It was a simple geographical incompatibility. The breakup hurt him badly, but he never questioned his decision. He came from a modest background in a small town in the Midlands. His father, in his own way a brilliant man and a wasted talent, was an inspector of primary schools and his mother, the catering manageress at the local hospital. He was an only child, and his ambition from his earliest recollection was to escape to a bigger world with broader horizons. His father encouraged him to look to education as the way out. He didn't live to see his son win a top scholarship to Cambridge.

The step from primates to people was an obvious one but surprisingly difficult to manage. He'd made his name in animal behavior and, in the specialized academic world, that was his niche. As an arts student, however, he'd been struck by how

poets and novelists were constrained to describing human feelings and behavior through metaphor; though powerful in arousing emotions, metaphor could only ever be a description at one
remove. Behavioral science, on the other hand, offered the
promise of a precise and immediate account. More, it suggested
that feelings could be inferred from behavior, and that opened
up an exciting vista of opportunity. Why couldn't one, in theory,
read a person's facial and bodily cues just as clearly as one read
a book? Using a modified Facial Affect Scoring Technique pro-
cedure, he began to make detailed observations of people's eye
movements, recording minute changes in pupil size and eye
shape and lid positions under different emotional states. It was
during this research, which he began at Columbia on the side,
that he realized the significance of micro-momentary expressions—those tiny, fleeting facial cues which the naked eye
missed but which, when filmed and replayed in slow motion,
showed, for instance, a smile flicking to a grimace and back to a
smile again in the space of a mere fraction of a second. These
covert cues offered a window onto the subconscious and, when
correlated with overt facial cues, could be codified into a kind of
dictionary and analyzed by a computer so as to provide a scien-
tifically accurate definition of any person's true state of mind
and feelings. Science had unraveled man's genetic makeup,
revealed the organic workings of his body, and analyzed the
chemistry of his brain. Now the last bastion of the human mystery could be breached—the privacy of human thought. The
implications were mind-numbing.

To anyone with a mind, that was.

Stephen kicked the gravel and swore aloud. Screw the
Board. He'd damn well find a way of carrying on. He'd be first
into that breach. In his mind he began composing the postcards he'd soon be sending from Stockholm to Don Weitzman
and Warner Friedman and the whole pack of goons. He
glanced at his watch. In Europe, the labs would be closed and
the professors gone home; on the coast, they'd be having
breakfast. He'd give it a couple of hours and call Lou Whittard
at Berkeley. Berkeley was in a different league from Columbia.
Lou had funds, and he'd always made overtures when they'd
met at conferences. San Francisco was the place. Pretty girls,
perfect weather, great food, a relaxed lifestyle. It was another

world over there. And one where money wasn't the only god and king.

Money. More exactly, Joanna's money and his lack of it. That was the rock on which their ship had foundered. It had pervaded their lives from the very first, an insidious parallel force that whispered behind doors, poisoned minds, and varnished everything with a false value. He'd met Joanna at a dinner party in the first week of arriving in New York. It never occurred to him to wonder if she was rich. Everyone in the city was rich by his standards. He just fell for her vitality and sense of fun and, frankly, her looks, at once soft and strong, and her body, the body he still hungered for. She listened to him with the enthusiasm of a fresher student, she made him feel master of the universe, and in return she showed him the wealthy insider's New York of restaurants and clubs and private mansions. When they went to the Metropolitan Museum of Art, the Director would show them round; after the opera, they joined the conductor in his dressing room; at Emmerich's, Andre himself would come out to greet them, at Hirschl & Adler they'd be made at home by Stuart in person. Only gradually did he realize that the common denominator in all this was money. And by then Joanna and her lifestyle were inseparable in his mind. He couldn't imagine loving one without having the other.

Her friends and advisers were unanimously hostile to him. Her cousins, who stood to inherit if she died, made blatant representations to Warner Friedman, as head of the Trust, to invoke a vaguely drafted term of her grandfather's will and disinherit her should she marry this opportunistic English fortune hunter. Friedman was only stopped by the intervention of her father who, alone of her family and friends, had her happiness at heart. Bella was his only other ally—partly because she was an adolescent rebelling against material values, but also because the two of them, stepfather and stepdaughter, got on so well together. He heaved a sigh. He missed the girl.

But all that was past. A new chapter was beginning, and the pages were blank. He looked about him, waiting to feel once again the thrill of excitement and awe at the majestic beauty of the city, at the fearless expression all around of the raw strength and energy of man. But all he felt was anger and disgust. The buildings looked like shallow cardboard film sets, their beauty paper-deep, and the strength of man was all arrogance and his energy all neurotic bombast. He felt bitter and betrayed.

Slowly, filled with sorrow for his lost dream, he turned and retraced his steps along the path he'd come.

At the entrance to the Athletic Club he met Galton, Joanna's chauffeur, coming out. Galton greeted him with a broad-lipped grin, but his large, soft bovine eyes peaked in compassion.

"Hi, Mr. Stephen," he said. "I just delivered you a package from Mrs. Lefever. At the Department they said to find you here. They said you don't work there no more."

"That's the way it goes." He clapped the older man on the shoulder. "Thanks. I appreciate it."

"Any time, Mr. Stephen." He paused. "Anything I can do—"

"I'm doing fine, thanks, Galton. Just fine."

A moment of awkward hesitation followed as the two men stood on the sidewalk, going their opposite ways yet reluctant to part so abruptly.

"It's not my place to say," began Galton, "but I wanted you to know how sorry we all are. I mean, the guys on the front door. And the girls in the salon. Maybe it'll all come right."

"That's very kind of you. Yes, maybe it will."

Another brief pause followed. Irritated passersby were having to step aside.

"Well, I'd best be getting along," said Galton finally.

"I'll walk you to the car," offered Stephen.

"I'm parked round the corner."

They walked to the corner in silence. Stephen mustered a casual tone of voice.

"How's Joanna?"

"Business is crazy. We're rushed off our butts."

"Kind of you to find time now."

"My pleasure."

The conversation was getting nowhere. He was constrained by his English manners, Galton by his divided loyalties. The limousine was now coming into view: the opportunity was disappearing. Yet why should he care what Joanna was up to? He didn't want to know. He couldn't afford to care.

"And Joanna herself? Is she okay?"

"She'll be sorry to hear you quit your job."

"I got fired. Ever got fired yourself, Galton? It's strangely liberating."

"I have a wife and kids."

"So did I, Galton, so did I." He smiled, admiring the chauffeur's discretion in refusing to be drawn into talking about his mistress. "Can you make time for a beer?"

"I don't drink."

"Of course you don't. Coffee, then?"

"Another time I'd like that. She'll be expecting me back already." He unlocked the car and turned to face him. "If you ever need some place to stay, it's only small, nothing like you're used to . . . "

"You're very kind. No, the world's a big place. I'll be on my way soon."

"We'll miss you." He offered his hand. "Don't forget. Anytime . . . anything . . . "

"Take care, Galton."

"You too, Mr. Stephen." He climbed into the car and swung the door closed. "Any message to deliver?"

"You haven't seen me. You don't know where I'm staying. And you don't know I've left the Department." He paused. "Look after her, will you? Do what you can to see she's okay, huh?"

The older man nodded and, with a small wave, engaged gear and swept off into the stream of traffic.

Stephen stood on the sidewalk watching the limousine disappear. *You haven't seen me. You don't know where I'm staying. Look after her, will you?* He should have said more. Not given an explicit message maybe, but something Galton would transmit, some word of affection, something to show her he was thinking of her. Which, goddammit, he was every moment of the day, especially the moments when he was trying *not* to. A thousand times he'd passed a phone and been on the point of calling up. He'd begun letters, he'd been through the common friends he could call, he'd even thought of intercepting Bella at school, but then he didn't want to put pressure on her and cause her the pain of a conflict of loyalties.

He turned abruptly and made his way back to the club at a fast and angry pace. This was no way to think. Trying to reopen a dialogue with Joanna was hopeless. She was a prisoner of her own guilt; he'd thrown open the doors for her, but she refused to leave. Tell himself what he might, he loved her, but there was nothing more he could say or do.

So now he had to put the past behind him. And that meant no nostalgic backward glances, no sentimental bad habits. Joanna had made her bed and she must lie in it. And he mustn't care who with.

Lou Whittard, dean of the Experimental Psychology faculty at Berkeley, was unreservedly enthusiastic. At a conference at Tulsa just two months before, they'd talked late into the night about Stephen's work on developing a lexicon of human crypto-language. At that time, he had believed the Trust would fund the project, and a whole associated department besides, and he hadn't pursued Whittard's interest. Now everything had changed.

"Come on out," said Whittard. "Let's talk."

"Lou," said Stephen, biting the bullet, "there's something you'd better know. The work doesn't bring its own funds."

"The best never does. Don't worry. We have budgets for horseshit you wouldn't believe. No problem diverting a bit here and there. So, when can you make it?"

"Tomorrow?"

"Call my secretary with your flight details, and I'll have a car meet you. And Stephen," he warned, "don't speak to nobody else, but nobody, okay?"

Stephen put the phone down and let out a whoop. *Tomorrow.* He shouldn't have sounded so keen, so available. But what the hell? He *was* keen and available. Not everyone in the world was a political double-dealer, Joanna. On the west coast they had different values.

He went to the mini-fridge and poured himself a Michelob. This was more like it. The dice were rolling again. Contacts were what really counted, not cash. Contacts and, of course, a bloody brilliant idea. Stand by, Weitzman, for your postcard from Stockholm.

When the stewardess came to check seat belts were fastened prior to landing, her gaze lingered longer than usual on his lap. As he hastily drew a magazine over the rampant evidence, she met his eye and a brief, amused smile lit her milky complexion.

When the aircraft had come to a standstill and the other passengers stretched to reach the overhead racks, he alone remained seated. Once in the terminal building, he headed for the first door bearing the international symbol of *homo lavatorius*, but even the act of micturition failed to soften the unyielding stiffness of his member. He walked toward the limousine pick-up point with an awkward gait, his hanging bag held in front of his crotch like a shield yet knocking against the thrusting prong at every other step. Even as the car drove over the endless sweep of the Bay Bridge and headed toward Berkeley and the tall campanile that dominated the university campus like a priapic totem, the swelling obstinately refused to subside. Only an act of onanism in his bedroom at the hotel in a leafy avenue off Tilden Park, followed by a long and flesh-mortifying cold shower, finally restored his organ to its normal dimensions. Which was just as well, since at the very moment of climax, the phone rang and Lou Whittard's voice came on the line to say he had arrived at the hotel and was waiting downstairs in the lobby to take him to dinner.

Yet reprieve was short-lived, and no sooner had he sat down to his *langoustes a la facon du chef* at Chez Panisse than the warm, insistent swelling in his loins began again. For a moment of alarm he wondered if he had contracted that dire condition he'd read about in *Forum* or some similar magazine in which a man was afflicted with a permanent erection, but just at that moment Whittard made a remark about nonverbal body cues, and suddenly he realized this was exactly that, the spontaneous statement of his own body, and that all the time in the plane it had been pointing him west, like the needle on a compass, directing him where his destiny lay. He had a compass cock, a homing horn. He'd navigate by his nuts. They weren't rocks, they were lodestones. At the absurd thought he burst out laughing. He heaved with laughter until the tears ran down his cheeks, obliterating the puzzled face of his host opposite and washing away all the past and its tribulations in a great cleansing of his soul.

13

Joanna sat on the couch, naked to the waist. She held her left breast between the thumb and middle finger of her right hand, cupping its fullness in her palm. The attitude bespoke a Madonna-like innocence, yet it carried an implication of wantonness suggested partly by her positioning, leaning as she was slightly forward as if to proffer the breast to a lover, and partly by the blatantly erect state of the small, pink nipple at its tip. Partly, too, though it had nothing to do with the pose itself, by the lingering flush on her chest that still shone out like a beacon declaring the heights of ecstasy she had reached during their lovemaking a while earlier.

She kept her eyes lowered modestly, for though she was still half-clothed she had never felt so naked as she did now, exposed beneath the relentlessly intense gaze of the figure in the black shirt who sat crouched over a sketchboard so close that she could hear every scratch of the hard pencil.

Though she avoided his eye, she felt the heat of his scrutiny and knew he was studying every curve and delineament, every pore and particle of that chosen expanse of her flesh. More, she knew he could see *through* the skin to the subcutaneous structure of her body, to the sinews and muscles and fatty membranes, to her bones and organs and through to her very core.

He knew her more intimately than she ever could know herself. "Painting is drawing," he said. "And drawing is anatomy."

The day before, in the lull between one bout of love and the next, he had shown her a folio full of studies he'd made of corpses undergoing postmortem operations. There were sheet after sheet of these meticulous drawings, all in fine silverpoint and undertaken at the city's morgues over the space of years. One showed a closeup of a disemboweled stomach, with a heap of glistening, snaking intestines piled on a dish at the side. Though in gray and white, they looked alive and still pulsating.

"Too macabre for me," she'd shuddered, though unable to tear her gaze away. "Too ghoulish."

"Leonardo cut up his own cadavers. You'd call his work ghoulish? I'd call it genius."

"It was different in those days."

"Genius is genius, in any age. Like beauty."

"So, you call this *beautiful?*"

"Exquisitely beautiful."

She'd laughed. "It's just bowels."

"Nothing about the human body is 'just' anything," he'd responded, almost affronted. He pointed to a long, convoluted rubbery tube. "Take the small intestine, here. It's a foot longer in women than in men. And it varies from fifteen to thirty feet in length. A person's stomach is as individual as their face. Look in this case, how the left kidney is lower than the right, way down below the duodenum, in fact. You can understand why the Greeks and Romans peered into the entrails of animals to divine the future. And just look at the structure of the intestine wall, here, where it's been cut. See how amazing it is, how perfect. First it has a serous coat, which comes from the peritoneum here. Then a muscular coat, with the fibers going lengthwise and crosswise. Then you've got a connecting layer of loose, filamentous tissue. And finally the mucous membrane, thick and rich in blood vessels at the top and gradually thinner and paler below. Can you see the flaps of mucous membrane projecting on the inside? They're the valvulae conniventes. Sometimes they're spiral in shape, a characteristic we share with sharks, believe it or not. Maybe that's a vestige of our evolution from the sea, like our salty tears. Then over the whole inner surface are the villi, which are responsible for absorbing food, a whole web of tiny blood vessels, about four million in all, so tiny and fine that they give the surface this velvety appearance."

"Fascinating," she'd said.

She'd meant to sound serious, for it was indeed awe-inspiring, like discovering an unknown universe, but her tone came out as ironic.

He'd regarded her with a sudden distance.

"I find it so."

"I didn't mean . . . "

"That's enough."

Without a further word, he'd grasped her by the wrist and led her back to the bed. There he'd thrust her face down onto the pillows and taken her forcefully, even violently, from behind.

The thought sent a quiver of pleasure through her, and briefly she let her pose falter. Her hand slipped from her breast, and she drew up her legs in an effort to contain the pang of desire that gripped her stomach. The room about her seemed to retreat into a blur.

"Straighten up, please."

The command was whispered, but it jerked her to attention.

"I'm sorry," she mumbled.

She heard her voice muttering the apology, but she scarcely recognized it as her own. Sorry? she thought, who is this person inside me saying it's sorry? In her mind she stepped outside herself and looked down upon her half-naked figure, sitting on a couch upon a raised platform, lit only from above by the cool afternoon daylight streaming in through the skylights and shrouded all around by tall deep-hued drapes, this figure with pale soft skin and waves of blonde hair just breaking on the shoreline of her shoulder, with eyes demurely cast down and one breast cupped in her hand, and she wondered to herself, Who is this compliant, submissive person who looks like me and sounds like me? What is she doing here?

She knew exactly who this person was and what she was doing there.

His voice cut in as if in response to her thoughts.

"That's enough for today, Cristina."

He always spoke her name slowly, rolling the *r* and giving each of the syllables equal weight. It lent the name a Latin seductiveness yet also a curious pointedness, as though he *knew*.

But of course he couldn't. He knew only what she had chosen to reveal to him. Her name, Cristina. The address and phone number of her apartment. And her body. All of her body.

Similarly, she only knew what he'd chosen to reveal to her. She knew his name was Louis. She'd learned this from a message on her answering machine. She didn't know his second name. She knew the address of this house but not, now she came to think of it, the phone number. Nor his body—in half such intimate detail, at least—for he always wore at the very least a black silk kimono-like robe, even when making love.

But she knew, or was getting to know, something deeper about the man. What drove him, what inspired him, what excited him was his art. His own nature could be inferred from the nature of his work. And yet, as she reached for a shawl to cover herself and, stepping over to where he'd laid the sketchboard down, she saw what he had drawn, she smothered an involuntary shiver. Perhaps she wouldn't make the inference after all. Perhaps she'd leave his nature like the rest of him, and like almost everything about her, too—untouched and unknown.

The drawing was an anatomical study. The hand was sketched as a skeleton on which sinews and muscles had been added in layers. The breast, being without bone, was drawn as a network of tissues, some fatty, some fibrous, converging on the areola, and as with the hand only a thin pencil line suggested the actual final outline and surface. It resembled a bizarre combination of a photograph and an X-ray plate.

"It's . . . beautiful," she said. Remembering their previous conversation, she added, "And I mean it."

He handed her a glass of chilled wine.

"You believe in beauty?"

"Believe in it? I guess I *recognize* it when I see it."

"You recognize beautiful things, sure, but do you recognize *beauty*, as an absolute, an ideal, a transcendent principle? That's a question of faith."

"You sound like it's a religious experience," she smiled.

"It is, exactly."

She glanced at the drawing.

"It's beautifully executed," she began, "but I'm not sure I'd want to fall down and worship the subject matter."

"In Plato's world of Forms, there is the Idea for everything.

There's an Idea—an *ideal*—of Beauty. The whole purpose of art, the thing a real artist is striving to do, is to get as close as he can to that ideal."

"Why this in particular?"

"Because the female human body is the most sublimely beautiful of all living things," he replied quietly, with reverence. "And of all the parts of the female body, the breast is the most perfect." He reached forward and removed the shawl from her shoulders, letting it drop to the floor. "It's a shame to hide them, Cristina."

She swallowed. Why did she feel stripped bare so much more utterly than she had a few minutes before? Perhaps it was a question of role and context: it was one thing to pose nude as an artist's model and another thing to share a drink with him afterward in the naked flesh.

She considered the glass and sought for something to say to cover her state of confusion and arousal.

"I've heard of people having wine glasses made in the shape of breasts. Didn't Ivana Trump have her own copied?"

He refilled her glass with a smile.

"The *ancient* Cleopatra certainly did. Mark Antony had golden goblets modeled on her mammae." The dark pools of his eyes softened in humor. "I wonder if he had the wit to choose the left one. It's generally bigger than the right."

"Are mine different sizes?" she challenged.

"Cristina," he said, articulating her name in the precise way of his, "you need to be taken on a guided tour of your body."

She laid down her glass and looked at him expectantly.

Instead, he picked up the sketch and began making a minute comparison with the original before him. Ignoring her entirely, he reached forward with his pencil and gently prodded her breast with the flat end, studying the texture of the skin and the resilience of the flesh beneath.

She found herself unable to move. She felt shocked at allowing herself to be handled like this, like a slave at an auction, yet that very thought sent a shiver of thrill through her. She wanted to be as anonymous as an item offered for sale, without identity and responsibility. She wanted nothing more than to be the source of aesthetic delight and carnal pleasure for another person. Her legs would hardly support her as she stood there, waiting for him to finish his work and fulfill his delicate threat. How deeply she yearned to be led back to the bed, or to be taken there and then on the floor, or to be sent back to the couch, as he had one day the previous week, and positioned with all the careful attention of an arranged pose and then and only then, when everything was finally to his satisfaction, abruptly and savagely possessed.

Casting a downward glance she saw he was growing aroused. The memory of the drawing he'd shown her the previous day flashed back to her mind, and for a brief moment she found herself wondering if it was the ghoulish fact of human flesh being cut open or a genuinely higher aesthetic ideal of the perfection of form in the structures within that actually turned him on. Perhaps it was both. Could it be simply that what she saw as bestial, he saw as beautiful?

The thought swiftly vanished from her mind, however, for quite suddenly he put aside the sketch and the pencil and drew her toward him by the waist. Clasping her by the hips, he took the breast in his mouth and began caressing all around the tip with his tongue, then gently he slid to his knees, leaving her standing upright and swaying slightly, with her head thrown back and a low gurgle rising from her throat, as slowly, agonizingly slowly, the tongue began to descend toward her stomach and to the unquenchable pool of desire smoldering below.

Afternoons became their time. From two to five. Not every afternoon, for that would have taken on the quality of a routine, but as often, or as seldom, as he would leave word on the answering machine.

Around midday she would call through to Cheryl to say she wasn't to be disturbed, then slip the remote beeper from her purse and call the number at the apartment. Sometimes there was no message. More often than not, however, there was just the terse instruction waiting for her: "It's Louis. Come today." Or just occasionally, simply, "Tomorrow."

With a speed that left her dazed, the whole ritual soon developed the compulsive allure of an addiction.

It unfolded each day along the same unerring path.

As the hands on her desktop clock approach noon, she becomes aware of her heartbeat quickening and a restless impatience entering her dealings with people. She has to consciously control her voice as she calls through to Cheryl, but the irrevocable process really begins as she reaches into her purse for the beeper and senses the feel of that small plastic hand-held unit that seems, like a vibrator, redolent with forbidden pleasures. Her hand never fails to tremble slightly as she dials the number of the apartment, just as though she has leaped forward three hours in time and already reached the climax that lies in promise at the end of the relentless chain of events now just beginning.

Next comes the sound of his voice, soft and short. He never mentions her by name, nor does he always announce himself by his own either, and that makes the message seem somehow all the more intimate. The final abrupt *click* as the message ends, allowing no possibility for discussion or any excuse for disobeying, throws a switch deep in her psyche. Suddenly, with unquestioning clarity, she knows what she will do. She knows where she has to be, and when. Meetings, phone calls, appointments, everything else in her life now has to fit around this imperative. Her body has taken over control. Her will is robbed of independent power.

She leaves untouched the open sandwich Cheryl routinely brings her back for lunch, for she has no stomach to eat. She refuses coffee, for that only makes her nerves jumpy. She has to relieve herself every ten minutes, just like an adolescent awaiting her first date. No one sees any of this, of course. She dictates letters, handles meetings, makes phone calls in a perfectly normal way. She alone is aware of the sick throb of excitement pulsating within her and growing louder and more insistent as the hands of the clock reach one o'clock, then five, then ten after the hour.

On the quarter hour, she leaves the shop. She carries a briefcase if she is ostensibly going to a meeting, otherwise it's the small purse she keeps in a locked drawer in her office that contains just some money, keys, and the credit cards bearing her other name. She hails a taxi, and within a minute she is heading across the park to the Upper West Side.

Things move fast. She pays the cab, hurries down the pathway, and lets herself into the apartment. Throws off her jacket, kicks off her shoes. Pours herself a glass of Perrier from the fridge and takes it down the spiral stairs. With every step she sheds a bit more of Joanna and takes on a bit more of Cristina. In the dim-lit, womblike bedroom she steps out of her clothes and walks naked to the bathroom. In the shower she soaps her body and shampoos her hair with meticulous care, repeating the process a second time, for she is washing away the old skin and assuming the new.

Back in the bedroom she sprays perfume on her wrists and behind her ears and finishes with a general waft over her body and sometimes an extra spray to her chevelure. She steps into her lacy panties, which she prefers to be ivory color, though red will also do, then puts on a matching silk slip. She wears no brassiere: the garment is not merely unnecessary but positively forbidden. She now goes over to the dressing table to dry her hair and put on her makeup. For the afternoons she favors a hot vermilion lipstick called Temptation and a palate of warm, creamy blushes and shaders that she knows will hold up under the ruthless light that pours down vertically from the tall skylights in the studio.

Then she selects her clothes. A simple but stunning red crepe dress is her favorite, with a wrapround belt and a full skirt that swirls and billows as she walks. It is cut low to reveal the descending curvature of her breasts, though not so low as to appear vulgar. He has a particular fondness for women's breasts, she isn't afraid of calling it a particular *fetish*, and in this, as in everything else, she wants to please him.

Finally she is ready to don the blonde wig. He knows, of course, she is not a true blonde: his first glimpse of her completely naked would have told him that. A fine hair-net with a stocking mesh smooths down her own copper-dark hair and presents the base upon which the full and flowing blonde wig is then carefully placed. The underside of the wig is fitted with minute combs that hold it in place, firmly enough (and this caused her much anxiety at first) to stay in place under the most violent onslaughts of sexual passion.

The moment she turns to the mirror and sees herself in this wig, she invariably feels a tremulous rush of sexual excitement. She is Cristina.

It is perhaps ten minutes before two, and although she hurries out of the apartment and catches a cab passing her very door, she is going to be late. She sits forward on the cab seat, feeling her stomach loose inside her and her nether parts swelling with the jolting movement, squeezing her legs closed to smother the urge to touch herself, determined to keep herself intact until the release should come, until finally the cab draws up outside the gaunt and grimy house way over off First Avenue.

She pays and gets out. Ten paces take her to the front door. She takes the steps like a sleepwalker, looking neither to left nor right, for the teeming world of the street does not exist for her. She presses the buzzer, her hand already heavy with the etiolation of desire. The door clicks open without a word being exchanged.

She is inside. She pauses to accustom her eyes to the penumbra. The faint, cool smell of turpentine sends her head reeling. She starts up the stairs. She is already breathless. Her limbs are leaden, her body is soused with desire, there's not enough air in the world, she is going to faint.

None of this will he see. She will enter the studio looking fresh and cool. He will be standing there, half in shadow, appraising her. Maybe he will just be drinking black coffee, maybe cleaning his brushes, maybe performing some alchemy among the bottles and vials marked ACID and POISON. In the background stands the large canvas he is working on, his masterwork as he calls it, which always remains veiled. The smell of turpentine is now stronger and overlaid with the aroma of coffee, a heady combination that has become erotic by association.

Then he will step forward and touch her somewhere, maybe he will stroke his fingertips over her cheek, maybe mold his hand round the base of her buttock, and she will try to conceal the volcano quietly erupting through her body.

Maybe he will offer her a glass of wine, or talk through the drawing he is working on. Maybe he will discuss a book with her, or show her slides through a viewer. Yesterday it was a slide. A twelfth-century fresco in the crypt of the church of St. Nicholas at Tavant, in southern France, entitled *The Personification of Lust,* showing a woman with a long spear piercing one breast, painted rather crudely in pastel eau-de-nil and ochres ... she remembers everything. The day before, it was a book of fifteenth-century Gothic painting, and in particular a plate portraying the martyrdom of St. Denis, painted in 1416 and attributed, controversially, to Henri Bellechose, and which showed on one side the cardinal receiving his last communion and on the other being beheaded by an executioner—evidently a clumsy executioner, for he had his bloodstained cleaver raised for a second blow—while to the side lies the same body, now decapitated, the neck spewing blood and the severed head, in startling contrast to the rich gold and lapis lazuli, a deathly gray. He reminded her of the painting they'd met over at the Blum gallery showing the story of Adam and Seth, where Seth appears simultaneously carrying the branch in the background and kneeling at the graveside in the foreground, and pointed out how in the martyrdom painting the saint appears no less than three times in the same painting, a primitive condensation of time yet not so far in concept from the modern strip cartoon. . . . No, she forgets nothing. Every word he says falls on thirsty ears. Every thought he imparts seems imbued with magic and originality. Through his eyes she is beginning to see the world afresh.

The paintings are arousing him. This man, she thinks, is turned on by art! The aesthetic is, for him, erotic. One slides into the other, and with a seamless transition that always surprises her, she finds herself, naked or half-clothed, standing or kneeling or lying, spread over the couch or stretched out on the bed, greedily satiating the desperate hunger that has been building up ever since the stroke of noon and which has driven her, step by inevitable step, to this refined chamber of lust.

Three weeks had passed since Stephen left home. He had *left*, she told herself repeatedly, she hadn't thrown him out. It was, in Warner Friedman's phrase, a voluntary redundancy. Which, of course, it wasn't.

She tried not to think of Stephen. It was, quite simply, easier that way.

She had Maria field calls for him and redirect his mail to the Department. She deflected the conversation whenever Bella turned it in that direction, though despite herself she found herself making occasional innuendos that denigrated Stephen and carried the implicit message that she'd prefer the girl to have nothing to do with him. She threw out such of his shaving gear and socks as had failed to make it to the parting suitcase and anything else of his she found lying around, such as the back issues of the *Journal of Behavioral Psychology* and holiday brochures he'd ordered and even the bottles of Islay malt that were his personal special stock, all these she stuffed into his study and locked the door. When a plumber came to repair a leaking waste pipe and asked for the "john," she directed him to Stephen's private lavatory, without a moment's hesitation before or remorse afterward, and in that simple act she saw the proof that the place was exorcised of his presence and that she herself was on the road to freedom.

His birthday was approaching, and the question arose in her mind whether she should note it in some way. Whatever she did would lay down a marker for their future relationship, and she would rather not address that issue. Even a birthday card carried a message of some kind. The simplest form of words, just *Happy birthday, love from Joanna and Bella,* conveyed its own subtext, in that case one of cool formality, suggesting this or that about their status or whatever with his devious mind he might read into it. She didn't want to be suggesting *anything.* She didn't want to have to make a statement of any kind for him to bring his formidable mental apparatus to bear on it, decoding what was in her mind and picking his way into the secrets of her heart. She was still afraid of his power to subvert her will. Perhaps, too, she was afraid of what she still felt for him.

She mustn't weaken. She had to cling on to the overriding truth that it was no *use.* The relationship died not because of any particular infidelity or misdemeanor, though those were her pretexts, but because of actions further back that had been done and couldn't be undone.

But there was Bella. She knew she was effectively asking the girl to make a choice between her mother and her stepfather. She knew this was unfair, too. In a normal separation between consenting adults, the child might chose to live with one parent but it needn't be deprived of access to the other. Yet she found herself deliberately discouraging Bella from even talking of Stephen, let alone trying to make contact with him. Maybe she was afraid that if they got together he would subvert her to his side. Or, worst of all, that he would tell her the truth.

Her strategy was simple. She'd starve him out of their lives. She'd deprive her heart of the oxygen of feeling, and that way, in the course of time, the flame would go out by itself. As for Bella, she'd act as if he had never existed. He would just die out of their thoughts. That, she determined, was how it was going to be.

And to facilitate it, she threw herself avidly into her work at the salon and into her family life with Bella. Indeed, it worked well. Apart from those few exceptional hours of the afternoon which remained untouchably private, before long she found herself with such a busy schedule of activities that even if she'd been of a mind to dwell on deeper thoughts of Stephen she simply wouldn't have had the space to do so.

One evening at the end of the third week, however, between seeing Bella off to a start-of-year sorority party and going to *Tosca* at the Met, she found her thoughts turning to Stephen and, for once, she allowed them their rein. The remarkable thing was, she felt, that everything seemed, actually, *all right*. It was contained. Things were in place. In balance.

It was a warm, gentle evening. She stood on the balcony with a glass of cool white wine, surveying the city spread out below. The sorrowful notes of approaching autumn wafted over from the leafy park. As darkness took over the baton from daylight she sensed a palpable quickening in the pulse of the city. People were driving faster, as if to cheat the encroaching twilight, hurrying toward the life that began as the day ended. She took a sip of the wine. She closed her eyes. It was an '89 French Chablis, shipped by Barton et Guestier. It was not a particularly distinguished wine, but it was the wine of the same type and shipper and vintage that she'd noted her stranger lover always served—a dangerous and otherwise forbidden leakage from her other life, and not exactly the first either, for that same afternoon she'd found herself down on Madison Avenue near 60th Street and stepped into Shelley Marks' small perfumery store, a kind of alchemist's coven set in the lobby of a fine turn-of-the-century office building, and bought a bottle of his exclusive, rare potpourri, which even at this moment, as just putting her head round the glass door would confirm, filled the living room with its musky, Arabian aroma just as it filled the space curtained off from the main studio area that served as the bedroom, an aroma echoing the musky aura, infinitely more subtle and potent, that enveloped his body. . . .

She checked herself. Wasn't that exactly the proof? She'd

started reflecting on Stephen and her thoughts had turned away by themselves. Wasn't she then *cured?*

In fact, now that she came to think of it, she had almost to grope to get an image of Stephen at all. Was he tall or short, slim or big, dark or fair? Of course she knew, only the image seemed blurred, out of immediate reach and recall, like the memory of someone met on holiday and forgotten with the return to reality. For the new and sharp reality was the taste of the wine and the aroma of the potpourri and the power of these fragrances with their echoes of erotic delights to stir her senses to giddy oblivion.

Another sharp reality was lying in wait for her, and it chose this moment to resurface.

That Saturday morning, she drove Bella to her basketball practice, twenty blocks north on Madison. The court lay in a large open area behind the castellated facade of the former National Guard armory, now a high school playground. She stayed for a while, but as it was only a practice and not a proper game, she went for a stroll round the nearby streets to pass the time.

The day wore the quiet, benevolent smile of early autumn, and from the fallen leaves on the sidewalk rose a rich, mulchy scent that filled her with an indefinable longing. She made her way up to the secretive Conservatory Garden, where the quinces and crab apples were in full fruit and all around spread the gentle, sorrowful colors of the season in its declension. She sat on a bench in the pale sun and allowed her mind to grow still. She felt a profound contentment settling over her, like the gentle fall of a leaf in a windless sky. After a while she closed her eyes. The sounds of city life gradually receded into the distance, her eyes grew heavier and she slipped into a light doze.

She woke to find she was already late for collecting Bella. She hurried out of the garden and caught a passing cab to take her the ten blocks back. As the cab drew up alongside the fortress-like wall, she spotted Bella at the front entrance.

Bella was talking to a young auburn-haired woman. Their conversation was clearly ending, and just as the cab pulled up the woman turned to go. She looked up and met Joanna's eye. Her gaze lingered, and a knowing smile fleeted across her freckly complexion. Then with a parting word to Bella she turned on her heel and headed off down the street at a self-consciously nonchalant gait.

Joanna gave the cab driver a ten-dollar bill and, waiving the change, climbed quickly out.

"Sorry, angel," she said. "I had no idea of the time."

Bella ran forward, flushed from her exercise, her eyes shining.

"Hi, Mom. Did you see who *that* was?" she exclaimed. "I thought she was in Canada."

"Yes, I saw. So, how did it go? Was the coach pleased?"

"She's back in New York. She's got an apartment right around the corner." She linked arms with her mother and together they headed for the car. "She asked all about you and the business. And my school. And Stephen. We had a good chat."

"Bella—"

"I'm sorry, Mom. I didn't think it was a state secret."

"Bella, I don't want you having anything to do with that woman!"

"Karen's a friend. She used to *live* with us."

"She is *not* a friend," she snapped. "And she's not going to become one."

"Come on, Mom. I think she's great. She's kind, too. She was really sweet to Luke. She loved him. I remember going into his room at night and she'd be singing to him . . . "

"Stop it!" she cried. She took a deep breath and fought to control herself. "I'm sorry, darling," she muttered. "I guess I'm a bit overwrought."

They reached the car in silence and climbed in. As she leaned forward to start the ignition, she felt Bella's hand on her arm. The girl's eyes were peaked with concern.

"Are you okay, Mom? You've been acting a bit strange recently. You know what I think . . . "

"Strange? How do you mean, strange?"

"Just this and that. You seem kind of . . . preoccupied."

"No, I don't. I'm right there, on the ball. In fact, I haven't felt so good for ages. If you think I miss Stephen, you're wrong. I don't. Not in the least."

She was shocked by the sharpness and the hint of suppressed hysteria in her tone. It clearly surprised Bella, too, for she sat back in her seat and gave her a long, considered look.

"The lady doth protest too much, methinks," she concluded.

"Well, *me*thinks the past is the past and we don't need any of it in our lives, not Stephen nor that woman nor anyone else. We're the home team, right?"

"Right, Mom," said the girl wearily.

"Tell you what, let's go down to Fraser Morris and get something delicious for lunch. You must be starving."

Within a minute she was back in control, her equilibrium restored. She needn't have reacted like that. She was insulated from the tragedy, and threats that relied on her feelings of guilt couldn't touch her anymore. She was strong, and everything was in balance.

Her strength was put to the test that evening, just as she had foreseen and feared. It was late, and she was in her study, sitting up waiting for Bella to return from a party. She was seeing to the piles of bills and domestic correspondence that had built up over the past frantic weeks when the internal phone rang.

It was the porter downstairs.

"Sorry to disturb you, ma'am," said the man, "but I have a young lady here asking to see you."

"Say I'm not at home."

"She says you know what it's about."

"Show her out. Any trouble at all, call the police. And please make a note never to admit her. I'm not at home to that woman."

She replaced the phone quietly. She hadn't raised her voice. She'd remained calm and composed throughout. She was shaking, but she had done it. She had closed the door on the worst of the reminders. Her present was contained here, in this small book-lined room, with the smiling photo of Bella prominent on the desk and, beside the lamp, the glass bowl of potpourri whose fragrance sent its forbidden shivers through her, and as she surveyed the room and the gaps here and there where she'd taken down their wedding photo and removed the various witty and sentimental little gifts he'd given her on birthdays and anniversaries, she realized that Stephen was one of the reminders on whom she had closed the door. His fault was not the fool he'd made of himself at the show or yet the fool he'd made of her, nor the affairs he'd been having behind her back, nor any incompatibility of cultures and values or any of the dozen other reasons she'd given herself to legitimize her action. His ultimate crime was simply having *been there at the time.* He *knew.* His very existence in her life was itself a reminder of what had happened back then and a living reproach for her complicity in it. That wasn't his fault, he couldn't help it. If he'd been a saint and perpetually sober, if he'd been a paragon of fidelity and pathologically stage shy, she would only have had to invent a pretext. As it was, he'd offered her pretexts enough, and she'd merely had to bide her time and take her pick.

That door was now closed, and all that lay behind it was shut out forever. She leaned forward to the glass bowl and inhaled the musky aroma. Closing her eyes, she drank in its heady, erotic scent. It was the scent of freedom.

14

STEPHEN CHOSE TO SPEND the better part of his birthday on the
flight back to New York. There could be no presents by his
breakfast plate this time, no lunchtime treat at Il Cantinori as a
prelude to a surprise afternoon, no drinks with close friends
later, followed by an evening at the opera. He was now, anyway,
just past the halfway mark of his allocated three score and ten
and in that broad plateau where the count stood still before
eventually starting to go in reverse. Marking birthdays was for
those who were establishing their patterns and roots, not for
those uprooting to a new life.

So, it was to be a business day like any other, and to fill the
evening he had arranged to have supper with one of his former
research assistants at the Department, a bright girl called Helena,
whom he wanted to poach and take with him to Berkeley. Their
relationship was set firmly on a professional footing, which was
to say he didn't find her in the least sexually attractive, and he
was looking forward to an early night in preparation for a busy
morrow closing down his affairs on this coast.

The trip had been successful beyond all imagining.

Lou Whittard had thrown a dinner party at his home to
which he'd invited key figures in the Psychology faculty, including the Dean of Appointments and the Chairman of the Finance
Board, and the evening had been nothing short of a triumph.

The next day, Lou had told him they were putting together a package he was sure he'd find very acceptable: full professorial status, substantial research funds, an establishment of up to five assistants, and a review in six months at which he could expect a salary rise, coupled with tenure. The contract would be sent by courier to New York, and all Stephen had to do was sign and return it and, using the generous relocation allowances, get himself over to Berkeley and be in a position to take up the post at the beginning of October. That was just five days away. The deal was made in heaven.

He arrived in New York feeling like a conqueror. As the cab thundered through the Midtown Tunnel and broke surface among the towering cyclopean landscape of office and apartment blocks, he felt a sudden glow of fellow-feeling. The spectacle of raw power and certitude that had awed him as a young man on his first visit and which barely a month before had alienated him as a refugee from his home and his job, now fired him with empathy. He understood this place, he was part of it, he belonged to it. He shared in its power and certitude. More still, he knew how to master it. Given a fulcrum he could move this world.

He gave the cab driver a recklessly generous tip. As he strode into the leather-and-paneling lobby of the Athletic Club, he slipped the doorman a fifty-dollar bill. Collecting his keys and mail, he asked the concierge to do him the favor of booking a table at Aurora, he would dine at the sign of the goddess of dawn, the patron of new beginnings, and damn the cost. He was no longer the waif who rolled back soused and satiated in the early hours and who had to be steered to the elevator and chaperoned to his door. He was rich and famous, or at least he was going to be rich and famous, and in style and from strength he would bid farewell to those years of his life this island city had claimed. The words of a nursery rhyme came into his head: *When he was up he was up, and when he was down he was down.* . . . Never could there be a more apt anthem for this most wonderful and hateful, most seductive and perfidious place.

As he rode up in the elevator, humming the tune, he flipped through his mail. Most has been redirected from the Department and were in official stamped envelopes or bore their senders' names on self-adhesive labels. None of these looked either urgent or interesting. One, however, was addressed to him directly at the Club and had been delivered by hand.

Instantly he recognized the handwriting. He tore it open.

It was a birthday card. It showed a monkey in a frilly bonnet blowing out candles on a cake. Inside, beneath the rubric, *Apey Birthday*, was a handwritten message.

> Hi, Stephen,
>
> *Yuk! Sorry! It's the best I could find.*
>
> *I'd really like to see you. Mom needn't know. Call me this after noon if you can, around five. Mom never gets back before six these days. She's not keen on me seeing you. I'll explain.*
>
> *Ring twice, then hang up and ring again. I'll get to it before Maria.*
>
> *Don't worry, I'm not going to try and get you back together! It's just I miss you.*
>
> *Hopin' to see you, Birthday Boy.*
>
> Love 'n' kisses,
> B.

The card was not dated, but the envelope bore a small pencil mark showing the time and date it had been taken in. Today, just after one o'clock. Bella must have slipped out during her lunch break. How did she know he was living there? Did Joanna? Or had Galton told her?

Call me this afternoon if you can, around five. He glanced at his watch. It was just gone six.

The sound of the elevator doors shuddering closed broke across his thoughts. It had arrived at his floor, waited for him to disembark, and was now on the way down again. *I'd really like to see you.* He hammered at the *Stop* button, but it wouldn't respond, and he had to travel all the way down to the lobby and up again before he could get to the right floor. Outside his room he dropped the keys in his haste and stabbed his forehead on the doorhandle as he bent to pick them up. Once inside, he flung down his cases and made a grab for the phone.

His hand hovered over the cradle as it rang, poised to hang up if the maid or Joanna herself answered. He felt a flush of anger. What right did Joanna have to forbid Bella from seeing him? It was Bella's decision, goddammit. She had a right to whatever friendships and relationships she chose. Joanna and he might separate or whatever they liked as adults, but Bella had no part in it. She was innocent.

He let it ring twice, then hung up and rang back.

It was answered at once.

"Stephen?"

It was Bella's voice, in a hushed whisper.

"Hi, angel," he replied quickly. "Can you speak?"

"I can hear Mom just coming in."

"Right. Listen. There's a restaurant called La Scala. I'll meet you there at seven."

"But—"

"Say you're going to a movie with Lorri."

"Stephen," a low chuckle entered the voice, "something tells me you've done this before."

"Before you were born. See you later."

As he put the phone down he felt a surge of delight. Just to hear her voice was so wonderful. She'd missed him? God, he'd missed *her!*

He reached into his briefcase for his address book. This was a question of priorities. He could meet up with Helena anytime. He'd think up an excuse. No problem. Goodness knew, he'd done *that* enough times before.

For a moment he didn't recognize the young woman coming toward him through the tables, led by the maître d'hôtel. She walked with such grace and poise, her blonde head erect and her youthful, lissome figure demure in a simple midnight blue sleeveless dress. People looked up as she passed and followed her with their gaze to the table in the corner where he now rose to greet this nubile beauty of half his age.

"You look a billion dollars," he breathed.

She blushed lightly.

"I stopped by at Lorri's and changed. I wasn't going to tell you that."

"We don't have secrets, you and I." He leaned forward and squeezed her hand. "I'm really happy you made it. I can't imagine anyone I'd rather celebrate my centenary with."

"Well, I thought if it can't be Mom, you'd better make do with me."

"Make do?" He gestured around the room, deflecting the

conversation away from reference to Joanna. "Look at them all. The whole place is green with jealousy. That waiter's just dropped his pen, and as for that old bloke over there, he's spilled half his gazpacho down his shirt front."

"You're kidding me."

"Angel, you're talking to the world expert in body language."

The maître d'hôtel returned with menus and asked what they'd like to drink. Bella made Stephen choose first. He'd have a Manhattan, he said. She ordered a Coke.

As she opened her menu she frowned.

"This is a bit embarrassing," she began. "Mine doesn't have any prices."

"Price doesn't matter! Have whatever you want."

"It's just that I didn't bring a lot of money." She was blushing again.

"Money? You don't need money!"

"But it's my treat. It's your birthday and I haven't got you anything. I bet no one else's given you anything. Not even lunch."

"United Airways gave me lunch," he smiled. "You're wonderful and sweet and crazy, and it's the kindest thought, but *no way*. I invited you. This is my date. Okay?"

"Okay," she agreed, reluctant but relieved. The drinks arrived, and they shared a toast. She sipped her Coke thoughtfully. "I'm sorry about your job," she said after a pause. "Was that why you were traveling today? Does that mean you'll be leaving New York?"

"How did you know I'd quit the job?" he asked quickly.

"Mom told me. Does it matter?"

"Well, I didn't want her to know. I suppose I thought it might make her feel bad. I didn't want to put her under the burden." He checked himself. That was only partly true. At the time, he'd wanted to harbor it as his own secret pain, to justify his self-pity. "So she knows where I've been staying?"

"She's always known, though she only just told me. She found out the day you moved in."

"Keeping tabs on me, huh?"

"Because she cares. She won't admit it, but she does care."

"You can read her body language?" he smiled. He didn't want to go down this avenue. But she ignored the remark.

"And so do you, Stephen. You care about her."

"You read that in mine?"

"Otherwise you wouldn't be so concerned about not making her feel bad."

"And does she feel bad?"

"She covers it up. She's full of fun and life and rushing around and everything's okay. But it comes out in little things. She flies off the handle for no reason at all. She's sorry afterward, and there's a lot of stuff about us girls sticking together and we're the home team and all that. Just like the other day."

"Oh?"

"I was at basketball practice, and while I was waiting for Mom to pick me up, guess who I bumped into, right there in the street? Karen. You remember, the nurse we had for Luke."

"And Joanna saw her?"

"She left just as Mom arrived. Mom went off the deep end. 'I don't want you having anything to do with that woman!' and 'She's not a friend, and she's not going to become one!' It was weird. She's in a bad state, but she won't admit it."

"It's tough all round," he muttered.

"I'm sorry," she said, abashed. "I didn't mean to bleat on about Mom. It's been tougher for you, I know. But you can take it, Stephen. You're not so . . . fragile. Like you won't break if you're dropped."

"I was," he smiled. "And I didn't."

"I'm glad," she said tenderly. "I can't bear to think you'd have nobody to pick up the pieces."

The wine waiter was hovering at his elbow. Stephen looked across at Bella. She was gazing at him with such a softness in her blue-gray eyes that he felt a stab of anguish at the prospect of a life without this exquisite, kind child. Would they ever meet again except occasionally, in clandestine moments like this, snatched on fleeting visits through the city? For a moment his resolve faltered. The future beckoning him from the west coast seemed suddenly frivolous and unimportant and far removed from all that mattered.

He swallowed hard. This was no moment for sentimental second thoughts. He turned to the waiter.

"We'll have the 'eighty-five Puligny Montrachet," he ordered, "and could you bring it while we chose our meal?" Then he turned back to Bella with a smile. "You can handle wine on top of Coke?"

"You'll have to drink most of it."

"We can take our time. You're going to tell me all that's been happening to you."

It was a wonderful evening. When finally he took her back home to the Park Avenue apartment and paid off the cab on the corner of the block like an illicit lover, she flung her arms round him and kissed him with a desperate passion.

"Don't go forever," she whispered. "We need you."

"I'll be back and forth, angel," he mumbled through the lump in his throat. "And you're coming out to check out Berkeley, right?"

"Take care. Be happy. Write me at Lorri's." She gave a small smile. "Mom will come round to it. We won't always have to do this cloak-and-dagger stuff."

As she drew back, he saw there were tears in her eyes. She wiped them away briskly and shone him a brave, self-deprecating smile, then she turned and ran down the sidewalk, stopping only to give him a brief wave before disappearing into the canopied entrance.

The night was sweet and balmy, and he walked the fifteen-odd blocks back to the Club, savoring the bittersweet memories of the evening. His thoughts of Joanna and Bella seemed to merge into one deep pool of love and regret. More than once he had to pause in his tracks as he felt the stabbing physical pang of loss.

But as he cut the final corner through the park zoo and let his eye rise above the treetops to the towering buildings with their facades a maze of lights and their ziggurated pediments profiled against the indigo sky, he realized that he was at a watershed in his life. He had to make a choice. The past, or the future.

He steeled his heart and quickened his step. His direction lay ahead, not behind.

His resolve was tested almost at once. As he entered the lobby of the Club, he was distantly aware of a young woman rising from one of the deep leather seats in the lounge area and coming forward. At the sound of her heels hastening up behind him, he turned.

Her auburn hair was smartly coiffured, her freckly complexion had been retouched professionally and she wore a crisp gray two-piece suit, but behind the image he recognized instantly the wilder demeanor and scruffier deportment of the nurse they'd formerly employed.

He stood waiting for her to make the opening move, his body instinctively braced for a confrontation.

Karen cast around her with an amused eye.

"I thought I'd find Professor Stephen Lefever at the Metropolitan at least," she smiled easily. "Still, I guess when you're down on your luck . . ."

"I have no business with you," he muttered between gritted teeth. "Now, if you don't mind, I want to get to bed."

"But I have business with you, Stephen. You want to talk here or go someplace else?"

"Karen, just bugger off. I don't know you."

"You want me to make a scene right here?" she challenged with steely sweetness.

"God, you miserable bitch," he growled. "I'll give you three minutes outside."

"I know a club around here serves a mean scotch," she offered as she hurried alongside him to the door. "Don't say you've given up drinking. Pigs don't fly."

He stormed out into the night and hauled her by the arm fifty yards down the street. There he stopped and turned on her.

"Now listen," he began savagely. "I know what you've been doing. You're going to lay off them. Both of them. No more chance encounters with Bella. No more threatening Joanna for money."

"You disappoint me, Stephen," she said, pulling her arm free of his grip. "I came to offer you a deal. A partnership deal."

"If you think for one minute . . . "

"She's *loaded*. She kicked you out and cut you off. You won't see a penny. She's got the smartest lawyers in town tying it up. Think, Stephen. Here's you chance to get back."

"And yours to destroy a woman's life, a woman who never did you any harm, a woman whose only mistake was in hiring *you*. You disgust me!"

"Don't you come on all high and moral! Anyway, she can afford it. I'm not going to bleed her dry. If she didn't think she'd done something wicked, she wouldn't pay up."

"She is paying with her *sanity!*" he almost shouted. "You're destroying her. She can't get free of it until she's free of you."

"Tough."

He froze. *Tough?* Was that all she could say? He felt his hands turning to steel pincers. Another word from her, and he would grab her by the throat and slowly, mechanically, crush the life out of her.

He raised a finger and pointed it directly in her face. He held it no more than two inches from between her eyes.

"If I ever hear you have been in touch with Joanna or Bella again," he said in a deadly whisper, "I will come after you, and wherever in hell you are, I swear to God I will find you and break you in pieces."

She backed away. Her expression faltered, then she gave a cracked laugh.

"Horseshit!"

He made no reply. He just stood icily still, focusing all his venom upon her. She took another step back, then another. He felt as if the power of his stare were physically propelling her backward. She laughed again, pulled a face, stuck her finger to her temple.

"Screwball!" she cried. She was retreating now. The distance between them was widening all the time. "Asshole!" she yelled. "I'll get you! I'll tell them what you did! You wait! Fuck the both of you!"

She went on hurling abuse until she reached the end of the block where, jabbing a final one-finger insult at him, she turned and disappeared, leaving him to make his way slowly back to the Club, quaking with shock and fury in every fiber of his being.

His sleep during the nights that followed was tormented by bizarre, uninterpretable dreams, and he woke tired and confused. He struggled to regain the elation of the previous days and that heady sense of his unfolding destiny, with all its bold promise of new beginnings and sweet sadness of old partings, but all he could feel was worry and outrage.

He spent the final morning finishing his packing and settling his bills and, with the better part of the day still left before his flight in the late afternoon, he put the last arrangements in place for the move. He called the realtors in Berkeley to check all was fixed on the house he was renting, he wrote letters to his solicitor and bankers back in England, and he paid a visit to his own bank round the corner from the Park Avenue apartment where he made arrangements to open an account in an affiliated bank in Berkeley and to transfer the dwindling remains of his funds there. He checked the shippers and insurers, he called Helena with an improved offer, and rang round old friends and colleagues to say good-bye. But all along he felt something was missing. His mind wasn't on it and his heart wasn't in it.

Finally, with his bags packed and ready, he addressed himself to the issue.

He was worried for Joanna.

He paced his small room uncomfortably. Dammit, why should he get involved anymore? She was never going to change. He'd washed his hands of her. What she did with her life was her own affair. If she couldn't get to grips with the past and insisted on laying herself wide open to this bloodsucking harpy, that was her own lookout. He'd done all any man could to help her see it. But she was obstinately blind to what she was doing to herself. Some people just couldn't be helped.

And yet he couldn't leave with an easy mind unless he made just one last attempt. His conscience, as she herself had once remarked, was his Achilles' heel. He knew he'd never be able to close this chapter of his life satisfactorily otherwise. Maybe now, with the distance of separation, if he talked to her as a concerned friend and not an implicated partner, she would listen to him.

He glanced at his watch. A quarter to one. She'd be at the salon. Working through lunch, as usual, grabbing a sandwich Cheryl had brought in from the deli down the block in between phone calls.

He'd take her out to lunch. Somewhere new, somewhere without memories. Somewhere where they could talk in a businesslike way, adult to adult.

He reached for the phone. Then he thought again. He didn't want to give her the chance to make an excuse.

He'd just turn up. She'd have to see him then.

Grabbing a jacket and tie, he headed for the door. There he stopped and hastened back to the bathroom to brush his teeth. He sprayed aftershave on his cheeks, then abruptly rinsed it off. What the hell was he doing? He didn't want her to think he'd made a special effort. This wasn't some young kid's first date. It wasn't a date at all.

He waited impatiently for the elevator, and when it finally delivered him to the ground he dashed through the lobby, knocking into a group of soberly dressed men speaking in hushed voices, and burst out into the street. The autumn day was dazzlingly bright, and he paused for a moment to collect himself before engaging with the rush and swirl all around. Was this folly? He was acting on a whim, not on calculated thought, and likely as not he'd regret it later.

A cab drew up outside the Club and discharged a young man with a squash racquet and sports bag. As it was about to pull away, he stepped forward and climbed in. He gave the address of Designing Woman on Madison Avenue, and a moment later he was on his way.

Looking back later on what then transpired, he found himself unable to imagine what possessed him to act as he did. As his cab approached the salon, he saw Joanna standing on the edge of the sidewalk. She wore a gray tailored suit and she carried a black Gucci purse, and she had her arm upraised to hail a cab. A short way ahead of his own cab, one duly pulled out of the stream of traffic and drew up alongside the curb, and she climbed quickly in.

Instead of paying off his cab or directing it to take him back to the Club, without forethought or conscious reason he leaned forward to the armored plastic divider and told the driver to follow Joanna's. And thus, with one tailing the other, the two yellow cabs set off up Madison Avenue. At 79th Street, the leading cab swung left and, crossing Fifth Avenue, headed into the park.

Through the scratched and blurry divider he could see the back of Joanna's head in the car in front. She was sitting very erect and looking straight ahead. Even when the cab lurched round the twisting bends of the cut, she seemed to remain absolutely upright. It may have been his imagination, but the cab seemed to be in a particular hurry.

As the minutes ticked past, he began to question the good sense of this. What was he going to do when she finally arrived? What business took her to the Upper West Side, anyway? The garment industry was located mainly in the midtown area. Maybe she was visiting a client. She couldn't be delivering, for she wasn't carrying anything, and her clients came into the salon for fittings. All the art galleries she frequented were around 57th Street, Warner Friedman's offices were down in Rockefeller Center, Conde Nast and the fashion magazines were nearby, too. . . . As her cab left the park behind and, crossing Columbus, headed deeper into the residential area, a terrible realization struck him.

She was seeing a lover.

No sooner had the thought occurred to him, bringing in its wake a spontaneous stab of pain, than her cab drew in to the side of the road outside a large brownstone. She paid the driver and stepped out. His own pulled up twenty yards further down, and by the time he had settled his own fare, he only just managed to catch a glimpse of her figure hurrying down a narrow pathway that evidently led to a basement apartment.

He crossed the street, but instead of walking off he hung back in the shade of a tree from which he could watch the house. This was crazy, he told himself. She only had to look out of the window and she'd see him. The shame of being caught spying was unimaginable. And yet some force, whether jealousy or merely curiosity, rooted him to the spot. He'd always believed he knew everything about her and nothing she did could surprise him. Now he realized she was a stranger to him—perhaps she always had been—and this enigma both disturbed and fascinated him.

Once, moments after he'd taken up his position, he caught a fleeting figure crossing past the window, but after that he saw nothing. Twice he started to walk away, only to stop and come back again. The pain was biting like an arrow in his side. Why was he doing this to himself? He didn't want to know any of it, he didn't want to feel any of it. If she chose to take up with another man. . . .

By some acuity of his senses, above the growl of traffic, he heard the door opening. Abruptly it slammed. Footsteps clicked

up the path. And suddenly into his field of vision came the figure of a blonde-haired young woman in a simple red crepe dress
and high heels.

A wave of relief flooded over him. This was a girls' apartment, a pad shared by a couple of models: there was no man in
there. Joanna was probably right this minute signing up her
friend over a bowl of carrot salad and a glass of Perrier.

His eye followed the blonde girl as she skipped up the path
and swung into the street, the red skirt swirling and billowing as
she moved. Strange, he thought fleetingly, that wasn't how a
mannequin walked. Maybe she was a photographic model. Or
something quite different, why not?

That walk. He knew that walk. He knew that tilt of the body.
That angle of the head. That whole indefinable ensemble of car-
riage and movement that was unique to every individual. You
could pick out a friend at Grand Central at rush hour not by
their face or their clothes but just by the way they held their
body. He knew. He'd studied posture identification.

Then it hit him. It struck him with such force that it left him
literally stunned.

It was incredible.

He started along the street after her. He stumbled between
the trees and cars, trying to stay out of sight while keeping her
in view. At the corner of Columbus, she stopped. He shrank into
a doorway. She looked about her, searching for a cab. For a
brief moment she turned full face toward him. She didn't see
him, but he saw her. And with absolute, irrevocable certainty he
knew there was no mistake.

He watched her flag down a cab and climb quickly in. He
saw the cab drive off and disappear down the avenue. In an
unreal daze, he retraced his steps. This time he crossed the
road and went up to the house. Without hesitation he followed
the path between the raised brick flowerbeds down to the door
of the basement apartment. It was unmarked but for the number 7. He rang the doorbell. There was no sound of movement
inside. He rang again. Still silence. He pressed his face to the
window, cupping his hands against the pane, and peered
inside.

There was not a soul there. The tailored gray jacket lay flung over the sofa and the black Gucci leather purse and matching shoes were scattered over the floor.

The copper-dark haired woman in the gray suit who had gone in and the blonde-haired woman in red who had come out were one and the same person.

15

FROM HIS LABORATORY WINDOW in the monolithic Life Sciences building, Stephen looked out over the campus grounds and watched the season imperceptibly turning. Four hectic but highly productive weeks had passed, and with that efficiency characteristic of a nation constantly on the move, he'd scarcely had time to draw breath before he found himself fully established in his new Department, with dedicated video recording and playback systems and two on-line computer terminals and his own letterheaded paper inscribed, FROM THE DESK OF PROFESSOR STEPHEN J. LEFEVER, not to mention the gunmetal Buick compact in the leafy parking lot outside and the fully furnished rented home in a colorful avenue off Wildcat Canyon Road, which he'd chosen for no other reason than the ring of the address. He had, after all, made it to the western frontier, the eternal El Dorado of the heroes of those early pioneer movies that he associated with wet Saturday afternoons spent at the local movie theater and which belonged among the happiest memories of his childhood.

He was pleased, he was content, but he wouldn't say he was happy.

Lou and the rest of his new colleagues did all they could to make him feel at home. They invited him to their homes, each in turn. A welcome party was thrown for him at the Depart-

ment. Everywhere he turned there seemed to be girls, each
more alluring than the last. He had often thought of America as
one vast spinning disk that centrifuged all the nation's beauty
and brains to its two opposite shores, but now he had to admit
the system was off-center and undoubtedly this side was favored
with the fairest and the finest.

But wherever he looked, whether gazing out across the bay
with the setting sun burnishing the water a coppery bronze or
reading through a stack of periodicals in the library or scrutinizing a face on the video monitor frozen in mid-expression, there,
seared indelibly on his mind and interposing itself between him
and the screen or the page or the world outside, was the one
perpetual and ineradicable image: the woman in the red crepe
dress and blonde wig. The woman he knew as Joanna.

What the hell was going on in her mind?

One lunchtime over a steakburger and salad in the Senior
Common Room dining room, he put the scenario—hypotheti-
cally—to Lou Whittard. He'd just been reading a fascinating
case study, he said with contrived nonchalance, about a married
woman who ran a clandestine parallel life. She had a secret
apartment where she went in the afternoons, and there she
dressed up as someone entirely different . . .

"A cross-dresser?" inquired Lou, chewing as he spoke. "We
had one last semester. Called himself Alex. Alex for Alexandra."

"No, no, she dressed as another woman."

"What did she *do* as this other woman? Moonlight?"

"She's got money. She doesn't need a job."

He checked himself, realizing his mistake. Lou stopped
chewing and eyed him wryly.

"I get it. She's the wife of a friend of yours." He prodded his
gums with a toothpick. "Maybe she does afternoons as a high-
class hooker. Ever seen *Belle du Jour*?"

"I don't think she'd need to do that."

"Not need to get laid? Show me one married woman who
doesn't."

"I mean, she wouldn't need to *dress up* to have an affair."

"Why not? Suppose she wants an affair but she feels guilty.
Solution: do it in the guise of someone else. Assume a different
identity. Then it's not *her* opening her legs to the tennis coach or
whoever, it's her alter ego. Mind you," he added, "no one *I* know

would feel guilty at laying the tennis coach. Round here it's *de rigeur.*"

Stephen couldn't echo the professor's smile. In this place you couldn't get an analysis that didn't center around sex. Sex was the first thing on people's minds. But not with Joanna, surely not. There had to be a different explanation.

"Suppose she just likes looking and feeling like someone else," he wondered aloud. "Just to walk the streets, go shopping, have a drink in a bar. She might get a buzz from the freedom. Maybe she lives quite a public and stressful normal life, and this is how she escapes the responsibilities."

"Maybe," Lou echoed doubtfully. "But then, maybe she'd do better to see a shrink."

"Maybe she is. Maybe she puts on this facade to see him."

"Uh-hu. On your side of the pond, Stephen, going to a shrink is cause for shame. Here, it's like having your daily dump. In August when they're on holiday, everyone goes round psychologically constipated."

Stephen finally managed a smile.

"You're not so long out of clinical practice, Lou," he said. "What would you diagnose?"

"Well, I'd say it's neurotic, rather than psychotic. She's no schizo if she can control the switch-over so well. My guess is it's an hysterical condition. A defense mechanism. She's running away from some deep-rooted image or memory she can't face up to. Some deep-rooted guilt, maybe. Seems she can control it okay so far, but watch out, this kind of thing can easily turn into a serious dissociation or some other personality disorder. You might even be talking of multiple personality. If you believe such is possible." He stabbed the toothpick into the remains of his bun like a matador delivering the *coup de grace*, and looked up. "Am I on target?"

"Spot on, Lou," replied Stephen quietly, and the two men rose from the table.

But what could he do about it, especially at such a distance? Nothing, except worry.

Even if there were some way to communicate, though, he wasn't qualified. She was too far gone for his kind of reasoned talk-it-through-together approach. She needed professional help. *A serious dissociation. . . . You might even be talking of mul-*

tiple personality. He was no professional, but he wasn't a fool either. Surely he could read the literature and make an informed guess of his own.

That afternoon he went to the library and read all he could find on the subject.

He skimmed the literature from Morton Prince and Pierre Janet at the turn of the century up to Ellenberger and Sizemore recently, and he ended up more confused than before. Psychiatrists didn't seem able to agree whether the self was a single unity or divisible into separate personalities. Certainly the case studies of Prince and Janet, where the patients were invariable young women and a high level of erotic charge ran throughout the sessions, looked suspiciously like artifacts of the process itself. On balance, he felt that hysterical dissociation states—if such was indeed Joanna's case—were really about deception and self-deception. The red crepe dress and the wig represented a *mask.* And here he was on home ground. A mask worked to deceive not only the viewer but the wearer himself, too. In primitive society, the man *became* the mask; it actually gave him powers he otherwise lacked. The danger was that the two identities became disconnected. What if, in Joanna's case, the masked and the unmasked selves grew so separated in her mind that they became entirely unconnected, with neither able to influence the other? What if her alternative self developed into an independent personality with its own self-sustaining life? The implications were shocking and distressing.

As he walked slowly back to his laboratory, he tried to tell himself he was fabricating a whole edifice of anxiety based on the slender evidence of a single incident. He could have misinterpreted it completely. Maybe the apartment belonged to a friend, or indeed to one of her models as he'd first imagined, and this was the one and only time she'd done this bizarre thing. For all he knew, she might have been dressing up for a parents' play at Bella's school, or performing in a charity funfair and just stopped by her friend's place to borrow some clothes and wig. . . . Certainly, he had no evidence to assume the place was hers, or that she visited it regularly. *A married woman who ran a clandestine parallel life,* he'd said. *She had a secret apartment where she went in the afternoons.* . . . What kind of a fanciful, inductive piece of crap was this for a scientist to be voicing?

He quickened his step. He was the one with the neurotic problem. He'd allowed himself to become obsessed. And he only had to step aside to realize why. He was a typical egotistical male who'd been rejected by his wife and his pride was injured, and rather than admit she was a perfectly well-adjusted woman doing something perfectly reasonable in the circumstances, he chose to reconstruct her for himself as thoroughly crazy and dangerously unstable, inventing for her a whole elaborate complex of psychoses and fantasies. It was, frankly, all so much bullshit.

Why couldn't he just admit that he was hurt and angry and leave it at that? He'd let this mania distract him long enough. It was time to get a grip on himself.

All the same, that evening he sat down with a large whiskey at the kitchen table and, taking a sheet of paper from his briefcase, began to compose a letter to Bella. A lighthearted, uncomplicated letter, certainly with no reference to all this now-forgotten business. It was just to keep in touch.

A curious image frequently came to Joanna's mind. She remembered walking along the beach with Stephen in the early days of their love, listening to him enthusing about the frontiers of science and how, if he had his time again, he'd have been a physicist exploring the nature of reality and matter. In the mysterious world of subatomic physics, he'd told her, a particle could exist in two places at once. In fact, only the act of capturing it defined where, and thus which, it was. She liked to think of herself like that, as a being floating undefined and uncaptured in an evanescent realm, neither quite here nor quite there, neither wholly this person nor wholly that, but always potentially either. She was a single entity, but she existed in two forms. Which form she took was her own choice. Nothing defined her. No one captured her.

But of course, in cold reality each persona had its context, and the context had its claims. Appealing though the fantasy might be, she was not floating free in some indeterminate subatomic soup: she was either here or there, either Joanna or Cristina, either brunette or blonde, either her morning or her afternoon self. As the pressures from each side began to tighten, she found it harder and harder to juggle her commitments to prevent them clashing. But inevitably conflicts arose, and for all she might wish it, she finally came to the uncomfortable realization that though her mind might be capable of this feat of bilocation, her body simply could not be in two places at the same time.

The inevitable happened sooner than she expected.

One of her major European customers was in town and called up to fix a meeting. She was out, and Cheryl had left on maternity leave. The temporary secretary who replaced her looked in the diary and, finding a blank, committed Joanna to a lunch appointment for the following day. Twelve-thirty at the Aureole, on 61st Street between Park and Madison. She only learned about it in the morning, by which time it was too late to rearrange it.

Shortly after twelve, Joanna closed her office door and phoned into the answering machine. The familiar sweet and helpless melting feeling stole through her body as she listened to the whir of the tape rewinding. Then came the slow, silken voice she most wanted to hear and yet, this time, she most dreaded.

"It's Louis. I expect you today."

No business lunch took less than two hours; an hour and a half was exceptional. Today she was giving it one hour exactly, and even that would make her late for her assignation. The customer, true to his European *mores*, arrived ten minutes late and prepared to settle in for half the afternoon—and not just the afternoon, as the special warmth of his greeting implied. He was a handsome Milanese in his forties, and she'd long suspected he was attracted to her. He laid the menu aside as it arrived and, leaning forward, took her hand in his.

"Joanna," he said, his eyes expressing the unfazable sincerity of the Italian, "you are the most beautiful woman in New York."

"You're jet-lagged," she smiled.

"My judgment is unimpaired." His gaze grew keener. "Something has happened to you, Joanna. You're different."

"You mean, I was not the most beautiful woman in New York before?" she mocked, withdrawing her hand.

"You're just more beautiful than ever. Somehow . . . nobler. Like the Madonna. Unreachable."

"Hokum."

She turned to the menu and tried to study it. She felt in a turmoil of confusion. Part of her was flattered: perhaps she was different, though she saw herself more as a Madame than a Madonna. She snatched a glance at him and wondered how long he was staying in town and if, maybe, they could meet up properly one evening ... then she checked herself. What was she thinking of? Within a couple of hours she'd be in her lover's studio, completely naked, lying on the bed or spread over the couch, maybe talking first and then making love, or making love first and then talking, but always both, whichever way round. Her belly involuntarily clenched with anticipation.

Flushing, she hailed the wine waiter. She ordered a Pussy-foot, a nonalcoholic cocktail of exotic fruit juices. She never drank before seeing Louis. She liked to feel on the razor edge of her senses. But even as the waiter took her order, she changed it to a vodka. This time she needed a little help with the transition. Then she turned back to her guest.

"Shall we order?" she suggested, her throat dry.

Between the first and second courses, she excused herself to call her office. On the way back she stopped the maître d'hôtel and signed a blank credit card voucher. Then, composing an expression of anxiety and apology, she returned to the table. She didn't sit down.

"You must excuse me," she said hurriedly. "Something's come up at the salon. It's a crisis. I have to get back. Let me call you. Where can I reach you?"

"I fly back tonight." He rose to his feet. "I'll come back with you."

"No, no, I can handle it."

"We can talk on the way. I have a deal for you. A big deal."

"Hold onto it."

"I need a yes or no now."

"Okay, will it make me money and cost me nothing?"

"It will.

"Then yes. Send me the contract." She leaned forward and pressed a kiss full on his lips. "Unreachable? Bullshit," she breathed as she pulled away. "We'll talk on the phone. Stay and finish your meal. It's paid for. We'll have the other half in Milan."

It was twenty minutes to two as she climbed into a cab and

gave it the familiar address on the Upper West Side. For a fleeting moment she debated whether to go straight to the studio as
she was, but dismissed the idea at once. She would just have to
be late. Better late than *known*. And why not be late? She'd
chosen to make a habit of punctuality: he'd never explicitly
demanded it.

As the cab plunged across the park, she struggled to think
herself out of Joanna and into Cristina, yet she was beset by
anxieties and embarrassments. How rude to walk out on her
lunch date like that! And what a crazy excuse! He was bound to
call the salon later and ask about the crisis. And then, what was
she thinking of, agreeing to a deal blind? Maybe she could wriggle out of it at the contracts stage, but she'd given her word. She
would never do anything so reckless in her right mind.

But she wasn't in her right mind. She was sick. Sick with
love, sick with lust.

She sprang out of the cab as it pulled up outside the apartment and, telling the driver to wait, flew down the path and let
herself hastily in. Once inside, she kicked off her shoes and tore
off her clothes, skipped down the spiral staircase, raced to the
shower, no time to wash her hair today, just a quick freshen-up
sprinkle, then barely pausing to dry herself she powdered and
perfumed her body, wriggled into the silk slip and the red crepe
dress, fitted the blonde wig, snatched up her small purse and
stuffed her lipstick and makeup inside, then with a quick glance
to check her appearance in the mirror, retraced her steps up the
staircase and across the living room and out into the bright daylight and, with her high heels snicking the paving stones, made
her way up the pathway and back into the waiting cab.

At the first red light, she applied the eye liner and was feathering in the edges of the eye shadow as the cab took off again.
Bracing her body against the lurching motion, she managed to
work in the blusher before a violent jolt shot her across the seat.
She had to wait until Park Avenue before a temporary gridlock
allowed her to attend to her lipstick, and even so it wasn't until
the cab was drawing up outside her destination that she suc-
ceeded in putting the final touches of gloss to her lips.

She paid off the cab and paused for a moment on the sidewalk to focus herself on what lay in store for her behind that tall
and grimy stone facade. Her throat was desperately dry and her

heart pounded violently. She stood isolated in her own world.

For a while she stood there, motionless, her eyes clenched shut as, by dint of willpower, she gradually smothered the last lingering traces of the persona she'd cast off. Half opening her eyes, she saw the red high heel shoes. She saw the sheer silk stockings. The red crepe silk dress. The bracelet, the watch, the single string of pearls. Swaying backward, she caught the light, floral perfume of her body. Her eyelids felt the weight of the mascara, and a slight turn of the head brought into focus the curtain of fine blonde hair.

The metamorphosis was complete. She was Cristina.

She mounted the steps and pressed the intercom. After a pause, the door lock buzzed open. She went in. The sudden darkness engulfed her, and her senses lurched at the familiar cool aroma of polish and turpentine. With quickening pulse, she hurried up the stairs toward the beckoning light. She felt her legs weakening as she reached the top. She craved the oblivion that lay through the door ahead.

She did not see him at first. She sensed his presence more by the familiar faint aroma of body musk in the room. He was standing some way across the room, dressed, as usual, in black and all but invisible against the black drapes. Only when he spoke did she register his location.

"You're late, Cristina," he said in a soft, menacing purr.

"I'm sorry," she mumbled. "I was—"

"Close the door, please."

She closed the door. She was so suffocated with desire that she could barely even stand.

"Now undress. Just where you are."

She obeyed. Her ready compliance shocked her, and yet she yearned to be relieved of the responsibility for herself, for what she would do and for what, in the ever-present past, she had done.

The red dress slid to the ground, followed by the silk slip, the garter and the stockings, and within a moment she was quite naked. Instinctively she moved a hand to cover herself.

"Hands behind your head," he ordered her quietly. He still hadn't moved from his position across the room. "Now come forward where I can see you."

Like a sleepwalker she stepped toward the center of the

room, into the shaft of cruel cold light that seemed to fall vertically from the skylight. At last he now came forward. In his
hand he held a short stick, the length of a conductor's baton but
slightly thicker, made of dowel with a small wooden ball on one
end. He held it for her to see.

"A signwriter's stick. Simple, but very effective. You shall see."

He gripped her by the elbow and turned her to face away
from him. Out of the corner of her eye she caught the fleeting
movement of the arm with the stick raised. She heard it swoop
through the air and in the next instant she felt the blazing streak
of pain across her buttocks. She gasped with the agony and,
more, with the outrage, yet she was paralyzed beyond protest.
And even as she felt him place his hand upon her neck to position himself better for the next stroke, she made no attempt to
wrest herself free but rather, through a hot blur of tears, waited
expectantly for the biting shriek of pain, even welcoming the
redemptive chastening of the cuts that now began to fall thick
and fast, to wash away with their pain the unassuageable pain
in her soul.

He had marked her. The mirror that night revealed the bluish-
purple crisscross of stripes already turning a dark livid hue.
Next time, he said, he would mark her permanently. A small,
discreet, indelible sign that she would carry forever. She must
not ask what it was. She would come again in three days' time,
when it should be done.

She shivered at the prospect. Her spirit rebelled at this different yet infinitely more exquisite form of a blind deal, but as
the three days approached their end, she knew with a sick feeling of inevitability that she would indeed go blind into the
unknown. Not to ask and not to know, that was the unspoken
ground rule of their liaison, and this was no more than a reflection of that. In a way, it was the proof of it.

And, for her, it was working. Cristina and Joanna were
cohabiting successfully. There were bound to be logistical conflicts, but were they any more intractable than, say, for two people sharing the same car? She merely had to find a way of balancing the opposing claims of the two she was. But the rewards
were overwhelming. A profound calmness settled over her spirit
such as she had not known for these two years past. She felt

normal again, confident in herself, unafraid of herself. A door had opened onto the light, dissolving the dark shadows.

The three days fell over a weekend, and on the Saturday morning after basketball practice, she drove Bella out to the beach house. All around, the countryside was decked in fiery autumn colors in an extravagant final push to repel the encroaching winter. The air was crisp and rich with the aroma of burning leaves and falling sap. They walked all afternoon along the ocean shore and that night ate a hearty supper before an open fire before climbing exhausted to bed. Her sleep was calm and dreamless. In the morning, while Bella was still asleep, she stole out of the house and paid a visit to the Garden of Remembrance. She hardly realized until she was there that for once she hadn't put on anything black, not even a scarf. And as she stood in front of the small marble plaque recording the pitifully short life of her infant son, she felt her heart swelling with a tender, resigned sorrow. She felt at peace with her grief.

When she returned, she found Bella in the kitchen, laying the breakfast. The girl scanned her anxiously as she entered.

"Are you okay, Mom?" she asked.

"Fine, darling," she replied easily. "Never felt better. I went to pay my respects."

"I guessed." Bella frowned. "You sure you're okay?"

"Do I look like something's wrong?" she laughed.

"Well, no, actually. You look like everything's pretty good."

"It is, angel. It is."

That Monday she prepared herself carefully. She had drawn a red line through the whole day in her appointments diary and told the temporary secretary she would be away from the salon and out of reach from midday. At twelve, she called into the answering machine fearing a change of plan, but there was no message. She was at the apartment well before one o'clock, and there she took a long and meticulous shower, pomaded and powdered her body with great care and went to considerable pains over selecting underwear that was neither too provocative nor too demure. She wore red, as ever, but this time she chastened the effect with stockings and gloves of pure white. Her makeup was paler than usual, and she wore no jewelry whatever.

Once again, a cab whisked her back across town and, just as the dashboard clock turned two o'clock, set her down outside the gaunt town house in a street off First Avenue. Within a moment she was inside. She climbed the stairs slowly, and at last, her stomach knotted with tension, she entered the studio.

He greeted her with a glass of wine.

"I have something to show you," he said.

He took her toward the curtained window where, half in the shadow, stood an easel on which was clamped a wooden board. A small spotlight illuminated the painting with a low, yellowish glow. The painting itself was somewhat smaller than the board, being half veiled behind a small pair of dark velvet curtains, but these were drawn sufficiently for the image beneath to be discernible. Built up in careful layers of glaze and varnish, it showed a detailed study of a woman's hand cupping her breast. *Her* hand, cupping *her* breast.

She caught her breath. It was so perfect in detail and texture and the whole seemed so utterly lifelike, as though it existed not on a two-dimensional board but fully in the round, like a hologram image suspended in space. She reached compulsively forward to draw back the curtains.

"May I?" she asked.

But the instant her fingers touched the curtain, she realized the trick. The curtains were part of the painting! It was a brilliant piece of trompe l'oeil. Her hand hesitated above the surface, as though undecided whether to trust her sense of touch or of sight.

"Amazing," she breathed eventually.

He smiled faintly.

"Art is illusion," he said. "I think you understand illusion."

She looked up sharply. His dark eyes were penetrating her soul.

"I do?" she fumbled.

"A trick like this is easy," he gestured to the painting. "It plays up to your expectations. If I'd put a pair of fish instead of curtains, you'd have guessed at once."

"But I can *feel* the material just by looking at them."

"That's the artifice of art. Making one thing look like something different. People engage in artifice all the time."

She met his eye.

"Who knows who any of us really is?" she said in a half whisper.

"We are whatever we chose to be at the time," he responded. "Our realities shift. Who we chose to be depends on who we are with, where we are, how we feel, what is happening to us. On all those feelings and memories and fears and drives swilling around inside us all the time."

"But I thought you believed in absolutes," she hastened, wanting to deflect the conversation from its strangely pertinent turn.

"Absolute ideals, yes. Beauty. Love. Passion. Suffering. An artist's job is to work the absolute out of the particular. To draw the beauty out of, say, an image of pain and torment."

Her voice came out as a small, dry croak.

"Is pain something beautiful to you?"

A tense silence followed, filled only by her pulse pounding in her temples.

"Pain can be ennobling," he replied at last. "And therefore beautiful."

"How medieval," she shivered.

"As you like," he responded.

He produced a bottle of wine and refilled her glass. He did not seem to be drinking himself. She snatched a glance around the room. Her eye lingered on the couch. On it was draped a large white towel, and beside it stood a low fretwork table with an embroidered cloth on which were spread an assortment of what looked like bamboo pens and inks.

He caught her gaze.

"We'll come to that," he said with an enigmatic smile. It was the first reference to the promise he had made three days before.

He laid her glass aside and began slowly undressing her.

She closed her eyes and submitted to the delicate ravishment. His hands, rounding and molding her flesh, had the feel of a sculptor's, and far from peeling away her cladding of clothes, she fancied, he was somehow adding to her, as if deliberately *composing* her. His touch avoided the most sensitive regions of her body, tracing their boundaries in a way that merely inflamed her further. Her being was ablaze like a forest fire, and every touch, so exquisitely contrived, only served to fan the flames.

She heard the moan break involuntarily from her throat. Her legs were dissolving, her body melting. She felt his arm reach under hers to support her, she felt him draw her toward him like a soldier succoring a wounded comrade, she smelled the familiar musky turpentine odor of his body, she felt the roughness of his shirt grazing her skin, she felt the cold stab of his belt buckle as it pressed against her side. From afar off she felt herself being steered toward the couch and carefully settled on it, she might have said *arranged*, half on her side and half on her front, with her arms draped over the raised end and one leg bent with the knee pressed up against her breast so as to tauten the full naked area of one buttock. And her head angled so that she should see what he was to do.

He stepped back, made a slight adjustment to her position, then moved away. After a moment, low strains of music filled the room, early music, Palestrina maybe, or Boccherini, a slow lilting adagio weaving a timeless spell around her. She closed her eyes again and gave herself up to the agony of waiting.

The chief instrument, of which there were two, was a short length of varnished bamboo on the end of which a common sewing needle had been carefully tied so that its tip projected just a millimeter or two from the end. The thread was bound around the length of the needle so as to form a grip, but also, as she later saw, to act as a reservoir for the paint. One was for the black, the other for the red.

He showed her a shallow china dish in which lay a fine black powder. This was not the common lamp black, he assured her, which was made by burning resins and waxes and collecting the soot, but proper ivory black, which he had made himself out of the femur bone of a steer he'd bought at a butcher's, then degreased, burned in a crucible, and ground to a powder. Shortly he would add a quantity of denatured alcohol to turn the powder into a workable ink.

Red was more difficult. Red lead, he informed her, was both toxic and impermanent. Vermilion, a compound of mercury and sulfur, also known to the Greeks but only rediscovered by the

alchemists, was certainly of the right period—the twelfth century onward—but it was similarly toxic, and of course there
could be no question of introducing anything poisonous
beneath the skin. In the fifteenth century, Cennini detailed
many contemporary red pigments—sinopia, cinabrese, cinnabar,
minium, amatito, dragon's blood—but there was a problem with
each (cinnabar, for instance, was another form of mercuric sul-
fide). Finally, after some thought, he'd decided to go for a dye
rather than a pigment and he'd concocted a mixture of the scarlet from the Mexican cochineal insect and the pink from the
Dutch madder root. He held another dish close for her to
inspect. It contained a puddle of bright red fluid, the color of
fresh blood.

He drew up a stool and, taking a brush, began to sketch an
outline on an area of her flesh between buttock and hip. She
clenched involuntarily at the touch. Was he going to *paint* her?
He unscrewed a small pot and smeared Vaseline onto the area,
then reached for one of the instruments and dipped the needle
into the black ink.

He was going to tattoo her.

At the first prick of the needle, she flinched. It stung, rather
than hurt. He paused to press a hand against her flank, in the
way of a rider quieting a horse, then applied the needle again. It
left a black smear over the Vaseline which he wiped off with a
swab of cotton wool to reveal two tiny black pinpricks set indelibly beneath the skin. All the time he was speaking to her in a
soft, mesmeric voice. In the background the music continued
quiet and stately. But she was hardly listening. She felt dazed,
unreal, robbed of her will. What was he drawing? His *initials?*
Why was she submitting to this? She didn't know. Even the
question itself seemed unreal.

He was telling her about an early Christian martyr, the subject of paintings since the fourteenth century. He talked matter-
of-factly, as if recounting an event that had happened in this city
the previous week, not in Sicily seventeen centuries before. The
incongruence between his tone of voice and the torments he
was describing shocked yet fascinated her.

"She was a virgin," he was saying, "and exceptionally beautiful. She had blonde hair, rare for a Mediterranean. Long blonde
hair. Tiepolo gives her dark hair, but that's an eighteenth century

gloss. Painters always personify images in their own idiom. Northern figures of Christ show him as fair-haired and blue-eyed. In Latin countries, he's dark and swarthy. I've seen black Christs in Alabama and sallow ones in Mexico." He paused. "My St. Agatha is blonde. It's important."

"What happened to her?" she whispered.

"The local Roman prefect, a man called Quintianus, wanted to have her, but she refused him. She was a Christian, and it wasn't advisable to refuse. He ordered her to sacrifice to the gods, a test of loyalty to the emperor, and she refused that too. While she was a virgin, he couldn't touch her. So he had her sent to the *lupanar*, the brothel, to be ritually violated. That was always the trick. The same happened to Lucy of Syracuse, who was martyred under Diocletian fifty years later. So, Agatha went to the brothel, where the *madame*, a famous courtesan of the time who traded under the name of Aphrodisia, tried everything she could to break her, but miraculously she preserved her virginity. Quintianus was furious at being thwarted and threw her in jail. There he had her tied to a column head down and stretched on the rack, then branded with the mark of the *fasces* . . . "

"What's that?"

"Fasces? The Roman symbol of imperial authority. A two-headed ax in a bundle of rods. It was carried in front of emperors and generals when they appeared in public. The rod symbolized beating, the ax, cutting."

A dull pain smoldered through her flank, sharpened every moment or two by the continued relentless prick of the needle. She told herself she was there voluntarily, she could stop at any time, she only had to get up and leave. But the pain seemed distant, as though she were an observer watching from outside and driven by curiosity.

"And then?"

"And then they performed the *mamillarum abscissio*. What the French refer to as *L'ablation des seins*. In German, if you prefer, *Der Abschniedung der Bruste*."

"And in English?"

"The removal of her breasts."

A silence fell. The word *removal*, so ordinary and practical, sent a chill shiver through her. Her mouth felt desperately dry.

"I should like a drink," she said in a small voice.

"We're almost finished."

She looked down to her buttock. He had finished with the black and was now working with the red. The design was no larger than her thumb, but through the Vaseline it was hard to make out the image.

"Although versions vary," he continued distantly. "In the Latin it reads, *pectoris papilla tollitur*. Does *papilla* refer to the points of her breasts, perhaps just the nipples, or the whole breasts themselves? Painters tend to assume the latter. The Luini in the Borghese in Rome, for instance, and the del Piombo in the Pitti Palace in Florence—not to mention the Antonio Ricci in the Prado and, of course the most famous of all, the Tiepolo in the Berlin Museum. Tiepolo shows both breasts fully cut off and presented on a platter. Certainly in Catania where she was born, at the foot of Etna, they celebrate her saint's day by baking bread breasts and serving them two on a plate."

A brief silence fell while he continued his work.

"Was that the end of her?" she asked eventually.

"St. Peter healed her. Then Quintianus had her stretched naked on a bed of glass and hot coals. That finished her off." He sat back and, taking a swab of cotton wool, wiped clear the surplus blood and ink, then quickly pressed a square of lint on top and taped it down with sticking plaster. "There, that's finished too. Leave the dressing on for three days."

He rose and fetched her glass, then held it to her lips to sip.

"It won't come out?" she murmured.

"Never."

"I'm a marked woman?"

"You're much more beautiful like that."

"You want me more?"

"More than ever."

He moved behind her and raised her onto her knees. She could feel the material of his clothes rough against her thighs. His hand was working around the boundary of her thirsting sex, the region he had so cruelly skirted before, moving in closer, closer, until with a sharp involuntary gasp she felt herself suddenly entered and the first convulsions of pleasure shudder through her body.

He sent her away numb and drained. He told her he would not see her for one week. By then, all final traces of the mark would have healed.

Three days later, in her bathroom before retiring for the night, she carefully pulled off the sticking plaster and removed the lint pad. At first she didn't make anything of the curious image in red and black she saw there, inked indelibly under the skin of her right buttock. It looked like a series of black lines with some object in red sticking out of the top. She looked in the mirror, but that revealed nothing further. Then, quite suddenly, with a sickening lurch she realized.

It was a tiny bundle of rods tied around a two-headed ax.

The rod to symbolize beating, he'd said. The ax, cutting.

16

THE SORENESS WORE OFF QUICKLY, and part of her was almost disappointed for that. It served as a reminder of her secret other self. Now she was only conscious of the mark when she accidentally brushed against something or when she took a shower or went to the bathroom, when she would twist round to glance at it with forbidden fascination. The local swelling subsided just as quickly, and within days her skin was as smooth and intact as ever, only it bore this ghostly brand beneath. Positioned as it was, the mark would be concealed by all but the skimpiest of panties or bikinis, so that no one except herself or her lover would ever know it existed. But it did indeed exist, there under the skin, as secretly and ineradicably as Cristina existed under Joanna's.

Most of the time, making calls or meeting clients or mingling in the crush at the opera, she did not really think of it. Yet it existed as an unseen reassurance, like the safety net of a tightrope walker, and its very presence somehow gave her strength and confidence.

People noticed the outward change. Warner and her family ascribed it to her being rid of Stephen. They said she was like a flower blooming from out beneath a stone. Bella, being closer and cleverer, said nothing but remained cautious and watchful.

She herself, being too close, failed to notice how reassurance created its own dependence. Like an addictive drug, comfort turned rapidly to craving. It took an incident of extreme force to reveal how far down the road she had gone. But by then it was too late to turn back. The tightrope walker was falling into the net. Joanna *needed* Cristina. The dissociation was set to become complete.

On the sixth day, a Sunday, a package arrived.

Bella was leaving on a school excursion to the Adirondacks for the day, to visit a wildlife study center where a new radio tracking program had been pioneered. She was running late as usual, and when the house phone rang, Joanna snatched it up, thinking it was the doorman to say the minibus had arrived.

"A package here for you, Mrs. Lefever," came the doorman's voice.

She wasn't expecting anything.

"Who's it from?"

"No name. It came by cab. You want I send it up?"

"Please. If the bus comes for Bella, say she's on her way down."

She turned to find Bella all set to go, wearing nothing but a thin sweatshirt, jeans, and trainers.

"You can't possibly go like that!" she exclaimed. "They had frost up there, and the forecast says it'll get colder. Get your skiing anorak and some gloves, and put on some decent boots."

"You're always fussing these days, Mom. I'll be fine."

"You'll be out of doors all day and it'll be dark when you get back. Come on, do as I say. And hurry."

With a sigh of exasperation, Bella ambled off to the coats closet. Joanna fetched the small parcel of iron rations she'd made up—chocolate chip cookies, a Hershey bar, a peach, a carton of apple juice—and waited to hand them to her. *You're always fussing these days.* More than before, when Stephen was around? Probably. But then, they were now a single-parent family. She didn't want to suffocate the girl, but she had to give her the love of two. And, though she scarcely dared put it that way, with only half of herself.

"Take this for the journey, darling."

"Mom, I'm not in first grade. The others won't be taking

stuff." She softened and gave her mother a kiss. "When I get carried off by grizzles it'll save my life."

Just as she was seeing her daughter out, the elevator arrived. The doors opened, and the assistant doorman stepped forward carrying a long, oddly shaped parcel in white paper wrapping. She took it from him and blew Bella a kiss.

"Have fun, darling," she called. "Tell me all about it tonight."

The doors closed, and with a soft whirring sound the elevator descended. A moment later, all was silence.

She took the package into the living room and laid it on the sofa while she went to fetch a pair of scissors. It was light, like a hatbox or a gift box containing a ballgown, and it bore her own name in small printed capitals. But its shape puzzled her. It had six sides, not four, and it widened in the middle and tapered at the ends. Somewhere in the back of her mind it registered an echo, but she couldn't quite work it out.

She cut the white tape and tore off the wrapper to reveal a white cardboard box of the same shape beneath. It was when she saw the three initials printed in crisp Roman lettering in the center that she understood.

R. I. P.

Her stomach took a sickening lurch. The shape was that of a coffin.

She snatched off the lid.

Inside lay a baby.

It took her a moment to realize that it was a life-size baby doll. Its eyes were closed. It wore a diaper, and it lay swaddled in a white baby blanket. Its skin was not pink and healthy but a deathly pale gray. Pale limbs, pale chest, pale head. And all over its body, on its temples and the bridge of its nose, on the veins in its arms and wrists, even on the inside of its ankles, on all the points where drips and tubes and catheters and feeds might be introduced to save a tiny, critically ill human life, were little patches of special infant sticking plaster.

She recoiled, choking. As she did so, the box fell off the settee as though the baby had come alive, and the creature fell to the floor. It landed upright, and suddenly its eyes swung open. She let out a shriek of horror.

The eyes were not blue or violet, but white. Porcelain white.

They were the eyes of a corpse with the lids peeled back.

And on the carpet by her foot where it had rolled out of the box, lay a small, real, hypodermic syringe.

In a flash she understood it all: the sender, the echo, the message. She staggered out the room and into the kitchen, where she bent over the sink and retched emptily. She turned on the tap and put her head under the stream of freezing water until the cold numbed her scalp. She was about to faint. Swaying and swooning, she slid to the floor and folded up in a sobbing, crumpled heap.

Cristina strolled through the park in the crisp October sunshine. She chose the park, as always, because it offered the perfect blend of anonymity and intimacy. She felt good, and from the glances of passersby she observed from behind her dark glasses she knew she looked good, too.

She wandered gently down the West Side to Strawberry Fields and into the Sheep Meadow beyond. Feeling a pang of hunger, she dipped briefly across the avenue to the Cafe des Artistes and ordered a smoked salmon hero at the bar. But food wasn't what she hungered for, and leaving the sandwich untouched, she paid the tab and headed back into the open parkland. Picking her way through the streams of Sunday joggers and mountain bikers, she wandered across the meadow and followed the edge of the central lake around to the Fountain. There she paused to buy an ice cream and sat down at a bench to watch the world go past. She had nothing to do but idle away the hours in pleasant people-watching.

Yet she couldn't settle. She tossed away the ice cream half-eaten and took to her feet again. She backtracked to the bridge and, crossing the lake, plunged into the ramble of undergrowth with its dense tulip trees and azaleas. When she emerged she saw her steps had been taking her inexorably eastward. She went on, and in a couple of hundred yards she was at the Conservatory Pond, with the swirl of the traffic on the East Side now within earshot. There she paused again to watch the flotilla of small radio-controlled boats speeding across the water, and it briefly amused her to see their owners, full-grown men, so delighting in their childish hobby. The sunlight coruscating on the surface of the water began to lock her gaze in a grip of fascination. She felt drawn into the flickering with its irresistible, seductive pull.... Abruptly she pulled away and headed off again at a quicker pace. She felt stirred by a restless, compulsive drive to keep moving. If she stopped, she would get sucked in. And yet when she reached Fifth Avenue and saw that her steps had by now taken her right across the park, she realized that her unconscious mind had led her in this direction with a purpose of its own.

What she did next came automatically, not from any conscious thought or choice. She felt like an automaton, governed by an unseen, outside hand.

She hailed a cab. She gave the driver an address six avenues away, in an almost direct line toward the East River. Even as she climbed in, the desire was swelling thickly inside her. Every street that took her closer to her destination quickened her pulse a beat. This was forbidden, and dangerous. Just six days had passed, not the full seven. She was breaking the rules. Would this break the magic? What if she caught him unprepared? What if he was with someone else? Or simply not in?

The cab set her down outside the familiar house. The street was quiet. People were indoors, watching the big Sunday ball game. She didn't stop to think further. Lifting the hem of her red skirt, she hurried up the front steps and without hesitation pressed the bell.

Silence. She looked around her in case ... she didn't know in case *what*. Either he was out or he didn't answer the doorbell when he wasn't expecting visitors. She felt disorientated, off balance.

Then suddenly the intercom crackled.

"Who is it?" came a voice she hardly recognized.

She turned back. Her heart was in her mouth.

"Cristina."

No reply.

"I have to see you," she said hoarsely.

Still no response. The agony was unbearable.

"I need to see you," she persisted. "Are you alone?"

A long pause followed, then quite abruptly the buzzer went.

She stumbled inside and closed the door. Breathing heavily, she made her way up the dark stairs. She reached the top, braced to face whatever she might find.

As she entered the room, she scanned the space about her quickly. Everything seemed normal, no nude models on the couch, no girlfriends hastily dressing behind the drapes, no dope-smokers scuttling into the wings. Only Louis himself, advancing toward her slowly, a quizzical, unreadable half-smile over his lips. Then she noticed a white thread caught in his cuff button and trailing on the floor. It seemed to belong to the large canvas which she'd never seen, the painting she'd always imagined he'd given up because it had a white sheet draped over it, like a sofa under a dustsheet in an empty house. She looked from thread to sheet and back again, making the connection. She had the powerful feeling that he had been working on that picture just now but that he didn't want her to know.

She turned to meet his eye. He raised a quizzical eyebrow and his smile grew more dangerous.

"Well, well," he said, coming forward. "This *is* a surprise, Cristina. To what do I owe the honor of this visit?"

Joanna bade the doorman a pleasant good evening. From the clock behind his desk she registered it was past ten o'clock. She'd often returned later from a day's business. Waiting for her private elevator, she met an elderly couple who lived on the tenth floor coming out of the communal elevator. They paused to inquire after the family.

"And how's Stephen?" added the woman, who clearly knew the answer to the question she was about to put. "We haven't seen him in a while."

"Stephen's in California on a research professorship," Joanna replied easily. She knew that from speaking to the accommodation manager at the Athletic Club. Word had got around the building here. Stephen was a popular figure.

"Shall we be seeing him over at Thanksgiving?" probed the woman.

"I doubt it," she smiled back. "Pressures of work."

The arrival of her own elevator cut short further interrogation. As she rode up to the top floor, she repeated the conversation in her mind. No fluttering in her heart, no knotting in her stomach. With some surprise she realized she could now talk about Stephen calmly and with ease.

As the elevator doors opened into the apartment, Bella came rushing forward. Her long, oval face was drawn with anxiety.

"Where have you *been*, Mom?" she cried. "I was getting so worried."

"Why, angel, I was just out," she replied, taken aback. "How did your day go? I see the grizzlies didn't get you."

"Anything wrong?" questioned the girl, scrutinizing her.

"Of course nothing's wrong. What ever should be?" She brushed past and led the way to the kitchen. "You hungry? I'm famished. Let's have a Spanish omelet and you can tell me everything you did."

Bella perched on a bar stool and kept up the scrutiny.

"Where did you go?"

"I had a business appointment."

"On Sunday? You didn't say."

"Darling, I didn't know myself till lunchtime. Warner called up. He had to get me to sign some papers."

"Mom," said the girl quietly, "Warner's out of town. He's in Florida for a week. You told me so yourself."

"He flew back early. I don't know why. I'm not responsible for his schedule." She struggled to keep the asperity out of her voice. She'd had a business meeting, that was all. Okay, it was late and on a Sunday, but so what? The world was getting to be a tougher place, and you did business whenever business was there to be done. She put her arm around her daughter's shoulder. "I'm truly sorry I wasn't here when you got back. I could have called, I know. I guess I just lost track of time."

Bella suddenly threw her arms around her and buried her face in her breast.

"I was so worried, Mom," she sobbed. "I thought you'd done something terrible."

"Bella, darling! Why on earth should you think that?"

"Because of that thing. You know."

"What thing? I don't know."

Bella pulled away and pointed to the corner of the room. There, on the floor by the service door, in the place where trash was put before being taken out, lay the white box. From amid a tangle of white wrapping paper projected one small ashen-white foot.

"I found it in the sitting room. I guessed what it's supposed to mean. Oh God, Mom, who could do such a thing?" She was shaking hysterically.

"It's nothing," replied Joanna easily, stroking the girl's fine long hair. She bit her lip. How could she have been so stupid to leave it where Bella might find it? She simply hadn't been thinking. "Just a dumb practical joke. I should have had Maria throw it out right away."

"It's sick! Evil! Whoever did it, I'd like to lock them away for ever."

"Don't let it get to you, darling."

"It doesn't get to *you?*" The girl looked up in surprise. "I thought you'd . . . I don't know what I thought."

"No harm's done. I'll get rid of this stupid thing right away and we won't think any more about it."

She reached into the closet for a large garbage bag and, picking the doll up by the ankle, dropped it inside. It fell with a muffled crack. She bundled in the blanket after it, then stamped on the box to crush it. The letters, R. I. P., somehow refused to be crumpled, so she folded the lid in half, then in half again, and rammed it down on top. In a minute there was nothing left but an odd-shaped garbage bag tied at the neck with Scotch tape, which a moment later went out of the back utility door to be dumped with the rest of the trash on the service landing.

"There, all gone," she said, brushing her hands as she returned. "Okay, is it to be an omelet, or what?"

"I'm not hungry, Mom," said Bella, red-eyed. She gave a convulsive shiver. "You know who I think it was."

"Come on, put it out of your mind."

"Karen. I bet it was her. You know you said to keep away from her." She shook her head in puzzlement. "But why would she want to *haunt* you?"

"Don't think about it. Just some crank sent it."

"A crank who was there when Luke was dying," Bella retorted. "I can't bear to think there's someone out there who wants to upset and hurt you."

"I'm *not* upset or hurt, darling," she reassured her.

"Really?"

"Truthfully."

She held her eye with unflinching conviction, and gradually the girl began to relax. Eventually she managed a smile.

"You know what," she said at last, "I could use a slice of pizza and a glass of milk."

"I could murder a pizza, too."

*   *   *

That night as she was taking a shower before bed, Joanna
looked with puzzlement at the small tattoo in the hollow of her
right buttock.

She stood still for a moment under the cascade of water,
angling herself so as to study this curious mark upon her body.
It seemed strange, mysterious. She seemed to have difficulty in
remembering quite how it had got there and what it signified. It
was somehow mixed up with the whole swollen ache that radi-
ated from her sex to the furthest outreaches of her body. Her
breasts were sore, her mouth and neck felt bruised, her elbows
and the small of her back were tender, and yet she didn't exactly
remember how this had come about. A link was missing
between the evidence and its cause. Yet it didn't seem to matter
that she couldn't make the connection. She didn't even want to.
She relished the sting of the hot water on her sore flesh, and the
immediacy of the sensation itself was all that counted.

Later, when she slipped into bed and, stretching luxuriantly
between the sheets, felt the touch of the cool soft material
against her naked skin, she had the sense that a great burden
had physically lifted off her and that nothing existed except a
perpetual present, unfolding from moment to moment.

In the early hours of morning, with the moonlight streaming in
the window and the traffic far below reduced to the occasional
whisper of a car speeding through the wet streets, Cristina rose
from the bed.

She couldn't stand by and let such a thing happen to the
poor little soul.

She wrapped her silk bathrobe about her and tiptoed bare-
foot along the corridor and down the stairs. At the bottom, she
hesitated. Distantly she could hear the soft whir of electrical
equipment, perhaps a fridge or a freezer, punctuated by the random hiss of the heating. Otherwise not a sound penetrated the
heavy slumber of the apartment.

The kitchen was illuminated by an angular shaft of moonlight that ran in a splinter along the floor and up the side of the
central table, exploding in a starburst from the crystal fruit bowl
lying on top. She skirted the table and chairs and made for the
back utility door that led onto the service landing, where a large
garbage bag lay waiting to be collected.

Kneeling down, she untied the tape at the neck of the bag.

Quickly she felt inside. Her fingers met a soft blanket, then thin hair, then cold infant flesh. Gently she withdrew the tiny form and, wrapping the blanket around it, drew it into her breast. Then slowly she made her way back to the kitchen, where she stood for a while in the light of the moon, cradling the tiny infant tenderly in her arms.

"Poor soul, who could think of doing such a thing to you?" she murmured softly. "My poor little precious, so small, so tiny, so cold. Cristina will see to you. She'll give you a proper burial. Come now, little treasure, come into my bed and let me warm your tiny cold hands."

Slowly, cuddling the inert little body close to her, she retraced her steps up the stairs, along the corridor, and back into the bedroom.

17

TWILIGHT WAS FALLING OVER the Berkeley campus. In his spacious laboratory office, Stephen sat at a video console, scrolling through a library of the mug shots of all the male criminals convicted by the San Francisco Police Department in the previous five years. Though they came in all shapes, sizes, and colors, each subject was photographed in a standardized way, one shot staring ahead in full frontal pose and the next in profile—but always, and this was the important thing, taken from exactly the same camera distance and under the same lighting conditions.

"Homicide. Negative. Negative. Nix. Homicide."

Beside him, recording his calls as he screened the faces one by one, sat a tall, long-legged girl in a fluffy white U.C.B. sweatshirt and tight aquamarine pants. Every few moments she gave an audible sigh. She'd been expecting a date and, instead, all she was getting was data. Her name was Yolande. Between his calls she would sweep back a stray wisp of her long fair hair and cast him a covert glance from beneath large-framed glasses. She scored A for sexuality and E for subtlety. Par for the course out here. (Would he rather have it the other way around? *E* for sexuality?) Yolande was studying the influence of pheromones on human behavior, a glamorous area of research being conducted in another department. She'd noticed him on campus and around the building and she'd contrived to bump into him twice, and that afternoon, coming upon him in the department coffee lounge, she'd asked keenly about his work and volunteered her services that evening. Sitting over a sheaf of continuous computer stationery and marking off names of a bunch of convicted villains was clearly not quite what she'd had in mind.

"Nix," he continued calling. "Nix. Nix. Negative."

And Yolande obediently made the relevant tick or cross.

He wound the tape forward in fast jerks, taking one mug shot every second so as not to allow himself time to make more than a snap decision. He looked at the full frontal shots only, ignoring the profiles, and he had taped two sheets of paper across the screen to form a window so that he could see nothing except the subjects' eyes. The cues he was reading lay in the eyes.

Beside him, Yolande was working down a corresponding list of names, checking the guesses as he called them out against the crimes noted against each individual and putting a tick or a cross depending on whether he'd guessed correctly or not. The whole thing was just a hunch, of course—one of those crazy ideas straight out of left field that Don Weitzman had so derided. But the humble hunch had fathered many a great breakthrough.

"Homicide. Negative. Negative."

On and on it went, minute after minute, until he finally came to the end of the videocassette. He reached for a bottle of whiskey from his desk drawer and poured out two generous shots into plastic beakers. He pushed one toward Yolande, who was in the process of totaling up. She pushed it back without stopping her work. With a shrug he added it to his own. He could never get used to the post-alcoholic society.

"So, how do I score?" he asked.

She arched an eyebrow over her glasses.

"Do you want to rephrase that?" she asked. "Or do I take it as heard?"

"Let's stick to percentages."

She smothered a smile and reached for a calculator.

While he waited for her to work out the result, he took his drink over to the window and gazed out over the campus. Below, a magical tracery of illuminated paths and roadways crisscrossed the lawns and wove around the university buildings that lay like stately liners at berth. It seemed, like all things here, to hold out a world of fantastical promise. He felt a shiver of excitement. This was fairyland, where everything was possible. Even hunches. And the implications of this hunch were mindboggling.

The idea had come to him two years before, in the winter following Luke's death. He'd been walking home one night after giving a talk to a conference at a midtown hotel—it was snowing, and cabs were impossible to find—when a young kid stepped out of a dark doorway and thrust a knife at him. Denizens of New York were inured to this, of course, and the wise victim handed over his wallet without fuss, but Stephen, not yet habituated to violence as a social norm, was outraged and immediately shaped up for a fight. But something in the mugger's eyes froze him. The kid had a knife, he was standing just a couple of feet away and staring him in the face, but he was looking *through* him, as if his eyes were focused on some point beyond, a point not in space but in the imagination. And in that instant Stephen knew that this kid was a killer.

What had told him? He remembered walking through the gently falling snow, robbed of his wallet, and feeling not so much anger and vengefulness as excited curiosity. The kid had not been on drugs, to judge from those students he knew who regularly were. No, here was a creature equipped with a masterpiece of evolution, the forward-pointing eyes and stereo vision that made the human animal capable of very precise movements and measurements of distance, holding a weapon to his opponent's throat and *focusing off target*.

When he reached home, Joanna had been furious. It had probably been out of relief that he was safe, but a quarrel ensued. She accused him of caring more for his work than his family, calling him selfish and irresponsible to risk his life without thought for those he might leave behind. . . . How absurd that all sounded now! He had disappeared from her life as surely as if he were dead, and she was living every bit as happily as before.

In the early hours of the morning, however, he'd crept downstairs to his study and worked until dawn, puzzling out the question. The two eyes converged and diverged, each one being controlled by six small muscles, and the tiny variations in the angle were fed back to the brain to signal the distance of an object. A person talking to a friend across a dinner table, say, was conscious of being held at the correct focal length. But to be stared at, close-to, by someone whose eye divergence suggested they were fixing on something behind them across the street, was a weird and chilling experience. Like any incongruence of body cues, too, it was a revelation of the state of the inner mind.

And this had told him he was looking into the inner mind of a killer.

He'd tried to explain it to Yolande earlier. She'd seen the paper masking the video screen and asked what it was for.

"The eyes have an unconscious language all their own," he'd told her. "You can't fake eye expression like you can fake a smile. You know how disturbing it can be when people wear dark glasses indoors? You don't know what they're thinking."

"Yeah, and mirror shades are really weird," she'd agreed.

"Right. But most studies of nonverbal cues concentrate on the mouth and lower face. Muscle control is greater there, but that also means expressions can be masked better. A Japanese, for example, will tell you about some horrific car accident with a happy, smiling face. He's masking. Watch him at the scene, and his face will look shocked and upset. All cultures register the primary emotions with the same facial expressions. Ekman showed that." He paused, aware this was beginning to sound like a lecture. "All I'm saying is, looking at the mouth for subconscious cues just makes another layer to decode."

"And eyes tell more?"

She was flashing her own. The message was coming across like the beacon from a lighthouse. This was before he'd sat her down to work.

"Eyes are the windows onto the soul."

"Hey, you believe in the soul?"

"The subconscious mind," he'd corrected himself briskly, wanting to avoid the inevitable trip down that astrological deadend. She'd be telling him next that in a previous life she was Yolande, Queen of Anjou at the time of Joan of Arc. What would he have been? *Saint* Stephen?

Eyes were, indeed, highly expressive. They softened in love and hardened in anger, they widened with surprise and narrowed with cunning. Staring eyes signified madness, lowered eyes were maidenly, and liars avoided eye contact altogether. Eyes flirted and seduced, they desired and deceived. Even the pupils told their story: pinprick pupils were a sign of a deceitful nature, dilated pupils a sign of erotic arousal. Yolande's were vast liquid pools, magnified to climactic levels by her glasses. He tried to look away.

But what else could be glimpsed through this window? Homicidal tendencies? The killer instinct? *Evil?*

Yolande's voice now abruptly cut through his thoughts. She had finished the calculation.

"You want the figure?" she asked wearily, laying aside the calculator.

"Give it to me."

"Sixty-seven percent," she declared. "Room for improvement. Could try harder."

"Hits or misses?"

"Hits. I only rate success."

"Jesus!"

It was astonishing. A 5 percent hit-rate was the odds on the basis of pure chance. But he had scored over sixty percent! In two out of three cases he'd been able to tell the homicide cases from the others. Just by their eyes.

He turned back to the window and stared out, lost in thought. Just suppose he had hit on something here. Suppose he could build a scientific diagnostic tool that could detect the potential killers in society . . .

"Tell me, Yolande," he said, scarcely moving, "what would you think of by evil?"

"Evil?" she echoed, surprised. "You mean, devil worship and all that shit?"

"Is killing and maiming evil?"

"Hey, what is this?"

"Or does it depend on the motive." He was talking more to himself. "It's okay to kill in war and to kill in self-defense. It's mostly okay when you're not responsible for your actions, say it's a pure accident or you're mentally unbalanced."

"Hannibal Lecter is evil," she offered.

"He's a sociopath. For him, morality hits a complete blind spot. To him, actions have no moral color at all. What he does is certainly evil, but he doesn't see it. Is he himself evil, then?"

"Okay. Take some goon who shoots up a shopping mall for the hell of it. Say he gets a kick out of wasting people. He knows it's bad, and he does it deliberately."

She was cooperating now in this strange Socratic dialogue he found himself impelled to pursue. He nodded.

"I agree that's one kind of evil."

"There's others?"

"I'm thinking of where a person does something terrible but believes it to be positively right. Hitler knew what he was doing in gassing the Jews, but he justified it by a higher principle, an ideal of racial purity. He didn't go to bed at night with a bad conscience. On the contrary, he felt he'd acted nobly. Isn't that the most terrifying kind of evil? Where a man does have a strong moral sense yet he does horrific things in the belief he's actually doing right? Evil done for good motives, atrocities committed in the name of an ideal?"

She was now giving him the who-is-this-weirdo? kind of look.

"Where's all this leading?" she queried uncertainly. "What's it got to do with those mug shots?"

"Quite so. I'm looking for the connection."

"Stephen," she said, considering him gravely, "is this your idea of a fun evening, tossing out a bunch of crazy ideas and seeing where they land? You treat all the girls to a lecture on evil?"

"These are important issues," he heard himself saying stiffly.

"God, you're so *serious!* C'mon, loosen up." She reached forward and switched off the video monitor, then rose and began turning off the lights at the door. "Closing time. I'll buy you a beer at Larry Blake's or someplace noisy. You need to chill out. You want to come?"

"Lead on," he sighed, defeated.

They never made it to anywhere either noisy or public. Her rooms just happened to lie en route, and she was driving. With no more than a sideways glance that it hardly took a degree in nonverbal cues to decode, she pulled her bright yellow beetle into the parking area beside a graduate dormitory block and, murmuring something about making him "comfortable," climbed out and led the way indoors.

She was an athletic lover, and she took her pleasure energetically and noisily. She performed the preamble with a certain artistry, though, offering him a selection of condoms like cigars from a cigar box and using her mouth to put on him his chosen sheath with a skill that clearly derived from years of chewing bubble gum in adolescence.

As so often, he felt functional: who was really there to make whom "comfortable"? Yet part of him was still the young man of his own student days, when the rule was never to turn down a screw on the principle that, like a hot meal, you never knew where the next one was coming from. Better to get it under your belt and then go out and tackle the rest of life.

That view, he now realized, relied on an image of male sexuality as a kind of unvalved lavatory cistern that filled up steadily and had to be bled off regularly to prevent overflowing—an adolescent image recently reawakened with his newfound bachelorhood, yet one that seemed far removed from how he really felt now. The different Ages of Man were to be respected. Making love with a girl fifteen years younger was fine so long as he allowed that he was fifteen years older, with all the changes in values and expectations and drives that the years had brought. On that basis, if he were honest, he'd have rather spent the evening discussing the nature of evil over a bottle of chilled Napa Valley in a seedy student dive than doing the trampoline act in some unknown private gymnasium that went by the name of a bedroom.

But then again, after closing time at the private gym and finding himself back in the street and alone—a quick bunk-up was okay, it seemed, but Spending The Night represented an unimaginable leap in the level of intimacy, when, God knew, all he really wanted still was the comfort of a young body sleeping curled up in his—he found the dreadful juvenile voice whispering in his inner ear, *Well done, take a medal, attaboy!*, while the exhaustion in his limbs and the soreness of the sheet burns on his elbows and knees took on the quality of trophies of a battle nobly engaged and honorably acquitted, so that when he did finally make his way to Larry Blake's and replenished his spent fluid with several beers, he felt suddenly and explosively terrific, remanned, ready to take on the world and game for anything.

The high continued through the third beer. The fourth tasted

sour, however, and the fifth brought a sudden decline in his
mood. The noise of the R & B band seemed no longer lively but
deafening; the figures dancing to the music were like mari-
onettes on an alien stage; the other drinkers at the bar were
physical reproofs of how he must look himself, a worn out,
fucked out wreck going through a premature midlife crisis.

He needed a break. He'd take the Thanksgiving week off and
drive down to Mexico. Maybe he'd find some ancient Mayan
herbal remedy to rejuvenate him. Hadn't he heard something
about lizard penis in cactus juice?

The sixth beer gave him a spurt of reassurance. His salvation
lay in his brain, not his balls. Sixty-seven percent! It was a shattering result. He'd put it to the test right then and there. There
was a latent murderer in the room and it was his job to spot
him. He began scanning the faces around, scrutinizing the eyes,
always the eyes . . . until a burly football jock gave him that very
particular look that was still seared on his memory from the
Irish bar in New York, and very quickly he looked away. This
was strictly a lab study, not fieldwork.

The seventh beer brought on a wave of melancholy, and he
left the glass half drunk. Everything he felt seemed contradicted
by something else. He was tired, yet his mind was feverish. He
was a free man, yet he couldn't somehow enjoy the freedom. He
had been seduced by a devastatingly pretty girl, and yet he felt
empty. He was swamped with crazy ideas, yet he couldn't make
anything of any of them. He was like a car, accelerating and
braking at the same time, with the result he was revving wildly
but getting nowhere. Nothing seemed to return him what he
wanted. Yolande, presumably, had got what she wanted out of
the evening, she'd sent him off into the outer world after elicit-
ing a promise of a repeat performance. These kids in the bar
were getting what they wanted, drinking and laughing and
dancing and sniffing and shooting God knew what behind the
scenes to keep the balance of high and low adjusted. Even the
respectable Lou Whittard was somehow *settled*, sitting in his
vast office like a fat spider and pulling the strings of the intri-
cate web of money and learning with the self-assured cunning
of a Machiavelli. And even Joanna, way on the other side of the
continent, knew what she was doing. At least, she'd known what
she was doing when she'd packed his suitcases and placed them

in perfect alignment by the front door. Why was he alone such a goddam mess?

He called a radio cab. The firm was busy, but a cab would come in ten minutes. Suddenly he felt he had to get into the open. On the sidewalk outside, he paused. He couldn't wait ten minutes. He didn't want to go back to his rented house, anyway. It was empty, he'd be alone, and he'd only drink some more in the hope of gentle oblivion settling over him. He didn't want to crawl the bars or clubs. For a crazy moment he thought of dropping back in on Yolande, but even in his present state he realized that would be a catastrophe: she'd be in bed watching television and eating a takeout pizza, or she'd be giggling with her girlfriends and comparing dates, or maybe she'd be out partying, trawling the student bars and clubs herself, luring fresh, younger meat into her parlor.

Then he knew what he wanted to do. Abruptly he headed down Telegraph Avenue toward the university campus. He had unfinished business at the lab. And a car to collect, if he were sober enough to drive by then.

The building was empty but for a security guard on the front desk, who sat with a pair of stereo headphones and his back to a bank of closed-circuit monitors so that he didn't see or hear Stephen approaching until he'd reached the desk itself. To make up for the lapse, he went through the protocol of signing him in and checking his identity at excessive length, and by the time Stephen had reached his office the effect of the beer was finally wearing off, leaving him feeling flat and uninspired and just wishing he'd taken the cab and got to bed. He poured a whiskey to restimulate the cortical cells, but the alcohol didn't seem to get beyond the limbic system and only served to dull his wits.

For a while he sat in front of the video monitor, scrolling through the mug shots of the various villains and spot-checking his guesses. The score still came out at around two in three hits. Incredible. But science was measurement. Could he *measure* why?

He froze one frame showing the face of a serial killer, a young man with a long, lean face, pencil-thin lips, and large, staring eyes. Again he had the sensation of the gaze being fixed at an inappropriate focal length: the eyes were staring *through* his own, and beyond, burning a hole in the back of his very skull like the rays of the sun focused through a magnifying glass.

The angle of the eyes' divergence could be readily measured in the laboratory using mirrored contact lenses: a light was shone onto the surface and its reflection registered, giving a very precise measurement of position. But you couldn't go around the street getting suspects to pop on a pair of contact lenses. Besides, his hunch seemed to work from photographs alone. How could he measure *that?* Could an optical reader digitize the eye-images into tiny bits and pixels so that it could be analyzed by a computer?

Abruptly he broke the stare. The eyes were mesmerizing him. He turned away from the screen with a convulsive shudder. He had been staring at evil in the eye.

He looked around the room for something of beauty upon which to rest his gaze. Electronic equipment in gray and white thermoplastic housings, desks and chairs in tubular steel, carpet tiles in a beige fleck to disguise coffee spills, overhead fluorescent lighting in functional polyvinyl casings . . . nothing of elegance or aesthetic uplift, not even anything fashioned by the hand of man from nature's own materials. Finally his eye lit upon a small, unframed photograph half hidden behind a pile of journals on the windowsill, the photograph he'd had tucked into the letter rack on his desk in the laboratory at Columbia and which he'd kept with him from place to place, the picture of Bella in her early teens, wading out of the ocean at the beach house in the Hamptons.

He took the photo and held it under the light. Her smile brought a smile to his own lips. Just to rest his eyes on this image of simplicity and joy made him feel cleansed. He began to chuckle. God, she was a great kid.

He reached into a filing cabinet and took out a videocassette marked only with the place, New York, and the date, early August past. Quickly ejecting the reel with the mug shots, he slipped the cassette in and rewound it to the beginning. Then, topping up his beaker and swinging his feet onto the desktop, he sat back to watch the tape.

It showed Bella in the kitchen of the New York apartment, sitting on a bar stool, with her long fair hair hanging down like a mane and dressed in nothing but a T-shirt and panties. She was painting her toenails and speaking into the phone at the same time. She looked up and pulled a face at the camera, then began wiggling her shoulders and playing the flirt. Suddenly she looked across to the door and quickly wound up her conversation. The camera swung around to show Joanna coming into the room. She waved it away irritably, but it only closed in tighter.

He leaned forward and pressed the Pause button. He tried to examine that face as though it were a stranger's, and in every line and muscle it shouted *stress*. It was the face of a woman on the verge of a nervous breakdown. How had he been so blind? How could the face he had once devoured with such kisses and observed secretly across a room or a table with such adoration changed so far? Couldn't it somehow be reversed, like a videotape, and restored to the one that he had first known and loved? People never really changed. They might change their partner or their circumstances, but they carried their own natures like baggage with them. Within everyone there was the person they had been. Even the child of simplicity and joy they were long before. Couldn't a loving hand peel back the layers of pain and experience that had accumulated since?

Not here, in this case. Not now. It was too late. Joanna and he were, in every way, too far apart.

18

THE SOCIAL ROUND THAT ROSE TO A PEAK around Thanksgiving had never been so hectic. Joanna declined as many invitations as she could, but there were still the business receptions and the fashion shows she couldn't cut, the charity galas and the vernissages, the bar mitzvahs and the birthday parties, not to mention the private dinner parties where well-intentioned friends, and worse-intentioned relatives, tried to match her up with a suitable new man. No woman of her wealth and looks should be without a man in her life, they reasoned. And indeed, all the eligible males she had thrust at her were at the very least High Net Worth Individuals, and some were even interesting and cultivated, too.

But she wanted none of it. A separation was a bereavement and called for a period of mourning, she explained to one of her girlfriends who accused her of being "unsociable" when she declined an invitation to a billionaire's private Caribbean island for a week's vacation. For herself, she felt no need of any explanation. In that area where "social" really meant "sexual," she felt quite complete.

Bella, of course, was openly hostile to the merest hint of any suitor. She couldn't believe things with Stephen were actually over, and she never missed an opportunity to champion his corner. Such was the sad sweetness of youth, thought Joanna, never to believe the world could really be other than you wanted it to be.

As the days grew colder and the evenings darker, their trips to the beach house became fewer. They planned to spend Thanksgiving there, however. It was now just ten days away. They would invite in a few local friends for an evening, but otherwise they'd stay by themselves and relax from the madhouse in the city. In the meantime, every minute of her time was spoken for. Her mornings were spent at the salon and her evenings at one function or another, while her afternoons, which remained indefinitely blocked out in her diary by a thick red line, were reserved for her special business meetings.

The breakfast television was on in the background. It was more for noise than for news. She had taken to having it on at breakfast since Stephen had left, to provide, as it were, the missing company. Bella was, as always, only half awake. She sat on a bar stool eating a bowl of cereal and apparently reading the strip cartoon on the back of the packet, though it wasn't easy to tell since the curtains of her hair still remained drawn.

Joanna was pouring a cup of filter coffee when the reporter's voice jerked to the front of her attention.

"A surgeon at this well-known East Side hospital," a smartly-dressed young woman was telling the cameras against the backdrop of a giant hospital building, "was yesterday indicted with unlawfully administering a lethal injection to a terminally ill patient in his care . . . "

Joanna looked up sharply. She laid down the coffee jug. A shiver ran lightly over her skin, like pebbles scattered over a frozen lake.

"Lillian Marks, aged seventy," continued the reporter with the high drama of a race commentator, "died within minutes of being injected with a fatal does of potassium chloride. . . . She was terminally ill . . . an incurable condition . . . chronic pain . . . refused medication . . . begged to be allowed to die . . . "

Joanna felt herself lock solid. She couldn't even turn her head toward Bella. She spoke like a marionette, in a kind of robotic squeak.

"Turn it off, Bella."

The curtains parted and the girl looked up.

"Mom?"

"Turn that thing off. Please."

She was frozen rigid like a person who had touched a high-voltage power line and could only be freed by cutting the supply. She was conscious, too, of a curious metallic taste in her mouth, like the taste of a coin but with an undertone of bitter almonds.

"Turn it off!" she barked.

Out of the corner of her eye she saw Bella reach for the remote control. She gripped the side of the breakfast bar as a wave of giddiness swept over her. It seemed as if the room momentarily dissolved, and for a second she was in that strange land of shifting forms between dreaming and waking where the very self became fluid and out of focus.

She heard Bella's voice repeat more anxiously, "Mom?" and she thought, "Who is she calling to?"

Gradually the room regained its shape and form, and she could see Bella's face looming close. Across the room the television was now just a blind screen. She blinked hard and shook her head to realign her senses.

Bella was tugging at her sleeve.

"What's the matter, Mom?"

Nothing was the matter. What was the girl talking about?

"I'm fine. What's up?"

"You look as white as a sheet."

"Do I?" She frowned. "I can't think why."

"You went all funny."

"I must have been daydreaming." She returned to pouring the coffee.

"What was wrong?"

"Wrong with what?"

"With the thing on television."

"Oh, I'm sick of the news. It's always the same. The *bad* news, that's what they should call it." She heard herself chattering on, under some conversational autopilot. "I really don't know why we have to endure a diet of shootings and muggings at breakfast. You'd think they could find something more cheerful to start the day off with."

"It wasn't a shooting or a mugging, Mom."

"Wasn't it? I wasn't listening." She paused. Bella was looking at her mistrustfully. "Either way, there's far too much violence reported these days."

"That's because there's so much out there." The girl's expression was cautiously beginning to relax. She spread a muffin with grape jelly. "They should bring back the electric chair."

"Bella!" she exclaimed, genuinely shocked. She took a sip of coffee. The hot, strong liquid seemed to revitalize her. "Anyway, the death penalty is no deterrent. That's been proven."

"Stuff deterrence. What's wrong with old-fashioned retribution? An eye for an eye. You kill someone, you get killed in turn. Very simple."

"Very primitive," she responded quickly. "We're supposed to be a civilized society."

"Yeah, and look what a mess we're in."

"But what that surgeon did," she found herself persisting, against all her instincts, "surely there's nothing really wrong in that."

"Taking life is always wrong." She cast her mother a narrow smile. "So, you *were* listening."

"Always wrong?" She tried to manage a laugh. "Everything's so black and white with you young kids. Life isn't like that. You'll see."

The girl was about to argue further, but she checked herself.

"You should know, Mom," she sighed ironically. She took her plate to the sink, then headed for the door. "I'm going to be late. Late is late, and no shades of gray."

Joanna listened to the footsteps climbing the stairs. She paused, feeling disturbed and strangely puzzled, as if the world were rushing to a summary judgment without giving her a chance to explain or defend herself. And yet explain what? Defend herself against what accusation? She had the uneasy sense that there *was* something, but she couldn't quite focus on what it was. It all belonged to someone else.

She checked her watch. Abruptly she swallowed back her coffee and followed Bella out. There was no time for such thoughts. A busy day at the salon lay ahead. The business of life had to go on.

The process of life itself went on, too, and on that same day her assistant Cheryl gave birth to a baby girl. The staff at the salon clubbed together to buy flowers and gifts, which Galton drove out to her home in Brooklyn. She had asked Joanna to be a god-mother, and that Saturday, at a Baptist church in Brooklyn, the newborn infant was christened.

The church was newly built in futuristic, angular forms, with the internal walls of bare shuttered concrete, the seats and pulpit in pale Oregon pine and the stained glass in the pattern of crazy paving. The gathering was small and the ceremony brief but intimate. Joanna and Bella stood at the front with the other godparents, who were local family friends, while a hymn was sung and a short series of prayers spoken. Then the group followed the minister back down the nave to the font that stood by the entrance.

There Cheryl handed the baby in its long lace christening robe over to the minister, who anointed its tiny forehead with the sacred water and gave a brief address welcoming the new life into the body of Christ's family and reminding the godparents of their duties toward its spiritual upbringing. He then handed it back to Cheryl, who was standing next to Joanna, and began around the godparents in turn, exacting their pledge to fulfill their duties. The chill of the water had made the baby cry, a soft, mewling sound, and instinctively Joanna reached forward to comfort it. Cheryl held the little creature out for Joanna to take.

Joanna saw her own hands advance, then suddenly freeze.

The soft, mewling sound suddenly amplified in her head to a terrible, broken scream. She stood rooted to the spot, unable to take the baby yet also unable to withdraw her hands. The baby hung midway between them, offered but not taken.

The others had noticed. The minister stumbled in the middle of his sentence. Cheryl's face registered hurt and dismay. Beside her, Bella caught her breath. The moment seemed to go on forever, with the baby poised just inches from her grasp, yet she just stood there, paralyzed, unable to do anything. Dimly she was aware of a faint, ferrous taste in her mouth.

The lace of the christening robe brushed her hands, and at the touch she abruptly shrank back, smothering a cry.

No! Don't bring it near me! Don't let me touch it!

The world about her went silent. Faces stared at her, frozen and aghast. They looked as if they were all in some vast tank of water, mouthing silently, their eyes bulging and expressions distorted, and she was standing there, quiet and composed and distant, watching these figures looming toward her and away again like fish in a vast aquarium, and the baby, now withdrawn into its mother's embrace, growing redder and more distressed and yet for all its howling making no sound whatever.

She looked at herself, at her clothes and shoes. What were they all staring at?

Then she understood. She wasn't wearing her red dress. Nor her silk stockings and red shoes. She had forgotten. Somehow, by mistake, she'd put on this crisp gray check suit. They knew it was wrong. They could tell. Cristina always wore red. And never without stockings and red shoes. Sometimes no panties, either. Could they tell *that?* Has the minister got X-ray eyes? she heard herself think. Dirty old bugger. There he is, leering at me again. What does he want, an eyeful of leg, a glimpse of naked stocking-top? I bet he's wondering if I'm wearing pantyhose, and do I have the panties underneath or on top? Men wonder these things. Like women wonder if men wash their hands before they pee or afterward. Important life-informing details. Why won't they stop staring at me? Have I messed up my makeup? My hair, it's my hair, my wig has come adrift. It's so hot. I can't breathe. Get me out of here. I need air.

Fingers were tightening on the tender flesh of her upper arm. She was being steered into a seat. Everything was beginning to unfreeze. There was movement and noise and a babble of voices.

"Loosen her collar." Cheryl's voice.

Then Bella: "It's okay, Mom, you just had a dizzy spell. Sit here for a bit and you'll be all right."

"Here, drink this." It was the minister now, holding a glass of water toward her.

She blinked, then frowned. Why all the fuss? She was absolutely fine. Perhaps she'd fainted. The glass was being tilted to her lips. If she didn't drink, it would spill. She looked up into the minister's large, concerned eyes.

"You blessed it, Reverend?" she heard herself asking.

"Mom, don't be blasphemous!" hissed Bella at her side.

She drank. It tasted metallic, like spa water dunk out of an iron cup, but strangely and recently familiar.

She struggled unsteadily to her feet.

"Forgive me," she mumbled. "I don't know what came over me. I'll get some fresh air and be right back."

She made her way to the door and stood in the porch, drawing in deep breaths of the crisp November morning air. She groped through her mind to remember what had happened, but it all seemed so foggy. She recalled the hymn and the prayers, then going up to the font and the minister baptizing the infant, but that was all. She must have blacked out. She couldn't have fainted, or she'd have hurt herself falling on the stone floor. Did she fall asleep? People could just drop off, even standing up. Had she got dropsy, or the sleeping sickness? Or was it a *fugue?* She'd read about fleeting moments when the world just faded out, when you became, literally, absentminded. She'd had a moment like that before, over breakfast earlier in the week. Maybe she'd make an appointment with the doctor. Or maybe she wouldn't. It was probably nothing at all.

Bella was beside her, supporting her arm. The others were coming out now, too. The service was over. She felt conscious that she had spoiled the event for Cheryl, but she still couldn't quite figure out how. She turned as Cheryl came up. The young woman's freckled face was full of sympathetic concern. The baby was in the other godmother's arms.

"I'm truly sorry," she muttered. "I don't know what happened."

"Stress of work," smiled Cheryl. "I said you couldn't cope without me. Just hold out till I get back. Don't crack, okay?"

It was meant lightheartedly, but Joanna couldn't return the smile. Bella linked arms and steered her toward the car.

"Come on, Mom," she said quietly, "let's get you home."

Late that night, after her mother had kissed her good night and gone through the usual fond routine of urging an early lights-out and a good night's rest, Bella took a yellow legal pad from her desk drawer and, sitting cross-legged on the bed, composed a long letter to Stephen.

She poured out her heart, saying how worried she was for her mother and how much she'd changed since he'd left. Something really odd and disturbing was happening, she said. There were times when Mom simply didn't seem to be *there*. She'd see or hear something—nothing obviously alarming—and suddenly she'd flip into this strange absent state, and you could talk to her and call her name as much as you liked and she'd look at you and talk back as though you were a stranger—not a complete stranger, more like someone she'd known long ago but whose name she'd forgotten. Then, a few moments later, just as suddenly she'd flip back out again, and when you asked what was wrong, she'd look at you as though *you* were the crazy one. It was as if she fell asleep on her feet for those few moments, or she'd been hypnotized by someone and then, out of the blue, she heard the trigger word.

It was truly weird.

And then there was what happened at the christening today, Bella went on. That really shook her up. She'd tried talking about it on the way home, but Mom just said she'd been daydreaming. But anyone there could see something was seriously wrong. Cheryl said it was stress of work, but you could tell she didn't really think that. Something far more worrying was going on. Mom was acting like a head case.

She covered five sides of paper when she heard footsteps in the corridor outside. She quickly folded the letter and hid it under the duvet.

"Remember what I said, darling," called her mother. "You've got a long day tomorrow."

"Night, Mom," Bella called back, obediently switching out the light.

In the morning, she put it in an envelope and slipped the envelope into her school case. During the lunch break, she went to the mail room in the administration offices and added it to the outgoing mail tray. She was just leaving the room, however, when the second thoughts that had been dogging her all day came to a focus all at once and, turning back, she quickly retrieved the letter from the tray.

It wasn't fair to get Stephen alarmed and upset over something that was no longer his concern and something he couldn't do anything about anyway. She was on her own, and she had to handle this by herself.

As she reached her classroom, she tore the letter into a dozen pieces and tossed them into the wastepaper bin.

At Bella's insistence, Joanna canceled the drinks evening she'd been planning for the Friday of the Thanksgiving break at their house on the beach. Under Bella's orders, too, they slept in late, ate a full breakfast, then went for long, bracing walks beside the ocean. In the evenings, they read or played card games in front of the fire in the snug room and retired to bed early. Bella rationed her vodkas and regulated her eating and even screened the movies she could watch on television. Joanna smiled to herself to observe this young girl ordering her around so firmly and competently, and she was touched. She didn't feel like the invalid that was being made of her, but she did admit to having felt a little dislocated recently and to showing other normal signs of stress, and she was grateful for the enforced opportunity to take a rest.

The one social event Bella did permit was an invitation to supper at the house of their immediate neighbors on Saturday, their final evening. She really wanted to see her friend Eddie, of course, but she dressed it up to appear a major concession, like an outing on parole for a convict, and Joanna had to promise to go easy on the predinner cocktails and be sure to leave no later than eleven. She played along, enjoying the role reversal.

By ten o'clock, however, the regime of exercise and early nights was taking its toll and the evening itself was wearing thin. Geographical proximity was really all that united the adults, unlike Bella and Eddie who had the whole uncharted future in common. Their conversation waxed as that of the grown-ups waned until finally Bella caught her mother stifling a yawn and, abruptly resuming her role as protector, stood up.

"We'd better be getting back," she declared. "Mom needs her beauty sleep."

"No, I don't," objected Joanna, coming alive.

"No, she doesn't," echoed her host chivalrously. "Beauty she ain't short on."

"Well, it was great you could come," mediated his wife wisely. "Even if the pumpkin pie wasn't . . . "

"It was just wonderful," Joanna cut in, rising to her feet, too.

Eddie was speaking to Bella in an earnest whisper. "Do you *have* to split? And you really go back tomorrow?"

"Eddie," reproved his father.

"You stay, Bella," said Joanna. "Eddie will see you back, won't you, Eddie?"

"Sure you'll be okay, Mom?" Bella was still in solicitous maternal mode, but she wasn't going to object.

She'd be okay, she'd be fine. She'd had a great evening, and wasn't that the real joy of close friends, the fact that you could just chill out when you wanted and nobody accused you of party-pooping? She heard herself intoning the ritual excuses for an unseemly escape from a boring evening. She felt overwhelmingly tired. She continued the exchange of noises until finally she was out of earshot.

Their house was on the neighboring plot, and although both of their grounds were quite extensive, it was too close to justify going by car. A path ran through the low scrub that lay between the house and the ocean. Fifty yards down, it led into a grassy clearing on her own land from which, in turn, fed a path that zigzagged up to their house. Her host insisted on seeing her to the boundary of his property, where he kissed her good night on both cheeks, and from there on, guided by the flashlight she had brought, she wove her way across the clearing and up the pathway, through the undergrowth and finally toward the broad, lopsided clapboard building that was their home.

The moon was veiled in broken cloud through which, from time to time, shone piercing shafts of pale greenish light. After a while she found it easier to walk without the flashlight, and with the bite of the chill air she began to feel her senses sharpening. Behind her, the ocean kept up the perpetual crash and hiss of flow and ebb. Ahead, the house rose proud of the landscape, its downstairs lights ablaze like a lighthouse. With her shawl wrapped tightly around her, she steered her path toward this beacon. At the pool she paused to check the cover was properly secured, and she made a detour around the rockery to pick a bunch of thyme to take back to the city next day. Finally she let herself in through the double glazed doors, hiding the key under a brick for Bella.

Once inside, she went around turning off lights and checking the windows and doors were secure. In the kitchen she warmed a glass of milk in the microwave to take upstairs to bed. With the warmth of the house her fatigue was returning and, with a final glance around to check all was fine, she turned her steps wearily toward the staircase.

She was half way up the stairs when suddenly she froze in her tracks. She'd heard a noise! A distinct sound of movement, coming from upstairs!

God alive, she thought, there's someone in the house.

She honed her ears. All was silent. Outside, far in the distance, came the plaintive whoop of some nocturnal creature.

Suddenly, from deep in the bowels of the house, came a soft, muffled explosion. She started violently, then realized it was just the heating boiler kicking in.

But there it came again, a strange shuffling sound, from down the far end of the corridor. Maybe some animal had got in, a raccoon fallen down the chimney, it had been known to happen. Then she heard a voice, a human voice. But the really eerie thing was, the voice wasn't talking. It was *humming*.

She stood frozen midway on the stairs. Should she go back down and call the police? She took a step forward. The stair tread creaked. She held her breath. The humming stopped. Then, oblivious to her, it started again. Quickly she scrambled the last few stairs to the top. On the landing she stopped to look down the corridor. A cry choked in her throat.

A light was shining from under the door at the far end. The door to Luke's room.

Impelled by numbing dread, she began down the corridor. Step by step she came closer to the door. Inside, the voice was speaking now, in a quiet indistinct mutter. With the remoteness of a trance, she saw her own hand reach out for the door handle and slowly, so slowly, turn it.

The door inched open. She recoiled with a gasp, releasing the handle so that the door swung open the rest of the way by itself.

In the center, beneath the light, bent over a makeshift cot, stood a nurse in crisp starched white uniform. Her auburn hair was pinned neatly back behind a white cap and her slim waist was gathered in by a broad blue belt. An array of pens and thermometers projected from her breast pocket.

Joanna's mind gave a sickening lurch. Times without number she had been there, in that very room, with that same nurse, at that late hour of night, bent over this same pitiful infant.

The nurse looked up. She put a finger to her lips.

"Ssh," she whispered. "He's asleep."

Leaning forward again, she pulled a small blanket up over the tiny pale form that lay in the cot. Joanna's head was spinning. Was this happening now, or was she back in the past?

"Look at him, the little treasure," the nurse was saying tenderly. "Asleep at last. I gave him his oral medication, and he took it like a lamb."

Wide-eyed with horror, Joanna took a half-step forward. In the dim recesses of her senses, she was aware of a familiar metallic taste in her mouth. She swallowed, but it only grew more bitter. The room seemed to be dissolving about her. Her whole vision seemed to tunnel in on the cot. Grasping the door frame for support, she stared into the cot.

The baby was fast asleep. Her baby. Her own little boy.

The nurse was speaking again, addressing the sleeping infant in the same cajoling voice.

"And now for your shot, honey," she said, producing a hypodermic needle from a tray. She took off the cap, then held it out to Joanna. "Would you like to do the honors tonight, Mrs. Lefever? There's no need to be squeamish. It's best done when he's asleep. Just a little prick, that's all he'll feel, and then it's over. Mrs. Lefever. . . ?"

Cristina stepped forward. With a swift movement, she reached into the cot and snatched up the baby. What was this nurse she'd never met before in her life doing to her poor little child?

"Who are you?" she spat. "What are you doing?"

The nurse seemed momentarily taken aback. She adjusted her smile.

"Don't you think you should be more careful with him, Mrs. Lefever?" she asked levelly.

"What's your name, girl?" she snapped.

"I'm Karen," replied the nurse, coming forward. "You hired me to look after Luke, remember? Now, why don't you just let me take him . . . "

"Keep away!"

"Come along, Mrs. Lefever. We don't want to upset the little one."

The nurse reached out and made a grab for the baby's arm. Cristina pulled back, but not quickly enough. There was a ripping sound, and the arm came off in the girl's hand.

"My God, look what you've done!" screamed Cristina. She snatched the severed limb and, muttering words of comfort to the lifeless form cuddled in her arms, began backing toward the door. "There, there, my sweet one, Momma will see to you."

"Now wait a minute . . . " The nurse was advancing, her eyes narrow and watchful.

"Get back!" she cried. "Can't you see what you've done? You've killed him! He's dead! Murderer! Get out of my sight!"

"He was dead already, Mrs. Lefever. Your baby was dead."

"Liar! Murderer!"

She had reached the door by now. There, with a howl of pain, she grasped the small, inert bundle to her breast and stumbled away along the corridor, down the stairs, and through the house to the door that led onto the back lawns.

Bella stood on the doorstep watching Eddie's tall, rangy figure loping away down the pathway. Just before the path disappeared in among the bushes, he turned and waved a kiss. She stood on tiptoes to catch the last glimpse before he was finally lost to sight.

For a moment she stood drinking in the chill of the night air and listening to the distant weary *plash* of the ocean. A light shiver rippled over her skin. She closed her eyes briefly and felt his parting kiss still smoldering on her lips. He'd always been the kid next door, the childhood pal. Now suddenly everything had changed. How was it she had never *noticed* him before like that? It was weird, as though it had been waiting all this time to happen. She sighed. She felt good, very good.

An owl hooted in a tree, returned a moment later by another more distant. Were they wooing, she wondered, or just warning one another? Birds sang to mark out their territory, but tonight she'd rather think they sang to serenade. She listened to the other sounds of the night, the shuffles and snuffles in the undergrowth and further away the eerie coughing of some larger creature, a fox perhaps. Then she became aware of one she couldn't place, a kind of sharp chipping sound, like a blackbird smashing a snail's shell on a stone. But no blackbirds were abroad at this hour. The sound went in relays of five or six sharp strokes, followed by a silence, and then it would start up again. It seemed to come from the small apple orchard that lay beyond the rockery.

Puzzled and curious, she made her way down the gravel path that skirted the main lawn and led to the rockery and the rougher ground beyond. The moon peered through a thin skein of cloud to illuminate her steps. The chopping, chipping sound was growing louder. As she reached the thick hedge that enclosed the orchard she suddenly recognized what it was.

It was the sound of a spade striking the ground.

Someone was digging at that time of night! She slowed in her tracks. A frisson of fear prickled her skin. This could be dangerous. But impelled by curiosity, she tiptoed forward. A twig snapped under her foot, and she froze. The digging abruptly stopped. For a moment all was silent, then it began again. Chip, wrench, shovel, chip, wrench, shovel. . . .

Hardly daring to breathe, she inched her way to the hedge and peered through a gap. She stifled a gasp.

At the foot of a large, bare-branched apple tree stood her mother. She had her back to Bella and she was digging a shallow trench about the length of a suitcase and half the width. On the ground beside her lay a small bundle wrapped in some kind of white blanket. Next to it, but detached from it, lay a curious pale bent object which suddenly, to Bella's horror, resolved itself into the arm of a doll.

Instantly she understood.

She stood gripped by an appalling fascination as her mother finally laid the spade aside and, gathering up the baby and its severed arm, swaddled it tightly in the blanket and pressed it tenderly against her breast. Then she slipped to one knee and lowered it gently into the grave. For a moment, she knelt there as if in prayer. Then she stepped back and, picking up the spade again, began shoveling back the earth, patting it down as she went to form a shallow mound.

All the while, Bella watched, unable to move. She was paralyzed by the scene itself, but, more than that, there was something wrong about her mother's movements, something dehumanized and robotic. She moved in small jerks, like a puppet. Her face bore a plastic smile of serenity and her eyes were staring and empty. This wasn't the real Mom.

The bizarre burial was over, and any moment Bella knew she'd be spotted. Coming back to life, she carefully retraced her steps back to the rockery, where she broke into a run and fled without stopping through the undergrowth and along the gravel path until she was safely indoors.

She rushed up to her room. Her eyes blurred by tears, she groped in her holdall for her address book. She listened at her door to check all was still clear, then she closed it quietly and picked up the phone by the bed and, with a shaking hand, dialed Stephen's number in Berkeley.

It rang and rang.

Come on, she whispered desperately. *Answer! Oh Stephen, where are you?*

But there was no reply. Finally, afraid the light on the set downstairs would give her away, she conceded defeat and slowly put down the receiver.

19

THE SKY WAS STILL GRAY AND COLD, with the first steely tinge of dawn unfurling over the ocean, when Joanna went into Bella's room to wake her. She shook the sleeping girl gently by the shoulder.

"Wake up, darling," she whispered. "We have to get back to town. I'm sorry."

Bella stirred from a deep slumber. She rubbed her eyes and looked up anxiously.

"Why? What's the matter?"

"I had a call last night. I have to get back for a meeting. I'll explain. Come on now, angel. Have a quick wash and slip your things on, then we'll hit the road."

"I'm seeing Eddie later, Mom. Couldn't I stay here and you come back after your meeting?"

"It could go on all day. I'm sorry, darling. I'll make it up to you." She began packing up the books and clothes Bella had brought. "We'll stop off for breakfast on the way."

She hurried her daughter downstairs and, grabbing a glass of juice on the way, steered her out of the house. The morning air was chill and damp, and a low autumnal mist shrouded the trees that lined the front drive. In the street, not a soul was abroad. Throwing their holdalls into the trunk, she ushered Bella into the front seat and climbed in beside her.

Bella was craning her neck to look behind her.

"Whose car is that, Mom?"

Joanna followed her line of vision. Half-concealed at the side of the house stood a small, bronze colored car.

"Oh, didn't I say? We had a visitor last night."

"Who?"

She started up the engine. "Karen."

"*Karen?*" Bella spun around.

Joanna slipped the car into gear and began to move forward.

"She dropped by," she replied casually. "I found her here when I got back from next door. I suppose she still has a key."

"What? You mean, that woman got into our house by herself. And she's still *there?* Aren't you going to do something about it?"

Joanna glanced back toward the house. At an upper window she caught a fleeting movement. A figure in white appeared briefly in the frame, then vanished.

"She knows her way around the place," shrugged Joanna.

"But I don't understand!" persisted Bella. "You know she did that dreadful, sick thing! She's a monster!"

"She apologized. She really didn't mean any harm."

The girl flashed her a look of incredulity, but checked herself. For a while they drove in silence along the broad, empty streets.

"Anyway," she said at last, more to herself, "you disposed of it."

"Yes, it went out with the trash," replied Joanna.

Bella's eyes narrowed.

"What were you doing last night, then, Mom?" she asked carefully.

"What was I doing? I saw Karen to her room, took a shower, and went to bed. Oh, and there was this call."

"I'm sorry, Mom. I saw you outside in the yard. I saw what you were doing."

She glanced across and met her daughter's hard stare. As she did so, she took her eyes off the road and suddenly she saw the car was veering across into the oncoming lane. She wrenched the steering wheel straight and the car skidded on the dew-damp roadway for some distance before she managed to get it back under control.

"That was a close call," she breathed, shaken. A Hardees came into sight ahead. "You ready for something to eat?"

"I'm not hungry," replied the girl, still holding her under puzzled scrutiny.

"We have plenty of time."

"When's your meeting?"

"Oh, uh, I have to call when we get to the apartment."

Bella was toying with the ends of her hair. A frown puckered her longish features.

"Mom, is there a problem at work?"

"No, no, it's a deal. Sometimes opportunities can't wait." She leaned across and squeezed the girl's arm. "What would you like to do this afternoon best of all?"

"I thought you were tied up all day."

"Oh, I'm sure I can wrap it up sooner than that."

Another silence fell. The day was brightening as they turned onto the freeway. Joanna put on a Bonnie Raitt tape, one of Bella's favorites, but the girl reached forward and switched it off.

"Can we talk instead, Mom? You don't like that, anyway."

"Sure, angel. What do you want to talk about?"

"I mean, *talk.*" A quaver had entered her voice. "I'm worried and confused, Mom. I don't know what's going on."

"Darling, what's upsetting you?"

"Can't you see? Everything's upside down. One minute Karen's a menace, the next she's staying in our house when we're not even there. One moment we're having a happy time enjoying the vacation and the next we're dragged out of bed and have to rush back to town." She looked down at her lap. "I thought last night had fixed it all. But it hasn't, has it?"

"Last night?" echoed Joanna, genuinely perplexed.

"When you buried that doll. I thought it was all because you never buried Luke, you had him cremated instead, and now you had."

"I did *what?* Darling child, you've been dreaming. You're right, I am upset we never gave Luke a proper burial. I let Stephen talk me out of it. I blame myself for that."

"But I thought . . . " She checked herself and turned toward her mother defiantly. "What were you doing last night then, out there, digging up the orchard? Sleepwalking?"

Joanna scrutinized the pale, troubled face. For a brief moment she wondered if this was some kind of game or joke that she wasn't comprehending, but the challenge in those eyes was too open, too uncompromising.

"Are you all right? Should I be worried about you?"

"Mom, don't play tricks!" pleaded the girl. "Please tell me."

"But I wasn't anywhere last night. You're imagining it. I went to bed straight away. I fell asleep with the light on. Believe me."

"You really believe that?"

"It's true. Now let's pull in somewhere and get something to eat and forget all about this absurd nonsense. Okay?"

But Bella made no reply. She had turned her head away, and behind the hand pressed tight to her face she was silently weeping.

Joanna changed hurriedly. She chose the Dior charcoal herringbone suit with the square shoulders and tailored waist that Bella called her "power-dressing" look. Her makeup was pale and understated, and she wore no jewelry other than her Rolex Oyster and a pair of simple pearl drop earrings.

Bella sat on the bed, watching her scurry into the bathroom and back to the dressing table with a strangely sad, puzzled look. It was tough to have to drag her back like that, but they'd had a few good days' vacation and they'd have had to come back that evening anyway—getting snarled up with the other returning traffic into the bargain. They'd do something together that afternoon, maybe take in the Thanksgiving parade and fanfare going on down in the Village, and they'd get Lorri along, too, and any other of her friends that were around. It was raining, but she'd find a way of making it fun.

"I'll be back by one, darling," she reassured her daughter as she gave her neck and wrists a light spray of perfume. "If you want to go out before, just call me at the salon. We'll meet up somewhere in town."

Bella looked up, her eyes peaked with anxiety.

"Everything is all right, isn't it, Mom?"

"Don't go on! Of course it is." She reached for the girl's hand. "Call Eddie and say sorry from me. See if he can come up here one evening and stay over. I'll get in a bunch of travel books and you can work on your trip." She squeezed her hand and smiled. "Are you getting sweet on him, Bella?"

"It's not that, Mom."

"Well, I like him. I don't want to interfere, but for what it's worth, I approve." There was a ring on the internal house phone. Her cab had arrived. She gathered her purse and gave her daughter a soft kiss on her forehead. "Love you, angel."

"Love you too, Mom."

"See you later."

With a final parting kiss, she left the room. She stepped briskly down the stairs and along the corridor to the elevator. She fiddled impatiently with her earrings while she waited for it to reach her. She was dying for a coffee or even just a glass of water, anything to take away the nasty metallic taste in her mouth. Finally the elevator arrived, and she stepped inside and hit the button for the lobby. As the doors were closing she glimpsed, far down the corridor, the wan figure of Bella, silently watching.

But the doors were closing and suddenly she was alone, with the pressure building within her. The elevator was descending fast, it was dropping like a stone, pulling her out of her skin like an insect emerging from its chrysalis. Through her mind flashed a kaleidoscope of images—the nurse in white uniform, the baby doll with its arm wrenched off, the glint of moonlight on the steel blade of the spade, the fleeting figure at the window, and always the burning urge to escape, to flee, to pack the car and slam the doors and run for it . . .

With a soft whir, the elevator abruptly braked its descent, then settled gently to its appointed level, inching itself to a final halt. She closed her eyes against the sudden rush of nausea, but that seemed to make the strange feeling worse. Her mind was fogging over. Desperately she looked about her. She was imprisoned in a padded cell. Why weren't the doors opening? She tried to compose herself by focusing on her hands, her clothes, her shoes. She glanced at her fingernails and wondered distantly why she hadn't painted them. And what was this charcoal herringbone suit she was wearing? She hardly recognized it. She must have dug it out from the very back of the closet.

Finally, with a light shudder, the doors parted. Ahead lay a lobby area, clad from floor to ceiling in bronze and marble. A man in the uniform of a doorman stepped out from behind a desk. Smiling, he ushered her toward the main door. He seemed

to know her. He called her by a name she didn't quite recognize.
A yellow cab was waiting at the curb outside. The doorman held
open the door for her and escorted her under the canopy to the
cab. He produced an umbrella from nowhere to shield her from
the rain as she climbed inside. He slammed the door for her and
stood back, touching his cap in a brief salute, as the cab took off
into the steadily falling rain.

She sat back in the seat. She looked about her. At the rips in
the seat covering, mended with brown parcel tape. At the
driver's identification card. At the rain-blurred windows through
which it was impossible to see where they were going, although
the driver knew, of course, for he turned here and braked there
and swung round the corner there until, somewhat sooner than
she'd expected, he drew into the side of the road and pulled up.

"Here y'are, ma'am," he announced, not turning round. "Five
bucks fifty."

Cristina pressed her face to the streaming window.

"Where is this?" she demanded.

"Where you said. Madison and Seventieth."

"I want the Upper West Side, mister. West 89th Street. You
got that? Jesus, what's with you guys?"

"You're the boss," growled the driver.

He stepped on the accelerator so savagely that the tires
screeched despite the wet road. He roared off at a punitive
speed, taking corners and throwing her from side to side with
deliberate vindictiveness. She let out a weary sigh. Another
macho retardate who couldn't handle simple criticism. Saying
he'd got the address wrong was like saying he had a frankfurter
for a dick. What did their mothers *do* to them at potty training?

Finally they drew up outside the old brownstone and she
handed the driver the exact fare. He looked at the coins and
notes in his hand as if it were animal droppings.

"Thanks for nothing," he snarled as she climbed out.

"Thanks for the grand tour," she replied brightly.

"Up your ass, lady!"

"Dickhead!"

She slammed the door so hard the handle should have fallen
off, then hurried down the path through the rain. A typical
exchange of views between city dwellers, nothing to get fazed
about. She fumbled in her purse for the key. The rain began
falling more heavily, in thick perpendicular sheets.

Finally, she got the door open and stumbled thankfully inside. She threw down her purse, turned up the heating, tossed off her wet suit jacket and shoes, then went to fix herself a double-strong coffee in the kitchen area. She turned on the television and the stereo together, snatched a shot of vodka from the freezer as she was going for the milk, lit a Turkish cigarette which she puffed once and left smoldering in an ashtray to serve as incense, then took the coffee downstairs to the bathroom where she ran a ferociously hot shower and stood for as long as she could bear it, letting the tensions and stresses and confusions gradually wash away, until finally she stepped out refreshed, renewed and, in her deepest self, released.

Bella prowled around the apartment, unable to settle. She called her friend Lorri, but there was no reply. The rain was sheeting down now, and there was no point in going out. She dialed Eddie's number but put the phone down before it answered: she'd call him later when she felt less confused and when she could give him the sweet attention this tentatively flowering love deserved. She switched on the television in the living room and sat on the sofa flipping through magazines, but gave up after a moment and went to the kitchen for a drink. Finally she perched on a bar stool and stared out of the window at the cityscape beyond, now reduced to formless outlines by the thickly falling rain. That's how the world is, she thought, just a jumble of random bits and pieces, without shape or meaning. Nothing connects up. Mom can't see it. *Darling child, you've been dreaming,* she'd said. But I *wasn't* dreaming! I saw her as clear as daylight, right there in the orchard, digging a hole in the ground and burying that hideous doll.

Didn't I?

A sudden doubt crept into her mind. The sands on which she stood were shifting. Maybe she'd somehow got the order of events wrong. Maybe she'd gone to bed in the normal way and fallen asleep and dreamed it all. The whole night seemed under a magical spell. Had she dreamed the kiss, too?

She reached for the phone and dialed Eddie's number again. This time she spoke to him. She explained Mom had had to get back and she was sorry they couldn't meet up. Quickly, before her unprepared feelings could betray her, she said she had a favor to ask him. It sounded strange, and she'd explain later, but would he go next door to their own place and check the orchard and see if a patch of earth beneath a tree in the middle had been freshly dug over, and then call her back?

She waited an eternity for the reply call. Finally, it came.

"Yeah," Eddie confirmed. "There's fresh-dug dirt. Looks kinda like a small grave. You buried a pet?"

"Just something we ran over," she replied quietly. "I'll call you, Eddie."

She put her finger on the cradle and held it there for a moment, deep in thought. Then she lifted the finger and dialed Mom's number at the salon. She'd go over and stay beside her. She could wait downstairs while the meeting went on. She wasn't going to let her out of her sight.

The phone rang and rang. Finally, she hung up. Mom had a phobia about unanswered phones. It meant she wasn't there.

She glanced at the wall clock. It would be dawn on the West Coast. If Stephen was there at all, she'd get him. Once again she rooted through her holdall for her address book and dialed his number. And once again, it rang endlessly, in vain.

A cold, creeping fear wormed its way into her soul. She was on her own, isolated and helpless. She could only wait it out until Mom called. And in the meantime, *think*.

Toward midday, she had an idea. Stephen's study had been under lock and key ever since he'd left. It contained all his stuff, waiting to be packed up and shipped out to him. Mom couldn't bring herself to touch it. Perhaps it meant that she was secretly hoping he would return? Or subconsciously expecting him to? God, adults were so *dumb* sometimes.

She found the key in the escritoire in the living room and gingerly opened the door. The blinds were down and the room smelled dusty. Books lined every inch of the walls, but the desk and floor space were littered with a jumble of his possessions: his exercise bicycle, his set of antique walnut-framed hunting prints, the pair of tennis rackets he took back and forth to the beach house but hardly ever used and, looming out at her from every shelf and surface, his collection of masks. Ghoulish faces and garish faces, some with popping eyes and others with small holes, war masks decorated with blood and hair and death masks fringed with white feathers and daubed in ash.

She switched on the light and looked about her. Stephen had

the answer to everything. He either knew it or had a book on it. Somewhere in this treasure house of knowledge lay the answer to Mom's problem.

She scanned the dusty shelves. Old periodicals, box files of cuttings, stacks of fanfold printout, and books upon books. She looked for a diary or a notebook in which Stephen might had written down his private thoughts. Maybe there'd be correspondence with a psychiatrist . . . or, wait, something on *Luke*. This was the key to it, she felt sure. Everything had gone wrong when the baby died.

Luke had been born with an incurable illness, he'd lived for six months, and then he'd died. That was all. It was tragic, but millions of parents had lost infants without becoming serious head cases. Why hadn't Mom, who was in every other way so tough, been able to cope?

Her attention was caught by a group of books shelved together. She shivered as she read the titles. *Bereavement: Studies of Grief in Adult Life:* C. M. Parkes. *Grief and Mourning in Cross-cultural Perspective:* Rosenblatt, Walsh and Jackson. *Attachment and Loss:* J. Bowlby. And a copy of the *American Journal of Psychiatry* with a yellow page-mark that opened to an article by E. Lindemann entitled, "Symptomatology and Management of Acute Grief."

This wasn't Stephen's field. Why did he have these books unless it was to do with *that?*

She sat down on the floor and skimmed the Lindemann article. She didn't make much of the tables and statistics, but the general drift was clear. It was all about the effects of bereavement on people who'd been in a fire at the Coconut Grove nightclub in Boston, Massachusetts, some years ago. It was the first study to show something she'd have thought was perfectly obvious, people who suppressed their feelings suffered later from delayed or distorted grief. Death ceremonies in traditional societies acted as a valuable vent for expressions of grief. But what happened in modern societies where ritualized mourning had died out? What happened today when a parent was deprived even of the simple ritual of seeing their child buried? *Pathological consequences might ensue,* she read with a shiver.

Like burying a plastic doll?

She didn't hear the elevator arrive, and she only registered footsteps approaching the study when it was too late. The door opened sharply, and she looked up into her mother's frowning face.

"Bella, what are you doing?"

"Just reading."

She hurriedly closed the journal and stood up. Her mother took it from her and glanced at the title. Her frown deepened.

"I don't know what you want with this," she said shortly. "You know, it's high time we cleared this stuff out."

"How did the meeting go, Mom?"

"Very satisfactory, thank you. And you've been keeping busy, I see."

Bella bit her lip. Why was Mom talking in this stilted way? She let herself be ushered out of the room. Her mother turned off the light and locked the door behind them.

"Sorry," she said mildly. "I didn't think it was out of bounds."

"It's not. I just want to keep it all together, that's all."

But surely that didn't mean locking it? Shaking her head, she followed her mother to the living room. It was getting worse.

"So, it was worth the schlepp back this morning?" she began more brightly. "You got what you wanted."

"Perfectly," her mother replied with a distant smile. "Have you thought what you'd like to do, darling? Bella? Why are you staring at me like that?"

Bella didn't reply for a moment. A new idea was dawning. Maybe she was barking up the wrong tree entirely. She cast her mother a sly look.

"Come off it, Mom, you can't kid me."

"Kid you, darling?"

"You've changed your earrings. You had those pearl drop ones on before. And you've painted your nails. And, hey," she reached forward and picked a long strand of hair off her dark gray suit. "A man with long blond hair! Is he a pop star or something? So much for your business meeting!"

She was laughing now. It all figured. *That* was who called last night and that was why she had to get back.

Her mother's reaction took her by surprise. She whipped forward and brushed the stray hair out of her hand, then tore off her earrings and slipped them into her pocket. She folded her arms so that her hands were hidden, then sank into an armchair and glared at her daughter defiantly.

"Is that better?" she snapped. "Is that what you want? Don't you like your mother looking good? Just because Stephen's gone, do I have to dress like a drab?"

"Hey," cried Bella, puzzled and distressed, "I was only teasing. I didn't really think . . . "

"You didn't think at all. You never do."

"Mom!"

"And for your information, Bella, I was not seeing a man. I was having a business meeting at the office. Like I told you."

"I don't care if you were seeing the President! Just don't pretend to me. You weren't at the office, Mom."

"Are you now your mother's keeper?"

"I called you."

"You called to check, huh? So, she spies on her own mother. What kind of a daughter have I raised?"

"For God's sake, Mom! This isn't you!"

She was in tears now. Abruptly, her mother got to her feet. As she did so, her hand caught the shade of the table lamp and the lamp, a delicate Chinese porcelain vase, fell to the floor. It snicked the edge of the magazine rack as it went and shattered into a dozen pieces. Joanna's hand flew to her mouth and she let out a small cry, but she didn't move. She just stood staring dumbly at the broken ornament.

Bella dropped to her knees and began scooping up the pieces.

"It's okay, Mom. It was only a lamp. Only a *thing*."

She looked up. Her mother had gone very pale. She was pressing her temples and blinking hard. She looked as though she were coming round from an anesthetic.

"I'm sorry," she said in a confused tone. "I don't know what came over me. What were you saying?"

"I don't know," said Bella. "I don't know anything anymore."

"Come here, my angel." Her mother reached out her arms and drew her close. "We've all been under a lot of stress lately. Sometimes I feel I'm losing my grip."

"Mom, do you think you should see someone?"

"You start to forget things when you get to my age. That's all it is."

"You're only thirty-seven, Mom. That's hardly geriatric."

"Thirty-six, if you don't mind." They exchanged a glance and laughed. "Come on," she said, "let's go someplace. We'll go see what gives in the Village. Right?"

"Okay," sighed Bella. The moment had passed.

"First, let me get out of these clothes. I won't be a moment." She headed to the door, glancing at her fingernails on the way. "I really don't know what possessed me," she murmured half to herself. "I hate shocking pink."

With a light shrug, she made her way out of the room, leaving Bella standing in a pool of resignation and dismay.

Stephen had driven through the night to be back in time for a mid-morning lecture he was due to give a class of freshers on gestural communication. As ever, he'd misjudged the scale of the distances in his adopted homeland, and despite taking the interstate rather than the scenic coast route he still arrived in Berkeley with only a couple of hours to spare for a nap.

He hauled his bags indoors and, dragging himself upstairs, kicked off his boots and threw himself on the bed. He felt exhausted but exhilarated. Images of the Sierra and all its raw beauty filled his mind as he closed his eyes, and in his ears echoed the rhythms of the language and song of Mexico. He vowed he really would learn Spanish at last and to hell with communication of the nonverbal kind. He set the alarm for ten o'clock and stretched out on the counterpane, unshaven and fully clothed. He felt raw and raunchy and travel-worn, like a gunpoke just ridden into town. Another time, another place, there'd be a holster slung over the chairback.

He smiled to himself. He liked the image of a freewheeling buccaneer, and he had felt for the first time, as the miles on the signposts counted down to San Francisco, that he was coming home. Driving into the blush of the breaking dawn and watching the vastness of the land unfold with the rising sun had filled him with wonder and delight. New York seemed so far away, a city lost in wintry darkness, with no room to move, no air to breathe. Studies of overcrowding among rats had shown identical patterns of violence. Nothing would entice him back. Here, life was altogether sweeter, the air warmer and cleaner . . .

Just as he felt himself sinking into a deep slumber, the bedside telephone rang. He turned over and waited for the answering machine to cut in. Then he remembered he didn't have one in this house. Blurrily he fumbled for the receiver and raised himself on an elbow.

"Hello?" he croaked.

"Oh, thank God! I've been calling and calling."

It was a young woman's voice. She sounded distressed and relieved at the same time. He couldn't place her.

"Who is it?"

"It's *me*. Bella."

He jerked upright. All his senses were suddenly awake.

"What's happened?"

"I'm calling from a pay phone. Shit. I'm out of money."

"Call me collect," he shouted, then the line abruptly went dead.

A minute later they were reconnected. Bella was calling from the street across from her school, it was her lunch break. She'd been trying to reach him for several days. She was struggling to keep control, but now and then she'd have to break off before regaining her strength to speak again.

It was Joanna. She was going off the rails. Her behavior was crazy, unpredictable, dangerous. It started when Karen sent that weird baby doll . . .

"What did you say? Karen's been in touch?" he snapped.

"She's back, Stephen," said the girl in a trembling voice. "And she's moved back in."

"Jesus!"

There was a brief pause, then Bella spoke again. There was desperation in her tone now.

"I know I've no right to ask this of you, Stephen, not after what Mom did to you," she pleaded, "but you've got to help. Stephen, you've got to save Mom."

His mind was whirling. Karen had surfaced again. And Joanna was losing her mind. His worst fears were coming true.

"Listen to me," he said, enunciating every syllable carefully. "Just act as though everything's normal. Go along with whatever Joanna says or does. I'll get a flight back tonight. I'll meet you out of school tomorrow, at the soda bar opposite. Tell Joanna you've got something on late. Okay?"

"Okay." Her voice melted with relief.

"And Bella," he added, "I understand what's happening. And I think I know how to handle it. I'll explain everything when I see you. So, don't worry."

"Thanks, Stephen, really thanks. See you tomorrow."

He replaced the phone in a turmoil of confusion. He didn't understand anything, frankly, and he didn't know how to handle it. He wasn't even sure if he should interfere at all. Yet he knew he would. For all he told himself that Joanna's problems were her own affair now, that she'd cut him out of her life and he had no reason to get embroiled again, he knew he couldn't stand by and do nothing. He was the only person who *could* do anything: he was the only person who knew Joanna and what she had really been through.

Stephen, you've got to save Mom. That cut straight to his heart.

God knew, he'd tried before. Time and time again. What was different this time? Nothing. And yet, by the same token, there was still that perpetual tiny glimmer of hope that, against all the odds and in face of all the evidence, something might happen to break the cast and to restore to him the love he had lost.

20

"I DON'T KNOW WHERE I AM ANYMORE," said Bella in despair as she came to an end of her account. "She's just not the Mom I know. One minute she's all affection and love, the next she has that weird look in her eyes like she'd forgotten who I am. She refuses to admit she's said and done things. It's like living with two people. What can we *do*, Stephen?"

He unclenched his fist and released the plastic cup he had been crushing as his anger mounted. The soda bar was noisy with boisterous students just out of school. He felt uncomfortable and out of place. He needed a proper drink.

"I'll tell you what we *can't* do," he muttered tightly. "We can't reason her out of it. I've tried. At a deep level, you see, she's repressing terrible feelings of guilt. What that nurse did has reawakened those memories. That's what she meant to do. There's really only one thing to do," he went on, more to himself, as the chilling solution grew inescapably clear. "Eliminate the source of the reminder."

Bella wasn't following his line of thought. She toyed with her straw. A frown settled over her pale oval face.

"It's to do with what happened to Luke, isn't it," she said. "But I don't get it. Cremating him wasn't such a sin. Millions of people believe in it. I think I do. I'd rather go up in a puff of smoke than rot away and feed the worms."

"Your mother feels strongly about certain things."

"I know. She believes we'll all rise again on the Day of Judgment in our old fleshly form. It's crazy. Suppose she lives to eighty, does she really want to come back as a wrinkled old hag? And Luke, would he be six months old and riddled with cancer, for all eternity? I suppose she thinks he'll now come back as a bunch of ashes. It's so *dumb*. Can't she see it?"

Stephen drew a deep breath. Every day since the infant's death he had known this moment would come. Sooner or later, whether voluntarily or not, he would have to face Bella with the truth. Now it could be avoided no longer.

He reached forward and closed his hand over hers.

"It's not that, Bella," he said quietly.

She met his eye sharply.

"How do you mean?"

"It's not to do with what happened after Luke died. It's about *how* he died."

"Sure, he was very sick. He was *born* sick, the poor little love. We knew he was going to die sooner or later, even though we pretended to each other that he wasn't going to."

"It's about her *part* in how he died," elaborated Stephen.

A look of startled suspicion flashed into her blue eyes.

"What are you getting at?"

"Listen," began Stephen, then checked himself. The noise, the airlessness, the crush, this was no place for what he was about to say. Abruptly he rose to his feet. "Let's go somewhere else. We can't talk here."

He left a pile of coins by his plate and pushed through the raucous press to the door. Bella followed, puzzled, returning her friends' greetings distractedly as she passed.

The wind outside was chill and bracing. He stood for a moment on the sidewalk as the cool revived him. Some way across the road a neon light flashed, *Bar*. Turning up his overcoat collar, he took Bella by the arm and steered her through the flow of traffic.

"Let's get a drink," he growled.

The bar was a dark subterranean dive, lit by low blue lights and arranged in a series of small alcoves set back from the bar counter. Soft, moody jazz played in the background. A waitress in a loose knee-length sweatshirt came up and took their order. It was their happy hour, she advised them with a long, sad face. Bella asked for a Coke, Stephen a large Johnnie Walker without ice.

"Strange, calling the blue hour the 'happy hour,'" mused Stephen as they waited for the drinks. "On the principle that you smile when the angel of death passes over, I suppose. The Greeks used to call the three evil old Fates the 'Kindly Ones.'"

"You're avoiding the issue, Stephen," reproved Bella gently.

"So I am."

He let the silence fall until the drinks eventually arrived. He took a long pull of the whiskey and waited for the welcome rush of alcohol. He lowered the glass and played with the reflection of the table light in the surface of the liquid.

"Pain is a strange thing," he began. "The old view of pain had it as a sensation going from nerve endings in a straight path through to the brain. The more the tissue was damaged, the greater the pain. Then they discovered a mechanism in the body, in the dorsal horn of the spinal cord, which acts like a gate to modulate the input from the nervous system. In the brain itself, the actual perception of pain is modified by all kinds of psychological factors—attention, anxiety, suggestion, and so on. A child can hurt himself really badly, but distract him and he'll be laughing a minute later. You've probably cut yourself and only felt the pain later when you actually saw the blood."

"Yes," she agreed cautiously.

"You can't know someone else's pain. You and I can crack our heads together, but you can't experience my actual pain. Maybe I don't feel it at all. How could you tell?"

"Well, I guess I'd look for signs. If it hurt, you'd rub your head and say 'Ouch.' If you're a kid, maybe you'd cry."

"What if I can't rub my head? What if I can't even speak? What if I'm crying all the time anyway, because I'm hungry or uncomfortable or any of a dozen other reasons and crying is my only way of signaling these things? *What if I'm a baby?*"

Her expression sharpened as she perceived his drift at last.

"How do you tell if a baby is in pain?" she echoed. "I suppose you infer it. If it hurts us, it will hurt it."

"A baby who misses a feed will scream. Is it in pain? I haven't eaten since breakfast and feel quite hungry, but I'm not howling."

"You're taking your food in liquid form," she smiled briefly.

She paused, then grew serious. "What are you saying, Stephen?"

"There's a school of thought that says babies don't feel pain as we do," he began carefully.

"Are you saying Luke wasn't in pain?" she cried, shocked and incredulous. "That's utter garbage! I was there. I saw. I heard him crying at night. Not just crying like a baby wanting a feed. Crying like a creature in agony. Like he wanted to crawl up the wall. Anyone with ears could tell."

"Those people," he went on quietly, "put babies under major surgery without anesthetic. Partly, I have to say, it's not easy to judge the right type and dose of anesthetic for a baby. Scaling down an adult dose of thiapentone, say, just doesn't work. But partly there is this belief that though they may feel discomfort, though they may try and wriggle away to avoid the cut of the knife, nevertheless you can open up a tiny baby and operate on its organs in a way that would be unthinkable in a child or adult."

"My God," she shuddered. "Why are you telling me this?"

"Because it's important so that you understand what we did and why we did it."

"I don't see. They weren't going to operate on Luke, were they?"

"No, no. Surgery was no use."

He signaled to the waitress for another drink. He knew he was stalling. He had to steel his nerve to relive the terrible trauma.

"What, then?"

"They quite simply refused to recognize the amount of pain the wee infant was in." He swallowed thickly. He could feel tears pricking his eyes. "Your mother and I knew, though. Like you, we were there. We saw. We *heard*."

The fresh drinks arrived. Bella didn't touch hers. Stephen took a stiff pull of his own. He spoke to the glass he held nursed in his hands.

"They did their best to make him 'comfortable.' Basically, that meant tranquilizing him into a semicoma half the time. He was fed by tube, of course, but he couldn't be kept too deeply tranquilized or the food uptake failed. Toward the end his autonomic systems began to break down, so they had to keep him closer to the surface. On top of that, of course, there was the treatment itself. The chemotherapy, the blood transfusions, the endless tests. And all completely and utterly hopeless. We were prolonging a life that had no hope of a future. Prolonging misery.

"I remember sitting night after night at the side of the crib, way into the early hours of morning, praying. Yes, even the godless reprobate I am, I prayed. I appealed to some divine principle of harmony, maybe I invoked it by the name of God, I don't know, but I pleaded with whatever force inspires the universe and guides the human heart and fate, I pleaded for my boy's life. In my mind I would envelop the little soul in a kind of womb of love and harmony, I'd even visualize the infected cells and imagine obliterating them with an army of healthy ones, I'd struggle to the limit of my mental power to *will* him better. But every night he got just a it worse. He'd surface for a little, just as though he were drowning, and I'd stand over him and watch him fighting this impossible fight, crying aloud in that terrible strangled way, with that tube down his throat and his mouth half taped up to hold it in position, wrestling and struggling so pitifully, and I couldn't do anything about it, nothing at all, except stand there and rage inside and plead with some nonexistent and unfeeling deity . . .

"On the morning he died, he suddenly seemed better. Do you remember? He opened his little blue eyes. He seemed to *see* us for the first time. His breathing came easier. He lay very still. I even thought he was smiling. It was wonderful. Like the clouds parting. We were filled with this wild joy. Everything was going to be all right. He was on the mend, he'd turned the corner, the treatment was working at last. All those cruel, brave hopes. Your poor mother was drained by it all, and I was even planning to take her away for a couple of days' holiday, not too far but somewhere different, just for a break. I'd called the travel agents and we were thinking of checking into a country house hotel in Vermont. The doctor had been and gone, and Luke was once again sedated. Karen was due for time off, and we'd told her to take the rest of the day. She wanted to do some shopping in the city, and you wanted to see Lorri, so you drove up together.

"Then some time around four, Joanna had gone down to the mall and I was in the kitchen, with the baby alarm on, making a call—there was a problem with the pool filter or something— when I heard this cry over the alarm. I've never heard such a sound. It was hardly human: I half thought some animal had got into the room. I rushed upstairs. It was just terrible to see. Luke was in agony. He was sobbing and howling helplessly. It went on and on. It wouldn't stop. I called the doctor, but I only got his answering service. I didn't know what to do except to hold the poor infant. So I picked him up and stood just rocking him backward and forward, with all those tubes still connecting him to the machines. I sang to him to try and drown his screams, but it was no use. Nothing anyone could do could help him.

"And then Joanna returned. I'll never forget that look on her face as she came into the room. The world seemed to crash about her. She took the little mite and just pressed him close to her. We looked at one another, and we knew we had to do something."

Bella's words came out in a hoarse whisper.

"What happened? What did you do?"

"I had already come to the decision. I suppose it's easier for the man. I hadn't borne the child, it didn't come literally out of my body. Anyway, I suppose I have a different attitude to life. More pragmatic. I don't believe in the sanctity of life as an unconditional absolute . . . "

"Stephen—"

"Right, right. We managed to get some sedative into him through the drip, and we put him back in the crib. He was quieter, but clearly much weaker, much worse. The upturn in the morning had been a false dawn. We went downstairs to the kitchen. I remember we stood on other sides of the breakfast bar and we discussed it together. She was in tears. I refused to get emotional. She was horrified at what I was proposing, but gradually I wore her down. I guess I just outargued her. She will say I forced her. I felt just as strongly as she did, but I didn't have the ingrained moral revulsion." He paused and met her eye. "But I did one thing which, looking back, I bitterly regret."

"What was that?"

He let out a breath. The simple truth was now the best.

"I would have done it myself," he said quietly. "But I knew Joanna would never forgive me. So I made *her* do it." He looked back into his drink. "It never occurred to me she would never forgive *herself*."

"You mean you—?" Bella was aghast.

"We facilitated his death."

"My God."

"Around seven o'clock the sedative wore off and the sobs of agony began again. We resedated him, and again, about ten o'clock, it started up. Joanna finally broke. At last she saw the uselessness of keeping him alive like this, and the cruelty of it." He rubbed a hand over his face. The skin felt like someone else's. "We wanted to make it beautiful. I took him out of the crib and disconnected all the tubes and lines. Joanna dressed him in his christening robe, and we took him downstairs and out into the open. The evening was warm and silky, with that surreal stillness you get up there on high summer nights. We found ourselves going to the apple orchard. I don't know why, maybe it was just especially peaceful there. Some days before, I had prepared a needle with a shot of sodium pentobarbital I'd got from the labs. They use it as an anesthetic during experiments on animals. Anyway, I had this needle in my jacket pocket. I hadn't really thought it through. So, there we were, Joanna carrying the baby in her arms, so light and insubstantial it already seemed to have given up life, and we . . . we just had to do it." His voice was choking. "She sat underneath a tree. The light was a warm soft gray. They looked so goddamn beautiful together, mother and child, my heart was breaking. Luke was whimpering again in pain. He was at the limit of his strength. She looked up at me for what to do. I suppose I was hoping he would give up, expire, just like that. But he was beginning to writhe. So I took him in my arms and I got out the needle. She hated needles. She knew how to give injections, but whenever they did it to Luke, all those times they inserted catheters and drips, she had to look away. I handed her the needle. Because I was holding him, she had to do it. I wanted her to do it. She gave me this horrified look I'll never forget, but I kind of willed her to do it. I held his arm out for her. 'Go on,' I told her, 'quick, do it, you must, spare him any more suffering.' It was terrible. She seemed hypnotized, as if she were being manipulated by some other force. A strange, glazed look came over her eyes, and she began talking to him, saying how much she loved him and how the pain was now over and he would rest sweetly forever and she would be reunited with him in the course of time and we would all be together in the Happy Land. . . .

"She did it. She was very brave. The sight of a needle going into a baby's tender flesh is one of the most awful things a parent can imagine, but she managed it. She emptied the syringe, then took him in her arms. He grew very quiet, very suddenly. It was just as if a hand had passed over him." He brushed away a tear, then went on more brusquely. "She wanted to bury him there and then, on that very spot. She wasn't really with it. She hadn't taken in the practical consequences. I mean, this was, technically, first degree murder. So I covered our traces the best I could. I put him back in his cot and hooked up the things again. That was truly awful.

"Then Karen and you came back. Luckily I got you to go to bed thinking he was just asleep. But Karen knew at once. And she knew we'd done it. She could tell from everything. She was very clever. She said absolutely nothing. We called the doctor, who came out and certified the death. We broke the news to you in the morning. The cause of death was obvious, after Luke had been so long at death's door, and there wasn't even an autopsy. That was one small mercy. But there was still Karen."

"I see." A nasty ironic glint lit Bella's eyes. "Most inconvenient for the partners in crime."

He swallowed back the whiskey. It wasn't having the analgesic effect he craved. He didn't want to have to face Bella's moral onslaught. And yet, he couldn't expect otherwise. Luke was her brother.

"Karen left the next day," he said shortly. "I saw to that. But she had words with your mother first, and I'm afraid Joanna gave in to her. Karen went away a few thousand dollars better off. She promised that would be the end of the matter. But of course it wasn't. Blackmail never ends." He shook his head. "The money doesn't matter. It's the effect on Joanna that counts. If only she would stand up to Karen. But she won't. Karen hasn't got a shred of a case in law. The evidence is destroyed. It's one word against another. Of course, Joanna can't see that. All she can ever see is her own guilt."

"So that's why you insisted on having him cremated. To destroy the evidence. You can dig up a body that's buried, but ashes tell no story, right?"

"Yes, but you must understand . . . "

Bella's glance silenced him. She sat frozen rigid, like a judge over the damned.

"I understand everything," she said quietly.

He shook his head in sorrow. There was no more he could say.

"I'm truly, truly sorry," he managed finally.

"You're not sorry you did it. You're just sorry you had to tell me."

"I'm sorry for everything. Most of all, for not doing it myself. No one would have known. You'd have been spared all this. And Joanna wouldn't have suffered all that she has. We'd probably still be together. I often think of that."

"Why did you make *her* do it, then?"

"Because I loved her and I wanted her to be free. I thought it would force her to face up to his death and not find ways to suppress it. Frankly, I don't know what the hell I thought. I only know I was completely wrong. And we've been paying for it ever since."

The silence lengthened. Bella's expression was inflexible. He reached forward to touch her hand, but she withdrew it quickly. Oh God, he groaned inside, had he forfeited her compassion, her forgiveness? Why hadn't he imagined how it would sound from her point of view before unburdening himself on her? People didn't always want the truth. Bella wanted the comfortable belief that she'd been fed at the time, that her little brother had died quietly and naturally, at night, in his sleep. But he couldn't maintain that deceit any longer. Keeping the truth buried would condemn Joanna forever to a life of torment and madness.

She was regarding him with shock and loathing. He could guess what was going through her mind.

"Luke was dying, Bella," he persisted, leaning forward. "They only gave him a matter of weeks. Weeks of hell."

"Letting someone die isn't the same as killing them," she said tightly.

"Isn't it?" he responded. "Someone is starving to death, you have spare food and you don't give it to them. Is that morally different from shooting them? One is a sin of omission, if you like, and the other a sin of commission. But both are sins. From that viewpoint, morally equivalent."

"Luke would have died in his own time," she retorted.

"In the doctors' own time," he corrected. "He was being kept alive by medical technology. His 'own time' was up the moment he was born. He was living on borrowed time."

"And you just withdrew the loan. Great."

"Look, it's not a question of whether you pull a plug out or stick a needle in. Those are morally identical. What matters always is the *intention*. If you ran over an animal and it was obviously in terminal pain, wouldn't you want to put it out of its misery? For its sake?"

"Yes, all right. But who's to say that was best for Luke's sake? He could hardly be consulted. You made the decision for him."

"We were putting him out of his misery," he repeated, seizing the opportunity of her admission. To get her to accept mercy killing in principle was nine-tenths of the argument won. He sat back, not wanting her to feel checkmated so quickly. "I agree," he conceded, "it's difficult when a person can't give their consent. That's a real ethical mine field."

"It's the slippery slope," she objected, withdrawing her admission. "Why stop at people in terminal comas and disabled babies in intractable pain? Why not kill off the mentally ill, the mentally retarded, the senile, people with Alzheimer's? In your brave new world of euthanasia, would *Mom* be safe?"

"Come on, you draw a line."

"Sure, but *who* draws *what* line?"

"Someone has to decide," he responded. "Take the case of a kid who needs surgery to save his life: it's the parents who make the decision and give the consent. Most people find that ethically acceptable on the grounds the parents love the child and have its best interests at heart." He paused. "Your mother and I did what we did because we loved Luke and had *his* best interests at heart."

She shifted uncomfortably.

"It's still taking life."

"Yes," he agreed. "It is."

"And that is wicked."

"When done for the wrong reasons and with the wrong motives."

"For whatever reason."

"You don't really mean that," he contradicted her gently. "Remember what you just said about when you'd hear him crying in the night. 'Not just crying like a baby wanting a feed,' you said. 'Crying like a creature in agony. Like he wanted to climb up the wall.' Right?"

She sank her face in her hands.

"I feel so . . . dirty. Like I've been an accomplice to a murder."

"You can imagine how your mother feels."

She looked up. Tears were pouring silently down her cheeks.

"Poor Mom," she muttered.

"And how it is each time Karen reappears and opens the wound," he went on, pressing home. "Giving in to the black-mail is just endorsing her own guilt. She has to get free of that somehow."

"Burying baby dolls is no answer," said Bella bitterly.

"The bitch knows exactly what Joanna's going through. I had it out with her just before I left New York. She didn't care. She actually laughed. What was Joanna's state of mind to her? I think she relished the torment she was inflicting."

"God, I wish she'd gone to Canada and never come back. The heartless, selfish, cruel monster."

"I can't stop thinking of that vicious trick with the doll. I find it hard to imagine anything so sadistic and vindictive. It's wicked. Evil."

Bella's eyes were burning through the tears.

"You can't let her get away with it, Stephen! You've got to do something!"

He smiled sadly. Even as he was speaking, and speaking sin-cerely, a hidden observer within him was watching with a devious eye. Bella needed to pin her anger on somebody. He had deflected it from himself by sleight of argument, but it had to find a focus. And just as he needed her forgiveness for what he'd done, he needed her implicit blessing on what he was about to do.

"I don't even know where she is."

"I do!" she cried triumphantly. "I told you. She's at the beach house. She's moved in. Laying siege to Mom."

"You're sure?" He leaned closer.

"Eddie next door told me. He's been watching the place for me." She grabbed his hand. "Come on, let's go there right now."

He squeezed her hand. He didn't want her party to *this*. He didn't even want her to think about it. He would just do what had to be done.

"Leave it to me, angel. I'll take care of her."

"So she never, ever, pesters Mom again?"

"So Mom will be free."

He swallowed back his whiskey and reached for his overcoat.

"Come on, angel. I'll get you back home."

Eliminate the source of the reminder. His words echoed in his mind as he waited in the cab as Bella hurried the twenty yards from where he'd dropped her and disappeared with a brief wave into the apartment building. The driver was waiting for instructions, but for a moment he couldn't speak. How many times had he slipped back into that building at some late evening hour, into the warm light beneath the blue and gold canopy, past the uniformed doorman, down the marbled foyer to the private elevator with its scented upholstered walls, and finally into the apartment that had, until recently, been his home. The home he shared with his family. With Bella, his blonde-haired girl, always laughing and teasing and playing practical jokes. And with Joanna, his woman love, so complex and sensuous, and so eternally intriguing. And here he was, sitting in a cab outside in the cold dark night, locked out, excluded, rejected. And why? Because of one malicious young woman whose petty greed had poisoned Joanna's mind against him, playing on her guilt until, step by step, she ended up destroying her life and love. And, in the process, his own life and love, too.

He recalled the scene in the street outside the Athletic Club and the vow he had made then. The words came back to him now like an awesome curse. *If ever I hear you have been in touch with Joanna or Bella again, I will come after you, and wherever in hell you are, I swear to God I will find you and break you in pieces.*

"Where now, sir?" The driver was growing impatient.

Stephen unclenched his fist. He felt the prick of pain where he'd been jabbing his nails into the palm.

He met the driver's eye in the mirror.

"You want to earn a couple of hundred bucks?"

The Department building reared tall and forbidding against a bright, cloudless sky. Here and there, in laboratories and offices, lights burned where cleaners were at work. The foyer was in semidarkness but for pools of light illuminating the front desk and the main elevator concourse. Behind the desk sat a security guard, reading *Hustler* magazine. He made no attempt to cover it as Stephen approached and, picking up the pen chained to the registration book, signed in under the name Don Weitzman. He flashed his Berkeley university identity card too quickly for the guard to register more than the photo and, diverting his attention by asking him to keep an eye on the cab waiting outside, hurried to the elevator concourse. He stepped inside the first and hit the button for the penthouse.

Once at the top, he let himself through the security door with the electronic pass card he had never surrendered and which had remained in his wallet all this time. As he entered the chimp dormitory, he was met by the familiar odor of fur and urine and the rustle of activity as their alert senses picked up his presence. He hurried down the passageway between the cages, trying not to look to left or right in case he would linger among these clever creatures that had been his friends, until he reached a white armored door at the end. The pass card opened this, too, and a moment later he was inside the small laboratory where the feeds and drugs were prepared.

Little had changed. Even the key to the drug cabinet lay still in its hiding place on top of the sterilizer. In a flash he had opened the cabinet and was searching for what he wanted. Tranquilizers, sedatives, stimulants, analgesics, antiseptics, anticoagulants, antibiotics, hormone additives. . . . Finally he found it. A simple, base chemical: potassium.

In large quantities, potassium was lethal. The body naturally contained small quantities of potassium in the cells. At death, this was released into the blood stream, resulting in an amount that would be fatal in a living body. At an autopsy, therefore, a high concentration of potassium in the body would register as quite normal. But who could tell if this were the effect of death, or its cause? Murder by potassium injection, he reckoned, would be virtually undetectable. Especially if—and this was a nice refinement—so as to avoid telltale bruising and puncture marks, the needle were inserted into a mole.

He found a large syringe and filled it with the chemical at full concentration—more than enough, he reckoned, to cause instant heart failure in a heavy adult—and, slipping it into his overcoat pocket, cleared his traces and made his way back through the low-lit jungle world of the primates.

As he passed their cages, he paused. Hand up, palm outward, saying *Hi*. Finger wiped across smile, to ask, *You okay?* Clenched fists to heart: *I love you*. They looked at him with glazed eyes and stupefied grimaces. Orson raised a paw in the beginnings of a sign, but the arm dropped to his side and he began scratching himself. Lana's head lolled slack on her shoulders, robbed of its sharp vitality. He moved to the cage of his favorite, Marlene, and pressed his face against the bars. She sat in the inner depths, with her back to him, body rocking. He called her name. Slowly she turned. He reeled back with a gasp. Her eyes were just empty sockets with the lids sewn up.

My God, he cried silently, what have they done to you? What has that bastard Weitzman made this place into? A vivisectionist torture chamber?

Sick and blind with fury, he shot open the bolts and reached into the cage. The chimp cowered back in terror, snapping at his hand. Gently he coaxed her toward him and lifted her out. She whimpered pitifully as she recognized his voice and smell, and her withered arms tried to make the gestures of communication at which she had once so excelled. A lump rose in his throat. The others looked doped though otherwise unharmed, but this little one, the nimblest and cleverest, and the prettiest too, with her fine honey-colored hair and slender limbs, had been robbed of the very light . . .

He couldn't do otherwise. Reaching into his pocket, he slipped out the hypodermic and, easing off the cap, sank the needle quickly into her femoral vein. She squealed, writhed for a second, gave a sudden violent shudder, then abruptly went limp. Sick and shaking, he laid the little creature back in its cage, closed the door and, checking he still had plenty left in the needle, fumbled his way down the dim-lit room to the security door. He let himself quickly out and made for the elevator, and a moment later he was striding through the lobby, out of the revolving doors and down the steps to the waiting cab.

He would try persuasion first. He would plead with her. He would threaten, cajole, bludgeon, bribe her. He'd do anything he could to get her to go away. He felt for the needle in his pocket. Pray God he wouldn't have to use it.

21

MILLER POINT WAS A LOCAL BEAUTY SPOT, a low, wooded promontory onto the ocean on the edge of a nature reserve where, in high summer, young couples drove out to make love beneath the umbrella pines. It was also exactly two miles along the shore, over rocks, and along pebbly paths, to the beach house.

Stephen directed the cab to Miller Point, where he paid the agreed fare and got out. He waited until its taillights were lost down the long track back to the main highway then, wrapping his coat tighter about him, he headed off at a brisk walk along the shore path.

The wind blew off the ocean in slanting gusts that bit through the fabric of his coat. It sent the waves crashing against the rocks, flinging great flurries of spume high into the air. From time to time he slipped on a boulder or tripped over a tree root and fell, grazing his hands and bruising his shins. The moon was a sharp sliver, too distant and too cold to do more than cast a veiled sheen over the broken surface of the sea and reduce the trees and shrubbery to gray, two-dimensional forms. Soon, far to his left, began the houses, some lit and some dark, each presenting a different outline but all crouched low against the wind coming in relentlessly off the ocean.

He glanced at his watch, angling it to catch a glimmer of moonlight. Eleven-thirty. He would reach the house at midnight. Where would she be? In bed? He quickened his pace. A thousand scenarios had rolled through his mind during the long cab journey, but he still had no real plan. It all depended how she would react. Whether she'd be *reasonable*. But he wasn't ruling out the final solution. And he wasn't risking having the cab drive him to the front door.

Eventually, the boat house at the edge of their property loomed ahead in dark silhouette. The tide was in, and the waves lapped greedily against the wooden piers, swelling and sucking through the open slats that clad the sides. Behind the clapboard doors he could hear the surge buffeting the boat against the rubber tires that protected the surrounding boardwalk. He turned his steps sharply inland and, with the wind at his back, headed up the narrow sandy strand to the low scrubland that stretched along the foot of the lawns leading up to the house. He skirted the open ground, keeping tight to the shrubbery at the sides, until finally he broke cover by the pool. There he paused and studied the familiar low, asymmetrical structure ahead.

The house was in darkness but for a solitary light burning in an upstairs room on the far corner. His pulse quickened. This was the bedroom to the nurse's suite.

He moved rapidly, not allowing himself time for reflection. Keeping to the grass, he hurried noiselessly up to the French doors in the center of the rear facade. He felt around the ground on either side until his fingers touched metal. The key was there.

In an instant he was inside. He gently closed the door behind him and stood for a moment listening to the familiar night sounds of the house: the tick of the grandfather clock in the hall, the rattle of a loose casement in the wind, the creak of a floorboard settling after the heat had gone off.

He tiptoed forward, down the corridor, into the hall, and up to the staircase. But at the foot of the stairs, he hesitated. A glimmer of light filtered down from the upstairs landing: her bedroom door was open.

He'd planned to surprise her. That would at least give him a psychological advantage. But now he realized he'd never make it upstairs and down the corridor without being heard. Maybe, instead, he would terrorize her. Disorientate her. Trick her into coming downstairs. Spook the hell out of her in the dark. Then confront her.

Beneath the stairs was a closet with the fusebox and circuit breakers. Quietly he opened the door and, finding the main house breaker, threw the switch. Instantly the glimmer of light upstairs went out. He took up position in the darkest shadows behind the stairpost. Any minute she would fumble her way downstairs, looking for a candle or a flashlight.

He crouched motionless in the dark, waiting. The clock ticked, the windows rattled, the floorboards . . .

Suddenly he froze. His breath died in his lungs.

The floorboard *behind* him . . .

He keened his senses. The darkness was suddenly alive. The hairs on his neck bristled. He was not alone. There was someone else close by, so close he could almost smell their presence. Gradually, out of the silence, came the sound of breathing. Human breathing. Deep in the shadows, barely an arm's stretch away.

The voice materialized out of the pulsating dark. A soft, disembodied hiss.

"So. Shown up at last."

He whipped round. The darkness was moving, but he could see nothing. Then he became aware of something hovering in midair just inches from his face, something that glinted faint and dull. It moved into a pale shaft of moonlight that washed in through the window on the half landing.

He was staring into the barbed tip of a harpoon.

"We'll have the lights back on."

The voice carried an edge of steel. Reeling under the shock, he groped his way into the closet and switched the breakers back on. A moment later the hall lights sprang on, and before his dazzled gaze stood the figure of Karen, dressed in a crisp white nurse's uniform and leveling a harpoon gun at his chest.

He began to bluster, to remonstrate, to play outraged incomprehension, but she silenced him curtly.

"Cut it." She motioned with the weapon. "Take the coat and jacket off. On the floor."

"Now wait," he began again. "Let's talk this through sensibly."

"I'm not that dumb, Stephen," she warned quietly. "You left your car someplace. You came along the beach. No one knows you're here. No one's going to come looking for you. Besides, it would give me great pleasure to skewer you to the wall."

For a wild moment he thought of rushing her and trying to deflect the harpoon with his coat, but he knew it was madness. The trigger was already drawn past first pressure, and every ounce of her body was taut with determination.

He began to remove his coat, abandoning his own weapon with it.

"What next?" he demanded thickly.

"Just get me what's in the safe."

"The safe? I've no idea where Joanna keeps the keys."

"It's a combination," Karen corrected him wearily. "And you know the numbers. So be smart and move your ass."

Through a blur of unreality, he led the way down the corridor to Joanna's study and switched on the light. The small, book-lined room had been ransacked. The low door had been wrenched off the paneled cabinet that housed the safe, but the safe itself was intact. An anglepoise spotlight was directed onto the dials of the lock, and on the floor all around lay a profusion of paper scribbled with combinations of numbers she had evidently unsuccessfully tried. He crouched down before the dials.

He looked up. Karen had positioned herself in the center of the room where she could keep him covered.

"If I open this," he growled, "how do I know you'll leave Joanna alone?"

"If you don't, you'll never get to know."

"There could be a lot of money in here."

"I'm going to count to five. One . . . "

He'd miscalculated badly. What the heck had he thought persuading, appealing, cajoling would do?

He moved with the speed of a cat. Grasping the spotlight, he spun it round so that it shone full in her face. She threw up a hand, dazzled. Lobbing the lamp at her like a grenade, he dived forward at the same time and hit the floor at the foot of the desk. At the same instant came the *phthutt* of compressed air and the steel shaft whistled through the air. It splintered the edge of the desk above him and, gouging a shallow channel through the flesh of his left shoulder as it passed, shivered into the paneling behind him.

He leapt to his feet and lunged forward. With a cry she

backed away and, finding herself unarmed, abruptly turned and fled from the room. As she flew down the corridor she flung the empty gun at him in a vain effort to block him, but on he still came.

A vicious slash of pain from his shoulder caused him to stumble, but he struggled on and finally caught up with her in the kitchen. She had snatched up a knife and was edging round the central island, stabbing and slashing the air between them. He grabbed pots, plates, glasses, anything he could lay his hand on, and hurled them at her. An iron pot caught her a glancing blow on the forehead. She let out a howl of pain and, screaming abuse at him, began backing out of the room. He came after her, his hands outreached like a strangler's, the sheer ferocity of his advance driving her down the corridor to the double doors that led out onto the back lawns. Cornered at the doors, she rounded on him and began jabbing the knife around in wild, vicious slashes. He cast desperately about him. On the floor a few yards back lay the spent harpoon gun. Snatching it up, he stepped forward and with a single swift blow knocked the knife out of her hand, sending it clattering uselessly across the floor.

With a cry, she turned and wrestled frantically with the door handle. Suddenly the door swung open. She tumbled out and, a second later, she was engulfed in the night.

He crouched in the lee of a bush, waiting for his eyes to grow accustomed to the deceptive tones and shapes of the moonlit world about him. The low illumination played tricks, robbing objects of their color and turning shadows into solid substance. His shirt was damp with blood, and his shoulder throbbed painfully. Ahead, he glimpsed her white-uniformed figure fleeing down the winding pathway that led to the swimming-pool changing rooms. Breaking cover, he stumbled across the lawn at an angle to head her off. He prowled cautiously round the low building, every fiber of his senses sharpened. He crept round in a full circle, he scanned the stacks of cast-iron garden furniture laid up for the winter, he tiptoed round the pump house and searched the barbecue area, but she was nowhere to be seen.

Then, far away down the path that ran along the side of the shrubbery and down toward the beach, he caught sight of her fleeting form, darting and jinking in short zigzag spurts like a hunted hare. Yet there was something purposeful about her gait and the direction she was taking. She had now broken onto open ground and was heading directly for the ocean, glancing over her shoulder from time to time.

And then he realized. The boat house! It contained an angler's armory—marlin spikes, nets and snares, ropes and lines, gutting knives, cans of gasoline, a pistol for firing flares in distress. . . .

Clutching his shoulder to contain the pain, he ran fast and low across the open ground and plunged into the coarse scrub beyond. Even though he knew every twist and wind of the tracks, he reached the boat house just moments too late. She was already scrambling down the final steps onto the boardwalk and, before he could intercept her, she had crossed the porch and slipped in through the clapboard door.

Cautiously he followed, but instead of going inside he crept round the platform that ran round the sides. Some way beneath his feet, visible through the open slats of the walkway, the ocean fizzed and frothed. He tiptoed along the slippery boards, his ears keened for the slightest sound, but he could hear nothing apart from the continual crash and hiss of the waves beneath the building.

Suddenly came the straining whir of a starter-motor. She was trying to get the boat going! What was in her mind? He couldn't stop to think. Any minute, she'd have started the motor and be away.

Skidding on the planks, he tore round to the door and burst inside. Ahead lay the boat, its moorings slipped, slewing around in the wash of the ocean. She was inside, bent over the controls. The engine was coughing, but it wouldn't fire.

He cast around the shadows for some implement. A broken oar, a box of lead-weighted diving belts, various fishing rods . . . and, attached to a coil of rope, a small grappling anchor with four vicious curved barbs. He seized the anchor by the rope and, swinging it above his head, released it like a lasso. It whipped through the air and caught her round the middle. The barbs bit through her uniform into her flesh. She let out a scream. He began hauling her bodily toward him, but she managed to grab the rope and pulled against him with all her strength. For a moment she gained the advantage. Gradually she backed to the side of the boat and was mounting the edge when, quite suddenly, he slipped and let go. The rope shot out of his hands and, with the tension released, she fell backward. She fought to regain her balance, but just then the swell caught the boat, opening a sudden gap with the landing stage. With a shriek of horror, she toppled backward into the chasm, the anchor ripped free and, with the next swell, the gap closed again.

He scrambled round to find she had been swept underneath the boardwalk. He could see her through the gaps in the planks. The waves were battering her back and forth, one moment sweeping her up against the underside of the boardwalk, the next flinging her against the concrete piers, then dragging her back with the ebb only to carry her up and forward once again with the oncoming swell. She was screaming, choking, flailing her arms in a desperate attempt to catch hold of something firm. For a moment she got a grasp on one of the boards just at his feet, her fingers frantically clawing the edges for a purchase, and then the next wave curled through the open slats and swept her away down the channel beneath the boardwalk and into the inky dark.

For all his rage and hatred, he couldn't just stand there and watch her drown. He fell to his knees and tried to wrench up the boards, but they were nailed solid. He raced back to the door and fumbled around in the semidarkness for a crowbar, an ax, anything. Finally his fingers lit upon a heavy lump hammer. He began smashing the boards with the hammer, laying on blow after blow until he'd hacked away a body-size hole. He reached inside and waited for the ebb to suck her back past him. For a moment he caught her sleeve as she passed, but the resorbent current tore her from his grasp and flung her against a jagged metal girder.

He heard the next wave breaking far away, and when it arrived it seemed to lift the whole structure with it. It caught the weakly struggling form and swept it past him again with an irresistible force. He saw her pale face upturned in a final frantic plea, her eyes wide with ultimate terror. He grabbed at her, but the onrush was too strong: it carried her past him and broke with an explosive crash against the concrete pier. Nothing seemed to happen for a long moment, then she came back into view, floating gently on the ebb, face down and motionless.

Eventually, using the barbed anchor, he managed to hook her and haul her out. He laid her on the boardwalk. She was quite dead.

Twenty minutes later, about half a mile off the coast, he consigned her corpse to the ocean. Weighted with heavy lead diving belts strapped, round her waist, neck and ankles, she tumbled into the water and sank fast, leaving scarcely a ripple or bubble. Then, shivering with shock and cold and fighting waves of pain from his shoulder, he turned the boat about and chugged his way slowly back to the shore.

Several stiff whiskies restored him. Lint and bandages temporarily stanched his wound, a shallow but bloody gash through the muscle of the shoulder. Upstairs, he packed her few belongings into her holdall and tidied away all traces of her presence. Then he went to Joanna's study and, having cleared up the evidence of the fight, settled down at the typewriter to compose a careful farewell letter from Karen. He went through several drafts until he felt satisfied. Then, enclosing the key to the front door he'd retrieved from her purse, he sealed the envelope and addressed it to Joanna at the Park Avenue apartment.

The first glimmer of dawn was creeping over the ocean when he made a final tour of the house to check all was back to normal and finally took to the road. He took her car. Papers he'd found showed it was on hire from a rental firm in downtown New York. He drove slowly, conscious he had drunk well over the limit. At a rest area off the highway, he junked the holdall in a garbage bin. The first commuters were already swelling the roads as he reached Manhattan. On his way he stopped at the apartment and, relieved to find an unfamiliar doorman, handed in the letter. He headed on downtown, where he left the car outside the rental firm and returned the keys in the key-drop. Finally, overcome with exhaustion, he hailed a cab and made for the refuge of the Athletic Club.

Bella looked across the breakfast bar where her mother sat puzzling over a letter. She had just asked if she'd like her coffee poured but she'd received no reply. Usually she'd respond like Pavlov's dog at the mention of coffee: Stephen used to tease her about it.

"Who's that from, Mom?" she asked finally.

Joanna looked up, perplexed.

"Karen."

Bella started violently.

"Let me see."

She reached forward and snatched the letter. She skimmed it first for its sense, then read it again more carefully. When she'd come to the end, she let out a whistle. This was Stephen's doing. How the heck had he pulled it off?

"How about that, then!" she exclaimed. "Isn't it wonderful? Don't you feel relieved?"

Her mother's frown deepened.

"I'm not sure what I feel," she replied.

"But listen to what she says." She began reading the letter aloud. "'Dear Joanna, You may find this hard to believe, but I've been doing some thinking holed up in this dump here'—'dump' she calls it, what a nerve!—'and, I suppose, rattling round on my own I got a bit lonesome and called up Jake, he's the guy I shacked up with in Montreal and he wanted to get married but I said No. Well, his uncle just died and left him a whole bundle, and I guess I was missing him . . .' Gee, she does go on!"

"I've read it."

"But here's the point. 'So this is just to say I'm quitting the States and getting out of your hair, this time for good. The past is the past and the chapter's closed. I'm starting again, a new place, a new guy, a new life, and I don't want anything hanging over from before. I won't write or call again. I just want to forget all about it. Good luck with your life. Yours, Karen. P.S. I enclose the door key.' There you are, Mom. Rid of her at last!"

Joanna shook her head in puzzlement.

"First I heard of this Jake," she said.

"What does that matter? Just be thankful she's gone! Gone for good. And good riddance, I say."

"I'm surprised she makes such a song and dance about it." She shrugged and began sifting through the rest of her mail. "It was all so long ago."

"What do you mean?" cried Bella, startled. "Think of what she's done to you! Remember that vile doll she sent?"

"I always said the girl had no class. She did apologize, though."

"And what about milking you of all that money?"

"I don't remember anything about money."

"She was blackmailing you, Mom! I know she was. Don't pretend she wasn't."

Her mother's face registered surprise.

"Well, I suppose I may have helped her out now and again." She responded. "Karen was one of the family. She was a good nurse, very helpful and obliging. She never complained about the hours. She came back afterward to visit, from time to time. Never stayed long, though. Always flitting in and out. Not the kind to settle down. Maybe this Jake is the answer."

Bella listened, aghast. Her mother was talking in a strange, mechanical tone. She spoke as though she were reciting an account to a stranger.

"I can't believe you're serious, Mom," protested Bella.

Joanna rose and collected up the plates and glasses.

"Come along, darling, hurry and finish your breakfast or you'll be late again. We haven't got time to chat."

"But don't you *see?* It changes everything."

"Bella," retorted her mother crisply, "I don't know what's gotten into you this morning. Anyway, I have too much to do to listen to your stories."

Bella tried one last time. She got up and shook her mother by the shoulders.

"Karen's gone, Mom!" she cried. "Think about it. We're free. Don't you see? We're *free.*"

Her mother drew away with an expression, as though her daughter was going crazy. As she did so, a glass slipped from her hand and shattered on the tiled floor. She put down the other dishes and bent to pick up the broken glass. Bella went for a dustpan and brush and turned back to see blood streaming down her mother's hand. With a cry she rushed for a cloth, but Joanna went on picking up the splinters of broken glass in her bare fingers, with the blood pouring down her hand and spattering the floor in thick spots. She didn't seem to notice it or to feel anything. She carried on clearing up the glass, while Bella stood watching in a stupefied silence, then took the cloth and wiped her hand just as though it were water and not blood. Only then did she appear to notice the gash, now bleeding more profusely than ever. She looked at it in a distant, calculated way, rather as a doctor might examine the wound of a patient, then reached for the first-aid drawer and began dressing it. All the time she kept up an easy patter about the domestic arrangements for the day—she had meetings out round town all afternoon, and Bella would have to help herself to a snack from the fridge to keep the wolf from the door until she got back—but never once did she mention the letter from Karen or refer to anything Bella had said about it. Just like the pain from her wound, Karen simply no longer existed for her. She had rewritten the story.

The telephone woke Stephen from a sleep tormented by nightmares. On a reflex he had snatched up the receiver before the wave of anxiety and guilt hit him. The body had been washed ashore, the police had interviewed the cab driver and the trail now led inexorably to a small suite of rooms on the eleventh floor of the Athletic Club . . .

"Stephen? Are you there?"

It was Bella. He struggled onto one elbow. A streak of agony shot through his shoulder and he let out an involuntary grunt of pain. She asked if he was all right, but there was a deeper anxiety in her tone.

"Fine, fine," he replied quickly. "What's up? You got the letter? Joanna read it?"

"She read it."

"But?"

"Well, *I* think it was brilliant. A master stroke. Goodness knows how you got Karen to write it."

"But how did Joanna react?"

From the moment's pause at Bella's end, he knew the worst. He listened, numb, as the girl recounted the scene at breakfast that morning over the letter. He listened in silence until she came to the end. His heart was sunk in despair, but he knew he mustn't show it. And right now, he had to offer the poor girl some hope.

"Do you think it might help," he began, "talking to her away from home, somewhere where there aren't the memories? Why not get out of school early and go and see her at the salon?"

"You can never get her in the afternoons. Nobody knows her movements. She has meetings she fixes herself. Listen, I've got to get back now. I'll try and call you tonight. You aren't planning on leaving town quite yet, are you?"

He had a seminar to give the following day. He could cancel

that, but he had a series of vital commitments ahead in the closing weeks of the semester.

"I'll see it through," he promised rashly.

"Thank you, Stephen," she said with a fervency in her voice
that melted his heart. "I wish I could repay you somehow."

"Don't think like that. It's my own unfinished business, too."

"Well, maybe, you know, you and Mom . . . "

"Angel, you just get back and try not to worry. I'll work
something out. We're half way there."

She blew a kiss down the phone and hung up. He climbed
out of bed and took a couple of painkillers, then sat back down
on the bed with his head in his hands.

It hadn't worked. He had removed the cause of Joanna's
flight into fantasy, but it was too late to recall her. She was too
far gone. She had reconstructed the past for herself in a way
that wrote out her own guilt, and if she didn't have a guilty con-
science anymore, then Karen couldn't prick it. Quite simply,
Karen couldn't be a thorn in her side. So deep was her need for
this version of reality that she clung to it in the face of an otherwise clear reprieve.

But his analysis had been at fault, too. Disposing of Karen
had been a necessary, but not a sufficient, condition. She represented for Joanna the reminder of her guilt. Removing Karen
was to remove the reminder. But the guilt still remained.

He replayed his conversation with Bella in his mind, searching for any kind of lead to suggest where he might go from
there. For a fleeting moment he had a wild idea of going to the
salon himself and forcing Joanna to talk, but he knew it would
be fruitless. He, too, had been completely written out of her version of the past. In any event, as Bella had told him, she
wouldn't be there, anyway. *You can never get her in the afternoons. Nobody knows her movements. She has meetings she fixes
herself.*

Did she, indeed?

An idea slowly took form in his mind. It was an idea that fitted perfectly with everything he knew of her state of mind. And
it would prove conclusively whether, and if so how deeply, the
guilt still remained.

The afternoon sun was painfully bright for his unslept eyes, but
it carried no warmth. A low December wind prowled the streets,

stirring remnants of leaves about his feet. He stood, as once before, some way across the street, too far to be easily spotted yet close enough to monitor any comings and goings from the basement apartment. From time to time a passerby would cast him a suspicious glance, for in this hurried city you stood out if you stood still. He didn't give a damn, he was irritable and in pain. The resident Club medic had dressed his shoulder, but it still throbbed through the painkillers. But, most of all, he was angry. Angry with himself. Here he was, somewhere on the Upper West Side, standing watching an apartment like some half-assed private dick, following a wild way-out hunch for no better reason than that he *had* no better reason. Why did he imagine she would come here again at all? Why conceivably did he think she would come here *every afternoon?* He was grasping at straws. The fact was, he had no idea at all. Joanna's mind was an alien land to him, and he no longer had a passport to it.

He was turning away, cold and tired and frustrated, when he heard a door slam. A second later, hurrying up the steps and along the narrow path, emerged the figure he'd been waiting for.

She wore the red dress beneath a white Burberry raincoat, her blonde hair was swept back in a knot and her makeup was more striking than before, but it was *her*. The other Joanna.

A hundred questions crowded into his mind but, oddly, he could think of nothing except how unbelievably beautiful she was. He was stunned. Why had he never opened up this other side of her? Perhaps it wasn't too late. Maybe—the wild idea struck him—he could adopt a new identity, too, and reenter her life as a stranger, and they could become lovers . . .

But the idea froze even as it took form.

She already had a lover. Of course. That was where she went every afternoon. She dressed up and went to visit her lover.

The sudden stab of pain almost doubled him up. It left him sick and winded, as though he'd been kicked in the stomach. He gathered his coat about him and stumbled off down the road after her. He'd follow her, track her to this man's place, burst in on them, beat the shit out of him, grab hold of her, and take her away.

He followed her, as before, in a cab. Through the rear window he sought to read her body language. She hardly ever looked out of the window: didn't that imply she did this routinely? She kept checking her watch anxiously, as though afraid of being late. She constantly touched up her makeup and patted her hair, too, in the way of one nervous about her appearance. When held up in traffic, she sat forward on the edge of the seat, her whole form taut with impatience. Surely such a fraught state was no prelude to a romantic assignation.

When finally her cab pulled up in one of the rougher city streets off First Avenue and she hurriedly climbed out, he began to feel slightly easier. No woman like Joanna would possibly come here for such assignations.

But then, this woman was not Joanna.

She went quickly up the steps of a gaunt gray stone house and without announcing herself, she pressed an intercom bell. A second later, the door opened automatically and she disappeared inside, closing it quickly behind her.

He paid off his cab and, turning up the collar of his overcoat, slipped up the steps after her. There was just one intercom button, with no name. It was evidently a single house, not apartments. The windows of the upper two stories ran from floor to roof and were blacked out with blinds. Was this a photographer's studio? Why no company name? Who *was* she visiting?

He hurried back into the street and headed toward the avenue. Fifty yards down, however, he crossed the road and retraced his steps on the other side. Two youths with lank dreadlocks were sitting on the stoop of the house opposite, idling away the time. He struck up a conversation, and from them he gleaned the outline of what went on in that house.

A man named Louis lived there. Known in the streets as Lou. He was some kind of famous artist. He kept himself to himself. He always had these fancy chicks coming to the house, mostly blondes, each one a million dollars. They modeled for him—well, some of the time. His latest was the woman just gone in. She visited regularly, maybe three times a week, always afternoons. . . .

Stephen didn't wait to hear more. He stumbled away to the avenue and fell into the first bar he found. Two o'clock in the afternoon was a hell of a time to get drunk, but he couldn't think of anything else to do. He'd committed the nearest thing to first degree murder to save the woman he loved from certifiable insanity only to find she was indissolubly wedded to her new fantasy life and merrily off screwing some bloody painter, in fact so goddam happy at her regular rutting that the last thing she wanted was anything forcing her to come back to reality and give it up. The letter so carefully contrived to hit exactly the right psychological note, not to mention the body lying weighted hand and foot at the bottom of the ocean, was all very good for releasing the Joanna he had known, the Joanna *before*. But this Joanna was a stranger. She was a stranger even to her own daughter. She had crossed an irreversible frontier, and she now inhabited a land where she was far beyond his reach.

What had he just said, *the woman he loved?* The admission said it all. That was the real reason he was so angry. He was *jealous*.

He ordered a beer to chase the whiskey, then a whiskey to chase the beer. There was, simply, nothing else he could do.

22

CRISTINA SANK AGAINST THE BACK OF THE DOOR and waited for her thoughts to grow still. The cool aroma of turpentine and gutted candles sent her senses into a heady swirl, stirring within her the familiar forbidden yearnings. The ritual was under way, each stage following the last with an exquisite necessity. Gradually, as her eyes accustomed themselves to the dim-lit hallway, she began her ascent of the staircase. With each step the light ahead grew stronger until it filled the door frame at the top. She walked toward it slowly, already trembling with anticipation and desire. Nothing else existed outside this moment and this place. Eternity inched forward by the beats of her heart.

Louis came forward from behind the drapes. His dark eyes burned with a strange new intensity. He took her hand and kissed it lightly, then without a word he drew her closer and cupped her left breast in the palm of his hand, stretching the thin material as tight as a second skin. Her nipple hardened involuntarily, shaming her as always by its blatant betrayal of her desire. He coaxed it harder still with the point of his nail. But he was not so much fondling it as feeling it, rather as someone might assess fruit at a market stall. Then, nodding to himself with satisfaction, he turned away to a sideboard and a moment later returned with the two ritual goblets of wine. He still had not spoken.

She glanced quickly about the room, registering the slight changes. The easel with the large rectangular canvas had been drawn forward toward the center and was only half covered in white sheeting, although from where she was standing she still could not make out the subject. Beside stood a plate camera on a tripod. Canvas and camera were both directed toward the low dais on which was placed the large brass bed, its mattress and bolster laid with ivory silk sheets.

But what sent a tremor of fear and anticipation through her was the curious noose-like object lying on the bed. He must have followed her eye, for he led her over to the bed and handed it to her to examine.

It was a broad leather belt formed in a circle. Its flat surface was embroidered in silver braid and its edges were padded in the way of a saddle, while a series of thongs at each end served for a clasp. It had a pagan, primitive look, like some kind of armlet or anklet, yet it was too big for an arm or an ankle. A slave collar, perhaps, from early colonial days? It was clearly some implement of restraint, for it was affixed by a length of stout plaited rope to the upper rung of the bed-head. Yet a kindly implement, for pains had been taken to soften the hard raw-cut edges and to decorate its surface for a pleasing effect. But the real softness came from that supple gloss that only derived from contact with living flesh.

"Beautiful, no?"

He spoke in a half whisper, his tone pure velvet.

"It's . . . interesting." Her mouth was uncomfortably dry.

"Mexican," he went on, his eyes fixed upon her rather than the object itself. "It's old, of course, but not *that* old." He smiled faintly. "There's a limit to authenticity. At least as regards the props."

"What is it?" she managed.

"Let's say it's a kind of halter."

She shivered at the touch of the leather. Who else had worn this thing, and in what circumstances? She stared, mesmerized. Her breath came short and shallow. Already the numbness was creeping through her body, dissolving her strength and robbing her limbs of their force. Her flesh cried out in desire, but she could only wait, wait for the word that would begin the slow, magical, inexorable process of her release.

It was no word, but a gesture. A signal of the hand, quite careless, bidding her to undress. She laid aside the wine glass and, instinctively turning her back, slipped out of the red dress and the silk slip, the garter and stockings. In a moment she was quite naked. As usual, he remained fully clothed.

He began caressing her slowly, almost idly, letting his fingertips trace their way round the contours of her body, down her spine to her buttocks, hovering for a reflective moment upon the tattoo, the indelible mark of his authority over her, then rising again along the flat of her stomach, round her breast to her neck. Gently he angled her head back so as to stretch the neck, and for a moment his touch followed the line of tautened sinews and strayed over the soft underside. Then, tightening his grasp under her jaw like an angler carrying a fish by the gills, he led her over to the bed and slipped the tall leather collar where his hand had been. Finally, he positioned her so that she was half raised on her knees and leaning forward yet prevented from falling by the halter round her neck and the rope fixing it to the bed-head. Then, spreading her knees so that her neck was wrenched still further back and placing her hands upon her breasts, he began to work his fingertips up her soft inner flanks, up and round and higher and higher yet never quite all the way to the smoldering crux of her loins. Soon the thirst to be possessed was unbearable. She heard a low moan rattle in her throat. She writhed and twisted to try and bring her burning sex in contact with his hand, but all the time he deliberately eluded her. Then quite abruptly, gasping with the suddenness and surprise, she felt something big, impossibly big, work its way through the tight aperture of her anus and slide with shocking ease to penetrate deep inside her, and no sooner had she caught her breath again than another thick, rigid priapus sank simultaneously into her sex itself, and she felt her hands removed from her breasts and one made to grasp a strap at the front and the other a strap at the back and each, as she realized, attached to either end of a downward-curving strip of some stiff material on which the two upward prongs were mounted so that by pulling on the strap in turn she could oscillate the two prongs in and out of her in turn in a rocking motion, faster or slower or tighter or slacker as the command or the compulsion directed.

He had withdrawn behind the camera and was shooting off

film, triggering one exposure after another in quick succession, gradually faster and faster as she involuntarily quickened the pace toward a climax.

"Harder!" he spat the order. "Faster. More. Give it more. I want to see you go crazy. Drive yourself. Push to the limit."

Her neck was thrown back and straining against the collar. The world rolled wildly about her. Her whole body felt agape, melting in an ecstasy of abandonment. On and on he drove her, forcing her from one giddy peak to another, yet higher until she scarcely had breath left to scream and she felt she was bursting into fragments like a grenade exploding in slow motion. Through a dazed blur she was aware he had abandoned the camera and was tearing off his clothes. She had hardly registered a swell of joy that he was at last naked with her when the tension round her neck abruptly released, and as she fell involuntarily forwards she felt herself being caught and thrust onto her back, and with his lean, muscular body pressing down upon hers, an instant later, quite suddenly and ruthlessly, entered by him.

She was soaring high in the stratosphere of her conscious-ness where nothing existed except the pure sensation of ecstasy. She was floating beyond form or flesh, as invisible and expan-sive as the very skin of the ether, in a realm where there was nei-ther light nor dark, sound nor silence. She was the universe, whole and part. An eternity passed before gradually she felt the fragments of her being settling back to earth, gently floating down like leaves falling silent and unseen in a great void.

She awoke to find herself lying curled on the a beneath a light counterpane. Every muscle of her body was sore, every fiber trembling. She felt like a time traveler returned from a voyage into eternity, finding the world unchanged. She cast about her to reassemble the pieces of her context. The room with its long rich drapes, the cool afternoon light cascading down from the skylights above, the bed upon which she lay still with the halter affixed to the brass bed-head . . . Gradually it all came back into focus.

He was standing at the easel, now fully clothed, painting. As she stirred, he glanced over the top of the canvas. She could see just his eyes, but even from that distance she could feel the heat of their intensity.

"Think of today," he said softly, "as the prelude."

She swallowed.

"Prelude to what?"

"To tomorrow."

Tomorrow. The way he said the word, melding promise with threat, sent a chill shiver through her. His tone of voice was still of velvet but the undertone was of iron. She yearned to know what further extremity of pleasure he had in store, even just to be granted a hint of what it might be, but in all that passed between them, in all the unbridled freedoms of the flesh, this was the sole taboo. They lived in an Eden of the senses where the only forbidden fruit was borne of the tree of knowledge.

"Pain and pleasure," he mused. "One thinks of them as opposites, when in fact, at the extremes, they're identical. Like two ends of a strip joined to make a circle."

"Not to the person feeling them," she shivered.

He came round the front of the canvas.

"If I showed you two faces, one in agony, the other in ecstasy, I doubt you could tell the difference."

"Really?"

"At the ultimate, they're indistinguishable. The facial musculature used to express both emotions is exactly the same. Remember the Cranach painting of St. Catherine of Alexandria at the Dresden Gallery? And the Albrecht Altdorfer in the Vienna Museum? Put her in a different context, replace the torture chamber with a bedchamber and the flagellator with a lover, and you'd believe she was having an orgasm."

She glanced at the camera. Inside it was a roll of film showing a face contorted with the extremity of pleasure. A curious, chilling thought wormed its way through her consciousness.

"And the other way round, too?"

"Of course. A woman at the peak of her climax could be mistaken for a woman, say, in the last stage of labor." He retrieved her glass and refilled it. "Another drink, Cristina?"

"Thank you."

She took a deep gulp of the chilled wine. Whether it was the drink or a draft in the room, but a cold frisson rippled through her body, and even after she had put her clothes back on again and drunk a cup of hot black coffee it still remained with her, deep in the bones of her soul like an instinctual echo of some ancient and long since outgrown warning signal.

But from the moment she left that room and let herself out of that house, she was already counting the hours to the morrow and whatever delights and dangers it should bring.

It was already dark when Stephen tumbled out into the bustle and bright lights of the street. Passersby cast him the particular New York scowl of distaste reserved for dog shit on the sidewalk and anyone begging for money. So what if he was drunk? He had every right to be. She was still his wife, after all. It was bad enough that she'd taken flight from real life, the life that had once included him, and invented this insane fantasy role for herself. But to go so far downhill as to screw around in the dregs of society and, worst of all, to throw herself into it with such impatient eagerness, was more than deranged and dangerous: it was disgraceful and degrading. She was dressing the harlot and playing the slut. Was *that* what all this psychological trauma had driven her to?

He groaned aloud. How could his fine Joanna, always so soignée and scented, so refined in all her sensibilities, lower herself to the squalor of a cheap and gaudy hooker giving afternoon relief to some gross lecher calling himself an artist? Artist, indeed! Arsehole by any other name. Why, Joanna, *why?*

He found his steps taking him back to the house. He stood in the street outside, scanning the gaunt and grimy facade. High in the upper room, through the windows that sloped back along the roof, he could see lights burning. Downstairs, all was dark. He stumbled up the steps and leaned on the intercom buzzer. For a long time nothing happened. Then he heard the *click* as the receiver at the other end was picked up. No one replied.

He pressed his mouth close to the transmitter.

"Is that Louis?" he slurred. "Is that the creep who's screwing my wife? She's the one you screwed this afternoon, in case you've forgotten already. Maybe she's still there. So, what's she doing, modeling in the nude, eh? Let me tell you something, asshole. She's having you on! She's not who you think she is. She's faking on you, man!"

With another *click* the receiver went dead.

Enraged, he flew down the steps and stood in the middle of the street, shouting obscenities at the top of his voice until he was hoarse.

"Hey, Louis, you creep, come on down! I know she's in there! Come out so I can bust your fucking dick!"

A car swerved, narrowly missing him, and the driver hurled an insult at him. A window in the next house flew up and a voice yelled at him to do something colorful to himself he'd never even heard of. The youths still hanging around on the stoop opposite began cheering, or jeering, he couldn't tell which.

The light glowing through the skylight abruptly went out. The house remained silent and dark.

Sobbing with rage and frustration, he turned away and headed up the street. The chill evening air was beginning to sober him, and he quickened his pace, desperate to get clear. He was appalled at himself for losing control like that. And angry with himself for acting like a jealous, jilted husband. Hadn't he buried all that in the past? He was a new man, in a new world, with a new future. His feelings for Joanna had gone out of the door with the suitcase, hadn't they, and he'd been rebuilding his life quite satisfactorily on his own since. Besides, he'd been drunk, and that always made him maudlin and sentimental.

But the more he recited this litany, the more he knew that it was not true. He might chose to deny or avoid them, but his feelings for Joanna were as strong as ever they had been, and it had taken the sight of actually losing her to another man to bring this sharply home to him. He groaned inwardly. He was trapped. There was no countermanding the dictates of the heart.

Of all Joanna's acquaintances in the glitzy world of high art— the "arty-farty-glitterati," as he called them—Stephen felt most drawn to David Blum.

Short, balding, with thick frameless glasses and moist lips, Blum was not outwardly an appealing figure of a man. He carried a small aerosol in his palm which every few minutes he sprayed in his mouth to mask his halitosis, though with hardly more effect than tipping perfume down a drain, and his complexion was so smooth and polished that it reflected the gallery lights like a mirrored ball on a Christmas tree. He was grossly opinionated, too—he believed there were only two kinds of art, great art and crap, and nothing great had been painted since the Renaissance—but this gave him an appealing honesty in face of the fawning and fatuous world of dealers and collectors and

socialites that high-priced modern art attracted. He played the
social game, and very successfully, but with an irony that set
him above it. And of all those in Joanna's circle Stephen met in
his first months in New York, Blum had been the most assidu-
ous and attentive. He might have been courting Joanna and her
wealth through him, but at least there was charm in his devi-
ousness.

It was ten in the morning and Stephen was waiting in the
gallery when Blum at last swept in. He was wearing a black
broad-brimmed hat, white silk opera scarf, and a long fur coat
that trailed the floor. He handed his hat, coat, and scarf to the
receptionist, who told him in an outraged stage whisper he had
a visitor waiting without an appointment. He checked his watch
with an impatient frown before turning to see who it was. His
expression suddenly tightened, then relaxed in a wreath of
smiles.

"Stephen!" he exclaimed, advancing with outstretched hand.
"Good to see you."

"Hello, David. You're looking well."

"I thought you were lost to us. We were all so sorry to hear
about you and Joanna." He tightened his handclasp. "You're not
thinking of staging a comeback?"

"I'm just on a flying visit."

Blum's face assumed an expression of regret, but his manner
remained closely attentive.

"Well, then, to what do I owe this pleasure?"

"I need your help, David. You know everyone on the scene."

"Oh God," he groaned, "not you, too. Don't do it, Stephen.
There's no money dealing in art. They're jumping off bridges,
even on the coast."

"That's not it. I want some information about a painter."

"Romanesque or medieval?"

"His first name is Louis and he lives on the Upper East
Side, off First Avenue." He gave the address. "I want to get all I
can on him."

Blum faltered. He seemed to be searching for time.

"What's your interest?" he asked.

Stephen leaned closer.

"Come on, David, we're old friends."

Blum hesitated, then cast him a hard, calculating glance.

"You'd better come into my office," he said.

He led the way down a corridor off the main gallery and into a small, club-like room smelling of cigar smoke and varnish. He closed the door behind them and placed himself on the other side of a partner's desk. He spread his hands on the leather top like a pianist striking a chord.

"Louis van Nyman," he announced. "I know Louis. I deal in his work." His eyes sharpened behind his glasses. "You're interested in acquiring some of his art?"

"It's more personal."

"I'm strictly a dealer, Stephen. I don't get involved in the private lives of the artists I represent . . . "

Stephen interrupted him bluntly.

"There's a girl he's been seeing. Someone I happen to be crazy about. I just need to know who he is and what's going on."

Blum sat abruptly forward.

"A girl?" he echoed. "She wouldn't be tall, blonde, a smart dresser?"

"That's her," replied Stephen uncomfortably, not wanting to be pressed for her name. But the dealer volunteered one.

"You mean Cristina?"

Stephen nodded. So she'd assumed a name, too.

Blum was watching him closely, as if judging how far he should go. Abruptly his face broadened into a smile. A connection seemed to dawn upon him.

"Son of a gun!" he chuckled. "Poaching Joanna's models! And the nuptial bed still warm. Still, I guess it's always open season in love and war."

Stephen's mind was working feverishly.

"I didn't know you knew her," he said innocently.

"Cristina came to my last opening, though I hardly recognized her. I could say I know her better without her clothes on." He smiled at Stephen's reaction. "Take it easy, my friend. She may lie with Louis, but she also sits for him."

"Portraits?"

"Nudes, mostly."

Stephen swallowed.

"You have any of his work here I could see?"

"Nothing much."

"But something?"

"I wouldn't want to distress you, Stephen."

"It's okay."

"Well, we do have some of his nudes. Just small studies, though."

"Show me."

Affecting a resigned shrug, the dealer led the way out of the office and took him down the corridor into a small, windowless back room hung with paintings.

This was clearly a private salon for special collectors. Stephen followed him over to one wall on which a series of nudes in oils were displayed. Each was no larger than a book, being painted on board rather than canvas in thin glazes that gave a finish as smooth as the body itself. Something strange and chilling about the quality of the flesh made him look closer. He repressed a shiver. The naked skin was but the surface, and beneath, built up stage by stage and just visible in its layers, lay the elements of the body matter itself—blood vessels, glands, muscle fiber, fatty tissue, organs, bones—giving the whole a ghostlike translucency. It was as though he were looking *through* the body, stripping away the very skin and rendering the nude itself naked.

They all portrayed a woman, the same woman, in various erotic poses. In one, she wore a red dress that was opened so as to expose a broad ribbon of flesh from her throat to her sex. He gave a start. It was *that* red dress, the very one he'd seen Joanna wearing! She had long blonde hair and a high-boned oval face and sensuous lips that gave full expression to her state of plea- sure. It was a face that bore a distant resemblance, but it was not Joanna's face. Nor, and he should know, were they at all Joanna's breasts or Joanna's sex.

Blum was regarding him closely.

"True to life, would you say?"

Stephen grunted his agreement. So, Louis van Nyman was screwing all his models, and this Cristina was just another one, after all, who came to sit and to lie interchangeably, perhaps on the evening shift. Maybe they were all tall blondes who dressed smartly. Would a painting of Joanna in such a pose appear in the gallery? He shuddered at the thought. At least, Blum didn't seem to know Joanna had any part of this squalid setup and he himself had managed not to reveal it.

"It appeals to a special taste," the dealer was saying. "Not quite your cup of tea, isn't that what you say?"

Stephen shook his head.

"To think a man can make a living out of this!" he muttered.

"Oh, these are just potboilers."

"You mean, there's more?"

Blum hesitated. His mouth betrayed agitation.

"You'd expect a man of this talent to have his real work."

"What *is* his real work?"

Blum took off his glasses and began polishing them, transparently a displacement activity. His creaseless face suddenly screwed up like a newborn infant's.

"Once in a while, Louis produces a masterwork," he began carefully. "He's working on one now. It's his most ambitious project to date. That's why we haven't had anything in from him lately."

"What's different about a 'masterwork'?"

"Well, it's on a far larger scale altogether. Life-size. And the subject. . . . Let's just say it is for a collector with a *very* special taste."

"Like how special?"

Blum inspected his glasses but, as if unsatisfied with the result, continued polishing them. Small beads of perspiration had sprung out on his bald pate. Perhaps it was the heat of the spotlights in that small, airless room.

"They used to say of Paganini that he was possessed by the devil," he remarked by way of reply. "His music was, literally, diabolical. I would say the same of van Nyman's art. His work— his *real* work, not these sketches—is the closest I've ever seen to the living hand of the devil."

He turned to face Stephen. He gave him the full intensity of his naked stare. Something disturbing about the stare sent a deep shiver through him. Maybe it was just the apparent vulnerability in the pink, plump, screwed-up face in contrast with the words he was uttering. . . .

A momentary silence fell. Stephen gave an uneasy chuckle.

"I heard, in his street they call him Lou. Like short for Lucifer."

The small, dark eyes bored into Stephen's. When finally the dealer spoke, there was no corresponding chuckle in his voice.

He paused. "Very appropriate."

"And it doesn't trouble you? I mean, how do you feel about handling this stuff? After all, you represent him."

"I represent his art, not his principles."

"And you can dissociate one from the other?"

"It's called business." His voice lowered. "My own private tastes don't come into it."

"That's what all hardcore porn merchants say."

"I didn't hear that, Stephen." He cleared his throat. "I'm only telling you this because you asked. And, I suppose, I would rather you heard about him from me than got a wild garbled version from someone else."

"I'm sorry. Tell me more. So, what's his 'real' work actually like?"

"Very well, then," began Blum, cautiously mollified. "The first of these masterworks, and I still think his finest, was his *Martyrdom of St. Lawrence.* He based it on the frescoes in the chapel of San Vincenzo at Volturno. You're familiar with them? Of course not." He paused to replace his glasses. His eyes sprang forward like darts. "His is quite the most remarkable work. You can almost smell the flesh burning."

"That's their general theme?" gulped Stephen.

"Van Nyman is fascinated by the torments of the early Christian martyrs, the flagellations and beheadings, the violations and mutilations. It's a vision of the ennoblement of the human spirit through the degradation of the human flesh. The sublime and the obscene, meeting at the extremes. Or that's how he would see it." He spread his hands as if to dissociate himself. "But his technique is brilliant, prodigious. The effect he creates is so lifelike that you almost believe he was there in the torture chamber, sketching the body being flayed alive or broken on the rack."

Repulsive!" muttered Stephen.

"His work is much sought after, Stephen. It appeals to a small and very specialized market. Men with a certain taste for the erotic bizarre. They're always sold privately, of course. Never appear on the open market."

"And the one he's working on now?"

"Already gone to a wealthy Swiss collector. Sight unseen. I won't shock you with the price, but think of a very large and very round number. In fact," he went on, relaxing into a more conversational mode, "the buyer is due in town any day. He's paid half on account, and he wants to see what he's getting for his money. It has been somewhat embarrassing, actually. Louis had a slight setback back in the summer, and that set him back several months. All's well now, though, he has his model back." He smiled sympathetically. "They always come back. I wouldn't lay money on your chances, Stephen. He has a strange power over women. They *smell* his power. They don't easily leave his net."

Blum held open the door but, instead of returning to the office, led him to the main gallery. It was a signal that the meeting was drawing to its close.

"You know, David," remarked Stephen, playing for time. He felt confused: his mind was inundated with evidence and impressions, yet he still sensed there was something more he needed. "I miss all those glitzy opening parties, when people come to see and be seen and no one even gives a passing nod to the art. You see those red stickers but you never see anyone actually buying anything. I suppose a lot gets sold privately, as you described."

The dealer patted him on the arm.

"The real business is done behind closed doors. The parties are just public relations exercises. A man like Klaus Schumacher, for example, wouldn't be seen dead at a vernissage."

"Klaus Shumacher?"

"People of that kind," responded Blum quickly.

"What kind?"

"I mean, collectors with special tastes—"

"In the erotic bizarre?"

"—who prefer to remain anonymous."

Stephen felt a shiver of comprehension. Blum had unwittingly named the buyer of the new Louis van Nyman masterwork. An idea was taking shape in the recesses of his mind.

"Completely anonymous?" he persisted, assuming a note of incredulity. "Surely the artist knows who his patron is?"

"Not necessarily."

"You mean, a man like van Nyman might never meet his buyer? Not even privately, in the gallery, or at his studio?"

Blum smiled comfortably.

"Stephen, the dealer who puts artist and client in the same

room together is a dealer who has just gone out of business. And forty percent of a very large and round number is, let me tell you, quite a large round number itself." He held out his hand. "But it still has to be earned, and so you must excuse me. Good to see you, Stephen. Call me ahead next time you're in town and we'll have lunch." He smiled levelly. "And you can tell me why the hell you've given up the queen for her handmaiden."

"Prepare for a long lunch," smiled Stephen wryly. "Thanks, David. I appreciate your help."

Blum sat down at his desk, reached for the phone, put it down, then stood up again. He buzzed through to his secretary to say he wasn't taking any calls, then went to the window and stood staring out at the ugly urban roofscape with its water butts and generators and elevator housings streaked in pigeon droppings. He stood there for fully five minutes, without moving.

Then he returned to the desk and picked up the phone. His hand was trembling slightly as he dialed, and his throat was thick with tension as he gave curt instructions to the person at the other end.

Stephen's step began to slow. He bumped into a mailbox and tripped over a tray of ethnic jewelry displayed on the sidewalk. Eventually he took refuge in a doorway and took stock.

Cristina.

One of Joanna's models. Wasn't Cristina was the one who . . . ?

Surely there couldn't be *two* Cristinas?

Fumbling for a coin, he headed for a phone booth on the street corner and dialed Designing Woman. He put on a false voice for the receptionist so that she wouldn't recognize him and asked to be put through to Cheryl.

Cheryl was overjoyed to hear from him. Joanna was in her office next door, she said in a conspiratorial whisper, so she couldn't talk for long. He inquired after her baby and how she was coping with sleepless nights, then steered the conversation round to the question burning in his brain.

"Cheryl, I know this sounds crazy, but didn't you have a girl called Cristina working for you a while back as a model?"

"Cristina?" came the surprised echo. "You mean, Cristina Parigi? But—"

"Tall? Blonde? Lived on the Upper West Side?"

"That's the one. But you heard what happened—"

"Didn't she come to grief, some time back in the summer?"

"Threw herself into the East River. It was terrible. They still haven't found the body."

He had to make absolutely sure.

"You couldn't just check her address for me, Cheryl. Do you still have it on file? It's important."

"Hang on." She put the phone down while she went to look. He could hear phones ringing and even fancied he could hear Joanna calling out, but a moment later Cheryl came back on. "One-oh-one West Eighty-ninth Street, apartment number seven," she said. "Stephen, will you tell me what this is all about? Stephen? Are you there?"

But Stephen was far away in a world of his own. His mind was spinning. So, this was, after all, the name and the *persona* Joanna had assumed.

But then, what had Blum been talking about? He was Louis's dealer, he must know about Cristina. At least, he *seemed* very well informed. He'd even referred to a "mishap" back in the summer. *But all's well now . . . he has his model back.* What did that mean? Nothing made sense. Stephen racked his brain. Connections with apparent sense formed one moment, only to dissolve again the next in a sea of absurdity. A picture was inexorably emerging, but a picture so crazy and so terrifying that it had to be impossible. Or else the world was mad.

There was only one way out of the maze. He had to find out for himself.

He headed for Madison Avenue. Just before reaching the salon, he turned into a side entrance that led down a broad ramp to an underground garage.

He found Galton bent over the black limousine, polishing the wheels with a chamois leather. The chauffeur straightened at the sound of his name.

"Galton, I need your help," said Stephen briskly. "Like right now."

The chauffeur flashed a broad grin. He lobbed the leather into a bucket and reached inside for his uniform cap. He held the passenger door open for Stephen with an ironic show of courtesy.

"Where are we going, chief?"

"First Avenue, around One Hundredth. I'll direct you."

The limousine rolled out into the street and was soon purring away down the straight. Within fifteen minutes it was drawing up outside the tall, gaunt fortress which housed the studio of Louis van Nyman.

He directed Galton to park directly outside and leave the engine running. Then, reaching forward, he took the chauffeur's dark glasses off him and, turning up his coat collar in his best approximation of middle-European *chic*, stepped quickly out of the limousine and up the steps to the front door.

He cleared his throat and, thinking himself into an appropriate accent, pressed the intercom.

It was a while before a low, silken voice answered.

"Hello?"

"Mr. van Nyman?"

"You got him."

"Here Klaus Shumacher. . . "

23

THE AIR IN THE HALLWAY WAS COLD—colder, it seemed to Stephen, than the December day outside. Partly it was its churchlike atmosphere, the smell of candles and the gloom with only a dim tasseled lamp to light the dark gloss staircase and the maroon and gold wall coverings. But partly, too, it was the presence of the man standing before him. He seemed to move within a ghostly pool of cold air, as though he sucked the very warmth from his surroundings. And yet from his eyes emanated two such deep smoldering darts of fire, like St. Elmo's fires on a ship's mast, that Stephen felt almost the physical heat of their flame. There was something else, too, that slowly filtered through to Stephen's senses: a potent, all-pervading aroma of musk that seemed to surround the man, an aroma somehow more refined and yet more feral, like the alluring odor of animal fur. *They smell his power.* Stephen felt his muscles involuntarily tighten.

The man stood in the center of the hall, barring the way. He was tall and lean, and he wore nothing but black. Even his slicked-back hair was raven black. He watched, waited, listened, limiting his replies to terse remarks and subjecting Stephen all the while with an intense, suspicious scrutiny.

"This is something of a surprise, Mr. Shumacher," he said slowly. "What can I do for you?"

"I am early in New York," replied Stephen stiffly. "I have come to see how is my painting."

"It's nearly finished."

"Then lead me to it. I wish to see it."

Louis van Nyman did not move.

"I never show my work unfinished," he replied in the same slow tone. "You understand the delicacies of the final stages."

Stephen had not expected a rebuttal. He took refuge in bluster.

"This is not right! I shall speak to Blum! I have already paid one half. I demand to see the work!"

"No way, Mr. Shumacher."

"You artists, you are so sensitive. I understand. At least you will have the courtesy to invite me in. I am most interested to see your studio."

"With pleasure. When I am finished."

For a moment, Stephen was in a mind to abandon the pretense and storm his way upstairs, but he checked himself. That would achieve nothing. He was caught in his own trap. Suddenly he lost heart in this absurd game. It was getting him nowhere.

"And when will that be?" he demanded with all the irritation he could muster. "I have a tight schedule."

"Come back in two days and you shall have it."

Stephen stood like a dummy, utterly outwitted, as the other man opened the door and ushered him out. He made some token noises of protest, but nothing could alter the fact that he had basically been thrown out on his ear. He'd never even got to see the studio for himself, and the hall where he'd been kept standing like a lemon was so dark he hadn't even had a fair chance to decipher anything from the man's body or facial language. As he heard the door close behind him and retraced his steps to the waiting car, he had to admit that he felt, in a phrase that came back to him from his student days, a right bloody prat.

He slammed the door with spiteful force and sank into the soft leather seat.

"Let's go," he groaned. "Drop me back at the Club. I'm going to have a long sweat in the steam."

Galton caught his eye in the rearview mirror.

"You want company?"

"You want to get fired?"

"Mrs. Lefever ain't around, afternoons."

Stephen gave a bitter smile. He knew where she'd be *that* afternoon. Well, good luck to her. He'd done all he could, and sod the rest.

He tossed aside the hat and scarf, loosened his tie, and settled back in the seat.

"Tell me, Galton," he began more easily, "how've the Giants been showing out recently? I'm out of touch with the important things in life."

Cristina took her time over her preparations. She showered until her skin was numb, she perfumed her body in all its most intimate parts, she took meticulous care with her makeup and hair, and she wore, as instructed, not red but white. A simple white dress like a Greek maiden's, round at the neck and gathered at the waist. Beneath it, though, she wore nothing. Even clothed, she wanted to feel naked. *Think of today as the prelude . . . to tomorrow.* A compulsive shiver rippled through her. An erotic shiver, mingling fear and anticipation of the unknown.

The ritual was under way, and she was again in the hands of powers outside her.

She left the basement apartment and headed down the street to the avenue, she hailed a cab and gave it the address, she sat bolt upright in the back throughout the ride, then climbed out at the end and made her way up the steep stone steps, all in the semidelirium of a sleepwalker. She saw nothing of the world about her, neither people nor traffic nor any of the incidentals of street life, for her mind was focused down that long tunnel that snaked across the city and turned up the steps of that building, through the front door and into the cool, scented twilight of the hallway, up the dark gloss staircase and finally into the pool of light flooding out from the studio doorway.

She stood just inside the studio door, her heart pounding and a swollen ache weighing in her belly. He was standing in the center by the dais, watching and waiting. She could feel the magnetic pull of his eyes drawing her inexorably forward, and the familiar musky odors of the room, somehow more potent than usual, working like a drug upon her senses to lull her into

submission. Mesmerized, numbed, she stepped over the threshold, delivering herself into the hands of the unknown.

He came forward. Taking her by the wrist, he drew her
toward him and brushed a kiss on her neck. Offering him the
vulnerable, naked flesh seemed like a sacrificial surrender.

"My beauty," he whispered, almost inaudibly. "My love."

She felt a dampness on her skin, and she realized he was
silently weeping. She ran her hands through his hair and drew
him into a closer embrace. His body was trembling.

"I am yours," she murmured.

He slowly sank to the floor and, grasping her buttocks in his
hands, buried his face in her sex—no, she realized, not her sex
so much as her *womb*, and this was an act not of erotic foreplay
but of worship. He was kneeling at the feet of his Madonna.

"Forgive me," he mumbled.

A wave of love and tenderness flooded through her. She felt
as abundant and generous as the earth itself. Her body was a
haven of comfort. It was the ageless vessel of suffering and the
eternal bountiful source of pleasure and perpetuation.

Eventually he rose to his feet. He took her hands and kissed
them in turn, then he kissed her face, first on the forehead, then
on each cheek and last on the lips, almost as if making some
pagan sign of benediction, and finally turned away to the table
on which the wine cooler stood, so that his back was to her
when he spoke.

His voice came out thick and distorted.

"Would you, please . . . ?"

It was the first time he'd ever asked her politely rather than
instructed her. She smiled inwardly. He only had to say the
word.

"Of course."

She turned away with instinctive modesty. It was then for
the first time she registered the *tableau* he had created around
the bed. The familiar shiver of excitement and dread ran
through her. As on the previous day, there was the neck collar
attached to the brass bedhead, only this time two longer straps,
like a horse's traces, were affixed to the foot of the bed and met
in a broad belt that evidently was designed to tighten around
the waist. The coverlet was still white, but draped all around in
an artfully casual manner was an opulent swathe of purple silk
edged in gold in a curious step motif. The motif became clear

from the plaster bust of a Roman emperor set upon a column behind and, lying on the floor in front, amid the swathe of purple, a strange object that revealed itself as a bundle of rods laced up with ribbon with a two-headed ax projecting from the top. Her mouth went dry. Instinctively she glanced down at her own naked buttock to find the corresponding mark. The *fasces*. The rods for beating, he had said. And the ax for cutting.

She turned to see him advancing with the ritual goblet of wine in one hand. In his other he held a wine decanter. His eyes did not leave hers as he handed her the glass.

"Drink it," he said.

It tasted slightly sweeter than usual, with a bitter aftertaste. She drank it obediently, and he refilled her glass and made her do the same again. Then he took her by the hand and led her toward the bed.

"Come now," he said quietly. "It is time."

He had possessed her, like that, strapped up and opened. He had taken her from behind, greedily, savagely. She yearned to be released, even just to close her legs, but the bonds held her in position on her knees, her arms and neck pinned back and her torso thrust forward, tightly enough to prevent escape yet with sufficient play to allow her to squirm beneath the onslaught of his pleasure.

The room seemed to be receding in and out of focus. She closed her eyes and waited for her senses to settle back to earth. But still her head was spinning, and when she looked about her again the figure in black was in double. She could hardly make out what he was doing. She blinked hard. Everything was becoming blurred.

He had wheeled the large canvas on the easel forward and was studying her pose. Then abruptly he met her eye and stopped.

"Curious?" he inquired.

She nodded, confused.

"Of course," he went on in a conversational tone. "You must see the work. Then you'll understand what we're going to do." He smiled. "I say, 'we.' The highest art is often achieved in collaboration. Master and pupil, master and subject. Integral parts of the whole."

He turned the easel round so that the painting was facing

her in the full light. She squinted to focus. Something was wrong with her eyes, or the light, or maybe the canvas itself. Through a shifting blur she could make out the essential form of the subject.

The figure of a naked young woman, thrust forward on her knees, dominated the picture. Her head was thrown back and her long blonde hair streamed down almost to the floor. Her arms were pinned back like wings and her body twisted so that her sex was fully presented to the viewer and yet at the same time, on the flat of one buttock, a small, familiar tattoo mark in red and black was clearly visible.

The whole painting was finished in its full detail except for the two breasts, which were left as patches in bare canvas, as was a section of the marble floor lying directly beneath. Behind the girl, seen only in lower half and recognizable by their leather tongued sandals and tunics, stood two centurions, pinioning her by her arms, their rough dark-skinned hands biting deep into the pale soft flesh. A third, half-hidden in the background shadow, was forcing her head back by means of a broad leather collar and leash—that very same collar as around her own neck—while to the left of the frame, leaning against a fluted column that bore a marble bust, his face indistinct but his eyes staring greedily out of the half-shadow of the background, stood the purple-robed figure of an imperial Roman governor.

The picture was fading in and out now. She looked back at the girl's face and struggled to bring it into focus. It was hard to make out, with the head wrenched back and the features twisted in a gasp of pleasure—or was it pain?—but something told her she knew that rounded, sensuous mouth and those high cheekbones . . .

"You recognize the subject, of course."

His voice, close to her ear, interrupted her thoughts. He was scrutinizing her face.

"But—?" she mumbled.

"Ah, the model. You recognize her, too?"

It was Cristina. The real Cristina.

In the wake of that sudden flash of comprehension followed a sickening shockwave. The unspoken trust. The implicit confidence. The world created together these past months, the magical intimate world of silence and unknownness, the whole fabric of her wondrous fantasy, the very lifeline of her escape. . . .

All betrayed. Betrayed as thoroughly if it never had existed. The entire fantastical creation was crashing about her like a cardboard city in an earthquake.

She was sullied. Disgraced. Embarrassed beyond embarrassment. Shamed beyond shame.

He had known all along! All the way through, every single moment, every time she'd come to him, every time he'd touched her, with every kiss, every word, he had known!

No, no, no, no!

Through her growing horror she was aware he was speaking. His words seemed to address the canvas and his voice sounded full of regret. Even in that last moment she prayed that he would say something to quell the nightmare. He would explain, he'd share her surprise, it was a coincidence, an aberration, some confusion of her own making. . . .

But the name he uttered sealed the truth.

"Poor Cristina Parigi," he sighed. "Such a tragedy. For me. For you. For art."

Through the blizzard in her brain, she choked out her protest.

"You knew? All along, you *knew?*"

He reached out and stroked her face.

"Easy, now. Only you and I know. And I'm not about to tell anyone." His tone was soft, seductive. "You're my Cristina. Why, see, you both even share the same mark. Now isn't that beautiful? You're one and the same. Who is to know otherwise? And you, my new-found beauty, shall finish where she left off, so suddenly, so tragically."

Her vision lurched. His face, his smile, his burning eyes, all seemed to dissolve in a swirl of unreality. What was happening to her? Suddenly she realized. My God, the wine! He fixed the wine! She was drugged.

A wild frenzy of panic seized her. She wrestled frantically against her bonds, but nothing would give. She was pinned, trapped. Slowly shaking his head, he went round each in turn, tightening the buckles and straps. She was imprisoned in his web. Cristina, Joanna, she didn't know who she was any longer, she didn't care, she was just fighting to get free and save herself before she passed out and it was too late. . . .

"Let me free!" she choked. "Get me out!"

Suddenly she felt a thick wad being forced into her mouth and tightened round the back of her head. She shrieked, but all that came out was a muffled cry that resonated round her own skull. She was bound, gagged, drugged, and utterly helpless.

Raw, blind terror seized her.

He was working slowly around her. He had turned the canvas back and was lighting a small spirit lamp on the worktable beside his paints and varnishes. All the while, he kept up an easy, conversational chatter.

"One makes mistakes," he was saying. "But one learns. A single glass is just not enough. It was not a pleasant scene, I can tell you. She came round in the middle of things. Astonishing, the strength a woman can muster. And the speed. She was out of here like a scalded cat. Mind you, I didn't have the safety straps then. As I said, one learns."

He was heating some kind of implement in the flame. She caught a glint off a blade. Another wave of drowsiness washed over her. She was holding onto her consciousness by her fingernails but the waves were sweeping over her fast now, each one more powerful than the last, sucking her away in their ebb.

His voice was coming from a far distance.

"Of course, I went after her. But there was nothing I could do. She was possessed. She just ran and ran. No one could stop her. I was on a bridge when she jumped." He shook his head. "A tragedy for art. An irreplaceable loss. Or so I thought at the time."

She wrestled again, violently, but the numbness was creeping through her limbs and she could scarcely feel her own body. She scarcely had any sense of anything except that she was staked out like a sacrificial beast, suspended forward and exposed to whatever torment or pleasure he might chose to inflict. . . .

She screamed, she bit, she writhed, she fought, she wrenched, but it was no use. The shades were coming down over her eyes, and a vast dullness was seeping in through every corner of her brain.

"Only you and I know," he was repeating. "It's our secret." He paused. "They never found Cristina's body. Perhaps they will. Perhaps we'll give them a body. Shall we? Hair your real color, just like hers, and a little tattoo mark to make sure they get it right."

She was ebbing fast. In a moment she would give herself up to merciful oblivion. The light was fading. Only his voice seemed to come through, distorted as though he was speaking underwater. Through the blur came a word that jolted her back to consciousness.

"Oh, something it might amuse you to know. About your husband, or ex-husband, Stephen."

Stephen?

She scrambled the dying embers of her senses.

"He has taken to impersonation, too. Is this a family fetish? My apologies, that was in poor taste. He was here, in this very house, just a few hours ago. He came round posing as a Swiss art collector who'd bought this painting. Well, you'll be glad to know the work has indeed found a home. A very wealthy and very private collector in Denver, Colorado. Not called Klaus Shumacher and not from Switzerland. Still, I was most courteous and told him to come back in a couple of days. We don't want any interlopers spoiling our work, do we?"

He moved over to her and, reaching forward, gently pulled down the lower lid of her eye.

"Almost there."

He stroked the side of her face.

"Nothing great is achieved without suffering. The sacrifice is the measure of the art. What is one life, one beauty, one pain compared with the eternal life of a great work of art? *Ars longa, vita brevis.* Your beauty will perish, if not today or tomorrow then in years to come. But the Primavera's beauty is as fresh as the day she was painted. Yours will be as eternal. Your face, your skin, your flesh, even the image of your pain—you will become immortal. Capturing that to perfection is my task. I will enshrine your beauty and your being in a medium that is beyond the power of time to corrupt and destroy. I have studied you, scrutinized you, learned you. I know my work exactly. You must trust me to do you honor and do it well."

He moved forward. His eyes burned through the fog of her senses. In his hand he held a thin, polished metal object. Somewhere in the far recesses of her mind she registered this was a small surgical knife.

His other hand reached forward and cupped her left breast.

He hesitated.

Her scream burst from her skull and echoed round the

canopy of the universe, as blackest night gradually closed in over her.

Stephen sat in the hot room, surrendering himself to the scalding heat of the steam that hissed out from hidden grilles beneath the marble banks. His shoulder ached, his head throbbed, his very soul cried out in an agony of despair. But he could do nothing except vent his fury and frustration upon himself. His skin felt flayed raw, and the air was so hot it scorched his lungs and so humid he was all but drowning, but he forced himself to stay sitting there, beyond the threshold of pain, far beyond Galton's own tolerance, as other seminaked figures came and went like ghosts in some infernal mist.

He sank his head in his hands. The hissing grew louder, the steam burned his back like fire jelly. Perhaps he would melt to nothing, or boil away and shrivel into oblivion. Either would be a relief.

"Excuse me."

Someone had stumbled into him. He looked up to see the bent figure of an oldish man fumbling his way through the fog of steam. One hand held up a towel round his waist, while with the other he groped along the edge of the marble seats. His thick, wire-framed glasses were misted up, and as he settled down beside Stephen he took them off and wiped them with a corner of the towel. He turned to Stephen, his face screwed up in an apologetic grimace.

"Can't see a darn thing," he remarked.

Stephen made no response. He had seen something.

The man peered closer, focusing his bright, dark eyes on him.

"Hot today, huh?" He drew back with a frown. "Something wrong?"

Stephen was staring. The glasses . . . the eyes. . . . Gradually, from the well of his memory arose the image of another man, a man who hid behind glasses, too, until just a while back he'd chanced to take them off and reveal his eyes, *those* eyes. . . . A convulsive shiver ran through him. He now understood what he had seen that very morning. It was the look he'd first seen in the eyes of the kid who'd mugged him in the dark city streets two winters back, the look he had *studied*, goddammit, in face after face on police videotape back in Berkeley. The unfocused gaze of the eyes of the criminal sociopath.

How had he been so *blind?* This was his very speciality, and it had been staring him in the face!

He'd only seen the look in the places he'd most expected to find it—in the feral scowl of the young street mugger, in the villainous mug shots of convicted homicides.

But not here. Not in such a suave and cultivated exemplar of the refined upper crust of society.

He leapt to his feet. The rush of blood to his head almost made him black out, and he clutched at the old man's shoulder for support. With a mumbled apology, he groped his way through the scalding steam to the heavy sealed door and the cooling-off room beyond. There he yelled to Galton to follow him and, abandoning a shower and scarcely troubling to dry himself, threw on his clothes, grabbed his overcoat and headed for the exit, hauling the chauffeur after him.

Skin has its own surface tension, and even the sharpest blade causes a slight indentation before entering.

The skin of the female breast is particularly readily penetrated in that it is, to some extent, stretched by the gland tissue of which the mamma is composed. This tissue, when freed from fibrous tissue and fat, is of a pale reddish color, firm in texture and circular in form. It consists of numerous lobes, and these are composed of lobules connected together by areolar tissue, blood vessels, and ducts. Fibrous tissue invests the whole of the surface of the breast and sends down septa between the lobes, connecting them together. The fatty tissue, which determines the form and size of the gland, surrounds the surface of the gland and occupies the interval between its lobes, although there is no fat immediately beneath the areola and nipple. The arteries supplying the mammae are derived from the thoracic branches of the axillary, the intercostals, and internal mammary. The veins describe an anastomotic circle round the base of the nipple, known as the *circulus venosus,* from which large branches transmit the blood to the circumference of the gland and end in the axillary and internal mammary veins.

An ablated mammary would present an image somewhat resembling a bisected pomegranate. The blood flow would be copious and would require stanching to prevent fatal loss.

It is the practice in any surgical operation to describe the line of the intended cut by means of a mark drawn in ink or some other dye. Here, a fine sable brush with black gouache was used, and the line itself began at the upper point of the breast, just below where the curve began, and followed round to the crease underneath. The instrument of ablation was a surgical scalpel, heat sterilized, and with the deployment of absorbent towels beneath the area under operation and the establishment of a sufficient level of anesthesia in the subject, the work was ready to be commenced.

Stretching the skin between two fingers, Louis pricked the flesh with the point of the blade. The naked woman, her body limp and slack, did not stir. He grasped the knife more tightly and, with a single slow movement, made a long, shallow cut along the top of the breast.

A line of blood, like a thin necklace of rubies, sprang out behind it. He reached for a swab and dabbed the blood away, then settled closer for the next and deeper incision. . . .

A sharp buzzing broke through his concentration.

He looked up, momentarily confused. It came again. Longer, more insistently.

The intercom. Someone was calling from the street outside.

He turned back to his work. But the buzzing went on, rhythmically, like a message in Morse code. Who the hell was it? On and on it went, tapping out its insistent signal. He couldn't concentrate with that intrusive noise going on. Angrily, he rose from his stool by the bed and, crossing to the door, snatched up the receiver.

"Get lost!" he spat.

"It's David," interrupted an urgent, strangled voice.

"David?"

"Blum, for God's sake! Let me in."

Christ, the man was early, too early. What was he dreaming of?

"That crazy fool's been back," the voice went on rapidly. "We've got to talk. Open up. Fast."

Smothering an oath, Louis pressed the buzzer and hung up.

Stephen took the stairs two at a time. With no idea where he was going, he just launched himself toward the light. At the top, a short landing led to an open doorway.

He burst in. The image of that room would be seared on his mind for the rest of his life.

The man in black, over by the bed, scalpel in hand. The bed, a web of collars and straps. The woman, naked, suspended in the web, caught by her arms and waist, her head wrenched back by the throat, not moving, unconscious or maybe already dead, a thin line of blood starting from the top of her left breast, her face almost out of view, unrecognizable, dear God, no. . . .

The man had sprung forward, the flash of shock on his face turned to rage and hate. He crouched like a panther, the scalpel clutched in his fist. For a moment the two men stood squaring up to one another, eyes leveled. Words from Stephen's memory rose to the surface of his mind. *His work is the closest I've ever seen to the living hand of the devil.* It hit him with the force of a physical blow. He was staring into the face of the incarnated devil. Blum, the mugger, the convicts: none of these began to compare with the immeasurable depths of evil in this man's eyes.

The man moved suddenly. Darting in a zigzag, he lunged forward and slashed at Stephen's face with the knife. Stephen instinctively threw up his arm. He felt the blade slice through his overcoat and jacket and bite into his flesh. He caught a powerful waft of the man's odor—strong, musky, feral. He stumbled backward, knocking a receiver off its hook and sending a side table of drinks crashing to the floor. With a howl of rage, he grabbed the neck of a broken bottle and advanced.

The man was backing away, stabbing and slashing the air between them, then suddenly he spun round and, seizing a heavy stone pestle from a work bench, hurled it at Stephen. Stephen ducked, and the weapon shot past his head, shattering a large mirror on the wall behind.

Stephen plunged forward, fired with maniacal fury. He would kill him with his bare hands, he would grind the broken bottle into his face, he would throttle and crush and beat and bludgeon the life out of the bastard. With a wild cry, he lunged with the bottle. He caught his opponent on the cheek, gashing deep into the flesh and sending him reeling backward. Tripping, the man fell into the folds of one of the tall drapes hanging from the ceiling. In clambering to his feet, he wrenched the sheet from its fixing and found himself smothered in a sea of loose fabric. The scalpel skittered away uselessly across the floor.

Stephen rushed for it and, throwing himself onto the bed, began frantically slashing at the leather straps. Her head came free and slumped lifelessly forward. He felt her neck. She was half throttled, barely alive. Just yards away, Louis was wrestling his way out of the ensnaring drapes. He reached out for something to hold on to. His fingers closed around the base of the easel. As he tugged, the easel toppled over. It fell against a table, scattering paints and brushes and bottles of turpentine and varnish tumbling and sending a large glass spirit lamp crashing to the floor. In an instant a pool of flaming liquid spread across the floor and onto the end of the sheet enveloping him. With a bestial howl, he climbed to his feet and managed to struggle free of the flaming sheet. He was now coming forward, relentlessly, step by step, like an automaton, his arms outstretched, fingers poised like mechanical claws. But to Stephen's horror he wasn't coming after him, he was making for *her*, he was going to mangle her, throttle her, finish her. . . .

He cast around desperately. Jars of brushes, rolls of canvas, copper etching plates, glass apothecary jars full of chemicals, one labeled ACID. . . .

He snatched the acid jar, ripped off the stopper and, stepping between the maniac and his quarry, flung the acid in his face. The burning liquid caught him full in the eyes. For a moment, Louis just stopped in his tracks, blinked, and rubbed his eyes. Then with a shriek like a stuck pig he reeled backward and, with his hands pressed to his eyes, began stumbling his way blindly round the room, howling for water.

The fire was spreading. A tall drape hanging some way behind the bed caught at the foot and quite suddenly burst into a tall column of flame. The smoke was growing thicker. Choking, Stephen threw himself at the remaining bonds, frantically sawing and cutting and tearing with his hands and teeth, until finally the naked corpse slumped forward in his arms.

Hauling her over his shoulder, he made his way through the choking fumes to the door and, casting a fleeting glance behind him to see the crazed figure of the painter at the sink, desperately sluicing his face with water, as the flames crept closer with the suddenness of an ambush and the smoke grew thicker and more acrid, he stumbled down the dark stairs, along the hall and out through the front door.

And as he went down the steps and across the street to the waiting limousine, all he could hear was the sound of the inferno in the studio upstairs coming loud and clear over the intercom speaker, the crackle of flame and the crash of glass and, above it all, the frantic screams of the man inside, blinded and trapped in his dark prison of fire.

As the car pulled away, holding the semiconscious form of Joanna wrapped tight in his overcoat, Stephen glanced back through the rear window. The skylight of the studio was lit a bright orange. Suddenly, like a volcano, it exploded. The entire roof seemed to lift a few feet, hover momentarily, then burst into a billion fragments which rained down in a flaming shower of glass and debris.

24

FOR STEPHEN, the days that followed passed in a timeless blur. He would not leave Joanna's side. He held her hand as she underwent an emergency stomach pump at the hospital and kept vigil by her bedside while she spent the night under observation. In the morning he took her home by ambulance, where he put her to bed and nursed her himself as the doctors came and went and the long wait began. He took to sleeping in a chair in her bedroom, telling himself it was so that he could be near her if she needed him in the night, but in reality it was because he didn't want to confront the issue of what he was doing back in the apartment and on what basis he was there by making assumptions about beds and bedrooms.

Physically, she was weak, but she had suffered no lasting damage and the doctors were confident she would make a full recovery in a very short time. Mentally, however, she was profoundly confused. Her speech was slurred and rambling and she seemed greatly agitated by the sight of Bella—so much so, in fact, that the poor girl was forced to stay hovering in the doorway out of her line of sight.

"What's wrong?" she kept asking, pale and distressed. "Mom won't even look at me. It's like she's trying to hide from me."

"Give it time," he'd reply with as much conviction he could muster. "She's had a deeply traumatizing experience."

"But I wasn't part of that. I don't even know what happened. I'm only trying to help her, and she won't let me near."

"Time, angel, time," he pleaded.

But as the third day became the fourth without even the anticipated improvement in her physical condition, he could no longer convince himself that time alone would heal. Poorly slept and wearied by his own exhaustion and pain, he wasn't confident at trusting his judgment—and he certainly couldn't ask the doctors theirs—but he felt sure that, at a deep level, she didn't *want* to be better. She wanted the safety of the sick bed where she was maintained in a state of benign semiconsciousness with no demands made upon her to explain or justify or in any way account for herself. She seemed to be living in a mental no-man's-land between Cristina, whom she could no longer be, and Joanna, whom she dared not become again. Consciously or unconsciously, she was refusing to let herself return to Joanna because she could not bear to live with the knowledge of what she had done and been. And this unassuageable sense of her own shame, he was convinced, lay behind her bizarre and contradictory behavior toward Bella. Above all others, she had to be honest with Bella. Bella represented purity and innocence, and she was never to be corrupted by deception. That was why she couldn't—literally—face her own daughter.

But a return to Joanna was a return to Joanna's guilt, too, to the horror and self-disgust at that act of infanticide which she had carried deep within her and which lay at the root of all the trauma since. Would any amount of time heal *that*? Two years had not: far from it, the wound was deeper still. Would love heal it? His own love, faulty and frail as any human love was, had failed. No amount of remonstrance, no argument or reasoning, no unburdening to a friend or self-analyzing with a psychiatrist would make a blind bit of difference.

The only hope of liberation was in action. But what, and how? He was defeated. All that remained was to trust to chance that something, sometime, would happen to bring about the change.

The chance came soon, and from an unexpected quarter.

Toward the end of the fifth day, he came to the conclusion that the apartment and its ever-present associations with her double life was not helping her recovery and that a change of atmosphere was essential. He decided to take her to the beach house. There, beside the ocean and surrounded by the possessions she'd known since childhood, she might find some thread of continuity that would lead her back to herself. Perhaps he, too, would find there the time and space to reflect on his own confused feelings toward her and to consider what effect all this was to have on his own life.

Though still quite weak and often wandering in mind, she was lucid enough to latch on to the proposition eagerly, and despite the disapproval of the doctors he made up his mind that they would go. He had Maria pack a suitcase and Galton bring the car round for him while he made her ready for the journey. She was able to walk slowly, with assistance, and between them they helped her down to the waiting car. Bella saw them off. She had another few days of her semester to run, and then she'd come out and join them. It was no bad thing she had to stay, he felt. The break would do both mother and daughter good.

It was growing dark as they left the city, and the evening ebb of commuter traffic was already beginning. He drove gently, without hurry. From time to time he looked across at Joanna in the passenger seat, sitting upright and staring sightlessly ahead, and occasionally, too, he ventured a quiet remark without expecting any particular reply. The car was warm inside, and a tape of operatic arias played softly in the background. As they joined the Long Island Expressway, a light rain began to fall. The warmth, the music, and the gentle swish of the wipers conspired to create a hypnotic, womblike ambience. He looked across at her once again. She had relaxed back into the seat and her wide, vacant eyes were moist.

He reached across and tentatively stroked her knee.

"Feeling okay?" he murmured.

"Fine, thanks." Her tone was flat, almost disembodied.

"Maria's packed us enough food to stand a siege. We could go out for supper, though, if you feel up to it. Take in some soft-shell crabs at Chez Harry?"

"If you like."

"No, if *you* like."

A brief silence fell. Then she turned to him with such a helpless look of puzzlement and pleading in her eyes that he felt his heart would break.

"Stephen?" she asked quietly. "Why?"

He swallowed uncertainly.

"Why are we going here? So I can take care of you and get you well."

"I mean, why—?" Her voice trailed off. "Why did it happen?"

"Maybe it just had to."

Maybe the grip of sexual obsession was unbreakable. Maybe it was, literally, chemical. That man had *smelled* of sexual power. That was it! That musky smell pervading the space around him: that was raw androsterone, the human sex pheromone. Androsterone had the same chemical footprint as musk, its molecular structure had the identical perimeter length. . . . Men gave off this invisible sexual signal to attract women. It worked subliminally on the brain to create a mood of relaxation and sexual susceptibility, and women were powerless to resist its effects. Some men emitted more than others, but he had *reeked* of it . . .

Her voice, abrupt and brittle, interrupted his train of thought.

"I won't visit him this time," she said suddenly. "I won't. You'll have to do it. Tell him I can't."

"Visit who, Joanna?"

She jerked her head at the mention of her name, and a worried frown settled over her pale face.

"Make sure they're white," she went on abruptly in a rapid whisper. "I always have them white. Not lilies, though. Lilies smell of death. Fresias are probably in season. Look out for those little white narcissi, too. I like snowdrops best of all, only it's too early for snow."

He felt the lump rise in his throat. She was talking of Luke.

"Whatever you want," he replied softly. "I'll see to it. Now, why don't you close your eyes and rest for a while? We'll soon be home."

They drove on in silence. As she began to doze, a deep calm softened the lines of her face. He kept on going, his teeth clenched. God alone knew how he was going to pull her out of this.

Eventually, the first signs for the Hampton Bays came into view. Shortly afterward, he turned off the freeway onto a smaller road. A mile from the beach house, the road became little more than a wide track and the going grew rougher. The night was dark and the track only sporadically lit by street lamps. Set back from the road and well apart from one another, crouching among the wind-bent trees and the broad swathes of wiry sea grass, stood other beach houses of the same style, and though lights burned in a few, most were dark and heavily shuttered up for the oncoming winter.

He rubbed his weary eyes and stretched his aching limbs. Now comfortably on the home straight, he put his foot down and went a little faster. They'd stay in tonight, he'd make a fire, have a stiff whiskey . . .

Suddenly an animal flashed into the beam of his headlights. Furry body, pointed head, long striped tail.

Momentarily blinded, the animal stopped in midtrack. Stephen wrenched the wheel over to avoid it, but at that moment it bolted. Just as his foot was hitting the brakes, he simultaneously heard and felt a jolting thud. He shot a glance in the rearview mirror. The creature was writhing and squirming around in the middle of the road behind. Instinctively he hauled the car to a stop, flipped on the hazard lights, and reached for the door handle.

Beside him, Joanna had jerked awake.

"What's wrong?" she cried. "What's happened?"

"We hit something. A raccoon, I think."

He climbed out and hurried the twenty yards back up the track to where the animal lay thrashing around and yelping in agony. He knelt down. It was a large dog raccoon. A glance told him its pelvis and hind legs had been completely crushed beneath the car wheels, and the creature was trying to crawl away with its fore legs but only managing to skate around in a circle.

Joanna was running toward him. He looked up to see her face filled with horror and distress.

"It's had it," he said shortly.

"What are we going to do?" she cried.

It was then that, in a flash of absolute clarity, he knew what he had to do. Reaching forward with both hands from behind, he picked it up under its arms in the way he would hold a monkey he was separating from a fight, and began to carry it, wriggling and howling, back to the car.

"Get my coat out," he told her.

"You're taking it to the vet?"

"We're going to put it out of its misery."

"You mean, *kill* it?" She was aghast.

"Get my coat and look in the right-hand pocket. You'll find a hypodermic there. Get it out." He went round to the front of the car and held the struggling creature in the beam of the head-lights. "Just do it!"

She brought the coat to the light and, trembling, produced the needle.

"You can't!" she spluttered. "Not like that! Not in cold blood!"

"Take the cap off."

"I won't! I can't let you do this!"

The raccoon was trying to bite his hands. Its whole lower portion was dripping blood and flapping loosely against his trousers. He couldn't hold it much longer.

"What do you want, to let the poor thing die in agony? It's had it, Joanna! It's going to die. Leave it here and it'll die a slow, terrible, agonizing death. You decide. You're the judge. It's your decision. Abandon it to a horrible death or put it out of its misery. Which is it to be, Joanna?"

"I can't! It's not for me to say."

"All right, we'll dump it here."

He put the animal down on the road. From its throat came a frantic whimpering as it tried pitifully to claw its way to the verge, dragging its mangled legs behind it.

"Okay, okay." Joanna was pressing the needle on him, her voice cracking. "Do it, then. Do it."

"Why, Joanna? Tell me why."

"Just spare the wretched thing! Go on, quick!"

He stooped to the ground and grasped the wriggling crea-ture behind the neck, then he took the needle from her shaking hands and in a swift movement sank the point into the furry flesh. The raccoon gave three quick, convulsive jerks and abruptly went limp. He withdrew the needle and crushed it under his foot. Then he took the bloodied, broken corpse and laid it beneath a thorn bush at the side of the road.

Slowly he turned back to Joanna. She was standing in the beam of the headlights, ashen-faced and shivering convulsively. Putting his hands on her shoulders, he slowly drew her to him and held her in a tight embrace as the shuddering gradually subsided and gave way to a helpless flow of tears.

* * *

Two days later, Stephen was on his way back to Berkeley.

In addition to his regular workload, he had a major report for the Faculty Board to write before the end of the semester as well as a series of time-consuming funding applications to conclude. His work was no longer academic, it was real. It was of vital importance. What he had witnessed over those past days had given it a desperate new urgency. In his hands lay the potential to save society from the evil within it.

He'd called Lou Whittard one day after the next, postponing his return. The dean had been very accommodating, but the subtext was clear: Stephen was still on probation and he was pressing his luck to the limit. If he was serious about keeping his new job, he'd better stop playing truant and get his ass back over there. Academia worked by court politics: out of sight was out of favor.

Such was the reason he gave himself for returning.

In reality, he was going back because of Joanna. His mood was alternately bitter, depressed, angry, and truculent. Above all, he was angry with himself. What had he expected? The Joanna he'd first met, the vivacious firefly that swept into his life, all laughter and light, suddenly to emerge from the ugly carapace of experience accreted over the intervening years? Was he seriously expecting that, after that moment of self-confrontation and primal release in the deserted roadway, the clock would suddenly turn back and she would fall into his arms and drag him with lustful intent into the bushes as she had at virtually that very spot when taking him for the first time to the beach house, or at least snap out of her strange entrancement and, with the suddenness of a light being switched on in a dark room, smile and laugh and talk and frolic with all the zest and passion of the time before this all began?

Perhaps he was that dumb after all. Perhaps he'd let the fantastical affect his grip on the real and translated his hopes into expectations. Yes, he *had* hoped for more. He'd written the scenario: faithful hero rescues helpless beloved from clutches of evil demon. The facts of life were more cruel, however. Nobody ever loved the one that saved their life. And nobody could live with another who had seen them as naked and degraded as he had seen her.

Their good-byes were awkward and stilted. Most farewells carried the softening promise of a reunion. Theirs did not. The furthest he could go was a clandestine conversation with Bella about her paying a visit to Berkeley early in the New Year to check out the university for her own future. But at his parting with Joanna he couldn't even say, "See you," for he couldn't conceive of how or when or where he would actually see her again.

Too much had been said and seen that couldn't be unsaid and unseen. Several times he'd had it on the tip of his tongue to propose "making a fresh start" and "starting over" and "trying again," but each time the words seemed to wither away, unuttered. She was indeed Joanna again, and, it seemed, released now from the self-blame that had haunted her, but she wasn't a Joanna he could talk to. She was nervy and anxious and quick to misread innocent remarks. Innocuous comments carried unintended slights, and surrounding all that passed between them was an atmosphere of awkwardness and unease. It was as if she could perpetually see, indelibly reflected in his eyes, the image of the woman he'd burst in upon in that nightmarish scene at the studio. Perhaps she simply could not contemplate a future in which he would not always view her this way. And, although he'd studiously avoided admitting it all along, she would indeed be right. He had toyed as much with ideas of "having it out" and "laying it all in the open," but something in her attitude, at once defensive and aggressive, prickly and steely, made such a frank confessional impossible. She had to resolve it within herself first. Until she presented herself as the old Joanna he knew and loved or, better, as a new Joanna grown wiser from her experience, there would forever remain between them the shadow of that naked figure on the studio bed, abandoned in a delirium of degradation.

A stiff breeze blew off the ocean, scouring the leafless scrubland and buffeting the two figures in scarves and anoraks as they struggled along the shingle strand. The cry of seagulls carried eerily on the gusting wind, one moment piercingly close, the next snatched away into the distance. It was Christmas Eve, and the beach was deserted.

Joanna inhaled deep gulps of the bracing air and turned her face into the lash of the fine spray.

"Wonderful," she breathed. "You can feel it doing you good."

"Ever heard of ozone poisoning, Mom?" grumbled Bella striding along beside her.

"Nothing like a good, strong breeze to blow away the cobwebs."

"What cobwebs?"

"Don't nitpick." She linked arms. "What's bugging you, darling? You've been so grumpy lately. Would you rather we'd stayed in the city? We could go back for New Year's."

"It's not that, Mom."

Joanna knew, of course. She slackened her arm. Did they have to go through *that* business again? Treating a daughter as a sister had its downside. Everyone had a right to their emotional privacy.

"Would you like to invite Eddie over for supper tonight?" she asked. "You haven't seen much of him this time, and I thought you were so fond of him." She checked herself. Bella had a right to her emotional privacy, too.

Bella stopped and turned to face her. The wind strewed her blonde hair in wild flurries across her face.

"I don't understand you, Mom," she said. "What does Eddie mean to you? Yet you're all for having him over. 'Come to supper, come and do this and do that.' And there's Stephen, who's got no one to be with at Christmas, and you don't even call him. You just sent him packing as soon as it suited you. 'Thanks for all you've done, pal, now get lost.'"

"He had to go back," she replied stiffly. "He has his commitments."

"What about *your* commitment to *him?*"

"Bella!" she frowned.

"I'm sorry, Mom, but I think you behaved really badly. He only left because he didn't want to pressure you. He didn't want to put you under an obligation."

"I owe him no obligation!" she retorted hotly. "Whatever he did was his decision. I didn't ask him." She broke off, shocked to hear herself speak this way. "Anyway, you don't understand. It's too complicated. There are things you don't know."

"Listen to you! That's what you say to *him* when he's telling you the truth and you don't like it." Her eyes were blazing with passion. "Well, I think he *does* know everything. Only you find it too uncomfortable to admit."

Joanna clenched her teeth and said nothing. She set off into the teeth of the wind, relishing the sting of the spray on her cheeks and the chill bite of the breeze scouring her lungs. Bella skipped alongside her.

"Sorry, Mom," the girl was saying. "I didn't mean to hurt you."

"You're right, though," admitted Joanna sorrowfully. "The trouble is, he *does* know everything. He knows too much. He's seen too much."

"But that's crazy! I'll want the man I marry to know everything about me. I won't want to keep a single thought or feeling secret from him. And I'll expect the same from him. What I don't like, I'll forgive."

"Sweet child," she smiled.

"You're being patronizing! I'll tell you what your trouble is. You don't *want* him to know you. Because you're ashamed of yourself. You can't expect him to forgive you if you don't forgive yourself."

"It's easy for you to say that," murmured Joanna, feeling the force of the truth.

"It's easy for *you* to say *that*, Mom. I'm not so dumb I don't know you can't love someone who doesn't, deep down, love themselves."

"Maybe I don't want his love," she objected, deliberately missing the point. But Bella wouldn't let her get away with that.

"Stephen or anyone else, it's the same. You've got to forgive yourself. Love yourself a little."

They walked on for a while in a silence broken only by the crash of the waves and the plaintive cries of the gulls wheeling overhead. Finally, swallowing her pride, Joanna turned to her daughter.

"But how?" she asked simply.

"Draw a line. Everything behind it is past history. Everything ahead is the future. A clean sheet."

Suddenly the girl bent down and, finding a stick washed up among the flotsam, described a long, deep line in the sand just ahead. She looked up. Her eyes were shining.

"The line is here, Mom," she said. "Come on, step over it. The new life starts now."

In the shower that evening, neither the first nor the last for the day, Joanna saw again the mark.

She paused from her incessant scrubbing and scouring and stood for a moment beneath the cascade of steaming water, looking at the indelible red and black cipher. She gave a convulsive shudder. It sat there like some leech or scarab that nothing could shake off or wash away. She hardly knew what it meant, and only dimly could she recall how she'd come to carry it, except that she knew it was evil, a mark of Cain which she was cursed to bear forever. Suddenly her spirit rebelled. That belonged to the life before the line! In the new life, it did not exist. And it would *not* exist.

Over the next weeks, back in New York, she launched herself into a whirlwind of activity.

A short and relatively painless operation at a cosmetic surgery clinic removed the tattoo without, she was assured, leaving any trace or scar. She threw out mountains of her clothes and every stitch of her underwear, she had her hair restyled short by a top coiffeur from Paris who flew over twice a month to visit wealthy clients, she seized again the reins of her business which she'd badly neglected, and she even took the decision to put the Park Avenue apartment on the market and look for a new home.

Most of all, though, she *thought*. One afternoon she visited the street off First Avenue and, sitting in the back of the car staring at the burnt-out shell of the house, tried to piece together what had happened and where it had gone wrong. The past few years stretched in her mind like a course of stepping-stones, beginning with an initial error, blindly taken and fatally suppressed, from which each subsequent step, though seemingly insignificant at the time, had accumulated with frightening speed to drive her to the very edge of perdition. She simply hadn't been able to *see* what was happening. Stephen had tried to show her, but how could she accept absolution from one who, in her mind, shared in the guilt? In the end, as she now realized, only she could absolve herself. Bella was right: she had to forgive herself, to love herself a little.

It was not until mid-January, however, that she had attained the understanding, or maybe found the courage, to settle one major piece of unfinished business.

The first snows had fallen, late for the time of year, only to turn instantly to ice in the bitter winds that swept in from the north. The traffic ground by slowly, gridlocked at every intersection, smothering the lower levels of the city in a blanket of choking fumes. Pipes froze up, water butts burst, and sheets of ice fell dangerously from high overhangs, while on the sidewalks below, for all the grit and salt, pedestrians struggled and slipped about in their heavy rubber overshoes, adding one more element conspiring to slow the pace of life and raise the level of stress.

On such a day, at one o'clock precisely, Joanna left the salon and took a cab across town to 101 West 89th Street, to lay the ghost once for all.

The apartment was cold and dark. It was eerily quiet, too, in the dead, flat way a soundproofed room was quiet, and the air was heavy with the lifeless smell of a place long abandoned. She stood in the center of the room with her fur coat wrapped around her and with only the winter's day filtering in through the windows at each end for light, looking about her with the eyes of a stranger. The sofa and chairs, the coffee table and magazines, the pictures and mirrors and little ornaments here and there, all shared the look of familiar objects, and yet they seemed divested of any connection with her. She felt she had entered a room in a dream, a room she had once inhabited, with a sofa she'd sat in and glasses she'd drunk out of, but only in a different realm of consciousness. The room and its contents returned no living echo.

Trembling slightly, she crossed the room to the spiral staircase. At the top she hesitated, then, gritting her teeth, she slowly began to descend. She stepped through the star-spangled tunnel, past the bathroom, and finally into the bedroom. Her hand automatically found the light switch. The bed with its canopied drapes sprang to life with a luminous red glow, reflected a dozen times in the mirrored walls. . . .

Suddenly she gave a violent jolt.

There was someone in the bed! Blonde hair, red dress . . .

My God, Cristina!

Sick with horror, she edged forward. Then, with equal suddenness, a wave of relief flooded over her. The face was empty, the figure bodiless. It was just a blonde wig lying on the pillow, with a red dress stretched out on bunched-up sheets.

But as she stood shaking from the aftershock, she had the feeling that someone had indeed been lying there, but a person without substance, a being without form or body that had fled at her footfall. This place was a mausoleum, a hollow, empty chamber, and all that inhabited it were shadows.

And yet, something palpable existed in the atmosphere. A presence she could *feel*.

A fold of drapery was stirring! She stifled a cry. Cristina was there, in the room, in the very air about her. A sad presence. Restless. Unresolved. Pleading for rest.

She moved so fast she knocked over a chair, ripping the fabric of the canopy. She pulled open the bedside cabinet and snatched out the silver photograph frame showing a smiling dark-haired girl with an older couple, then, clutching it tight to her breast, backed quickly out of the room, snapping off the lights on the way, and retraced her steps up the spiral stairs and into the gray natural light above. She paused for a moment to recover herself, then headed for the door and let herself out, closing the door firmly and finally behind her.

That evening she wrote to Warner Friedman. She enclosed the photograph, a set of documents, and a silvered brass Union key.

Dear Warner,

   The name of the girl in the enclosed photograph is Courtenay Ann Chambers.

   Her place of birth was Paris, Texas. Her age would be 22, maybe now 23. She came to New York about a year ago and rented apartment #7, 101 W. 89th. I enclose the door key to this apartment, along with the rental documentation.

   Warner, I want you to arrange for a search agency to find the parents of this girl. I want you to send them a check for $100,000, strictly anonymously, then inform Lieutenant Portillo of our local precinct station of their address, reference the Cristina Parigi case . . .

In the morning, she had Galton hand-deliver the letter to the lawyer's offices. At one o'clock that afternoon, she closed the salon and took Cheryl, the staff, and all the models within call to lunch at her favorite Upper East Side restaurant, Mortimer's. In the afternoon she had a workout at her exercise club, followed by a full body massage and a sauna. In the evening, she took Bella to *La Bohème* at the Met, and that night she slept, for the first time she could recall in ages, like the long-forgotten child of innocence she once had been.

Stephen pressed forward across the terminal concourse to the gate through which the New York flight was now at last arriving. Bad weather on the East Coast had delayed its departure, and the passengers, a demographic cross-section of all America, looked too tired and travel-worn to face the evening ahead with relish. But he did. He'd been looking forward to this moment for weeks now.

Then, like a burst of sunshine on a dull day, he saw her. Her blonde hair danced as she walked and her gait was light and easy. She dropped her luggage when she saw him and, bounding forward, threw herself into his arms.

"Bella!" he exclaimed fervently. "God, it's good to see you!"

"You, too, Stephen."

He moved to pick up her luggage.

"That's all you brought? Let's go, then. I hope you didn't fill up on airline food. We can go Cantonese, Vietnamese, any-ese you like. I want to hear all your news. And tomorrow I've fixed a whole program of people for you to meet."

She held him back and eyed him critically.

"Stephen, you look a real mess," she said and began to straighten his collar and smooth his lapels. "C'mon, let me tidy you up."

"Hey, what is this? You want a chauffeur in uniform? Angel, out here we hang loose."

She had a strange look in her eye which he didn't at once comprehend. She went on hurriedly trying to spruce him up, while he tried equally to stop her. For a brief moment he wondered if there was somebody on the plane she'd met she thought would be important for him to meet, too, but by then the flow of arrivals had dwindled to barely a trickle.

And then he understood.

Just inside the gate, holding him with a cautiously soft gaze, a tentative smile on her face, stood a smartly dressed young woman. She seemed to look familiar, but. . . .

It was a full second before he registered. He caught his breath. Her hair, her clothes, her manner, her *look*, everything was different.

"My God," he gasped. "Joanna!"

She moved forward slowly, holding his gaze with a wry yet cautious smile. The world about him froze. A thousand questions surged through his mind, a thousand hopes that he dared not allow himself feel. Unconsciously he found himself moving toward her. A short distance apart, they both stopped. Then together they reached out their hands, each to the other. Their fingers met, interlaced, clutched tightly.

She stood her distance, waiting. Holding her at his arm's reach, feasting his gaze upon this reborn spirit and seeing in her gaze such an awakening, such fearless understanding, he felt the gladness welling up within him and break to the surface in a great swell of joy.

"You're looking just wonderful," he breathed.

"You look terrible," she smiled. "Still drinking too much and sleeping too little. Or sleeping with the wrong people."

"You've come all this way to tell me that?" He bit his lip to smother his smile as he sensed the familiar games beginning. "Or are you here to chaperone Bella?"

"Let's say I'm here on a tour of inspection."

"Checking out the pitch, like Bella?"

"Looking to the future."

"Whose future?"

"Could be ours."

"Well, we could give it a spin, I suppose."

They looked at one another and broke out laughing.

"Stephen," she said, "did I hear you say Cantonese? What are we waiting for? Let's go for it."